C000163488

A...

Liz Fielding has ... Middle East, setti... inspired by her tr... nominated for RW... Traditional Romance ... *the Bridesmaid*, and the Best Short Contemporary Romance in 2006 with *The Marriage Miracle*. She was awarded the annual Outstanding Achievement Award by the Romantic Novelists' Association in the UK in 2019.

Caroline Anderson's been a nurse, a secretary, a teacher, and has run her own business. Now she's settled on writing. 'I was looking for that elusive something and finally realised it was variety – now I have it in abundance. Every book brings new horizons, new friends, and in between books I juggle! My husband John and I have two beautiful daughters, Sarah and Hannah, umpteen pets, and several acres of Suffolk that nature tries to reclaim every time we turn our backs!'

Three-times Golden Heart® finalist **Tina Beckett** learned to pack her suitcases almost before she learned to read. Born to a military family, she has lived in the United States, Puerto Rico, Portugal and Brazil. In addition to travelling, Tina loves to cuddle with her pug, Alex, spend time with her family, and hit the trails on her horse. Learn more about Tina from her website, or 'friend' her on Facebook.

Unexpected Surprises

Unexpected Surprises:
One Miracle Night

LIZ FIELDING

CAROLINE ANDERSON

TINA BECKETT

MILLS & BOON

First Published in Great Britain 2022
By Mills & Boon, an imprint of HarperCollins*Publishers,* Ltd
1 London Bridge Street, London, SE1 9GF

www.harpercollins.co.uk

HarperCollins*Publishers*
1st Floor, Watermarque Building,
Ringsend Road, Dublin 4, Ireland

UNEXPECTED SURPRISES: ONE MIRACLE NIGHT
© 2022 Harlequin Enterprises ULC

Her Pregnancy Bombshell © 2017 Liz Fielding
One Night, One Unexpected Miracle © 2018 Harlequin Enterprises ULC
From Passion to Pregnancy © 2017 Tina Beckett

Special thanks and acknowledgement are given to Caroline Anderson for her contribution to the *Hope Children's Hospital* series.

ISBN: 978-0-263-30456-5

MIX
Paper from
responsible sources
FSC **FSC™ C007454**
www.fsc.org

This book is produced from independently certified FSC™ paper to ensure responsible forest management.

For more information visit: www.harpercollins.co.uk/green

Printed and Bound in Spain using 100% Renewable electricity at CPI Black Print, Barcelona

HER PREGNANCY BOMBSHELL

LIZ FIELDING

To Kate Hardy, Scarlet Wilson and Jessica Gilmore, who helped bring Villa Rosa and L'Isola dei Fiori to life.

It was a joy working with you.

CHAPTER ONE

Be not afeard; the isle is full of noises,
Sounds, and sweet airs, that give delight and hurt
not...

William Shakespeare

'MIRANDA...'

Andie Marlowe lifted her coat from the rack, took
a breath and fixed her face into a neutral smile before
turning to face Cleve Finch, the CEO of Goldfinch
Air Services.

It had been nearly a year since his wife had been
killed when the little six-seater she was flying was
taken down by a bird strike but his grief was still un-
bearable to watch. He'd lost weight, his cheekbones
were sharp enough to slice cheese and right now the
pallor beneath his runner's tan gave him a jaundiced
look.

'Cleve?'

'You're off this afternoon?'

'I stood in for Kevin last weekend.'

'I wasn't questioning...' He shook his head. 'I just
wondered if you could spare me a couple of hours.'

She did her best to ignore the totally inappropriate

way her heart lifted at the suggestion he needed her. He was her boss. He simply wanted her to take on a last-minute job.

'No problem. The ironing can wait.'

'Ironing? It's Friday. Shouldn't you be getting yourself ready for a hot date?' He almost managed a smile.

She almost managed one back. 'Men don't date any more, they just want hook-ups.'

'Men are idiots,' he said.

'You'll get no argument from me.' She'd tried Internet dating in the vain hope that it would take her mind off the only man with whom she'd ever wanted to get naked. It didn't so she'd stopped. 'My evening involves nothing more exciting than a darts match in the village pub but if anyone on the visiting team is under fifty I might get lucky.' She glanced up at the white board on which the flight schedule had been written but couldn't see any obvious gaps. 'Has someone called in sick?'

'No.' He lifted a hand, curled his fingers back into his palm. 'Imogen called.'

'My sister?' The sudden heart-pounding obliterated the uncomfortable sensation of being out of control of her limbs whenever she was around Cleve, taking her back to another time when her twin had been the sole focus of her concern. But Immi was fine now, happy, about to be married… 'Has something happened to Mum and Dad?'

'No!' He reached towards her and, for a moment, his hand hung in the air between them. 'I'm sorry, I didn't mean to alarm you. She called to let me know that the new aircraft…' He stopped as if the words were stuck in his throat.

Every instinct was to take his hand, hold it, give him

her warmth, comfort, whatever he needed. Before the message reached her brain and she could do anything so stupid he was dragging his fingers through thick dark brown hair that had once been streaked by the sun but was now shot through with silver.

Cleve's grief in the year since his wife's death had been painful to witness. And he wasn't the only one. The Mayfly, the six-seater aircraft she'd been flying when she died, had been built by Marlowe Aviation, the company started by Andie's family right at the beginning of aviation. Both companies had wobbled in the aftermath.

The Air Accident Inquiry had absolved everyone from guilt; it was clear from all the evidence that the aircraft had been brought down by a bird strike. The shocking revelation that Rachel had been in the early stages of pregnancy—something Cleve had kept to himself until the inquest—and the coroner's suggestion that, since she was such an experienced pilot, nausea or fainting might have contributed to the accident, had made it a double tragedy.

When the enquiry was over Andie's mother, fearful that her father would follow their grandfather into an early grave, had insisted he take a complete break and, leaving Marlowe Aviation in the capable hands of Immi and her fiancé, her parents were crossing India by bus like a couple of old hippies.

Cleve, on the other hand, had not taken a day off since the funeral, insisting that his responsibility was to his staff and Goldfinch, the company he'd built from nothing.

Andie suspected that deep down he was afraid that if he walked away, didn't get straight back in the cockpit, he never would. And, once the insurance claim had been settled, Cleve, in the most selfless, most support-ive of acts, had ordered a replacement for the wrecked aircraft from Marlowe Aviation. The exact same model in which his wife had died.

Now her sister had called to tell him that it was ready to be collected.

'I can pick it up,' she said, quickly. 'I'll take the train, stay overnight and fly back tomorrow.'

'No.' He shook his head. 'There are procedures. En-gineering checks to sign off.'

'I can handle all that.'

Andie had a degree in aircraft engineering and would have been in the design office right now if a good-looking flier, negotiating the purchase of one of her father's aircraft, hadn't promised her a job if she got her CPL. If he hadn't sealed his promise with a kiss that'd had her flying without the need for wings.

Cleve had been wearing a newly minted wedding ring by the time she'd completed her degree and ar-rived at his office clutching her CPL, but he'd given her a congratulatory hug and kept his promise. His wife, no doubt able to spot her crush from ten thousand feet and used to fending off silly girls, had smiled sympa-thetically, confident that with her in his bed he was oblivious to such distractions.

'I just need you to fly me up there, Miranda,' he said. 'If it's not convenient just say and I'll take the train myself.'

'I just thought…' Obviously this was something he felt he had to do but she wasn't about to let him go through it on his own. 'When do you want to go?'

'Now? Oscar Tango is free this afternoon. If the darts team can spare you.'

'They'll probably heave a collective sigh of relief,' she said. 'I was flying home tomorrow anyway. Immi's been nagging me about...' Her sister had been nagging her about a fitting for her bridesmaid dress but she couldn't bring herself to say the words. 'If you don't mind squashing into my little two-seater?'

'Whatever suits you.'

He held the door for her as she took out her phone and sent a quick text to her sister to let her know she'd be available for the fitting the next day.

'Is it pink?' he asked as they crossed to the control office to file a flight plan.

'Pink?'

'The dress.'

'You read my text?'

'I didn't have to. I received an invitation to her wedding and I imagine she wants her sisters as bridesmaids. The rare sight of you in a dress is almost enough to tempt me to accept.'

She glanced up at him but the teasing smile that had made her teenage heart stand still was now rarer than a sighting of her in a skirt.

'If it's pink with frills there's no way I'm going to miss it,' he added.

'Please... Not even as a joke.'

'I hope her fiancé has done his duty and lined up a best man to make your day memorable.'

'Portia's the oldest.' The glamorous one that not only the spare men but those who were firmly attached would be lusting after. 'She has first dibs on the best man.' And if he was anything like the groom she was welcome to him. 'Posy and I will have to make do with the ushers.'

'You're not impressed with your future brother-in-law?'

'I didn't say that.' Had she?

'You pulled a face.'

She lifted her shoulders a fraction. 'Marrying the boss's daughter is such a cliché. As long as Immi's happy that's all that matters.' Feeling a bit guilty that she hadn't quite taken to her future brother-in-law, she added, 'Dad seems to like him.'

'I congratulate him. Your father has very high standards.'

'Er...yes...' Talking about weddings with Cleve was too weird and, relieved to have finally reached the control office, she said, 'Will you go and fuel up for me while I deal with the paperwork?'

His brows rose a fraction. 'I've never known you let anyone but you touch her,' he said. 'You even service herself yourself.'

'I'm cheap,' she said, rather than admit that he was the only person she'd allow to touch the aircraft her father had given her on her eighteenth birthday.

The day she'd got her PPL.

The day Cleve had kissed her.

'Do not drip any fuel on the fuselage,' she said, taking the keys to the security lock from her pocket.

She would have tossed them to him but he reached out, wrapping his long, cold fingers around her hand to keep her from turning away. His eyes locked onto hers and she stopped breathing.

'I'm honoured.'

'Make that *suckered*,' she said, just so that he wouldn't

think she was going soft. 'You'll be using your card to pay for the fuel.'

She would have turned away but he held her hand for a moment longer until, with a nod, he took the keys and walked away, leaving her normally warm hand like ice.

'Do you want to take the stick?' she asked, out of courtesy rather than any expectation that Cleve would say yes. He wasn't a back-seat flyer and had no hang-ups about women pilots—he'd married one after all. The fact was, he hadn't been flying much since the crash.

He complained that his time was fully occupied running the business these days, setting up the new office in Cyprus. And, when he was forced to leave his desk, the murmurs reaching her suggested that he was taking the co-pilot's seat and letting his first officer have the stick.

That he had lost his nerve.

He shook his head, climbed aboard and closed his eyes as she taxied out to the runway. His attempt at humour on the subject of her bridesmaid dress had apparently drained him of conversation and any excitement about picking up the new aircraft would be inappropriate.

Forty silent minutes later she touched down and taxied to her personal parking space on the Marlowe Aviation airfield.

She didn't wait for him to thank her. She signed off, climbed down and, before he could dismiss her, crossed to where the chief engineer, no doubt warned by the tower of their arrival, was waiting for them.

'Hello, Jack.'

'Andie...' He took her hand, kissed her cheek, then

looked up as Cleve joined them. 'Cleve. Good to see you,' he said, not quite quick enough to hide his shock at Cleve's pallor. Any other time, any other man, Jack would have made a joke about women pilots, she would have rolled her eyes, and they would have got on with it.

'Jack.' Cleve's brief acknowledgement did not encourage small talk.

'Right, well, we're all ready for you.' He cleared his throat. 'Andie, you'll be interested in seeing the updates we've incorporated into the latest model of the Mayfly to come off the production line.'

It was a plea not to leave him alone with Cleve but, with the tension coming off him in waves, she wasn't going anywhere.

'I can't wait,' she said, touching her hand to Cleve's elbow, a gentle prompt forward, and she felt the shock of that small contact jolt through him. She caught her breath as the responding flood of heat surged back along her arm, momentarily swamping her body.

She held her breath, somehow kept her smile in place as he pulled away from her.

'The new tail design is largely down to Andie,' Jack explained to Cleve as they walked towards the hangar. 'The sooner she gets tired of life at altitude and gets back to the design office, the better.'

'Miranda was born to fly,' Cleve said before she could answer.

'No doubt, but my time will come.' Jack grinned confidently. 'Some lucky man will catch her eye and she won't want to be up and down all over the place once she starts a family.'

Desperate to cover the awkward silence that followed Jack's epic foot-in-the-mouth moment, she crossed to the aircraft, sleek and gleaming white but for the new tail that bore the stylised red, gold and black goldfinch identifying the ever-growing Goldfinch Air Services fleet.

'She's a beauty, Jack.'

She turned to Cleve for his reaction but he looked hollow and she thought, not for the first time, that this very public support of Marlowe Aviation and the aircraft her father built had been a mistake.

'Why don't we go and deal with the paperwork first?' she suggested. 'If Immi's in a good mood she might make us—'

'Let's get this over with,' Cleve said, cutting her off before she could suggest a bracing cup of tea. But she was the one making all the right noises, asking all the questions as Jack ran through the new design details.

The chief engineer's relief when a loudspeaker message summoned him to take a phone call was palpable.

'I'm sorry but I have to take this,' he said, handing her the clipboard. 'We've just about finished the externals. Why don't you take her out, try a few circuits? Get a feel for her.'

'Thanks, Jack,' she said, when Cleve did not reply. 'We'll see you later.'

'I'll be in the office…'

She gave him a reassuring nod when he hesitated, then turned back to Cleve.

He was staring at the aircraft, his face set as hard and grey as concrete. Her hand hovered near his elbow but she was afraid that if she touched him again he would shatter.

As if he sensed her uncertainty, he said, 'Go and find your sister, sort out your dress. I've got this.'

'I don't think so.' He turned on her but before he could speak she said, 'You're not fit to fly a kite right now.'

They seemed to stand there for hours, staring one another down and then, as if a veil had been lifted to reveal all the pain, all the grief he was suffering, his face seemed to dissolve.

Before she could think, reach for him, he'd turned and stumbled from the hangar.

The airfield was bounded on one side by a steeply wooded hill and in the few moments it had taken her to gather herself he had reached the boundary.

'Stop!'

She grabbed his arm and he swung around. For a moment she thought he was going to fling her aside but instead he caught hold of her, pulling her to him and, his voice no more than a scrape against his vocal cords, he said, 'Help me, Andie...'

He hadn't called her that since the days when he'd teased her, encouraged her, kissed her in the shadowy corners of her father's aircraft hangar and her stupid teenage heart had dreamed that one day they would fly to the stars.

He was shaking, falling apart and she reached out, slid her arms around his chest, holding him close, holding him together until he was still.

'I'm sorry—'

She lifted a hand to his cheek and realised that it was wet with tears.

'I can't—'

'Hush...' She touched her lips to his to stop the

words, closing her eyes as he responded not with the sweet, hot kisses that even now filled her dreams, but with something darker, more desperate, demanding. With a raw need that drilled down through the protective shell that she'd built around her heart, that she answered with all the deep-buried longing that she'd subsumed into flying.

She felt a shiver go through him.

'Andie…'

There was such desperation in that one word and she slid her hands down to take his, hold them.

'You're cold,' she said and, taking his hand, she led the way along the edge of the runway to the gate that led to her parents' house. She unlocked the door and led him up the stairs and there, in the room filled with her old books, toys, dreams, she undressed him, undressed herself and then with her mouth, her hands, her body—giving him all the love hoarded inside her—she warmed him.

CHAPTER TWO

EXHAUSTED, A LITTLE SHAKY from a rough ferry crossing, Andie handed her passport to the border control officer.

'*Buongiorno, signora.*' He glanced at the back page of her passport and then gave her the kind of searching look a Roman traveller landing in the ancient port of Sant'Angelo two thousand years ago would have recognised. The kind of look that would bring even the most innocent traveller out in a guilty sweat. 'What is the purpose of your visit to L'Isola dei Fiori?'

'I'm running away,' she muttered.

From her job, her life, from the man she'd been in love with since the life-changing moment when he'd applauded her touchdown in a treacherous crosswind.

Hiding the secret she was carrying.

'*Scusi?*'

She swallowed down the lump in her throat. 'I'm on holiday.'

He did not look convinced. She didn't blame him but the clammy sweat sticking her shirt to her back had nothing to do with guilt.

'You are travelling alone?' he asked.

That rather depended on your definition of alone...

She nodded. 'Yes, I'm on my own.'

'And where are you staying?'

'At Baia di Rose. The Villa Rosa.' His brow rose almost imperceptibly. 'My sister inherited it from her godmother. Sofia Romana,' she added, in the face of his scepticism.

The man's eyebrows momentarily lost touch with gravity. Clearly the mistress of the late King Ludano would not be everyone's choice as godmother but Sofia had started school on the same day as their grandmother. Their friendship had endured through a long lifetime and by the time their fourth daughter had arrived her parents had probably been running out of godmother options.

He cleared his throat, returned to her passport, flipping through the pages. 'You travel a great deal?'

'Yes.' She was in and out of airports all over Europe and the Middle East on a daily basis. 'I'm a commercial pilot.'

'I see.' He gave her another of those long, thoughtful looks but it wasn't his obvious suspicion that was making her feel faint, cling like a lifeline to the edge of the desk that separated them. 'You look unwell, signora Marlowe.'

'I'm not feeling that great,' she admitted. Her skin was pale and clammy and her hair, blown out of the scarf she used to tie it back on the blustery deck of the ferry, was sticking to her cheeks and neck.

She knew exactly what he was thinking and in his place she'd probably think the same.

'I have to ask you if you are carrying—'

'A baby.'

She blurted out the word. It was the first time she'd said it out loud. She'd told her sister that she was tired, needed a break, and Posy, unable to get away herself, had been so happy that someone would visit the villa, make sure everything was okay, that she hadn't asked her why she wasn't going to some resort where she could lie back and be waited on.

The first person in the world to know that she was going to have a baby was a border control officer who was about to ask her if she was carrying an illegal substance… 'I'm carrying a baby,' she said, her hand instinctively rising to her waist in an age-old protective gesture as she backed away from the desk. 'And I'm about to be sick.'

The ferry crossing from Italy had been choppy. The sandwich she'd forced herself to eat had gone overboard within minutes of leaving the harbour but her stomach seemed capable of creating a great deal out of nothing. It had been years since her last visit to the island but the Porto had not changed and she made it to the toilet before she disgraced herself.

Once the spasms had passed she splashed her face with cold water, retied her hair, took a breath and opened the door to find the officer waiting with her passport, wheelie and a sympathetic smile.

'Complimenti, signora.' She hardly knew how to respond and he nodded as if he understood that she was feeling grim and might just be having mixed feelings about her happy condition. As if that were the only problem… 'My wife suffered with the *vomito* in the early days but it will soon pass,' he said. 'Relax, put your feet up in the sun and you will feel better. Is anyone meeting you?'

'I was going to grab a taxi.'

He nodded, escorted her to the rank, spoke sharply to the driver who leapt out to take her bag.

'I have told him to take it slowly, *signora*.'

Out of the noisy terminal building, standing in the fresh air, the afternoon sunshine warning her face, she managed a smile. 'Did he hear you?'

His shrug and wry smile suggested that his words might well have fallen on deaf ears.

'Could you ask him to stop at a shop…*il supermercato*? I need to pick up some things.'

He exchanged a few words with the driver. 'He will take you and wait.'

'*Grazie.*'

'*Prego. Bon fortuna, signora.* Enjoy your holiday.'

Andie lay back against the cool leather of the seat as the driver drew carefully away from the taxi rank, out of the port and after a few minutes pulled into the car park in front of a small supermarket.

Her sense of smell, heightened by pregnancy, had her hurrying past the deli counter. She quickly filled her basket with some basic essentials and returned to the car.

'Baia di Rose?' the driver asked.

'*Sì. Lentamente,*' she added, using the word that the border official had used and Sofia had called after them as they'd raced down the path to the beach. *Slowly…*

'*Sì, signora,*' he said, pulling out into the traffic with exaggerated caution.

It didn't last.

He was a native of this ancient crossroads in the Mediterranean; his blood was a distillation of the Greek, Carthaginian and Roman invaders who had, over the millennia, conquered and controlled the island. His car was his chariot and the hoots of derision from other drivers as they passed him were an affront to his manhood.

She hung onto the strap as he put his foot down and flung the car around sharp bends, catching glimpses of the sea as they climbed up out of the city and headed across the island to Baia di Rose and the villa that guarded the headland.

She'd left London on a cold, grey day that spring had hardly touched. How many times had she and her sisters done that in the past when her grandmother had whisked the four of them out of England in the school holidays to give her mother a break?

She still remembered the excitement of arriving in a spring so different from the one they'd left behind. Being met in a sleek Italian car by Alberto who, with his wife, Elena, looked after the Villa Rosa, its gardens and acted as chauffeur to Sofia and who treated them as if they were little princesses. The exotic flowers, houses painted in soft pastels and faded terracotta and the turquoise sea glittering in invitation.

The house was only a few hundred yards up the hill from the village, perched on an outcrop in a swathe of land that stretched from the coast to the rugged, forested lands that led to the peak of the mountains in the heart of the island that King Ludano had declared as a national park.

Portia, her older and more worldly sister had shocked them all by suggesting the real reason was to keep his visits to his mistress from prying eyes.

Whatever his motive it had preserved this part of

the island from commercial exploitation, the ribbon development of hotels along the east coast.

The last stretch to an elevated promontory was reached by a narrow, twisting road. As children, they'd competed to be the first to catch a glimpse of the pale pink Villa Rosa. With its tiered roof and French doors opening onto a garden that fell away to the sheltered cove below, it was so utterly different from home.

Inside was just as exciting. Endless rooms to explore and the excitement of being allowed to join grown-up parties in the vast drawing room with its arched ceiling painted in the pale blue, pink, mauves of an evening sky.

There were dusty attics filled with treasures to explore if you dared brave the spiders and, her favourite place of all, the cool covered veranda looking out to sea where you could curl up with a book in the heat of the afternoon.

When they were children the gates had stood wide open in welcome and as soon as the car came to a halt they'd tumbled out, rushed down to the beach, kicked off their shoes and socks and stood at the water's edge, shrieking with excitement as the water ran over their feet.

Today the gates were closed and it was too early in the year to swim in the sea. Too late in the day to go down to the beach. She just wanted to curl up somewhere and sleep off the flight from London, the ferry trip across from the Italian mainland.

The driver asked her a question in something that wasn't quite Italian, that she didn't understand, but his look of concern suggested he was asking if she was in the right place. She nodded, smiled, paid him and waited while he turned and headed back down the hill.

Once he'd gone she took the weighty bunch of keys that Posy had given her from her bag, opened the small side gate and stepped into the peace and tranquillity of the villa courtyard.

On one side there was a low range of buildings that had once been stables but, for as long as she had been coming here, had been used as garages and storerooms. On the other side of the courtyard was the rear of the house with its scullery and kitchen. The door that, wet and sandy from the beach, they'd used as children.

It had been eight years since their last visit. She and Immi had been sixteen, Posy fifteen. Portia hadn't come with them. She had been in her first year at uni and thought herself far too grown-up for a family holiday by the sea, even in a glamorous villa owned by the mistress of the island's monarch.

Those years had not been kind to the villa.

King Ludano had died and Sofia had been left alone with only her memories to warm her in their love nest. Alone without her lover to call whenever something needed fixing.

It was an old house, there were storms in the winter and the occasional rumble from the unstable geology of the island.

The pink was faded and stained where rainwater had run from broken and blocked gutters. There were some tiles missing from the scullery roof and there was a crack in the wall where the stucco had fallen away and a weed had found a home.

Posy's wonderful bequest from her godmother

needed some seriously expensive TLC and she would have been lumbered with something of a white elephant if it weren't for its location.

The Villa Rosa was the only property on this spectacular part of the coast. It had a private beach hidden from passing boats by rocky headlands that reached out into the sea like sheltering arms and, thanks to the island's volcanic past, a pool fed by a hot spring where you could bathe even in the depths of winter.

As soon as she put it on the market she would be swamped with offers.

The sea sparkled invitingly in the low angle of the sun, but this early in March it would still be cold and all she wanted was hot mint tea and somewhere to sleep.

Tomorrow she would go down to the beach, feel the sand beneath her feet, let the cold water of the Mediterranean run over her toes. Then, like an old lady, she would go and lie up to her neck in a rock pool heated by the hot spring and let its warmth melt away the confused mix of feelings; the desperate hope that she would turn around, Cleve would be there and, somehow, everything would be back to normal.

It wasn't going to happen and she wasn't going to burden Cleve with this.

She'd known what she was doing when she'd chosen to see him through a crisis in the only way she knew how.

She'd seen him at his weakest, broken, weeping for all that he'd lost, and she'd left before he woke so that he wouldn't have to face her. Struggle to find something to talk about over breakfast.

She'd known that there was only ever going to be

one end to the night they'd spent together. One of them would have to walk away and it couldn't be Cleve.

Four weeks ago she was an experienced pilot working for Goldfinch Air Services, a rapidly expanding air charter and freight company. She could have called any number of contacts and walked into another job.

Three weeks and six days ago she'd spent a night with the boss and she was about to become a cliché. Pregnant, single and grounded.

She'd told the border official that she was running away and she was, but not from a future in which there would be two of them. The baby she was carrying was a gift. She was running away from telling Cleve that she was pregnant.

He would have to know. He would want to know, but the news would devastate him.

She needed to sort out exactly what she was going to do, have a plan firmly in place, everything settled, so that when she told him the news he understood that she expected nothing. That he need do nothing...

She sorted through the keys, found one that fitted the back door. It moved a couple of inches and then stuck. Assuming that it had swollen in the winter rain, she put her shoulder to it, gave it a shove and her heart rate went through the roof as she was showered with debris.

'Argh...' She jumped back, brushing furiously at her hair, her shoulders, shaking herself, shaking out her hair, certain that there would be spiders...

Cleve tossed his cap onto its hook and crossed to the white board listing the flight schedule.

'Where's Miranda?' he asked. 'I don't see her on the board.'

'She's taken a few weeks' leave.'

Leave? He turned to Lucy, his office manager. 'Since when?'

'Yesterday afternoon. She flew down to Kent in the morning and picked up the guys from their golf tournament but she wasn't feeling too good after lunch,' she said, without looking up from her VDU. 'She hasn't been looking that great for a few days.'

'She's sick?' His heart seized at the thought.

She shrugged. 'She appears to have picked something up. The punters take exception to the pilot using the sick bags so I told her to take a few days off to get over it.' Lucy finally sat back, looked up. 'She hasn't taken more than the odd day off since last summer so she decided to make it a proper break.'

'As opposed to an improper one?'

'Let's hope she gets that lucky.'

He bit down hard in an effort to hold in the response that immediately leapt to his lips. 'Why didn't you run this by me?'

'You've been in Ireland for the last three days.'

'You've heard of email, text, the phone?'

'I've heard you tell me not to bother you with the minor details,' she reminded him. 'If you want me to call and ask you to approve time off for someone who never takes a day off sick, who hasn't had a holiday in nearly a year, then you need to start looking for a new office manager.'

'What? No...' Lucy might be a total grouch but he couldn't run the office without her. 'No, of course not, it's just that...' It was just that he'd finally geared up the courage to face Miranda, talk to her. 'She's…that is everyone…is supposed to give a month's notice before taking time off.'

'She could have taken a week's sick leave,' she pointed out, clearly not impressed with his people skills.

'I know. I didn't mean…'

He turned to the gallery of Goldfinch pilots on the office wall. Miranda looked back at him from her place in the top row, her calm, confident smile never failing to instil confidence in her passengers and guilt, sitting like a lump of lead in his chest, exploded.

He'd broken every rule in the book. He'd lost control, taken advantage of her kindness, behaved in a way that he would have utterly condemned in anyone else.

He'd been a wreck and Miranda's sweet tenderness had been a healing balm, a gift that he could never repay. Her scent, the softness of her skin, her hair falling from its pins and tumbling over his skin, the life-giving sweetness of her mouth…

Every time he thought about her he was swamped with the memory of that night. Waking with her spooned against his body, the curve of her neck just inches from his lips. Fighting the temptation to rouse her with a kiss and take more of her precious warmth.

Not moving because he knew what he would see in those tender green and gold eyes.

Understanding, pity, a smile that let him off the hook and the awkwardness of a morning after that neither of them knew how to deal with.

Not moving, because the moment she woke it would be over.

He'd drifted back into the kind of sleep that had

eluded him for more than a year and the next time he woke, hours later, it was to a note propped against a cold mug of tea.

I'm taking the new aircraft back to base. Take my two-seater, or the train runs hourly at seven minutes past.
See you Monday.
M.

Bright and businesslike, a forget-it-and-move-on message. He couldn't leave it like that and he couldn't wait for the train.

He'd flown her little aircraft back to base, his need to see her, reassure her, overriding the PTSD he'd been experiencing since Rachel's crash. In the darkness of that night there had been no thought of protection and he needed her to know that she was safe, but by the time he touched down no one was answering at her flat and her car was gone.

She must have anticipated the possibility of him turning up at her door, tongue-tied, not knowing what to say and chosen to put some distance between them so that she could face him in the office on Monday morning as if nothing had happened.

It was, undoubtedly, the sensible thing to do and, maybe, if he'd been there on Monday, a shared look would have been enough to get them past that first awkward moment, but on Sunday night the call had come from Cyprus. His local partner had been hurt in a car crash and he'd had to fly out to take control.

He'd told himself that he would call her; he'd picked up the phone a dozen times and then put it down again.

Unable to see her face, read her body language, have a clue what she was thinking, he had no idea what to say. Men were from Mars...

His father relied on flowers to cover the word gap and he'd got as far as logging onto an online florist but stalled at the first hurdle when he was invited to choose an occasion. Birthday, anniversary, every cause for celebration you could imagine. Unsurprisingly, there wasn't an option that would cover this particular scenario.

And what flowers?

His father had been lucky—all it took was a tired bunch of chrysanthemums from the garage forecourt to provoke an eye roll, a shake of the head and a smile from his mother.

His own experience of married life suggested that nothing less than long-stemmed red roses would do if you were grovelling. No power on earth would induce him to send them to Miranda.

She deserved more. Much more. She deserved to hear him say the words. If only he could work out what they were.

He'd arrived back from Cyprus determined to clear the air but she was in the Gulf picking up a couple of mares that were booked for a visit to stud. Then he was in France and so it had gone on. Maybe it was coincidence, but if someone had arranged their schedules to keep them apart they couldn't have done a better job.

Miranda couldn't change his schedule, but she could swap her own around. Clearly she needed space and he'd had to allow her that.

Until today.

He'd flown back from Ireland determined that, no matter what, he'd talk to her. He still could.

'I'll stop by on the way home and take her some grapes,' he said. It was okay to be concerned about someone you'd known, worked with for years. And grapes didn't have the dangerously emotive subtext of flowers. Red, black, white—they were just grapes.

'You'll have a wasted journey. She checked the times of the trains to London before she left and then called her sister to let her know what time she'd be arriving.'

'Which sister?'

'Portia was on the box covering the post-awards parties, she'd have flown home if it was Immi, so it must be the one with the Royal Ballet.'

'Posy. Did she say how long she'd be away?'

'She asked me to take her off the schedule for a month.'

'A month!'

'She's worked a lot of extra days covering for other people, including you. She's owed six weeks.' She gestured in the direction of his office. 'Maybe she said more in the note she left on your desk.'

A cold, sick feeling hit the pit of his stomach as he saw the sealed envelope with his name written neatly in Miranda's handwriting.

He didn't have to open it to know that she wasn't coming back.

He sat down, read the brief note saying that she was taking leave owed in lieu of notice. She didn't give a reason; she didn't have to. Determined not to let this happen, he reached for the phone.

'Imogen, it's Cleve Finch.'

'Hi, Cleve. What can I do for you? There isn't a problem with the new aircraft?'

'No… No, it's fine. I just need Posy's address.'

'Posy?' She sounded surprised, but there was nothing guarded in her response. Evidently Miranda hadn't shared what had happened with her twin.

'I'm going to be in London this evening and I wanted to drop something off for Miranda,' he said, trotting out the excuse he'd rehearsed. 'Obviously I'd have asked her for the address but her phone appears to be switched off. She is staying with Posy?'

'You're kidding. Posy has a room you couldn't swing a cat in. Andie was just dropping in to pick up the keys before catching her flight.'

'Flight?' So much for his plan to take her out to dinner somewhere, talk things through. 'Where's she gone?'

'To L'Isola dei Fiori. Didn't she tell you?'

'I've been in Ireland all week.'

'Oh, I see. Well, Posy inherited an amazing old house from her godmother. It's got a fabulous conservatory and the most glorious gardens…' Her voice trailed off. 'I imagine they're all overgrown.' There was a little sigh. 'We used to stay there in the school holidays. It was magic.'

'I'm sure it was wonderful, but—'

'Sorry, I was having a moment… Posy can't get away until late summer and she's been worried about leaving it empty so Andie's using her leave to give it an airing. It's a bit off the beaten track,' she added. 'She might not get a signal. Is it important or will it wait until she comes back?'

'What?'

'Whatever you were going to drop off at Posy's?'

'Yes… No…'

She laughed. 'Okay…'

'Yes, it's important. No, it won't wait,' he said, quickly.

'In that case you'll want her address.'

CHAPTER THREE

ANDIE GATHERED HERSELF AND, having braved the door for a second time, discovered that it was the scullery ceiling that had sagged and was blocking the door.

Afraid she'd bring the whole lot down if she tried to force her way in, she trundled her wheelie and shopping around to the main entrance, found the correct heavy iron key and let herself in.

There were no worries about wet sandy feet messing up the gleaming marble tiled floor now. It was thick with dust and there was a drift of feathers where a bird must have got in through the roof and panicked.

She gave a little shiver, hoping that it had got out again.

Everywhere was shuttered. The only light was from the open door and, as the sun slid behind the mountains, that was fading fast. Using her bag to prop the door open, she crossed to a light switch but when she flicked it down nothing happened. She tried another in case it was just a duff bulb but with the same result.

She'd remembered the house as inviting, full of light, air, laughter. She'd never given a thought to how it might be in the winter, to be alone here, but the damp chill, dark shadows were weirdly creepy and suddenly this didn't seem such a great idea.

She could manage with candles for light—there had always been tall white candles in silver holders throwing their soft light in the evenings—but she was going to need hot water to clean the place up.

If rainwater had got into the wiring she was in trouble.

She hurried through the house opening shutters, letting in what light remained before braving the cupboard under the stairs in search of a fuse box.

There was good news and bad news. The bad news was that this had to be a regular occurrence. The good news meant that there was a torch and fuse wire on top of the old-fashioned fuse box.

More bad news was that the torch battery was on its last legs and she checked the fuses as quickly as she could, found the blown one and had just finished when the torch died. She shoved it back into place and breathed a sigh of relief as a light came on in the hall.

She carried her shopping into the old-fashioned kitchen. Someone had had the sense to leave the door of the huge old fridge open. It would need a good wash down but holding her breath in case it blew another fuse, she switched it on at the mains, still holding her breath as it stuttered before reluctantly humming to life.

Better.

She tried a tap. Nothing. The same someone had sensibly turned off the water and drained the tank.

She left the taps turned fully on and looked under the sink for a stopcock. It wasn't there and she opened the door to the scullery.

It was a mess. Directly below the damaged part of the roof the rain had seeped down through the upper floor and the ceiling was sagging dangerously and she certainly wasn't about to risk switching on the light.

Using the little light spilling in through the kitchen door, she picked her way across the debris to the big old sink in the corner and opened the door of the cupboard beneath it.

Something scuttled across her foot and she jumped back, skin goosed, heart pounding.

It was a mouse, she told herself. Not a spider. She'd seen a tail. She was almost sure she'd seen a tail...

Swallowing hard—and desperately trying to think why she'd thought this was a good idea—she bent down and peered into the cupboard. It was too dark to see anything and too deep for her to be able to reach the stopcock without getting down on her hands and knees and sticking her head inside. She swallowed again, knelt gingerly and, with a little squeak as her face brushed against cobwebs, made a grab for the tap handle.

She was about to give it a turn when the bright beam of a torch lit up the inside of the cupboard to reveal the thick festoon of cobwebs and a startled mouse frozen in the spotlight.

Then, out of the darkness, a man's voice rapped a sharp, *'Come?'*

Already on edge, a notch away from a scream, she leapt back, caught her head on the edge of the cupboard and saw stars.

'Mi dispiace, signora...'

Too damn late to be sorry...

'Don't *dispiace* me!' Andie staggered to her feet

and, hand on top of her ringing head, turned furiously on the intruder. 'What the hell do you think you're doing?'

'Oh, you're English.'

'What in the name of glory has that got to do with anything?'

'Nothing. I'm sorry, I didn't mean to startle you.'

'Epic fail,' she retaliated gamely, but her shaky voice wouldn't have scared the mice, let alone the man standing in the doorway, blocking out what little light there was. Half blinding her with his torch. She put up her arm to shield her eyes from the glare. 'Who are you? What are you doing here?'

'Matthew Stark.' He lowered the torch, took a step forward, began to offer her his hand but wisely thought better of it. 'I've been keeping an eye on the villa for the owner.'

'Oh? She didn't mention you when I picked up the keys. Rosalind Marlowe is my sister.'

'Rosalind?'

'She prefers *Posy*.' She would have cursed her sister for not warning her that she had appointed a caretaker but she'd carefully timed her arrival at her sister's digs for the moment when she would be dashing off to warm up for the evening performance. Sisters had a way of looking at you and instantly knowing that something was wrong. 'I'm Miranda Marlowe.'

'Oh…' He sighed with relief, clearly not that keen on evicting a squatter. 'Of course. You were at the funeral. If she'd let me know you were arriving I would have come up earlier and turned on the water. Checked that everything was working.'

'It was a last-minute decision and, since I'm the

practical one in the family, she knew I could handle a stopcock—' spiders were something else and, stepping back to let him in, she said, '—but knock yourself out, Matthew Stark.'

'Of course.' He stepped forward.

'Don't stand on the mouse,' she warned.

'You like mice?'

'Not in the kitchen, but I don't want to have to clean up the bloody body of one you've squashed with your size tens.'

'Right,' he said, his tone clearly that of a man who wished he'd stayed at home. 'No squashed mice…'

That was one squashed mouse too many and her stomach heaved as he ducked beneath the sink. He immediately backed out again and looked up at her. Breathing through the wave of nausea, she was grateful for the dark.

'You'd better turn the tap on or the air—'

'It's already done,' she snapped.

'Of course it is,' he muttered.

He re-emerged from the cupboard a moment later with a cobweb decorating his hair, which made her feel marginally more generously disposed towards him.

They retreated to the kitchen; he brushed the dust off his hands. 'Shall we start again? And it's Matt, by the way. Nobody calls me *Matthew*.'

'Andie,' she replied discouragingly as the pipes began to clang and air spurted noisily from the tap. 'How did you know I was here? Did I trip an alarm?'

'Chance would be a fine thing. No mobile signal, no Internet. I saw the light.'

'Very low tech.'

'You work with what you have. We were Sofia's

nearest neighbours as we live at the edge of the village. I looked out for her.' He looked around. 'Are you staying here on your own?'

She recognised that his question was provoked by concern—obviously if there had been anyone else in the house they would have appeared by now—but, conscious of her isolation, she responded with a question of her own.

'You knew Sofia? How was she? I hadn't seen her for several years before she died.'

'Independent, crotchety, glamorous to the end and impossible to help but she was kind to my mother. She's crippled with arthritis, which is why we came to the island. For the warmth, the hot springs,' he added.

'I'm sorry.'

He shrugged. 'It is what it is. She was using the spa at Sant'Aria but when Sofia heard she invited her to use the hot spring here on the beach whenever she liked. I laid some decking across the sand which made it easier for both of them to access the pool. I think she enjoyed having someone to talk to.'

'My grandmother still came when she could.'

'Yes. I met her once... Posy is happy to continue with the arrangement until the house is sold.'

She sensed a question and nodded. 'Your mother is welcome any time.'

'Thanks.' He looked around. 'This isn't exactly home from home. Do you need any help clearing up? That ceiling is a mess.'

'Are you a builder?' she asked.

'No, but I can handle a broom.'

He obviously meant well but she just wanted to lie down.

'I think it's going to need a little more than that but if you don't mind I'll worry about that in the morning.'

'Are you sure you're okay?' he asked, frowning.

'Long day, rough crossing,' she said, letting go of the chair back she was clutching for support. 'And the taxi ride up here was rather more exciting than I'm used to.'

He didn't look convinced but he let it go. 'If you're sure, I'll leave you in peace.' He paused at the door. 'There's no phone line but you'll find a cord by the bed in the master suite and another by the sofa in her little sitting room. If you need anything, a tug will ring a bell I rigged up in the garden. I will usually hear it. Very low tech,' he added, a touch sarcastically, 'but—'

'You work with what you have.'

He'd put himself out, come running when he thought Posy's house was being robbed and she'd been barely polite.

'Thank you, Matt. You've been a very good neighbour and I promise you, I'm a much nicer person when I've had eight hours' sleep.'

'I'm sorry I gave you a fright.'

'You saved me from having to stick my head in a cupboard full of cobwebs,' she said, with a little shiver. 'You are totally forgiven.'

He smiled, nodded, headed for the door. She watched him out of sight then shut the door and locked it, returned to the kitchen. The water was now running freely and she turned off the taps.

She had light and water, all she needed now was somewhere to sleep. Sofia had a master suite on the ground floor but she couldn't bring herself to use that. As children they'd slept upstairs and she had fondly imagined curling up in her childhood bed, watching the lights of passing ships. Right now the prospect wasn't that inviting.

The stairs were cobweb festooned, littered with stuff she didn't want to examine too closely. No worries about what she was going to be doing tomorrow. Cleaning…

She brushed her teeth in the downstairs cloakroom, washed her face in cold water.

There was a throw on a sofa in the room Sofia had called her 'snug'. Andie opened the French doors, hung it over the edge of the veranda so that any creepy crawlies would fall down into the garden and gave it a thorough shake.

Out in the distance she could see the lights of a ship and she paused for a moment, leaning on the wall, breathing in the fresh air coming off the sea. Then a yawn caught her and she shut the French doors, climbed into her PJs and wrapped herself in the lightweight silk robe she'd packed, wishing she'd brought her fleecy one.

Having located the bell cord and tied it up safely out of harm's way—the last thing she needed was to set it off and have Matt racing back convinced that she had a concussion—she stretched out and was asleep almost before she'd closed her eyes.

She was woken, cold, stiff and with a crick in her neck, by the low sun streaming in through the open shutters. She lay very still for a moment hoping that her stomach had given up on the *vomito*.

No such luck.

Teeth brushed, hair tied back, she made her way to the kitchen in search of something that would stay put.

The rising sun exposed the state of the villa in a way that artificial light had failed to do as she crossed the gritty floor in search of a kettle. She let the water run for a few minutes before she rinsed the kettle, filled it and put it on the old-fashioned stove. While it was boiling she located the switch for the water heater and, holding her breath, turned it on. The fuses held.

She took a mug from the dresser, washed it under the tap and tossed in one of the mint teabags she'd brought with her. That and a plain biscuit usually stayed down.

She carried them out onto the veranda, planning to let the crisp morning air clear her head but the cushions were missing from the chairs. She crossed the garden to a bench, put down the mug and stretched out her neck. Then, enticed by the soft, lulling splash of the waves breaking over the sand in the enclosed little cove below her, took the familiar path down to the beach.

Kicking off her sandals at the edge of the sand, she walked to the edge of the sea and stood for a moment as the water, ebbing and flowing, sucked the sand from beneath her feet.

One bold ripple rushed in, covering her feet up to her ankles, chilly but exhilarating. She longed to plunge into the water but she'd have to go back for her swimsuit...

There were some moments you could never recapture and this was one of them. If she walked back up the steep path she wouldn't come back to the beach.

She looked around but the cove was private. Unless you knew it was there you wouldn't notice it from the sea and it was too early for a call from even the most diligent of neighbours.

Rolling her eyes at her totally British reserve, she

slipped off her robe, stepped out of her PJs and tossed them on a nearby rock.

The gesture was oddly liberating and it seemed the most natural thing in the world to raise her arms to the heat of the fast-rising sun, welcoming the soft breeze that rippled across her body like a lover's touch.

As she stepped forward the cold water swirled around her ankles and calves, goosing her skin. Another step and it was up to her knees, thighs, a chill touch against the heat of her body, and she lay her hand against her still-flat belly, reliving the moment when Cleve, insane with grief, scarcely knowing what he was doing, had cried out as he'd thrust inside her and made their baby.

She shivered, but not with the cold.

It had been wrong, selfish, she'd taken advantage of his moment of weakness and now, instead of saving him, she was going to bring him more pain.

She caught her breath as the water lapped at her belly and then she dived in, striking out for the far side of the cove.

There and back was more than enough; splashed through the shallows and ran, shivering, straight to the hot pool. She had just stepped into it, lowered herself up to her chin, when her brain processed what she'd seen.

She turned slowly and peered above the rocks.

Cleve was leaning against the rock where she'd left her clothes, arms crossed, and he was grinning. 'That was worth flying thirteen hundred miles to see,' he said.

Blue with cold and covered in goose bumps? She doubted that...

'How long have you been there?'

'Long enough.'

Of course he had. He must have been in the garden when she stripped off, witnessed her mad salute to the sun...

'A gentleman would have looked the other way.'

'Only an idiot would have looked the other way. A gentleman would have saved your blushes and pretended he hadn't seen you.' He kicked off his shoes, peeled off his socks then tugged the polo shirt he was wearing over his head and tossed it next to her robe. 'But as I'm sure your father has told you, I've no pretensions to being a gentleman.'

'So if you're not an idiot and not a gentleman, what are you?'

'Honest?'

He reached for his belt.

'Stop! What do you think you're doing?'

'Joining you in that oversized hot tub while we discuss why your resignation is not going to happen,' he said, then paused as he was about to slip the buckle. 'Unless you'd rather get out and join me over here.'

They had been naked together for an entire night, no holds barred. He'd already watched her take a skinny dip, seen her run across the beach. Modesty was ridiculous but nothing would induce her to climb out and walk over there with him watching her every step of the way.

'I didn't think so,' he said when she didn't move, and the buckle was history. He flipped the button at his waist and dropped his trousers to reveal a pair of soft white boxers that clung to his hips and buttocks like cream to a peach...

'That's far enough!'

She'd had her hands inside that underwear, her hands on that tight backside as she'd undressed him. In her head he was already naked. In her head she wanted him naked, beside her, inside her...

'Pass me my robe.'

He hooked it off the rock and held it out. She snatched it from him, wrapped it around herself, careless of the hem falling into the water.

She'd intended to climb out and go back up to the villa so that she could face Cleve wearing proper clothes, but he was already walking across rocks worn smooth by centuries of water running from the spring and foaming into the sea.

'I was going to get out,' she said.

'Why?' He found himself a comfortable spot to sit opposite her, stretched his arms out along the rocks and closed his eyes. 'Your sister's villa is a wreck but I'll put up with it for this.'

'Not necessary. You'll be on the next ferry out of here.'

'I don't think so.' His smile had a touch of the old Cleve Finch—like the devil in a good mood. 'Jerry Parker's been trying to sell me his Lear for months. We closed the deal yesterday afternoon and I thought I'd celebrate by taking a few days off and seeing what it could do.'

She frowned. 'There isn't a commercial airport on the island.'

'No, but there's a flying club. They gave me permission to land and one of the members gave me a lift here.'

The international camaraderie of flyers...

'Who's looking after Goldfinch?'

'I promoted Lucy to Operations Manager.'

'Oh… Well, not before time,' she said. 'She's been doing the job for the last year.'

'You might not be so keen when I tell you that she's brought in Gavin Jones to cover your absence.'

'Tell her to give him a contract because I'm not coming back.'

Cleve had always run an early morning circuit of the old wartime airfield that was Goldfinch's base but since Rachel's death he'd run longer and harder. His shoulders were wide, his body lean, the muscles in his limbs strongly defined and his long, elegant feet were just a toe length from her own.

Worse, while she was no longer naked, the thin silk of her robe was clinging to every inch of her body. Even in the warmth of the pool her nipples were like pebbles and she lowered herself deeper into the water.

He smiled. 'Was the sea very cold?'

'Why are you here, Cleve?' she demanded.

'Did you think I'd let you run away?'

'I'm not—'

'You pull a sickie, tell Lucy you're going on holiday and leave your resignation on my desk. In my book that's running away.'

Okay, he had a point but she'd needed time to work this out. To try and find a way to tell him about the baby without destroying him.

'I was sick.' Seriously. 'And I didn't want to tell Lucy before I told you that I'd got another job.'

'First you run away and then you lie. There is no job.'

'I've had plenty of offers.'

'That I don't doubt. I know of at least three com-

panies who've attempted to lure you away from me in
the last year. More money, the chance to get rated on
larger aircraft, but you turned them all down.'

'You knew?'

'There are no secrets in this business. If you'd accepted a job offer I'd have heard about it ten minutes
after you'd shaken hands.' He looked across the pool
at her, his face giving her no clue as to what he was
really thinking. 'If you'd got a great new job,' he continued, 'you'd have told the people you've worked with
for years, colleagues who care about you, who would
want to throw the kind of party that you'd never forget.'

'I don't need a hangover to remember you.' He'd
already given her the most precious gift… 'I'll never
forget you. Any of you,' she added quickly. 'And the
reason you haven't heard about my new job is because
I'm going to work for my father. In the design office.'
Because of course that was what she'd have to do. She
was effectively grounded, not by regulations, but by
the memory of what had happened to Rachel, and she'd
have to live close to home so that she'd have baby support, at least until the baby was old enough for day care.
'Jack was right,' she added.

'Are you telling me that you've caught the eye of
some lucky man and you're going to settle down and
raise babies?' His voice was low, but a muscle was tic-
cing in his throat. 'Only forgive me for mentioning it,
but a month ago the most exciting thing in your diary
was a darts match in the village pub.'

'Cleve…'

'Does he know about the pity—'

'Stop!' She stood up, water streaming from her,
the robe clinging to her body, her legs, the material

no doubt transparent, before he could say the word. Turn what had happened into something dirty. 'Not another word.'

She stepped out of the pool, grabbed her PJs and sandals and ran, dripping, back up the path to the house. And, lo, as if the day couldn't get any worse, Matthew Stark was hovering by the open veranda door.

Terrific.

'Did I trip over the bell and summon you like some genie, or is this a social call?' she asked.

'No. Yes,' he said, flustered by her attack. 'I was a bit concerned…' His voice trailed away and she didn't have to look around to know that Cleve was walking across the garden towards them. Matt's face said it all.

'Is this him?' Cleve hadn't bothered to put his trousers on over his wet underwear. Why would he?

'I'm sorry,' Matt said. 'I thought you were on your own.'

'So did I,' she snapped. 'How wrong can you get?'

CHAPTER FOUR

'A COUPLE OF WEEKS,' she muttered as she grabbed her wheelie and retreated to the privacy of Sofia's bedroom. A little time to get her head around an entirely new future. Was that too much to ask?

The shutters were closed and the light bulb didn't respond to the switch but there was enough light filtering through the louvres to find her wash bag. The water would be barely warm but at least she'd have the bathroom to herself while she grabbed a few minutes to take a shower and wash her hair.

She'd once crept into Sofia's private suite and it had seemed the most glamorous thing in the world to her. The windows had been dressed in something gauzy, the bed had been covered with an embroidered silk throw and in the bathroom there was a huge, claw-footed bath with brass fittings that had been polished to a gleaming gold.

There had been piles of fluffy white towels and, on recessed glass shelves, there had been an array of gorgeous scented bath oils, bubbles and soaps from the most expensive retailers.

Rosa Absolute, Gingerlily, Orange and Bergamot...

She placed her rather more basic shower gel and

shampoo on the shelf, turned on the shower and, looking for a towel, opened the cupboard and pulled one
out.

The water was emerging in fits and spurts that had
the pipes rattling and it was only lukewarm but it would
do and, having peeled off her wet robe, she stepped
into the tub.

Cleve watched Miranda walk, stiff-backed, into the
house. The effect was totally undermined by the wet
silk clinging to every curve and her hair, always sleekly
pinned up under her uniform hat at work, was loose
and curling as it dried. Catching fire in the sunlight.

Aware that he wasn't the only one enjoying the view,
he turned on the man standing beside him.

'How long?' he asked.

'I'm sorry?'

'How long have you known Miranda Marlowe?'

'To the nearest minute?' He glanced at his watch.
'Thirteen hours and twenty minutes give or take the
odd second. She told me that she was nicer after eight
hours' sleep.' He pulled a face. 'I'm not convinced.'

'But if you're not…' He let the unwelcome thought
die. There was no one. He was responsible for her decision to leave, although why she'd choose to give up
flying… 'Who are you? What are you doing here?'

'Matthew Stark. I live in the village. I kept an eye
on Sofia and now I keep an eye on the house. When I
saw the light…' He shrugged.

'You thought she was a burglar?'

'There was a time when you could have left the
door unlocked but these days there are villains who'd

have the lead off the roof and strip out the pipes for scrap metal.'

'You took a risk coming up here on your own.'

'If there had been a truck I'd have gone back to the village and called the *polizia*. I assumed someone had broken in looking for anything they could steal or a place to sleep.'

'And instead you got Miranda in a bad mood.' Realising that he'd been curt, he offered his hand. 'Cleve Finch.'

'To be fair the bang on the head couldn't have helped and the house is a mess. I'm glad she's got company,' he said, as he took it, then offered him the bag he was holding. '*Cornetti.* From the village bakery. They were supposed to be a peace offering.'

Cleve ignored the bag. 'What bang on the head?'

'She had her head in the cupboard under the sink looking for the stopcock when I arrived. She gave it a bit of a crack when she looked up. She looked a bit unsteady for a moment but she said she was just tired and wanted to sleep.'

'And you left her?'

'She didn't give me a choice. The phone line to the villa came down in a storm several years ago and was never repaired, but I did explain how to call if she needed help.' He gestured with his head towards the house. 'Have you known her long?'

'Six years.' Six years, eight months and four days. 'It was her eighteenth birthday, she'd just got her pilot's licence and had taken the plane her father had given her for a spin. There was a tricky crosswind as she approached the runway but she touched down as light as a feather.'

That perfect landing, her brilliant smile as she jumped down onto the tarmac with her newly minted pilot's licence in her hand, the sun catching the hint of cinnamon in her hair and setting it ablaze, was as fresh in his mind as if it had happened yesterday.

There had been kisses and cake for everyone. He wasn't part of the family or Marlowe Aviation. He'd been there completing a deal to buy his first freight aircraft and maybe he'd been on a high too, because he'd assured her that if she went for a commercial licence he'd give her a job. She'd instantly invited him to her and Immi's party and later, in a shadowy corner of her parents' garden, they'd shared a kiss that hadn't been about celebrating her PPL. It had been just about them. Would have been a lot more than a kiss if her younger sister—giddy on champagne—hadn't stopped him from doing something of which he would have later been ashamed.

There had been other kisses. She'd lain in wait for him when she knew he was flying in. And she'd never let him forget his promise to give her a job.

He realised that Matt Stark was waiting but there was nothing more he wanted to share. 'Thanks for these,' he said, finally taking the bag. 'Hopefully they'll sweeten her mood.'

'Good luck with that.' He let himself out through the side gate and a few moments later Cleve heard the unmistakable buzz of a scooter heading down the hill.

Deciding that some clothes might help his case, he pulled his shirt over his head, stepped into his trousers and had just made it to the kitchen when there was an ear-splitting scream.

He dropped the bag and ran in the direction of the

sound, bursting through the door into what, discon-
certingly, was a bedroom.

'Miranda!'

There was a whimper and he found her in the en-
suite bathroom, teeth chattering, backed up into the
corner of the bath, her gaze fixed on a seriously im-
pressive spider on the wall behind the shower.

He picked up a towel that was out of her reach on a
wicker chair and offered it to her. Frozen to the spot,
she made no move to take it. This was a full-on case
of arachnophobia.

He draped the towel over her and as he lifted her
clear of the bath she clung to him as he had clung to her.

'It j-just appeared out of n-nowhere,' she said, re-
gaining the power of speech now the spider was out
of sight.

'I'll handle it,' he promised. 'Can I put you down?'
She nodded and he set her down and walked her
through to the bedroom but she continued to cling to
him. 'Will you be all right on your own in here while
I get rid of it?'

'Don't kill it! It's unlucky to kill spiders.'

'Is it?'

'Don't laugh!'

'I'm not laughing, I promise.' He might just be smiling but then, with his arms unexpectedly filled with a
naked woman who was clinging to him for dear life,
he had a lot to smile about. That spider deserved to live
a long and happy life. 'I'll put it out of the window.'

'No!' She pulled back a little, looked up at him, her
eyes desperate. 'It'll just climb back in through the air
vent. You have to take it right away. Outside the gates.'

He didn't think it would be a good idea to point out

that a spider could just as easily climb the gates and make its way back inside. There was nothing rational about her fear.

'Outside the gates,' he promised.

'Not *just* outside the gates.'

'I'll take it over the road and set it free in the trees. Will that be far enough?'

She looked doubtful but she nodded and said, 'I suppose so.'

'You'll have to let go,' he said with regret but the last thing he wanted was for the spider to take the opportunity to disappear.

'Yes…' Her fingers were bunched tight around his shirt front and it took a mental effort for her to open them, to take a step away from the protection of his arms. He had his own battle with the desire to wrap his arms around her, hold her, never let her go. Instead he caught the towel, which was the only thing between her and decency, before it dropped to the floor and, his eyes not leaving her face, he wrapped it around her and tucked the end between her breasts.

'I won't be long,' he said, his voice struggling through a throat stuffed with hot rocks.

Andie fought against the urge to grab him, keep him with her. Working in such a male environment, she'd had to put on the anything-you-can-do-I-can-do-better façade. The slightest sign of weakness would have been ruthlessly exploited.

That didn't matter here and she didn't take her eyes off Cleve until he disappeared into the bathroom, backing as far away from the door as physically possible.

He left a few moments later with the spider caught in a towel and, released from her terror, she scrambled into the first clothes that came to hand: a pair of cropped trousers and a vest top.

She combed through her hair, tied it back with a hairband and went to the kitchen. The kitchen was old-fashioned, with a dresser that would have to be stripped down, the china washed, and a large wooden table that they'd sat around for supper.

A search of the cupboard under the sink revealed an inch of liquid soap in a plastic container and she filled a bowl with hot water. By the time Cleve returned she'd stripped one shelf of china and piled it in and was giving the draining board and plate rack a thorough going-over.

'Can I help?'

'You already have.' Deeply embarrassed by the exhibition she'd made of herself, she cleared her throat. 'Thank you for rescuing me.'

'Any time.' He picked up the kettle and leaned in close to fill it at the tap. She was still shaky and the brief touch of his shoulder made her feel safe all over again. 'Do you want to talk about it?' he asked, moving away to put the kettle on the hotplate. 'Miranda?'

'I've tried the talking cure. It didn't help.'

'Talk to me.'

She glanced up. He'd turned his back on the stove and was looking at her so intently that she forgot what she was going to say. The only thing in her mind was how it had felt to be held, trembling, in his arms. The beat of his pulse against her ear, his hands spread across her naked back, keeping her safe.

'It can't hurt.' He moved away from the stove, was one step, two steps closer and all she could see was his mouth… 'I don't want to scare you but this house has been empty for a while. That spider is not going to be the only creature crawling out of the cracks in the walls.'

'The lizards don't bother me.' She forced herself to look away, look up at the little gecko sitting high on the wall near the ceiling. 'They eat mosquitoes and flies.'

'So do spiders.'

'They also have a million legs and eyes.'

'A million?'

She heard the teasing note in his voice, knew that a tiny crease would have appeared at the corner of his mouth and, unable to help herself, she responded with a smile.

'Okay, eight,' she said as, suddenly self-conscious, she began rubbing at a stubborn spot of dirt, 'which is at least four too many and when they move it looks like a lot more. Plus they're hairy. And they have fangs.'

'That's all you've got?'

Still teasing.

How long had it been? Not since a party in the mess, when one of the engineers had had a crush on her and she'd had to hide in the ladies'. Rachel hadn't been there that night and Cleve had smuggled her out the back way.

Unable to help herself, she gave him a sideways look. His face was thinner, the crease deeper than she remembered.

'In my head I can rationalise it. I know that they're more frightened of me than I am of them. But then I see one and all that goes out of the window.'

He leaned back against the drainer and folded his arms. She'd seen him do that a dozen or more times when someone was rambling on, full of excuses. He never said anything, just waited until it all came out.

'When I was eight a boy at school put a huge spider down my back. I could feel it wriggling inside my blouse and I was hysterical, tearing at my clothes, screaming.' Even now, thinking about it made her skin goose. 'There were buttons flying everywhere and he and his beastly little gang were laughing so much that they were rolling on the floor when one of the teachers came running out to find out what was happening.' She swallowed. 'It wasn't even a real spider but one of those horrible rubber things you can get from a joke shop.'

'Why did he pick on you?'

'Apparently his father had called him a fool for letting a girl beat him in a maths test.'

'What a pity you can't suspend parents for bad behaviour.'

She shook her head. 'The poor kid was to be pitied but it doesn't alter the fact that every time I see a spider I'm eight years old again and I can feel all those legs wriggling against my skin.'

'That's classic PTSD.'

'Not the kind anyone takes seriously.' She rinsed the cloth under the tap. 'I've learned to deal calmly with the occasional spider in the bath and believe me I checked before I got into the tub. I was washing my hair and I'd closed my eyes when I rinsed off the shampoo. When I opened them it was right there on the wall, thirty centimetres from my face.'

'It would have given anyone a bad moment.' He turned away, looked at a damp patch in the corner of the ceiling. 'I hate to say this but, looking at the state of this place, I'm afraid you're likely to meet a few of that chap's relations if you stay here. Why don't you move into a hotel?'

'I'm not here for a holiday…' Before he could ask why she was here, she said, 'Probate is moving at the speed of a glacier, Posy is tied up until later this summer and meantime this place is going to rack and ruin.'

He frowned. 'Should you be here if the estate isn't settled? Where did you get the key?'

'Sofia gave a set to Grandma the last time she was here. She must have known she was dying.'

'Posy's godmother? Why was she living here?'

'Sofia Romana? I don't suppose you've heard of her but she was one of the early supermodels. There's a photograph of her in the hall. She knew everyone, mixed in high society and when she had an affair with King Ludano, he set her up in this villa.'

'An interesting choice as godmother.'

'She and my grandmother were best friends. They started kindergarten on the same day. Mum and Dad were totally tied up trying to keep Marlowe Aviation afloat after Granddad died so suddenly and Grandma used to bring us here for the holidays. It was enormous fun. Film stars used to come to her parties.'

'What happened?'

'We grew up and life got serious.' She looked up, gazed out of the window. 'We sent cards for Sofia's birthday and Christmas. Little gifts, but I wish…' She shook her head. 'Have you had breakfast?'

'No, but your kindly neighbour brought you *cornetti* as a peace offering.' He tore open the bag that he'd retrieved on his way back inside, releasing the scent of the warm, cream-filled pastries. 'I hope you're going to share.'

Her stomach gave a warning lurch and she looked quickly away. Not now... Please, not now...

'Help yourself.'

'Are you okay?'

'Fine.' She plunged her hands back into the water, produced a plate and put it on the rack. The soap had a faint lemony scent and she concentrated hard on that. Cleve picked up a cloth and reached for the plate. 'It's more hygienic to let them drain,' she said.

'Is it? What can I do to help?'

'Nothing. Why don't you take your breakfast outside? They'll taste better in the fresh air.'

'Will they?' He bit into one of them, releasing a wave of buttery, creamy, sugary scent. 'I don't think that's possible. Is there any coffee?'

Coffee...

She didn't need the smell; the word was enough. She just about managed a strangled 'No—' before, clamping a wet hand over her mouth, she ran for the cloakroom.

Afterwards, she splashed her face with cold water and when she looked up Cleve was leaning against the door frame, arms folded, his face unreadable.

'Am I the last to know?' he asked.

'No!' This was a nightmare. Exactly what she hadn't wanted to happen. 'No one knows.'

'I think Lucy might have a good idea.'

'I haven't told her. I haven't told anyone.'

He nodded. 'So when were you going to tell me?'

'Can I...?' She indicated the doorway he was blocking. 'I could do with some fresh air.'

He moved aside, following her through the snug to the veranda. She sat on one of the steps and if he'd sat beside her, reached out to take her hand, if he'd said something…

Instead he leaned against one of the pillars and the silence stretched out like an elastic band that you knew was going to come back and sting you if you didn't do something.

'I haven't seen you, Cleve.'

'You were the one who left that morning. You arranged your schedule so that we wouldn't be in the office at the same time.'

She stared at him. 'What? No.' She shook her head. 'You did that.'

'Me? Why would I do that? Damn it, Miranda, you saved me that night. If I'd got in the Mayfly I would have flown in a direct line to the coast and kept going until I ran out of fuel. You knew that,' he said. 'It's why you stopped me.'

'Yes…' The word was no more than a whisper. His eyes had been dead.

'It's why you flew her back the next morning and left me your Nymph. I understood that and I came after you but you didn't stay to see if I got her safely back to base.'

'I knew you'd never do anything to damage her.'

She'd seen him through his moment of crisis, given him the comfort of her body when he was in despair and then again in an act of healing. She'd seen him laid bare, held him while he'd wept in her arms. Watched him sleeping, all the tension of the last year wiped from his face.

'Immi was expecting me.'

'For the dress fitting. That was much more important, obviously. How did it go?'

'The fitting?' She frowned. Why on earth would he care? 'Fine. No frills,' she said, but in truth she scarcely remembered the dress, or Immi's excited chatter about food, flowers, music.

Her senses were totally swamped by the night she'd spent with Cleve.

It was as if he'd been starving and he'd filled himself with every part of her, filled her with every part of him and she was hanging onto the memory of every touch of his hand, his mouth, his tongue. Storing it up like a squirrel hoarding nuts for the winter.

The dressmaker, pinning the hem, had looked up as one of the tears that had been running, unnoticed, down her cheeks had dropped onto the dress. She'd passed it off, telling Immi that she had been remembering how sick she'd been, how there was a time when none of them could have imagined her becoming such a beautiful bride.

But the tears were for Cleve, still so desperately in love with Rachel. And for her. Because, as for him, there could only ever be one love.

Then, realising that he was making some kind of point, she said, 'Does it matter?'

'I imagine she'll have to let it out. The dress. If you're keeping the baby.'

'If—' She was on her feet without knowing how she'd made it, facing him.

'Isn't that why you haven't told anyone?' he demanded, before she could say another word. 'Why you're hiding away in this crumbling pink birthday cake of a house? Why you're running away?'

'No—' Her mouth was so dry that the word snagged in her throat.

'It never occurred to me…' He caught himself, staring up at the sky as if for inspiration. 'How could you have taken such a risk?'

'Risk?' She took a step back, stumbled and if he hadn't shot out a hand and grabbed her arm she would have fallen, but the minute she regained her balance she shook him off. 'The only thing on my mind that evening was you, falling apart in front of me. Not contraception, not STDs. And my only concern since the stick turned blue has been that the news would be the final straw that broke you. Well, clearly I need have no worries on that score. You're about to become a father. Live with it.'

'Andie—'

He reached out to her but she lifted her arm out of reach and, because she didn't want to go back into the house with its cobwebs and spiders, turned and headed into the garden, pushing her way through overgrown shrubs and weeds until she found the hidden stone arbour where she and Immi had hung out.

It was too early for the roses that scrambled over it but the buds were beginning to form. Another few weeks and the air would be full of their scent.

Cleve put his hand to his heart as if he could somehow slow it down, catch his breath. Miranda Marlowe was going to have his baby and it was as if time had just been turned back, he was twenty-four again with the most beautiful girl in his arms and a world to conquer.

He wanted to roar, shout the news to the world, punch the air, but he had to think about Miranda, how she must be feeling, and he rubbed his hands over his face to erase the grin before he went to find her.

The paint had peeled from the bench leaving bare, silvery wood but it looked solid enough. She was sitting, eyes closed, legs stretched out in front of her, when she heard Cleve thrashing through overgrown paths as he searched for her. Muttering a curse as something whipped back at him.

He didn't call out, maybe he thought she wouldn't answer and he was right, but eventually he stumbled onto the hidden arbour and the bench gave a little as he sat beside her.

'I'm sorry.'

She didn't open her eyes. 'I don't want you to be sorry, Cleve. I don't want anything from you. I'm nearly twenty-five years old and having a baby is not going to ruin my life.' On the contrary his baby was a precious gift... 'You can go now.'

'I didn't mean...' He paused. 'Will you look at me, Miranda?'

It was easier when she wasn't looking at him, but she raised her lids and turned to him. 'You've scratched your face,' she said.

He raised his hand to his cheek and his fingers came away smeared with a little blood. 'It was a rose that hasn't been pruned in years.'

'Sofia loved her garden.' She found a clean tissue in her pocket and, resisting the urge to lean forward and wipe the scratch, she handed it to him. 'It's sad to see it so neglected.'

'I think the house has more problems than an overgrown garden.' He pressed the tissue briefly to the scratch then tucked it in his breast pocket without looking at it. 'I'm sorry for what I said, implied...'

'It was the natural thing for you to think but I didn't

run away. I left that morning without waking you because I didn't want either of us to have to go through
one of those awkward morning-after moments where
you don't know what on earth to say.'

She'd lain, wrapped in his arms, until dawn. Not
moving, willing him to stay asleep, drawing out the
moment for as long as she could, only moving when
he'd turned over, taking the covers with him.

She'd held her breath, sure he would wake, but his
face had been pressed into the pillow, his finely mus-
cled back moving in the gentle rise and fall of the truly
asleep. She could have watched him for hours, but instead she'd written a note to tell him where she'd gone,
quietly gathered fresh clothes that she kept at home
and left.

'I was going to call you from Cyprus.' His arm
brushed against hers as he raised his hand to drag his
fingers through his hair. 'I picked up the phone a dozen
times.'

Confirming that she'd been right.

'We've been friends for a long time, Cleve. I didn't
need words. I'm just glad I was there when you needed
someone.'

'And now you need me.' He took her hand, wrapped
his cool, dry fingers around it. 'What are the legal requirements here?'

She frowned. 'Legal requirements?'

'How soon can we get married?'

CHAPTER FIVE

ANDIE SQUEEZED HER EYES tight shut against the sting of tears as she shook her head, took back her hand.

'Don't!'

'A baby needs two parents, Miranda. You can't do that on your own. The only decision is whether we do it simply, here and now before the baby shows, or wait until after he's born and have the whole nine yards in the village church.'

'I won't be on my own. I have a family who will do everything they can to support me.'

'That would be the family you haven't told about our baby.'

Our baby...

The words sounded so sweet. Cleve was offering her everything she'd ever wanted. Offering the big promise, the one about loving and honouring her for the rest of his life.

That had been the dream in her eighteen-year-old heart when they'd crept away from her birthday party and in the darkness of the garden his white-hot kiss had seared her lips, his touch doing unimagined things to her body. Would have done everything if Posy hadn't come blundering through the bushes and crashed into them completely pie-eyed from the champagne she'd been sneaking.

Except it wouldn't be like that. Honesty compelled her to admit that it had never been like that. She'd thrown herself at Cleve and he'd caught her with enthusiasm. She'd made sure she was there whenever he came to the factory that summer and there had been other hot kisses, stolen moments, but they'd never dated. He'd never come to the house and taken her out. It had always been hidden, a secret, never more than an opportunistic flirtation for him.

It would be a hollow promise now, with only their baby binding them together as he or she reached all those precious milestones. First steps, first words, first day at school.

She was nearly twenty-five, too old to fool herself with teenage dreams. She had to live with reality, and the reality was that Cleve was still in love with his dead wife. That her son or daughter would be a substitute for the baby Rachel had been carrying when she died.

That wasn't a dream, it was a nightmare.

She stirred. 'You are right about one thing. This—' she lifted a hand to indicate the house, the garden '—this was running away. You know how it is when people work together. You throw up once and you've got a tummy bug. Twice and they're looking at the calendar, trying to remember who they've seen you with.' She drew in a slow steadying breath and turned to look at him. 'I haven't told anyone about the baby because I wanted you to hear the news from me rather than overhear some nudge-nudge, wink-wink speculation in the mess about who the lucky man might be.'

'Because I'd know.'

She tilted her head in acknowledgement. 'What did Lucy say?'

'Nothing… You know Lucy, she's as tight-lipped as a clam. It was just the way she said that it bothered the punters when the pilot threw up in the sick bag. I didn't pick up on it because I assumed your "bug" was just an excuse to get away for a while. Knew it was once I'd opened your letter. My mistake.'

'I really wasn't fit to fly. If I'd told her I was leaving she'd have wanted to know all the whys and wherefores.' She lifted a hand in a helpless gesture. 'She's not someone who takes "no comment" for an answer.'

'I don't think she would have asked because she already knew. It seems pretty clear now that she was dropping a heavy hint and she wouldn't have done that unless she was certain I'm the father.'

'The fact that you immediately took off will confirm it.'

'Undoubtedly, but she'll keep her thoughts to herself.' He used the thumb of his free hand to wipe away the moisture from beneath her eyes, cradled her cheek, looked into her eyes. 'We've been friends for a long time, Miranda. We'll be okay.'

He was saying all the right things, everything expected of a decent man, everything she'd known he'd say, and she wanted to believe him with all her heart. But her heart knew that being 'okay' with Cleve Finch was never going to be enough. Knowing that she would never light up his life, that when he looked at her he would be thinking of Rachel and the baby that never had a chance…

Resisting the temptation to lean into his hand, the

arm waiting to go around her, she retrieved her hand and turned away.

'A baby is not a good reason to get married, Cleve.'

'It's not a bad one. It used to be mandatory.'

'Thankfully things have moved on. I doubt Dad will stick a shotgun in your back.'

'I'm sure he won't.' He sounded unexpectedly bitter and without thinking she put her hand on his, provoking a shadow of a smile. 'Is there any chance that he might put one in yours?'

'What would be the point when we'd both know that he'd never pull the trigger?' She squeezed his hand briefly. 'I'll be okay, Cleve.'

'Of course you will. You're an organised and capable woman but, even with all the support in the world, life as a one-parent family is no joke. Your sisters lead busy lives. Your parents are finally letting go of the reins after a tough battle to bring the business back from the brink after your grandfather's death, turn it into the success it's become. They deserve time to enjoy their freedom.'

'You think I'm being selfish?'

'Not at all. I just think you need a reality check.' He placed his other hand on top of hers, held it for a moment. 'Whatever happens I want you to know that I'll be there with you every step of the way.'

'Even in the delivery room?' The words were out before her brain was engaged.

'I planted the seed, Miranda. I'll be there for the harvest.'

She swallowed but her throat was aching with the tears she was fighting to suppress and she couldn't speak.

'Will you at least think about it while I'm gone?' he said.

'Gone?'

The speed of her response betrayed her and his eyes creased in a smile. 'I won't be long. I'm going to walk down to the village and pick up some food. I need something a little more substantial than mint tea and cake for breakfast.' He released her hand, got to his feet. 'Is there anything that would tempt you?'

Oh, she was tempted.

For a long time she'd only been able to imagine what it would be like to spend the night in Cleve's arms. Now she knew and she was being offered unlimited access. All she had to do was say yes.

She forced herself to concentrate on the question, letting her mind wander over the major food groups. It came to rest on the image of a banana and her stomach didn't actually recoil.

'I might be able to eat a banana. A soft one, squashed on a slice of proper bread.' Her stomach rumbled appreciatively.

'That's a start. Anything else? Pickles? A lump or two of coal?' he teased.

'Yes.' She lifted her hand to shade her eyes from the sun. 'Take a look in the garage and if there's a can bring back a few litres of petrol.'

'Milk will do you more good.'

About to laugh, she realised that he was serious but then he'd been here before. Like any excited father-to-be he would have read all the books, wanting to share every moment of such a life-changing event with Rachel.

'I'll need a little time for my stomach to adjust to

the possibility of dairy,' she said. 'Meanwhile, unless someone has spirited them away, there should be a selection of vintage vehicles including a two-seater sports car and a scooter in one of the sheds.'

'They should help pay for the roof repairs but I imagine they'll all need a little more than petrol to get them started.'

'They'll certainly need an oil top-up but there might be some in the garage. I'll come with you and check.' Cleve looked as if he was about to say something irritating about putting her feet up. Before he could she said, 'I'll need some form of transport while I'm here.'

'My vote is for the vintage two-seater,' he said, holding out a hand. She took it, let him haul her to her feet, because not to would make too much of it. But then he kept her hand in his, holding back the long whippy shoots from overgrown shrubs so they wouldn't catch her bare arms, not letting go until they reached the garages.

There was a padlock but the hasp was little more than rust and all it needed was a tug. Cleve opened one of the doors and they were all there. The scooter, a little runaround that you could park on a sixpence, still bright red beneath a thick coating of dust and, underneath a dust sheet, the shape of a long, elegant convertible.

The two cars had been jacked up so that the tyres were not touching the ground. Alberto had taken good care of them.

While Cleve looked for a petrol can, Andie slid onto the seat of the scooter and grasped the handlebars.

'We used to take turns riding this around the yard.'

Cleve turned to look at her. 'Portia snuck out on it one night to ride down to the village to meet a boy.'

'Why doesn't that surprise me?' he said, reaching for a petrol container he'd spotted on a shelf.

'She wheeled it out to the road so no one would hear her start it up and she didn't dare put the lights on in case someone spotted her. She only made it to the first bend before she landed in the ditch.'

Cleve, an only child, tried to imagine what it must be like to belong to such a close-knit family where no matter how you fought amongst yourselves, you always had one another's backs.

He turned the container over to check that the bottom was sound. 'Was she hurt?'

'A black eye and some colourful bruises. She told Grandma and Sofia that she'd had a bad dream and fallen out of bed.'

'Inventive. How did she explain the damage to the scooter?'

'Immi and I said we'd knocked it over getting it out of the garage. Alberto wasn't fooled but he cleaned it up and had it looking as good as new before they saw it and guessed what really happened.'

She stepped off the scooter and cautiously opened a dusty metal box sitting at the end of a workbench. Inside, neatly laid out, were folded cloths, chamois leathers, polishes—everything needed to keep the vehicles pristine.

'Alberto?'

'He and Elena looked after the house and gardens. I wonder if they still live in the village.' She opened a box of latex gloves and pulled on a pair, then picked up a cloth and began to carefully wipe away the dust to reveal the scooter's still-pristine pale blue finish. 'They seemed incredibly old to us at the time but I don't suppose they were.'

'No.' He raised the can. 'This looks okay. I won't be long.'

'Bring some marmalade.' She looked up, catching him by surprise with a grin that made her look eighteen again. 'For the vitamin C.'

It had been a long time since she'd smiled at him like that and he didn't spoil her joke by suggesting he pick up something a little more effective from the pharmacy. But then, unable to help himself, he said, 'Have you seen a doctor?'

She straightened and for a moment he could see her struggling for an answer because his question had been intrusive, personal, none of his business. Except that it was.

Everything about Miranda and their baby was going to be very much his business for the rest of his life. Convincing her of that might be a problem, but just when he thought she was going to give him a reality check her face softened and she put her hand against her still-flat waist.

'Not yet but I've been to the NHS website and I'm taking the folic acid and vitamin D as advised.' She pulled a face. 'Keeping it down is something else.'

It was all he could do not to reach out and cover her hand with his. To put his arm around her, holding them both, protecting them both, but, aware that she was totally in control of this situation, that she could shut him out at any time, he clutched the can a little tighter and stayed where he was.

'Can you feel anything?' The words struggled through the sudden thickness in his throat.

'Not yet. Not until about sixteen weeks. He, she is due around the second week in November.'

It was the first time she'd volunteered anything. It felt like an important turning point and for a moment neither of them moved, said anything as they absorbed the reality of what was happening to them.

'I'd better go.'

She nodded. 'I'll give the scooter a once-over.'

He wanted to demand that she sit down, put her feet up, do nothing until he returned but had the sense to keep his mouth shut and after a moment he forced his feet to move.

He'd assumed that his phone would come to life in the village but there was only the barest flicker. L'Isola dei Fiori was undeveloped even by tourist standards. For the first time in a very long time business was the furthest thing from his mind—his sole focus was Miranda and the baby—but he needed to check in to the office and he looked around for a post office, knowing that they would have a public call box.

He called Lucy, explained that he would be out of contact for a day or two and got a somewhat sarcastic response that he'd been out of contact for a year.

'It's fortunate that you're really good at your job, Lucy, or I'd have to fire you.'

'It's fortunate that I'm really good at my job or you'd have been out of business. Just take care of Andie,' she said.

She ended the call before he could reply and he was laughing as he replaced the receiver, crossed to the counter and joined the queue so that he could pick up some local currency.

He hadn't known what to say to Miranda until he'd realised that he was about to lose her. At that moment there was only one thing he wanted to say to her and he'd imagined flying in, finding her at some pretty villa, wooing her with good food, great wine, walks on the beach. Somehow convincing her to stay—not with Goldfinch, but with him.

The baby changed everything; he'd realised that she was never going to buy a desperate over-the-top declaration five minutes after he'd discovered she was pregnant. Five minutes after he'd practically accused her...

Just thinking about what he'd said made his blood run cold.

Hard as it had been to stop everything he felt from spilling out, he had managed to play it low-key, accepting that she wouldn't leap at his offer of marriage. Even without the baby, she'd have been convinced that his proposal was guilt-driven and rejected it out of hand.

There had been the possibility of something between them years ago. He'd been captivated by her smile, her love of flying, the way she'd looked at him. It would have been so easy to take everything she was offering, but Miranda Marlowe was the kind of girl you took home to meet your mother, a for-ever girl. She had been about to leave for university, a different life, while he'd had the kind of reputation that raised a father's hackles, a business that required every moment of his time just to keep it afloat and a bank calling in loans.

Back then their lives had been out of sync but now, magically, they had the chance to mesh if he didn't mess up.

For the moment he had to be content to sow the seed, put the thought of a future together in her head, nurture it with a show-not-tell campaign. He had to prove that he was serious, that he was with her for the long haul. That their baby was going to have two parents.

As he'd strolled down to the village, the sea shimmering on his left, the scent of wild rosemary clearing his head as he brushed against it, he'd had plenty of time to imagine how it would be.

He was going to be there for the scans, the prenatal classes, the birth. Be there for everything that came after.

He wasn't giving up on marriage, but he knew that was something he would have to earn and he was prepared to wait.

He paused outside a shop filled with exquisite baby clothes and soft toys. A small white teddy with a blue bow was practically begging him to come and buy it. He stepped away.

This had to be about Miranda, not the baby, and she wanted marmalade and *benzina*.

He bought groceries, stocked up on cleaning materials, filled the fuel can at the petrol station and was on his way back when he saw the name 'Stark' on a name plate by the gate of a large cottage. On an impulse he stopped, walked up the garden path and knocked.

Matt opened the door, raised an eyebrow 'Has Andie thrown you out?'

'Not yet.' He was planning to stay as long as she'd put up with him. 'She mentioned a couple who used to work at the villa. I wondered if they were still in the village.'

'Elena and Alberto? They're still here but they're

retired. I'm not sure they're up to helping clean up the villa. One of their sons keeps the grass cut in the spring. Unless it's watered it doesn't grow much in the summer.'

'It's not that. I think Miranda would like to visit them. Although if you know of anyone interested in a cleaning job we could certainly do with some help.'

'I'm sure they'd appreciate a visit. I'll point you in the right direction.' He stepped out of the cottage and walked towards the gate. 'If you go up that lane over there,' he said, indicating a turning a little way up the hill, 'they live in the third house on the right.'

'Thanks.'

'No problem and I'll ask around about help.' Matt hesitated. 'I usually bring my mother up to the villa in the afternoon to use the hot spring. I mentioned it to Andie and she was fine with it, but I don't want to be...' He stopped, frowned. 'Is that smoke?'

Cleve turned, looked up the hill where a thin plume of black smoke was rising into a clear blue sky.

'Miranda... She was in the garage...'

He dropped the bags and the can and began to run. He heard Matt shout something and then come after him on his scooter, pausing so that Cleve could scramble on the back before racing up the hill as the smoke began to billow out from somewhere behind the villa.

Cleve was off and through the gate before the bike was brought to a halt, then he was standing for a moment in confusion as he realised that the garage was not on fire. He spun around and saw Miranda, a dark smudge on her cheek and a small fire extinguisher in her hand, emerging from the villa.

'What the hell did you think you were doing?' he demanded, fear driving his anger.

'I, um…' She blinked, coughed. 'I saw the smoke, grabbed the fire extinguisher and rushed in.'

'Idiot,' he said, grabbing her, holding onto her, only too aware of what might have happened. 'The last thing you ever do is rush into a burning building.'

'I know,' she mumbled into his shoulder. 'But it's Posy's house.'

'It'll be insured. You'd have done her a favour if you'd let it burn down.'

'No!' She shook her head. 'This place is special. Magic…'

Matt came skidding into the courtyard. 'We saw the smoke. Are you okay, Andie?'

Miranda pulled away from Cleve, gave Matt a smile. 'I'm fine… I can't say the same for the kitchen and the house will probably stink of smoke for days.'

'What happened?'

'Someone, not mentioning any names, put the kettle on the hotplate and forgot to turn it off.'

The kettle? He'd done this?

Bile rose in his throat and unable to look her in the face he turned away and crossed the courtyard to stare, unseeing, at the sun sparkling on sea as the familiar veil of guilt descended, turning everything dark.

Less than an hour ago he'd been full of how he'd protect her, protect their child, imagining himself at her side through pregnancy, sharing the parenting, hoping that one day she'd look up and realise that they were a family. Instead he'd nearly killed her and their baby.

'Cleve?' He felt her hand on his arm, heard the concern in her voice. 'It was an accident. It could have happened to anyone.'

He shook his head, unable to look at her, to speak. It hadn't happened to anyone. It had happened to her and he was responsible.

'I saw you put the kettle on. We both forgot about it—'

'It was my responsibility.'

'You were a little distracted.' She was by his side and lifted a hand to his face, forced him to look at her. 'No harm, no foul.' Her smile was tender, she was doing her best to reassure him but she had no idea.

'Anything could have happened in that wreck of a house. The ceiling could have collapsed, you could have been trapped—'

They both turned at the sound of an approaching fire engine and Matt shrugged apologetically. 'I shouted to Mum to call them.'

A second later the big gates burst open, four firefighters rushed in and for a moment there was total confusion until Matt—who seemed to be passably fluent in the local patois—managed to convince them that the emergency was over. That signora Marlowe had put out the fire.

They checked to make sure that it was properly extinguished, that everything was safe, then they all kissed Miranda extravagantly on both cheeks, declared her *'bella e coraggiosa'* and then, with a little encouragement, finally departed, closing the big gates behind them.

'I'll, um, go and fetch your stuff,' Matt said, wasting no time in following them.

'Stuff?' Miranda asked, when he'd gone.

'I dropped the shopping at Matt's. When we saw the smoke. The marmalade may not have survived,' he said, remembering the crunch as the bag hit the path.

'You were at Matt's?'

'I saw his name on the gate and I stopped to ask about Elena and Alberto. I thought you'd like to visit.'

A smile lit up her face. 'I would. Thank you.'

There was a black smudge on her cheek and he took a step back before he lost all grip on reality, reached out to wipe it away, kiss her, hold her, keep her safe. He could keep no one safe…

'I bought a load of cleaning stuff.'

Andie had seen the colour drain from Cleve's face as he realised what he'd done, the lines bitten deep into his cheeks.

'That's handy,' she said, hoping to tease him out of it. 'The kitchen was a mess. Now it's a disaster area.'

'I'll clean up,' he said, heading for the door. 'Then I'll get out of your hair.'

Well, that had fallen flat. About to tell him that she'd been kidding, that they'd do it together, she realised what he'd just said. Out of her hair meant— 'Are you telling me that once you've washed the smoke from the walls you're going to leave?'

His face was pale but his eyes were no longer empty. They were haunted.

She'd taken part in regular fire safety drills, done all the right things. Switched off the power, thrown the damp tea towel he'd been using over the kettle and then doused it thoroughly with the extinguisher, but he was reliving what had happened to Rachel. Their baby.

'Cleve—'

'You're right, Miranda,' he said. 'Your family will be there for you and your baby.'

'*My* baby?'

'The last thing you need is me messing up your life any more than I have done. I'll sort out financial support when I get back.'

Financial…?

An hour ago she would have sworn that nothing would have shifted him. Now, because of a stupid accident, he was staring into the past, reliving the horror. He wasn't just pale, he was grey, but she didn't need a degree in psychology to know that leaving now would be the very worst thing he could do.

Behaving like a pathetic little diva was totally alien to her nature but needs must; she had to stop him any way she could and she grabbed at the first excuse that came to mind.

'What will I do if there's another of those horrible spiders?'

'I've brought you something to deter the spiders.'

He had? 'I'm not using some dangerous poisonous spray.'

'It's peppermint oil. I asked the woman in the grocery store and she recommended it.'

'Peppermint oil?'

'Apparently vinegar is just as good but I thought the smell of peppermint would be easier to live with. You add a few drops to water and spray in the cracks.'

'Oh…' Without warning her throat filled up and her eyes began to sting.

He frowned, took a step towards her. 'Are you crying?'

If that was what it took…

'It happens all the time,' she said, flapping a hand in front of her face. 'It's the hormones.'

He was wearing that helpless look of a man faced with a woman having emotional collywobbles and she took pitiless advantage. 'It's not just the spiders. There are storms at this time of year. Or a tremor might bring the rest of the roof down and there'll be no one to dig me out,' she said, piling on the drama.

His jaw tightened and the forward momentum stopped.

'I have no doubt that Matt Stark will leap on his scooter and come racing to your rescue.'

Without warning she lost it. 'I'm not having Matthew Stark's baby!' she yelled. 'I'm having yours!'

Andie heard the words leaving her mouth but it was like listening to a stranger. Not her but some mouthy, out-of-control character in a television soap opera.

She'd poked the hormone genie and, let loose, it was having the time of its life. Unfortunately, it had overdone the drama because Cleve's response was to retreat, not physically but mentally. The flash of concern that had momentarily lit up his eyes had gone. There was nothing coming back from him and in the silence that followed her outburst there was only the sound of a throat being cleared.

'I'll, um, just leave this here.'

Matt very carefully placed two carriers and a petrol can just inside the side gate before backing out and closing it behind him.

CHAPTER SIX

CLEVE LOOKED AT the bags then, as if nothing had happened, he looked back at her.

'You don't have to stay here,' he said. 'You can come back with me in the Lear.'

Andie shook her head. 'That's not going to happen.'

All that waited for her at home was an ending. Putting her flat on the market, saying goodbye to the people she'd worked with, to the job she loved. Saying hello to a direct-debit relationship with Cleve.

'Have you any idea how long it's been since I've had a holiday?' she demanded. 'More to the point, how long is it since you've had a holiday?'

He glanced up at the roof with its missing tiles. 'I don't know about you but I'm pretty sure that the last time I booked a holiday there wasn't a hole in the roof.

'It was thatch, as I recall.'

Rachel had been full of the exotic spa resort in the Far East but at the last minute some crisis had blown up that only Cleve could handle. Rather than cancel and rebook, she'd gone on her own.

How he must regret that now.

'I wasn't looking forward to the mud baths, steam wraps and heaven knows what other tortures were lined up for me,' he said, his face devoid of expression. 'Rachel had a much better time without me.'

She'd certainly come back glowing and then, just weeks later, she was dead.

'Yes, well, all that lounging about in the sun and swilling cocktails is so yesterday,' she said, as whatever demon had been driving her disappeared like early morning mist rising from a valley, leaving nothing but embarrassment. 'These days smart people go to Cumbria and pay for the privilege of repairing footpaths and building dry stone walls in the pouring rain.'

'No risk of fire, then.'

'Forget the stupid fire. What happened was nothing more than a minor drama.' Okay, if she hadn't smelt the smoke the house could have burned down, but she had and it didn't. 'The roof didn't collapse, no one was hurt. It will be one of those "Do you remember when…?" stories that we'll all be laughing about years from now.'

'Laughing?'

'Yes.' Laughing as they embroidered the story for a little boy who was the image of Cleve. 'Idiot Daddy, brave Mama, comic-opera firefighters…'

For a moment she saw them all at some family gathering: her parents and her sisters, sitting around a table, the children wide-eyed, the adults laughing at stories that had grown with the telling. The image was so real that a chill whispered through her, the realisation that unless she did something, something truly brave, it was about to slip away from them, be lost for ever.

Cleve would eventually get past his grief, marry someone else, have a family…while the bundle of cells, the promise of life within her, would become an awkward adjunct to his real life. Someone they would make an effort to include but who would always be on the outside looking in.

'Laughing?' he repeated furiously, bringing her back to reality. 'You could have died!'

His angry words echoed around the courtyard.

She could have died. Like Rachel.

As if a switch had tripped in her brain she was no longer playing the role. Rachel was dead but she was alive and this was for real. Her own feelings didn't matter; this wasn't just about her. This was for Cleve and their baby, and she'd fight tooth and nail, make a complete fool of herself if that was what it took to make him let go of the past, look to the future.

'Could have but didn't. I'm right here and so is our baby. What happened to your offer to be there for our child, Cleve? To make a home? A family?'

He seemed shocked by her sudden switch, her attack, and his blank expression was replaced by confusion; hardly surprising since she'd made it clear that she didn't need his sacrifice on the altar of marriage. She had been so focused on convincing him that she could and would cope perfectly well on her own, it hadn't occurred to her that Cleve might not.

'Did I say that?'

'An hour ago you asked me to marry you. Or were you just going through the motions? You must have known that I'd turn you down.'

She hadn't known how he'd react to the news that he was about to become a father but she had anticipated his proposal, been prepared to turn him down. It had been a hundred times harder than she'd ever imagined but she'd told herself that she was doing the Right Thing.

Now she wondered if she'd just been thinking of herself, unable to cope with the fact that Rachel would always be there, between them.

Selfish...

Cleve had already lost the baby that was to be his future and she'd as good as told him the baby she was carrying didn't need him. Of course it would need him and making a home for their baby, being a father, would give him something to get up for each morning. To live for.

'Isn't that what marriage is?' she asked.

Marriage...

Cleve watched a lazy bee, drawn by the scent of the fruit he'd bought, or more likely the marmalade leaking from the broken jar, head for the bags that Matt had left by the gate.

'Maybe we should have breakfast,' he said.

'Breakfast?' He heard the catch in her throat.

'I think better when I'm not hungry. We'd better eat in the garden. I don't think smoke is going to improve the flavour of your banana.' He looked up at the door behind them. 'I'll open this door so that the air can blow through.'

'It's blocked. The ceiling sagged when rain got in.'

'I'll take a look at it.'

'Do you have time?' she asked, challenging him.

Having done his duty and proposed, been given a clear pass, would he really opt out and become a chequebook father?

An hour ago, with the scent of rosemary clearing his head, he'd been full of plans for the future. Realising

how close he'd come to tragedy had been the kind of reality check he would wish on no one. One that had sent
him reeling back into the darkness of guilt. To stay and
wallow in it would be an act of gross self-indulgence.

Miranda had reached out to him at his lowest ebb.
He owed her his life; what poor specimen of mankind
would walk away when she needed him? If only to save
her from a spider in the bath.

'I take it you're not planning to include the word
obey in your vows?' he asked.

'Vows?'

'Love, honour…?' There was a moment of confusion as she absorbed his meaning followed by an emotion less easy to read. Relief, no doubt, and regret that
unlike her twin she hadn't been swept off her feet by
the man of her dreams.

'And obey?' she finished. 'What do you think?'

Then the green-gold of her eyes softened in a smile
that reached out to warm him, a smile that had always
made the sun shine a little brighter, and he knew he
was looking at his redemption.

He might not be the man of her dreams but he would
do everything in his power to make Miranda happy.
To give her, and their baby, a good life.

'I think I'll get the plates,' he said, picking up the
bags. He opened one to check its contents and handed
it to her.

'I'd better wash my hands.'

'And your face,' he said, brushing the backs of his
fingers lightly over her cheek before heading for the
door.

'I'll be out by the conservatory,' she called into the
kitchen.

'I'll be right there.'

Andie stood there for a moment, the bag of groceries clutched against her chest, a lump the size of a tennis ball in her throat, before following him.

She put the groceries on the hall table beside an exquisite bowl filled with little shells and pieces of sea glass that they'd found on the beach.

Above it, in a gilded rococo frame, was a drawing that Posy had made of the house. It must have been on one of their earliest visits because it was too naïve, unconscious, to have been drawn by a teenager and she took a tissue from her pocket and wiped away the dust.

If she'd thought about it, she'd have imagined that having a house full of noisy children, teens, was the price Sofia'd paid for having her oldest friend stay for a couple of weeks twice a year. But maybe the childless woman had longed for a family and they had given her that, if only briefly, and for a moment Andie lay her hand over it.

'What's that?' Cleve asked.

She let her hand drop. 'A picture Posy drew for Sofia. She couldn't have been more than six.'

'And this, presumably, is Sofia.'

He was looking at the black and white portrait, a head shot dominated by her huge eyes...

'She was older than that when we knew her but her skin, her bone structure... Well, you can see. She had the kind of looks that would have still been turning heads when she was eighty, ninety. If she'd lived that long.'

'No doubt. Put the bag on the tray.'

He was carrying a tray loaded with plates, glasses, cutlery. She picked up the groceries and added them to the tray, which he then handed to her. 'I'll be right with you. I just want to take a look at that door.'

'So long as you're not going up on the roof.'

'Not today.'

She put the tray down in the snug, carefully checked the bathroom for any signs of eight-footed livestock, then caught sight of herself in the mirror. Her cheek was smeared with sooty smoke and her hair had dried in ginger corkscrews. It was no wonder that Cleve had been ready to run.

She washed her face and hands then damped down her hair and quickly plaited it.

'I'll be outside the conservatory,' she called from the hall. The only response was a curse from deep within the scullery. She definitely wasn't getting involved in whatever he was doing out there, and instead opened the door to the painted drawing room. The furniture was covered in dust sheets but there was a crack across the beautiful arched ceiling, no doubt caused in the same tremor that had brought down the roof tiles. The patchwork of stained glass in the roof of the conservatory had suffered too.

She wondered if the house was listed. Did they even have a system of listing buildings of special importance in L'Isola dei Fiori or would whoever eventually bought it simply pull it down and start again?

She opened the doors and stepped out onto a terrace where they'd sat out in evenings watching the fishing boats return to the safety of the village harbour, the lights coming on along the coast.

Last year's weeds that had grown through the cracks were tall and dry, but bright new leaves were pushing through and if nothing was done they would soon dislodge the stones.

She put the tray on the long wooden table where they'd so often had breakfast and crossed to the wall built along the edge of the cliff. The villa might be a bit of a mess but the location was spectacular. Below them, the beach was only accessible from the villa or the sea—and even from the sea you had to know it was there to find your way in—but from here the entire Baia di Rose and the village climbing up from the harbour into the hill behind was laid out in front of her.

She didn't turn as Cleve joined her.

'I saw a promising café when I was down in the village,' he said after a moment. 'Right on the harbour.'

'Was it painted blue, with lobster pots outside?' She sensed rather than saw him nod. 'We used to walk down there for lunch sometimes. Just us girls. Sofia would give us some money and tell us not to spend it all on wine…' No doubt when she was expecting a visit from the King.

'What did you eat?'

'Whatever the cook had bought in the market. Deep-fried squid if we were lucky. Swordfish steaks. Pasta *alla vongole*.' Sweet, sweet memories. 'Was that my stomach rumbling or yours?'

'I think it was a duet. So? Shall we try it later?' he suggested. 'Only I'm not sure if the cooker survived the double whammy of the kettle and the fire extinguisher.'

'I don't know about the food but I'd enjoy the walk.'

He leaned forward to look at her face. 'Are you okay?'

'Fine.' She dashed away a tear that had spilled down her cheek. 'I was just remembering…'

'So long as it's not the thought of marrying me.'

'No.' She put out a hand and he took it, held it and for a moment they just stood there, staring at the view, neither of them knowing what to say. 'As you said, we've known one another a long time.' Reclaiming her hand, she tucked away a strand of hair that had escaped her plait. 'We'll be fine.'

'When are you going to tell your family?' he asked.

'Oh…' She gave a little shrug. 'Do we have to? Mum and Dad are having a whale of a time travelling across India. Portia's in the States. Posy is desperate to become a soloist and daren't miss a performance—'

'And Immi is up to her eyes organising something to rival the royal wedding.'

'That's about it. One wedding at a time in the family is more than enough to cope with, don't you think?'

'So you're going for Option A?'

'Option A?' She finally turned to look at him and saw the ceiling debris whitening his hair, his shirt.

'What on earth have you been up to?' she asked, as if she didn't know.

He looked down, attempted to brush the mess from his shirt but it was damp and it smeared into the cloth.

'Leave it. I'll put it to soak.'

'I'll see to it.'

'Right answer.' He glanced up and when he saw that she was laughing, he smiled back and without warning her heart did a somersault. This was going to be so hard…

'Tell me about the scullery ceiling,' she said, quickly.

'Do you want the good news or the bad news?'

'There's good news?'

'The back door is now open and there's a good draught clearing away the smell of smoke.'

'And the bad news is that the scullery ceiling came down on your head.' That must have been the curse she'd heard.

'Not all of it. Just the bit in the corner near the door. Fortunately, it was wet so there wasn't a lot of dust.'

'More good news.' Although what state the bedroom above would be in was another matter. 'Can it be fixed?'

'There's no point until the roof is repaired. I noticed a builders' merchant on the outskirts of the village. We can call in on the way down and order some tiles.' She must have looked as horrified as she felt at the thought of him on the roof attempting to fix tiles. 'I used to work for a local builder in the holidays to earn money for flying lessons.'

'Tiling roofs?'

'Carrying them up the scaffold to the tiler and, because no skill is ever wasted, I asked him to teach me how to do it.'

'In case the flying didn't work out?'

'The alternative was following my father into medicine. He had dreams of me one day taking over his practice. Heaven knows why. He's always complaining about the hours, the money, the paperwork,' he said, but he was smiling. 'The old fraud loves it.'

'Which is why he wanted it for you.' Andie had met Cleve's father. He was the kind of family doctor that they used to make heart-warming television dramas about.

'He hoped that if I had to pay for flying lessons

I'd quickly get over my obsession with my great-grandfather's heroics in a Spitfire and fall into line.'

'Two stubborn men.'

'I'm better with machines than people.' He looked across to the table. 'Do you feel up to a glass of orange juice and a banana?'

'I think so.'

He poured orange juice into a couple of glasses. Cut thick slices of bread and took out a pack of butter.

'No butter for me.' She peeled the banana and squashed it over the bread, picked up a jar of marmalade. 'It appears to have survived.'

'That's not the jar I bought. Matt must have replaced it with one from his cupboard.'

'I imagine we'll need a witness,' she said, as she dolloped marmalade on top of the banana, 'and he's been a total brick. Shall we ask him?'

'You're sure about not telling your family?'

'Quite sure.' She looked up. Cleve was piling thinly cut ham onto thickly buttered bread. Damn, it looked good. Maybe after the banana... 'I'm sorry, I'm being selfish. You'll want your parents here.'

'This is about what you want, Miranda. They'll understand.'

Would they? Would her own parents?

Probably not, but the thought of pretending that their marriage was more than it was, turning it into a celebration, was not something she could face. No doubt there would be a party of some sort when they got home but that was all it would be—a party. Not a wedding reception.

'Maybe we're getting ahead of ourselves,' she said. 'We'll have to make enquiries about the legalities.

There'll probably be all kinds of rules and regulations. A million forms—'

'No.'

'No?'

'It would be different in Italy. Yards of red tape, all the stuff we'd have to do at home and then a whole lot of other stuff on top.'

'But not here?'

'No. L'Isola dei Fiori is a small island, the communities are close-knit, relationships are well known. No one could commit bigamy or marry a cousin because everyone would know the minute they applied for a licence.' Cleve shifted his shoulders. It wasn't a shrug, more an expression of awkwardness. 'The clerk in the post office was very helpful.'

'You went into the post office to check up on the legal requirements for marriage? After I turned you down?'

'I went into the post office to call Lucy and pick up some local currency but while I was there I thought I might as well make enquiries.'

'It sounds as if you had quite a conversation.'

'A lot more information than I needed. One woman in the queue told me that if you wanted to marry your cousin you'd have to fly to Las Vegas.'

'She spoke English?'

'The clerk was translating.'

'Oh. Quite a party, then.' She was struggling not to smile at the image this scene was creating. 'Does that happen often?' she asked. 'Cousins marrying in Las Vegas?'

'Apparently not because you could never come back and being exiled from L'Isola dei Fiori would be as if you were dead. Like this.' He mimed stabbing himself through the heart. 'What the locals lacked in language skills they made up for in gesture.'

'Right.' She made a valiant effort not to laugh. 'Well, so long as you didn't go out of your way.'

'Why would I do that when you'd turned me down?'

'Because you're a pilot and you've been trained to anticipate every eventuality.'

She turned to him and discovered that he was smiling. One of those old-time Cleve smiles that had stolen her teenage heart and, hit by a wave of dizziness, she made a grab for the table. Before she made it his arm was around her shoulders and she was close against him breathing in a mix of smoke, old wet plaster, warm skin. It wasn't helping…

'Are you okay?'

'Just a bit dizzy.' His shoulder was just the right height for her head and she leaned against it. 'It's the sugar rush from all that banana, marmalade and orange juice on an empty stomach.' Had to be. 'I had the same training as you, Cleve, which is why I know that if you'd been here you would have done exactly what I did and I'd have been the one having kittens instead of you.'

'Kittens? I thought we were having a baby.'

She dug him in the ribs with her elbow.

'I'm just saying that I understand why you reacted as you did.' Fear driving anger… 'I'd have been the one yelling at you for being an idiot,' she said.

'Would have been? From where I was standing you were yelling like a fishwife.'

'Yes. Sorry. It's the hormones.'

'Of course it is.'

'Are you laughing at my hormones?' she said into his shoulder.

'I wouldn't dare.'

'Wise man.' Cleve's arm was around her, her head was on his shoulder and suddenly she was smiling fit to bust. Not cool. This was a marriage of convenience, an arranged marriage. She'd arranged it.

She straightened her face, cleared her throat, sat up. 'Could you spare some of that ham?' He raised his eyebrows. 'I haven't eaten properly for days.'

He made her a sandwich, she took a bite, groaned with pleasure. 'So what are they? These minimal legalities?'

'We have to swear a Declaration of No Impediment before a notary, present it in Italian and English at the local government office in any town, along with our passports and the *sindaco*, the mayor, will issue a licence.'

'That's it?'

'That's it. All we have to do is decide where we're going to hold the ceremony and who we want to conduct it.'

'Can't the mayor do that? In the town hall?'

'I imagine so. We can ask when we get the licence. Do you want to go into San Rocco tomorrow to make an appointment with a notary? We could have lunch, do a little shopping?'

'Shopping?'

'Unless you packed an emergency wedding dress?'

'All I've got in my bag are jeans, leggings and tops. Even for the most basic wedding I think I'll need something a little more elegant.' She felt a blush creep into her cheeks. 'Not anything—' she made a helpless ges-

ture with her hand, unable to bring herself to say *bridal*
'—you know...'

'Frilly?' he offered.

'That's the word.'

'But it should be special.'

'Yes.' She'd only be doing this once. 'Have you got
a jacket?'

'Not one I'd want to get married in. I need a new
suit.'

'Well, that's convenient.'

She would be in a special dress, Cleve would be
wearing a suit and Matt could use her phone to video
them making their vows and signing the register to
send to their parents, her sisters, with the news that
not only had they got married but they were going to
have a baby.

And afterwards, he would take a photograph of the
two of them standing on the steps of the town hall that
she could print out, put in a silver frame and tuck away
in her underwear drawer.

Just for her.

CHAPTER SEVEN

Andie cleaned up the kitchen and the stove while Cleve went to look for a ladder so that he could check the roof and see what he'd need to fix it.

He'd stripped off his shirt and left it to soak in the scullery sink and she paused as she crossed the yard with an arm full of bed linen to hang over the wall to air.

He'd lost weight in the last year and there wasn't an ounce of fat on him, but he ran every day and the muscles on his back rippled in the sunlight. She knew how they felt beneath her fingers, the silk of his skin, the scent of his body unmasked by the aftershaves or colognes worn by most men. No scent of any kind was worn by flight crew. Every moment of the night they spent together was imprinted on her memory and she turned away before he saw all that betrayed in her face.

'Will you hold the ladder, Miranda? I'm coming down.'

'You shouldn't have gone up without someone holding it,' she said as she grasped the ladder, watching as his jeans-hugged backside descended until it was on a level with her eyes. 'Next time, call me.'

'Always.' He turned to look down at her and for a

moment there was nothing in the world but his gaze holding her and she was melting into the cobbles. 'It's okay, Miranda. I've got it now.'

He'd got it, she'd had it…

She moved aside and he stepped down from the ladder giving her an unimpeded view of wide shoulders tapering to narrow hips, his chest sprinkled with dark hair that arrowed down in a straight line to disappear beneath his zip.

'What are you doing?' he asked.

She jumped, felt a hot guilty blush sweep across her cheeks, then realised it wasn't an accusation but a question.

'Oh, um, I've battled my way through the cobwebs, made it upstairs and now I'm sorting out the bedrooms.'

'Don't overdo it,' he said, frowning as he touched his fingers to her cheek. 'You look a bit flushed.'

'I'm fine,' she said quickly. 'The ones on the far side of the villa, away from the kitchen, aren't too bad. Just dust and—' She came to an abrupt halt. Did he expect to sleep with her?

What had happened between them had been one of those spontaneous moments; there had been no conscious thought, no need for words, but this was going to be so different. Awkward.

Forget expect.

Would he want to sleep with her? Really want to? Not just sex, which she knew from experience would be hot, but in his heart…

'Cobwebs?' he prompted.

'And dust.' She swallowed down the lump in her throat. 'They sound like a couple of fairies in a Cinderella pantomime.'

He grinned. 'If they aren't they ought to be.' When she didn't answer he said, 'You don't have to worry about me, Miranda. I'm perfectly capable of cleaning a room and making my own bed.'

Was that little ping somewhere in the region of her heart disappointment? Despair? She'd left him sleeping to avoid the awkward morning-after encounter. It was going to be nothing compared to the evening before. A wedding night in which the groom was marrying out of duty…

'I've cleaned the rooms but the mattresses and bed linen still needs airing.' Desperate to get away from the subject of beds, she said, 'If you're up for a close encounter with a pair of Marigolds I'd far rather you tackled the upstairs bathroom.'

'I'll give it a thorough bottoming when we get back. Is it okay to take a shower in your bathroom for now?'

'It's not my bathroom, it's Sofia's. I couldn't sleep in there. I've put my things in the room I used to share with Immi.'

'Right. Well, I'll put the ladder away, get cleaned up and then we'll walk down into the village. If you're still up for it? We could get a taxi for the uphill return?'

'Yes.' She swallowed. 'Cleve…' They were going to have to talk about this.

'Hang on.'

She waited as he folded up the ladder but when he turned around she lost her nerve.

'I just wanted to say thank you. For the roof.'

'Hadn't you heard? Working holidays are all the rage.' His hand brushed her shoulder, lingered for a moment, as he passed. 'I won't be long.'

'I'll shut the French doors.'

* * *

Cleve put the ladder away in the garage. Alberto had kept it pristine. Everything shelved, labelled, tools cleaned, oiled and hung in clips, the layer of dust lending a Sleeping Beauty air to the place. Clearly the cars were his Beauties and Cleve made a note to buy a new hasp and padlock for the door while they were out.

He took clean clothes from his grip and tossed them on the king-size bed in which a king had once slept with his mistress. Having just had a fairly heavy hint that Miranda did not intend to follow Sofia's example, he let the water run cold.

Twenty minutes later, following the unmistakable sound of a scooter engine, he found Miranda riding around the courtyard, wearing a smile as wide as a barn door.

She pulled up beside him.

'You managed to start it.'

'It was as clean as a whistle. I pumped some air into the tyres and put the battery on charge earlier. The tyres stayed pumped and the engine started first time. If you open the gate we can go.'

'When was the last time you rode one of these things?' he asked as he hauled open one of the gates and fastened it back.

'Years, but it's like riding a bike. Don't worry, I won't pitch you into a ditch.'

'If you say so.'

A dozen things went through his mind, not least the fact that they should be wearing helmets. He wanted to wrap Miranda in cotton wool, keep her safe, but that was his problem, not hers and he threw his leg over the saddle.

'Hold on.'

He needed no encouraging to wrap his arms around her waist as she shot through the gate and onto the road. He took full advantage of the opportunity to hold her close so that her back was close up against his chest, his cheek resting against her hair, which still smelled faintly of smoke, taking the curves as if they were one. His only problem was that they reached the edge of the village and the DIY warehouse far too soon.

Half an hour later, roofing supplies ordered with the promise that they would be delivered that afternoon, they were sitting outside the blue painted café, wine and water on the table, a waiter listing what was on the menu for lunch.

Miranda ordered a swordfish steak with a salad.

'You seem to have regained your appetite,' he said as he ordered the same with a side order of fries.

'Sunshine, fresh air...' She shook her head. 'The truth is that I was stressing over how to tell you about the baby.'

'Why would you do that?'

She looked at him helplessly. 'Cleve...'

'Stupid question.' She was stressing because she thought he was screwed up with grief but it was too lovely a day to darken with the truth—that he was simply screwed up.

He'd kept Rachel's secret but Miranda would have to know everything before she took an irrevocable decision about her future. Not now, though. Not here. 'I hope it hasn't put you off your food.'

'No.' Andie shook her head. 'I'm fine.'

Nearly fine.

Neither of them spoke for a while but the silence

was the comfortable kind between two people who'd known one another for a long time and didn't need to fill every moment with banal conversation. Instead they watched the bustle of a busy working harbour, the boats coming and going, men washing down decks, a skinny black cat creeping along on its belly, stalking something that only it could see.

'I like this place,' Cleve said as their food arrived.

'Me too.'

The waiter asked if there was anything else they wanted, wished them *'Buon appetito'* and left them to it.

They tasted the fish and pronounced it good. Andie helped herself to some of his fries. He asked why she hadn't ordered her own. It was the normal, everyday stuff that was no different from lunch in the mess or down the pub and within minutes they were talking about work. The performance of the Learjet. How the Cyprus office was bringing in more business from the Middle East. Nothing personal. No more straying into dangerously emotional territory where the past could trip them up.

Cleve ordered an espresso. She refused to be tempted by cheesecake. Cleve paid the bill, checked the time and stood up. 'The tiles are being delivered this afternoon. You can stay in town if you like but I'd better get back.'

She knew that nothing would happen until four o'clock when the shops would reopen and the town would come to life but she'd inadvertently invoked bad memories and sensed he needed some time alone.

'The village has grown since I was last here. It's almost a town now and I'd like to explore a little. Walk off lunch.'

'Take care riding back. See if you can find a helmet.'

'I will if you promise not to go up on the roof unless I'm there.'

He drew a cross over his heart. 'Scouts' honour.'

'If you need me just ring the bell.'

His steel-grey eyes softened. 'Never doubt that I need you, Miranda.' She was still taking in his words when he caught the back of her head in his hand and kissed her. His mouth lingered momentarily as if tasting her and then he was gone before she could catch her breath.

She raised her hand to her mouth. It hadn't been a heavy kiss, just firm enough to leave the faintest tingle and send sparks flying in all directions.

A promise.

The waiter returned with his receipt and, startling him with a smile, she said, 'I think I'll have that cheesecake after all.'

When she returned, there was a car outside and in the courtyard Cleve was erecting a scaffolding deck. 'Where did that come from?' she asked.

'I hired it. Health and safety. I don't see a helmet.'

'I couldn't find a motorbike accessories shop. Has Matt brought his mother? I thought we might have scared him off. Did he say anything?'

'I was inside when they arrived and he took her straight down to the beach.'

'I'll try and catch them when they come up. To thank them for the marmalade. I would have bought a replacement jar but the shop isn't open until four.'

'We can pick one up in San Rocco tomorrow and drop it off on the way back,' he suggested.

'You can ask him to be your witness.'

He nodded, tightened a clamp.

'I'm going to see if I can start the little runaround. I'll feel safer driving into the city in that and we'll have somewhere to put the shopping.'

'My knees will be under my chin. Why don't you see if you can start the convertible?' he suggested, testing the connection before adding another piece.

'That is a valuable vintage automobile and I've seen how the locals drive.'

'Like Ben Hur in a chariot race?'

That was so close to her own thought that she laughed. 'Exactly.'

'Point taken.' He was smiling when he looked up. 'My knees and chin will probably survive the indignity.'

The capital, San Rocco, was one of those enchanting old cities that had everything. Ancient buildings, tiny courtyards and alleyways, steep steps disappearing around corners, tantalising glimpses of gardens through wrought-iron gates. Wide open piazzas with cafés spilling out onto the pavement. Pedestrian-only streets lined with what had once been *palazzos*, built in some golden age when the island was a crossroads for trade, but which now housed elegant boutiques.

And perched above it was the castle, dominating the city and protecting its ancient harbour far below.

'I can't believe this place isn't overrun by tourists,' Andie said. 'It has everything.'

'Everything except an airport.'

'Why don't they build one?'

'Maybe they like it the way it is.'

'If I lived here I think I might, too,' she admitted. 'It's tough on the young people who have to leave to make a living, though.' She mimed a stab through the heart.

'Not many tourists but there is an information office,' he said, crossing the piazza. 'With luck they can direct us to a notary.'

An hour later they had sworn statements, paid to have them translated into Italian and were told they could pick them up the following afternoon.

'Well, that was easy,' Andie said. 'Now for the tough bit.'

'Tough bit?'

'I hate shopping for clothes. One of the great things about my job is the uniform. I don't have to think about what to wear. Immi got all the power dressing and high heels genes.'

'Come and help me find a suit and I'll help you pick out a dress. And high heels.'

'You can't do that,' she said, aghast at the thought.

'I can't? Why?'

'It's…you know… Unlucky.' She felt an idiot just saying it.

'Unlucky?' Cleve stopped. 'Who are you?' he asked, grinning broadly. 'And what have you done with the efficient, totally focused and thoroughly down-to-earth Miranda Marlowe?'

'That's the work me. This is the *me* me.'

'Are you saying that you don't walk under ladders?'

'Only an idiot would do that.'

'You toss spilled salt over your shoulder? Believe a

broken mirror brings seven years' bad luck, bow to a magpie… I wouldn't have thought you had a superstitious bone in your body.'

'I don't.' Cursing herself for making a mountain out of a molehill, she said, 'I never bow to magpies but some things are ingrained. Part of the DNA.'

'Like the groom seeing the bride in her dress before the wedding.'

'There's always something behind these old superstitions,' she said. 'I can imagine some poor lad, being forced to marry the next-door neighbour's middle-aged daughter in a land grab, catching sight of his bride before the vows were sworn and taking to the hills.'

'So you'll be wearing something old, something new, something borrowed?'

Stuck with her stupid superstition, she said, 'I'm sure I can find something amongst Sofia's things.'

'What about blue?'

Oh, good grief… 'Of course.'

'But not a sapphire. Your eyes are hazel. Green and gold.' He took her hand in his so that her fingers were laid across his palm. 'Maybe a yellow diamond?'

'What? No…'

He indicated the building behind her and when she turned she was looking into a jeweller's window. That it was a very expensive jeweller you could tell by the fact that there were only a few stunning pieces on display in the window.

'We're going to need rings. You could leave it to me but you'll be wearing them for a lot longer than the dress and no doubt you'd rather choose your own.'

'Ring singular, Cleve.' Something plain like the one her mother wore.

'And have everyone think we had a hole-in-the-wall wedding because you're pregnant?' he said as, still holding her hand, he pushed open the door and ushered her in ahead of him.

Inside, in the kind of hush provided by deep carpets and serious reverence accorded to expensive objects of desire, they were met by a man so exquisitely tailored that he had to be the manager. He showed them to gilt chairs placed before an ornate desk, before taking the seat opposite them.

'*Signor, signora. Benvenuto.* How may I be of service?'

'We would like to see engagement and wedding rings,' Cleve said.

'Of course.' He turned to her. 'Have you a stone in mind, *signora*, or do you prefer a classic white diamond?'

Signora wished she hadn't made a fuss about the dress and was safely ensconced in a boutique changing room right now.

'The *signora* has hazel eyes with a predominance of gold,' Cleve said, before she could begin to think of an answer. 'I thought a yellow diamond.'

'*Perfetto.* A deep yellow.' He nodded to a man standing beside him, who disappeared and a few moments later returned with a tray of rings that gleamed in the soft concealed lighting.

'These are paired rings. The wedding ring has matching stones and is shaped so that the engagement ring will sit perfectly against it. Your hand, *signora*? So that I can measure your finger?' he prompted when they remained in her lap.

She looked at Cleve, sending a desperate message that this was crazy. These rings cost a fortune…

His response was to take her hand, pick a ring from the tray and slide it onto her finger. 'How is that?'

She cleared her throat. 'It's a little loose.'

'Try these, *signor*.'

Cleve removed the ring and replaced it with a pair of rings handed to him by the clerk. First the wedding ring, in which yellow and white diamonds had been set alternately into a plain polished white gold channel, and curved so that when he placed it on her finger the simple yellow diamond of the engagement ring sat snugly against it. It fitted perfectly and was so unbelievably beautiful that she was unable to suppress a sigh.

'*È molto bella.*'

'Cleve, no…'

She made a move to slip the rings from her finger but Cleve stopped her. 'These rings could have been created just for you, Miranda.' He was looking at her rather than the diamonds glittering on her finger. 'Beauty without frills, designed for strength, made to last a lifetime.'

She swallowed in an attempt to shift the rock in her throat but in the end simply shook her head, unable to meet his gaze.

'You think it is too much?'

When she didn't answer he touched her chin, forcing her to look at him, and she said, 'You know it is.'

'Would it help if I told you that I followed you to L'Isola dei Fiori with only one thought in my head? To ask you to marry me.'

'But you didn't know…'

'No,' he said. 'I didn't.' He turned to the manager,

who was doing his best to appear oblivious to their conversation. 'This pair for the *signora*,' he said, allowing her to remove the rings and place them on the velvet mat in front of them. 'And something plain for me.'

For him? Andie looked at his hand and realised he wasn't wearing the ring that Rachel had put on his finger. He'd been wearing it when he broke down but there was no mark, no telltale whiteness, to suggest he'd worn it recently.

The manager clicked his fingers and a tray of men's white-gold wedding rings appeared.

Cleve picked up a plain, polished band. 'This one,' he said, without hesitation.

'A perfect match, *signor*. It will be a little large, I think, but we can adjust it.' He checked Cleve's ring size and made a note. 'You will be able to pick it up tomorrow afternoon. Shall I keep all the rings until then?'

'Just the weddings rings. The *signora* will wear this one.' He placed a card on the desk and while the manager whisked it and the wedding rings away, he picked up the engagement ring and placed it on her finger.

Miranda's hand was shaking so badly that the stone flashed golden sparks in the light. 'I d-don't know what to say.'

'There is only one word I want to hear you say, Miranda, and that is *yes*, although I suspect the staff are waiting for you to show your gratitude with a kiss.'

'*Scusi, signor*, but your bank would like to confirm the transaction.' The manager handed Cleve a phone and retreated out of hearing.

'Saved by the bell,' he said, with a wry smile before dealing with the bank's security check. He declined the offer of champagne, handed her the glossy little carrier holding the ring box and, having assured them that he would return the following afternoon, took her arm and headed for the door, which was opened for them by a beaming clerk.

On the threshold she stopped, said, 'Wait.'

He glanced back. 'Have you forgotten something? Changed your mind? If you'd rather have a white diamond…'

'No. I just wanted to do this.' And she rose on her toes, closing her eyes as she touched her lips to his. For a moment that was all it was and then Cleve's arm was around her and the kiss deepened into something intense, real. The kind of kiss a teenage girl could only dream about. That a woman might yearn for all her life.

Who knew how long it would have gone on but for a spontaneous burst of applause behind them. They broke apart and a touch shakily she said, 'It would have been cruel to disappoint the staff.'

Wordlessly he laid his hand against her cheek, then put his arm around her shoulder and they were back in the piazza.

Feeling decidedly weak at the knees, she made an effort at normality. 'Right. Time to find you a suit worthy of this,' she said as, still scarcely able to believe what had just happened, she looked again at the ring. 'Always assuming you can still afford one.'

'I'm going to need a restorative espresso before I do anything else.'

She looked up. 'Was the ring that expensive?' she asked, horrified.

'It has nothing to do with the cost of the ring.'

CHAPTER EIGHT

CLEVE FOUND A cream linen suit that he was happy with, but, stupid superstition or not, there was no way Andie was having him along while she shopped for a dress to wear for their wedding.

'I could go for a walk,' he suggested.

'No need.' She'd had a far better idea. 'Sofia has wardrobes, trunks full of fabulous designer dresses. She used to let us dress up in them when we stayed.'

'She sounds more like a fairy godmother. Will they have survived the dressing up and the passing of the years?'

'Not all of them, but they were stored in sandalwood-lined trunks. I'm sure I'll find something I can wear.' Anything would be better than having to stand in her underwear while elegant assistants, speaking in fast Italian, made her feel less than adequate. 'Vintage clothes are all the rage.'

'Like drystone walling?'

'But not so hard on the hands.'

He didn't look entirely convinced and he might be right. Mice might have got in and made nests in the couture clothes.

'Whatever happens, you have my word that I won't stand in front of the mayor smelling of mothballs.'

'Just as long as you're there.' He took her hand. 'Let's go and find a jar of marmalade.'

They had lunch in the village and then, on the way home, they stopped at Matt's cottage.

'We came to return your marmalade and ask you a favour,' Cleve said, when he opened the door.

'You'd better come in, then.'

'Thanks. We won't keep you long.'

He showed them through to the back where his mother was sitting, enjoying the warmth of the sun through the glass.

'Hello, Mrs Stark. I'm sorry to disturb you.'

'Gloria, please. And it's lovely to have visitors. Sit down. Will you have coffee?' She looked at Miranda. 'Mint tea, perhaps?'

'That would be lovely. Thank you.'

'We came to ask you a favour, Matt,' Cleve said, turning to look at him. 'Miranda and I are getting married in a day or two. Just a stand-up-in-front-of-the-mayor job. We were hoping that you will be a witness.'

'Of course, that would be my pleasure!'

'Congratulations, I hope you'll be very happy,' Gloria said admiring Miranda's ring. 'Have you known one another long?' she asked.

'Six years, eight months and four days,' Matt said. 'Actually, make that five days.' Gloria frowned. 'Cleve told me. It was Andie's eighteenth birthday, she'd just got her pilot's licence and he watched as she made a perfect landing in a tricky crosswind.'

This description of their first meeting was met with a moment of total silence.

'You fly?' Gloria asked, stepping in to rescue the moment.

'I'm a commercial pilot but Cleve's wrong about when we met. It's seven days. Six years, eight months and seven days.'

Gloria gave Cleve a wry smile. 'If it was her birthday, you'd better memorise the date. It's fatal to get that wrong.'

'Miranda's birthday is on the twelfth,' he said. 'It's the day we met and I will never forget that.' Andie risked a look at him. He was looking anywhere but at her.

'Perhaps you forgot to account for the leap years,' Gloria said, filling the suddenly awkward silence.

'So, are your families flying over for the wedding?' Matt asked. 'The villa is hardly fit for visitors but we have a couple of spare rooms if you need somewhere for your parents to stay.'

'That's very kind,' Cleve said, standing up. 'Would you mind if we take a rain check on the coffee, Gloria?'

'Not at all. Drop by any time.'

'Thank you. We'll see ourselves out.'

Cleve was in such a hurry to leave that Andie had to go back for her bag and was just in time to hear an exasperated Gloria say, 'Matt, you talk too much.'

'Do you think so? I thought I'd said just enough.'

She backed away and quietly shut the front door. Her bag would be safe enough where it was for the moment.

Cleve drove in silence back to the villa and Andie was too busy trying to work out what had just happened to speak.

He'd told her in the jeweller's that he'd come to the

island with the express intention of asking her to marry him. She hadn't known what to make of that. Guilt? Or had her resignation shaken him into the realisation that whatever they'd had six years, eight months and seven days ago was still viable? Or did he just need an anchor?

That was the role she'd chosen for herself, so that was all right. Except he knew to the day—minus the odd leap year—when they'd first met. Girls remembered things like that...

No. She refused to read anything into it. It had been her eighteenth birthday. The sort of occasion that stuck in the mind even without the close encounter in the shrubbery. She worked for him so he knew exactly how old she was and she supplied the office with cake on her birthday.

Which accounted for the years. But the months and days?

They were so close in the little car. His arm brushed against her when he changed gear and above the smell of hot metal, oil, there was a combination of warm cotton, the scent of Cleve's skin, the shampoo he always used, familiar as her own.

She stole a glance at him but his face was unreadable, his jaw set as they pulled up in front of the garage.

'Will you be all right on your own for a while?' he asked. 'I could do with a run.'

'Good plan. I might take a swim.' He looked as if he was going to say something. 'I'll be careful,' she assured him, before he started. 'Swimming is great exercise for pregnant women,' she said. 'No stress—'

'It's not that. I was just wondering if you'd brought

a costume with you. Just in case Matt decides to drop by with your handbag.'

'I didn't think you'd noticed.'

'You went back for it but for some reason changed your mind.'

She pulled a face. 'His mother was giving him a bit of an earwigging for talking too much so I chose discretion and made a strategic retreat. I'm pretty sure that he'll wait for one of us to go and pick it up.'

'I'll collect it later,' he said, taking the bag containing his suit and the rest of the clothes he'd bought and disappearing upstairs.

Miranda went through to Sofia's room and opened up the wardrobe.

It had a faintly musty smell but the clothes had been placed in individual garment bags and had escaped the depredations of moths and mice.

She unzipped a couple but, although all designer with luminous names, they were day clothes, not the jewel-coloured gowns she and her sisters had had such fun dressing up in.

Not that she was looking for a jewel. She'd remembered a pretty silk kimono-style dress, cream with small green and yellow motifs, that hadn't been nearly exotic enough for her teenage self. It was simple, dressy enough for a low-key wedding and would look stylish in a photograph.

She went upstairs, into the rooms she hadn't begun to touch, hoping that the trunks hadn't been put up in the attic.

She found two stored in a box room but caught sight of the sea glittering below, pale aqua, deepening to turquoise and then, in the gap between the cliffs, a glimpse of deep inky blue.

The afternoon was passing and while the trunk would keep, her swim would not.

She looked at the ring so recently placed on her finger by Cleve, blushing a little at the way she'd taken advantage of the moment and kissed him. Smiling a lot at the way he'd seized the moment and run with it. The fact that it appeared to have left him as shaken as she had been.

Just like the first time. Six years, eight months and seven days ago.

She shook her head, slipped off the ring, then realised that the box was in her handbag. There were china trinket dishes on the dressing table but, unwilling to leave it lying there with the house open, she opened the hinged box beneath the dressing table mirror. It was empty but for a large key.

She picked it up, turned it over, looked around, wondering what it would open. Nothing in this room.

It couldn't be important or it would have been with the other keys and she dropped it back into the box, carefully placed her ring beside it and then changed into her costume.

She paused for a moment by a full-length mirror, smoothing her hand over her still-flat belly. Holding it there for a moment. Then she grabbed a towel and headed down to the beach.

Cleve took an overgrown path that led up the hill. He hadn't run for a couple of days and he pushed himself hard, pausing at the top to look down on the castle and the city of San Rocco with its many spires, the houses painted in faded blues, pink, greens giving it a fairy-tale quality.

But this was no fairy tale. Miranda might have changed her mind about marrying him and she'd sworn her statement without a hitch, but he'd had to push her to accept his ring. He could have cheerfully throttled the manager for interrupting them when he was about to claim a kiss. But then, unexpectedly, sweetly, she'd kissed him and it had felt like a promise.

He could still feel the softness of her lips, her melting response as, weak with longing, lost to where they were, he'd taken it up a notch. It had been as if he were kissing Miranda for the very first time, with all the possibilities stretching out before them. With none of the mistakes or baggage that clung to him.

If they were to have that he would have to tell her everything. She had the right to know the truth, the right to change her mind. He owed her that.

Only then could it be a brand-new beginning.

Andie heard Cleve cross the beach, the splash as he plunged into the sea. She turned, raised her dark glasses to watch him carving a path through the water as he headed for the gap that led out into the sea. Held her breath.

They'd always been warned not to go beyond the entrance to the hidden cove because of the fierce currents and she stood up, about to call and warn him. But he'd stopped and was treading water and as he turned to head back she ducked down, not wanting him to see her fussing.

When he joined her in the hot pool a few minutes

later she was lying back, letting the heat seep into her bones.

He was wearing swim shorts, his body beaded with sea water, the dark hair on his chest and legs clinging to his skin and she was glad she was wearing her sunglasses so that her eyes weren't giving her away.

'Good run?' she asked.

'Yes. I went up the hill. You get a good view of San Rocco and the castle from up there. I didn't realise it was so close.'

'The road winds around the island, but you can walk to San Rocco in about an hour from here. Less to the castle.'

'A well-trodden path, no doubt.'

She smiled. 'Once upon a time there was a king who loved a beautiful lady…'

'A married king,' he pointed out, lowering himself into the pool, taking the same 'seat' he'd used when he'd caught her skinny dipping.

'It's a somewhat tarnished fairy tale,' she agreed.

'It's not any kind of a fairy tale.'

'No.'

Sofia had been glamorous, witty, full of life at the parties she'd thrown but, looking back with the eyes of an adult, Andie didn't think she'd been entirely happy. And there had been another woman, one who'd probably had little choice in who she married, waiting at the castle for her husband to return. Two lonely women…

'Marriage is not a fairy tale,' she said. 'It's something that takes effort, commitment, heart enough to see you through the rough patches.' She was going to need all of that, but she had a great example. 'My parents had a tough start.' They'd had to give up their dreams and buckle down to save Marlowe Aviation when her grandfather had died. 'They are the real deal.'

'How's your father doing?' he asked.

'Good. They're having a great time in India. I'll miss the weekly video chat with them tomorrow.'

'Where are they?'

'There is no itinerary. They've left schedules, diaries, appointments behind and they're pleasing themselves.'

He nodded, said nothing for a while but it wasn't the quiet comfortable silence that they'd shared over lunch the day before. He was looking in the depths of the pool where the hot spring bubbled up and he should be relaxed after his run, his swim, but there was a tension about his jaw, his shoulders.

'What is it, Cleve?'

He looked up. 'I need to tell you about Rachel.'

Her stomach contracted. It was obvious that he'd had something on his mind, that this conversation had always been coming, but she still felt a momentary touch of nausea.

Breathe, breathe…

'I was going to tell you yesterday, when we were having lunch in the harbour, but it was such a lovely day that I didn't want to spoil it.'

'That doesn't sound good.'

'It's not.'

After their earlier closeness, he now seemed so distant. She knew something had spooked him at Matt's cottage; he couldn't wait to get away, to put some space between them, run, and she felt him slipping away from her.

'Shall I come and sit beside you?' From being the

comforter, she was now the one who needed to feel him close, touch him. 'I'll hold your hand if it will help.'

He shook his head. 'I need to see your face.'

Rachel had been the love of his life and all this ring stuff, talk of dresses had forced him to confront the reality of what he was about to do. He was going to tell her that he couldn't go through with it. Or worse, that he would marry her but that their relationship would be platonic.

She shouldn't have kissed him. He'd responded because he hadn't wanted to embarrass her and because he was flesh and blood but now he felt guilty.

Breathe.

'Cleve, you're frightening me.'

'I'm sorry, but we're getting married in a few days and you have a right to know...'

And now he was the one taking a deep breath. How bad could it be?

'Know what?'

'You have a right to know, I want you to know, that the baby Rachel was carrying when she died was not mine.'

'Not...'

She stared at him in disbelief. She'd had no idea what was coming but that was the very last thing she could have imagined.

They had been aviation's golden couple. Andie'd been wretched when she'd discovered that Cleve was married but he and Rachel had been so perfect together that she'd accepted it with only a bucket or two of tears.

Her heart had ached but he'd kept his promise and given her a job when no one else would even look at a newly qualified pilot with no experience. And she'd got on with her life.

More or less.

'Who…?' She shook her head. It didn't matter who.

'No one I knew.'

'I'm so sorry.'

'We'd been struggling for a long time.'

'That's why you didn't go to Phuket.'

'Not exactly. When she booked the holiday I thought she wanted a break, a chance to restart our marriage and I was willing to give it a try.'

He looked so bleak that it was all she could do not to reach out and hold him but this was something he had to get off his chest and she held onto the rock to keep her anchored in place.

'You didn't go,' she prompted after a while.

'A couple of weeks before we were due to fly out, she told me that she wanted to go alone. That she needed space to think things through.'

'So you invented a crisis?' She shook her head, barely able to take in the fact that his marriage had been in trouble. 'No one would ever have guessed.'

'Rachel put on a good show but the fact is that she was well beyond thinking things through. After her death I found photographs on her phone. She wasn't alone.'

She didn't know what to say. The whole idea of Rachel being unfaithful to Cleve was so unbelievable…

'I suspected there was someone else. I didn't blame her for having a fling; she was unhappy and I was unable to do anything to make things better. I only discovered that she was pregnant when I picked up her phone by mistake and found myself looking at a message from the antenatal clinic.'

'But…'

'I'd been sleeping in the spare bedroom for six months.'

Without thinking she moved, crossed the pool, sat beside him because, like Cleve, she knew that Rachel, who'd always said that there was plenty of time for a family, was not the kind of woman to get pregnant by accident.

It had been a lot more than a fling.

She took his hand and he grasped hers so tightly that it was all she could do not to squeak but he must have felt her wince because he immediately eased his grip. 'I'm sorry.' He managed a smile. 'I knew it would be a mistake to hold your hand.'

'Hold on as tight as you want.'

He lifted it, kissed her knuckles then let go, leaving it, leaving her, feeling empty.

'What did you do?'

He shrugged, the droplets of water from his shoulders coalescing and running down his chest. She dragged her eyes away as he said, 'Pretty much what you'd expect. I told her that I wanted her out of the apartment, out of my life. She retaliated by saying that the way it worked was that I would be the one packing my bags and if I wanted a divorce she would take half of Goldfinch.'

'Cleve…' What on earth was he going to tell her?

'She said a lot more. Some of it true.' He was avoiding her gaze now and she knew that she had been included in the vitriol. 'She was angry. She said I'd never loved her, that I should never have married her and that our marriage was an empty sham, and she was right.'

'Why did you?' The challenge was out before she could recall it. 'Sorry, sorry...' She held up her hands. 'That's totally none of my business.'

'We are getting married, having a child together. Everything about me is your business, Miranda.'

He closed his eyes for a moment as if trying to summon up the words that would explain how it had happened.

'Rach flew for me as a temp when I needed an extra pilot. The business grew, she was a good fit and she joined the team. I had no time for a social life and when she invited me to a New Year's party we both knew where it was going. Midnight struck and we were kissing, by one o'clock we were in bed. Within months she'd pretty much moved in with me and by the end of the year everyone was asking when we were going to get married.'

Of course they were.

Cleve and Rachel, handsome, beautiful, clever, both flyers with their lives invested in Goldfinch Air Services. You couldn't make it up.

'Then Rachel's parents announced they'd sold their house and were moving to France in June, at which point the "When are you two getting married?" question had an answer.

'There was no big scene where I went down on one knee,' he said. 'The truth is I let it happen because there was no reason not to.'

And he was about to do it all over again, she realised, her heart sinking like a stone.

'What happened, Cleve?'

'I told her that I'd see her in hell before she got as much as a breath of Goldfinch's tailwind. She couldn't stay to argue the point because she had a flight booked but told me to start packing and left with a suitably dramatic door slam. It was my rest day and I went for a run. Despite what I'd said I knew she would be entitled to half of everything and I needed a clear head to work out how I was going to survive.'

Her hand tightened in his, knowing what was coming.

'I spent the rest of the day working through the figures and I was about to ring my accountant to make an appointment when there was a knock on the door. It was Lucy and a policeman.'

CHAPTER NINE

'You never told anyone.' Andie was struggling with what she'd just heard. Trying to imagine the shock, the horror of that moment. How everything would have been made a hundred times worse by what had just happened. 'About the baby.'

'Rachel died horribly. I felt guilty enough without dragging her name through the mud.'

'Guilty?' Was that what tormented him? Not grief, but guilt? 'Why on earth would you feel guilty?'

'I should have grounded her. I should have called Lucy and asked her to bring in someone else to take the flight but it was like with the kettle,' he said. 'I wasn't thinking.'

'The only similarity to the kettle,' she said, 'is that they were both accidents. You must have been pretty shaken yourself.'

'Shaken by the scene, by how much pain she'd bottled up, but mostly I was relieved.' He'd been looking over her head, staring somewhere out to sea, but now he was looking directly at her. 'I was going to have to surrender everything I owned, mortgage my soul to hold onto Goldfinch but it was over. I didn't have to pretend any more. While I was running, even with the struggle ahead, it was as if my feet had wings.'

He turned away but she reached up, took his face between her hands and forced him to look at her.

'It was a bird strike, Cleve. She was flying low, coming in beneath heavy cloud cover and had the misfortune to run into a flock of geese set up by dogs or a fox, or maybe a bird-scarer installed by a farmer desperate to protect his winter wheat. She didn't stand a chance.'

'I told her that I'd see her in hell.'

She ached for him, understanding how, psychologically, those words must have eaten at him.

'It's the kind of thing we all say in the heat of the moment. Rachel was an experienced, responsible pilot, Cleve. If she'd had the slightest concern about her fitness to fly she would have grounded herself just as I did.'

'If she'd been thinking straight. I would have given her everything, the flat, Goldfinch, whatever she wanted, not to have those deaths on my conscience.'

The faint stubble on his cheeks was tickling her palms and she wanted to slide her fingers into his hair and kiss him quiet, make him stop thinking about this, but he'd been bottling up all this guilt, blaming himself and right now there were some things he needed to hear.

'Tell me, Cleve, in what way wasn't she thinking straight?'

'She was angry—'

'Of course she was angry. She'd been found out, caught cheating, forced to confront the issue before she was ready and, like you, saying things in the heat of the moment. A little door-banging strop—'

He shook his head but she didn't let go. If she let go he'd walk away and she wasn't done.

'A little door-banging strop is to be expected under the circumstances but by the time she reached her car she'd have been feeling relieved that it was out in the open.'

'You can't know that.'

'I have three sisters,' she said. 'We've all been there at some time or another. Keeping secrets, getting caught out. Anger is always the first response and then almost instantly there's relief.'

He didn't look convinced.

'When Rachel arrived at the airfield no one noticed anything out of the ordinary. She checked the weather, filed a flight plan at the airfield office. The guys there said she'd teased them about having thrashed them in the pub quiz at the weekend.'

He must have heard all this at the Air Accident Inquiry, the inquest, but maybe it hadn't made it through the fog of guilt.

'She met her passengers, both of whom had flown with her before and knew her well. She flew them to Leeds for a meeting. They both said she was totally focused as always. She had lunch in the airport cafeteria. Soup of the day, carrot and coriander, with a roll. She chatted to one of the ground crew, asked about his granddaughter—'

'How do you know all this?' he demanded.

'It was reported in detail in the local paper.' Every word was engraved on her memory. She'd wanted to be there for him but she and other pilots had had to keep Goldfinch ticking over, deliver the cargoes, put on a bright face for the regulars who hadn't deserted them. 'She wasn't in a "state", Cleve. At least not the kind of state you're talking about. If she was distracted it was because, like you, she was free and imagining a new future.'

'What future?' he demanded. 'The father of her baby never stood up to be counted. He just disappeared into the woodwork.'

'What would you have done, Cleve?' She held up a finger to stop his protest. 'I know you'd never have had an affair with a married woman, but if you'd been in his position, what would you have done?'

He remained silent, a muscle working in his jaw.

'Isn't it possible that he kept his grief to himself because, like you, he chose to protect the woman he loved?'

'You see the good in everyone.'

Not entirely. She thought Rachel should have been honest with Cleve but that was easy to say. She'd struggled with how to break the news of her own pregnancy and, as a result, he'd found out in the same brutal way...

'I see the good in you,' she said. 'You feel you were let off scot-free and that has fed your guilt. Instead of letting go, moving on, you've been brooding on that last confrontation, blaming yourself. Her death was a tragedy, grief is natural, but you were not to blame.'

'I should have—'

'Should, could,' she said, losing patience. 'This life isn't a rehearsal, Cleve. You don't get to come back and do it better. We all have things we'd have done differently given the chance but if you spend your whole life looking back at your mistakes, you'll never notice what's in front of you.'

'I know what's in front of me.'

For a moment she'd thought he was going to say it was her, their baby, a future neither of them had ever expected, but he was not seeing her as he stood up.

'I've got a roof to fix.'

How like a man to grab for something solid, something he could touch. She'd seen her father deal with messy, emotional things in just that way. It was as if fixing a broken engine, cutting the grass, repairing a bike gave him back control.

'Be careful,' she said, forcing herself to remain where she was as he waded through the pool, stepped up onto the sand. 'If you fall off, I will blame myself.'

He turned to look back at her, his forehead buckled in a frown. 'Why would you do that?'

'You're only here because of me, Cleve. You're only fixing the roof because I blackmailed you into staying and because it's human nature to blame oneself for things that go wrong. To analyse everything you said and did and how, if you'd acted differently, things would not have turned out the way they did.'

'Is that it? Are you done lecturing me?'

'That depends. How well have you been listening?'

'Let's see. You're responsible for me being here. You're responsible for me fixing the roof? How am I doing?'

'You're listening but is any of it sinking in?'

'You want a demonstration?' He held out his hand. 'How's this? If you're responsible for me being on the roof, you're going to have to come and watch.'

She thought what she needed to do was leave him

alone to process what she'd said, give his brain a chance to work through it while his hands were busy setting the tiles.

'If you're on the roof and I'm on the ground, how will that help?'

'Every time I look down I'll see you sitting down there watching me and I'll remember to be careful. Of course, if despite all that I do slip, I'll expect you to break my fall.'

'Idiot,' she said, but tenderly because he'd got the message. She took his hand so that he could pull her up beside him. 'I'm not going to be sitting around watching you.' No matter how appealing the prospect. 'I'm going to be working on the convertible. I can't have you driving to your wedding with your knees under your chin.'

Cleve tightened his grip on Miranda's hand as they crossed the beach to the freshwater shower that was no more than a pipe run down the cliff face from the garden above.

He might be an idiot, but at that moment he felt like the luckiest idiot in the world.

He'd just unloaded his mess of guilt on her because she had to know the worst of him. He owed her that. She'd been shocked but her reaction had been to take it to bits, clinically examine every part and respond with calm logic.

He felt like a misfiring engine that she'd taken apart, cleaned up and put back together.

He could never feel anything but guilt for what had happened to his marriage. He'd never loved Rachel the way she'd deserved to be loved but they'd managed until Miranda had joined Goldfinch. He'd explained why he'd had to give her a job, but sensed the danger and, while he'd never given her any reason to doubt his fidelity, the row that had followed Miranda's arrival had been the beginning of the end.

He turned on the tap. Nothing happened.

'Does this thing work?' he asked.

'It used to but I don't suppose it's been used in years. Maybe it's rusted up?'

As he looked up, there was a warning clang, the shower head shot off, missing him by a hair's breadth, and he let loose an expletive as a deluge of cold water hit skin warmed by the hot pool.

Andie, well out of harm's way, burst out laughing.

'You think that's funny?' Before she could answer he grabbed her and pulled her under the downpour so that she was the one gasping and a word he'd never heard her use before slipped from her sweet mouth.

He lifted his hand and wiped his wet thumb across it as if to erase the word, the mind-blowing image it evoked. She responded with a whimper that only intensified a reaction that the cold shower was doing nothing to cool.

There was a moment when the earth seemed to hold its breath, waiting, and then he lowered his mouth to hers, retracing the path of his thumb with his tongue, tasting the salt on her lips and then sweetness as her mouth opened to him. It was as if they had slipped back in time and she was responding with a hot, sweet, wholly innocent eagerness that had ripped the heart out of him and haunted him ever since.

He pushed down the straps of her costume, peeling it to her waist until the only thing between the softness of her breasts and his chest was a film of cold water. Deepening the kiss until the need to breathe forced them apart.

Her eyes were closed against the water running over her face, long wet lashes lying against her cheek. As he kissed them she shivered.

'You're cold.'

The drenching was all that was keeping him from exploding, but as he reached for the tap, turned it off, she raised her arms and, with her hand curled around his neck, she drew him back down to her and said, 'Warm me.'

'Are you warmer now?'

The sun had set and there was only the faintest glow in the horizon. They were lying entwined in each other's arms and through the open window Andie could see Venus, bright in the west, and the faint pin-pricks of stars lighting up as the sky darkened.

Warm. How could she begin to describe how warm she felt? This had been so different from that desperate night they'd spent together. While the sex had been intense, beyond anything she had ever experienced or could have imagined, it had been dark, shadowed and the emotion had provoked tears rather than laughter. Tears for loss. Tears she'd hidden—shed later when she was alone—for what might have been, for what never would be.

She'd never had any doubt that he knew who he was with, it had been her name on his lips when he'd spilled into her, but she'd blocked out the treacherous hope, aware that she was no more than a conduit from a painful past, a light in the tunnel to guide him to a new future. She had not looked or hoped for more.

Today that future seemed to be within their grasp and every move, every touch had been as if it were the very first time. New, a little bit scary, a shared discovery and he'd been with her every step of the way, tender at first, then responding to her urgent cries. There hadn't just been the tears that Cleve had kissed away afterwards, but laughter too. And when they'd exhausted themselves he was still with her, not just in his body but in his head.

'Much.' He'd warmed her body and soul. 'It's a shame you missed a bit or I'd have recommended you for the *Good Housekeeping* seal of approval.'

'Missed a bit?' The words were little more than a growl, but he was laughing, looking every bit as deliciously dangerous as the younger Cleve who'd whisked her into a dark corner of an aircraft hangar and kissed her senseless with her father not more than ten feet away. It had been heart-pounding stuff then and her heart was pounding now. 'There isn't an inch of you that I haven't warmed.'

Ignoring the heat shimmering across her skin, she smiled right back as she said, 'Then there must be a draught because there's a spot behind my right knee that's quite—'

The word *chilly* was lost in the depths of a pillow as he flipped her over and began to warm up the back of her knee with his mouth, his tongue and then, just to make sure, he warmed her all over again.

Cleve, warm for the first time in as long as he could remember, lay spooned around Miranda, his hand on her belly, imagining their child growing there. Her eyes were closed but she covered his hand with her own, tucking it closer against her, and he kissed her shoulder.

'What are you thinking about?' he asked.

She raised her lashes, looking out of the window at the sea and the lights of the fishing boats that had put out from the harbour below them. 'I was wondering why we never did this before.'

That was so not what he was expecting that it took him a moment to gather his thoughts, come up with an answer that filled the gaps.

'I wanted it so much,' she said, 'and but for Posy blundering in…' She sighed. 'Why couldn't she have chosen to throw up in some other part of the garden?'

That had been his first reaction too.

'Maybe your guardian angel guided her to you.'

She frowned. 'Guardian angel?'

'There would have been tears after bedtime.'

She raised an eyebrow. 'Are you telling me that you had a girl at every airfield?'

'Not every airfield.'

None of them like her and all of them history after a night that had shown him something new, unknown, that had changed him. Until then he hadn't taken anything too seriously. After that night he'd known what he wanted and it hadn't just been an air courier and taxi service. He'd wanted the world to lay at her feet.

'Where could it have gone? You were off to university at the end of that summer. I was struggling to build a business. I didn't have time to get seriously involved.'

'I wasn't looking for serious,' she said, turning to him. 'I was looking for a hot man who would—'

He put his hand over her mouth knowing only too well what she'd wanted. He'd spent too much time wondering what would have happened if he'd stepped over the line that night. How different their lives might have been.

'It wasn't our time,' he said, lowering his mouth to hers to stop her talking about it. 'This is our time.'

'It's at moments like this that you wish there was a telephone so that you could call out for a takeaway.'

Andie stirred, eased limbs aching from so much un-accustomed exercise. 'What would you call out for?'

'Anything with sufficient calories to replace those I've used in the last couple of hours. Something hot and spicy.'

'You're a long way from an Indian takeaway. I'm afraid if your run took it out of you then the food of choice is going to have to be pasta.'

'My run?' He rolled onto his side and, propped on his elbow, he looked down at her. 'I have only one thing to say to you, Miranda Marlowe.'

'Just one?' He looked so delicious that she would have reached up, hooked her hand around his neck and pulled him down so that she could kiss him if she'd had the energy. 'And what is that, Cleve Finch?'

'Walk to the bathroom and say that.'

She laughed. 'You win,' she said, surrendering without hesitation. 'The downside of that is that you're going to have to carry me.'

He leaned over and kissed her. 'It would be my pleasure.'

The cooker was of the old-fashioned solid kind and it had survived both fire and the attack from the extinguisher. Between the stuff she'd picked up from the supermarket when she arrived and the things Cleve had bought in the village, the fridge yielded the basics for a decent tomato sauce.

Cleve put on a pan of water to boil for the pasta and then they chopped and sliced, making it up as they went along.

Once, when she realised that he'd stopped, she looked up and he was just looking at her.

'Problem?'

'What?' He seemed to come from a long way away. 'I was just wondering if you're okay with garlic.'

'We don't have any garlic.'

'Don't we?' He looked down at the table. 'Olives. I meant olives.'

'Olives are fine, but we'll add them at the end.'

'Okay. You're in charge.'

'Oh, no,' she said, removing the seeds from a large tomato and chopping it up. 'This is an equal opportunities supper. If it's rubbish, you're taking half the blame.'

Oh, sugar… That hadn't come out quite the way she'd meant it, but when she looked up he was grinning.

'Onions, tomatoes, what could go wrong?'

'Not a thing.' She put heat under a pan, added a glug of olive oil then, when it was warm, piled in the chopped onions and gave them a shake.

Cleve searched the drawers for a corkscrew and opened a bottle of red wine he'd bought while they were out.

'Can I get you something to drink?'

'I brought a bottle of elderflower *pressé* with me. It's in the fridge.'

He poured her a glass of the cordial, poured himself a glass of wine while Andie added the tomatoes to the pan and gave it a stir.

'Do you enjoy cooking?' he asked.

She took a sip of her drink. 'I think it's a little bit late to be interviewing me for housewife skills.'

'I'm not marrying a housekeeper, but I've just realised how little I know about you.'

'Excuse me?' She raised an eyebrow. 'You've known me for years.'

'I know what kind of person you are. Generous, kind, thoughtful, focused. I would, I have trusted you with my life in the air and I know you have a natural flair for design. Whatever you did to the tail of the Mayfly has certainly improved the fuel efficiency.'

'My father has never forgiven you for giving me a job,' she said.

'Is that what he told you?'

'He told me that in a recession no one would take a risk on a newly qualified "girl pilot".'

'Please tell me he didn't say "girl pilot"?'

'No,' she admitted, 'but he might as well have. I wrote hundreds of application letters, filled in dozens of forms but I never got a single interview. His fake sympathy made me so mad that I told him that you'd promised me a job if I got my CPL and I was going to fly down and see you.'

'Oh? And what did he say about that?'

'That times were tough and I shouldn't rely on a spur-of-the-moment promise given three years before and no doubt forgotten as quickly.'

'So, despite the promise, I was the last person you approached for a job?'

'I thought he might have been right. It was the kind of thing a man might say...'

'When he wants to get into the pants of a pretty girl?'

'Maybe,' she admitted, with the faintest hint of a blush. 'And I knew it was my last chance so I made him a promise that if you'd forgotten, or if you didn't have a job for me, I'd give up my dream of flying and join the design team.'

'It's just as well I did have an opening for a new pilot.'

'You didn't. Not really.' She looked at him. 'It didn't take me long to realise that you could have managed very well without me.'

'Business began to pick up right after that. By then you were familiar with all the aircraft and fully integrated with the team. It was one of my better decisions.'

'Maybe, but that's what I know about you, Cleve. You are a man who keeps his word.'

His mouth was dry and he took another sip of wine. 'We're talking about you.'

'Me? What you see is what you get. I'm scared of spiders. I don't like frills or shopping for clothes, although I'm going to have to make an effort now that I don't have a uniform to hide in.'

'You look good in pink.'

'Pink?' She frowned. 'I can't remember the last time I wore pink.' At least…

'You wore a pale pink dress to your eighteenth birthday party.' It had been made of something soft that floated when she'd spun around. 'And you love daisies.'

'Daisies?'

He dumped a couple of handfuls of pasta into the water. 'I wanted to send you flowers when I was in

Cyprus but couldn't think what would send the right message.'

'Tricky,' she agreed.

'It would have helped if I'd known what the message was, but you always walk around the airfield and pick a bunch of dog daisies when they're in flower.' He stirred the pasta. 'If I'd remembered that maybe you'd have told me about the baby.'

'I don't think online florists do dog daisies.'

'No.'

'I like cow parsley and rosebay willowherb too. All it costs to please me when it comes to flowers is a little effort.'

'What about on Valentine's Day?'

'February? Violets. Harder to spot but they grow in their millions in the woods above the Marlowe airfield.' She tasted the sauce. 'You can add the basil now.'

He tipped it into the pan.

'I'll grate the cheese.'

'Cheese?' She looked apprehensive. 'I didn't know we had any cheese.'

He unwrapped the package that the delicatessen had wrapped in waxed paper. 'I bought some pecorino when I picked up the marmalade—'

'No-o-o!'

She had her hands over her mouth and nose and he swiftly wrapped it up and pushed it to the back of the fridge. 'I'll get rid of it later.'

She nodded, clearly not quite trusting herself to open her mouth.

He crushed a stem of basil, held it beneath her nose and in a moment she was breathing again. 'Oh, my goodness. I'm so sorry about that.'

'Don't apologise but for future reference is that cheese in general, pecorino in particular, or is it a morning sickness thing?'

'I don't know why they call it morning sickness,' she said. 'The *vomito* can hit at any time.'

'*Vomito?*'

She told him about the scene at the *porto*, the border official who'd changed from suspicious to kindness itself once he'd realised the problem.

'He was the first person you told about the baby?'

'I'm sorry, Cleve. It should have been you.'

'Don't stress.' He kissed her forehead. 'If I hadn't hung around in Cyprus...' Delaying his departure, knowing that he would have to talk to Miranda on his return. Not knowing what he would say. 'If I'd been there...'

She waved it off.

'If *ifs* and *buts* were candy and nuts—'

'Every day would be Christmas?'

They both grinned then Miranda said, 'There are, apparently, a whole heap of things I can't eat. Until a couple of days ago it didn't matter because I couldn't face anything but now I've got my appetite back I'll have to look it up on the Web.'

'I'll take my phone with me tomorrow and check the list when we go into San Rocco.'

'No, don't!' She shook her head. 'Take no notice of me. I'm being silly. I'm just afraid that once the outside world breaks into this time alone it's all going to fall to pieces.'

CHAPTER TEN

'HEY...' CLEVE PUT his arms around her and drew her close.

'It's those wretched hormones on the rampage,' she said. 'Of course you have to check for messages.'

'No, I don't.' He wasn't immune to the feeling that this was too good to be true, that something would leap out of the woodwork and mess it up. 'Your hormones are working overtime to take care of you and we'll respect them.'

She shook her head, but her eyes were overbright and she was blinking hard to keep the tears from falling.

'Shall we have lunch out tomorrow?' he suggested. 'I noticed a restaurant overlooking the sea about a mile outside San Rocco. Maybe we could take a look around the island? This is supposed to be a holiday. I imagine even the drystone-wall builders are allowed time out to look at the view.'

'Only when they stand up to straighten their backs,' she said. Then grinned. 'Is the pasta done?'

He let go of her and turned to check. 'Just right.' He drained it, mixed it with the sauce, stirred in some olives and then shared it between the two bowls. 'A few olives on the top, a leaf or two of basil and we're done.' He checked to make sure he'd turned the oven off then said, 'Shall we take it outside?'

They ate their supper sitting side by side, not quite touching, with the lights of Baia di Rose below them.

'Mark Twain said that nothing improves the view like ham and eggs,' Andie said after a while. 'I think I'd add a bowl of pasta to that quote.'

'What this view, this food needs, is some Neapolitan love song playing in the background.'

She laughed, shook her head. 'I didn't take you for a sentimental old romantic.'

'Didn't you? What would you choose?'

'Sofia used to love Sinatra. When we sat out here in the evening she'd put on one of his mellow late night song albums. "In the Wee Small Hours…"'

Cleve reached for her hand and began to sing very softly.

'I've never heard you sing,' she said, when he'd finished.

'I've never had anything to sing about before.'

'Cleve…'

He lifted the hand he was holding to his lips. 'Is it too soon to be talking names?'

'Names?' Andie, her hand in Cleve's, enchanted by the sound of his voice, was jolted back to earth.

The baby… She had to remember that this wasn't about her. It was all about the baby.

'Far too soon,' she said, making an effort to keep up the smile. 'Whatever we choose we're bound to think of something completely different when we see him or her.'

'Where does Miranda come from? Are you named after an aunt, grandmother?'

'Shakespeare's heroine in *The Tempest*.'

'You're kidding.'

'Portia, Miranda, Imogen and Rosalind?' she prompted. 'Mum and Dad met at Stratford. They were sitting next to each other at a performance of *The Merchant of Venice*. The rest, as they say, is history.'

'I'd never made the connection but, just so you know, if it's a girl I'm putting in a bid for Daisy.'

'Daisy Finch? It's a deal,' she said, doing her best not to read too much into the fact that he'd chosen her favourite flower. 'Unless she looks like a Violet, or an Iris, or a Lily.'

'Or a Poppy. Or a Primrose. Or a Pansy.' He grinned. 'I think we've found our theme.'

Theme? 'It might be a boy.'

'Let's worry about that when you've had a scan. That's if you want to know?'

Did she? Suddenly everything was moving too fast. This was supposed to be thinking time but all she'd done so far was react to situations as they'd arisen.

'I'll need notice of that question. Ask me something simple.'

'Okay. What's your favourite movie?'

'While You Were Sleeping.'

'Why? Tell me about it.'

'It's a chick flick,' she warned.

'I can handle that.'

'Who are you?' she asked. 'And what have you done with Cleve Finch?'

'If I'm going to have a little girl I need to get in touch with my feminine side.'

Unable to help herself, she laughed and they spent the evening sharing the things they loved: food, music, films and then, when it was too cold to sit out, they went to bed and shared each other.

Afterwards, Andie lay awake in the dark, the only sounds the quiet breathing of the man beside her, the soft susurration of the sea lapping the beach below them.

She'd grabbed at marriage to stop Cleve from slipping back into the darkness. To ensure her child had a place at the centre of his world. But what about her?

She had wondered if Cleve would want to sleep with her. Question asked and answered. He was a passionate man and clearly he was taking their marriage seriously, anticipating more children. A posy of little girls…

But where was love in all this?

He had freely admitted to having sleepwalked into marriage with Rachel, to having failed her.

A divorce would have been financially painful but once there were children…

His arm looped around her, drew her against his chest and he kissed her neck, murmured, 'You're overthinking it. Go to sleep.'

The following morning, while Cleve worked on the roof, Andie went down to the village to pick up her bag and visit Alberto and Elena, where she spent a happy hour reminiscing and catching up.

She told them about the wedding, explaining that it would be a simple affair, but she would love to have them join her and Cleve and the Starks for a small celebration meal afterwards. She left, promising to let them know when, and went back to the villa to hunt down the dress she was hoping to wear.

The gowns had been laid in acid-free tissue and layered with silk lavender bags and she found the dress she was looking for in the second trunk. Inside the lid was an album of photographs of Sofia modelling the gowns and the colours of the kimono dress were as fresh and vibrant as the day she'd been photographed for *Vogue Italia*.

She swallowed down a lump in her throat, knowing that she didn't have that kind of style. That it would never look like that on her. And when she held it up against her there was another problem. She was not model height. Even with high heels the dress was going to be too long.

'Miranda...'

It didn't matter. She could take up the hem or there were plenty of dresses and not all of them were floor length.

'I'm ready whenever you are.'

Cleve appeared in the doorway looking good enough to eat in a dark blue shirt and a pair of lightweight grey trousers he'd bought the day before.

'Stay there,' she warned, holding the dress behind her.

He held up his hands and backed away, grinning. 'I'm doing nothing to anger the superstition gods.'

They had lunch on a restaurant terrace overlooking the sea near San Rocco. Afterwards they picked up the rings from the jeweller and the translated declarations from the notary.

'Shall we go to the *municipio* and see if they can fit us in some time this week?' Cleve asked.

'I'd rather ask the mayor of Baia di Rose if he'll perform the ceremony. It feels more like home.'

'If that's what you want,' Cleve said. 'You know it's not too late—'

'No fuss, Cleve.' Then, when he let the question hang, 'It's too soon.'

To him the last year had felt like a lifetime but maybe the kind of celebration he believed she deserved would seem indecent if you were on the outside looking in.

'You should write to Rachel's parents.'

'They cut me dead at the inquest but I wrote to them on the anniversary of her death. Sent flowers. The letter came back marked return to sender. I imagine the flowers went in the bin.'

'It must be so hard to lose a child.'

'It's a terrifying responsibility.'

For a moment they stood, their hands tightly clasped, contemplating the fact that, as parents, their lives would never be their own again.

The mayor of Baia di Rose was delighted to be asked to officiate at their wedding. All they had to do was choose a day and a time.

'I'll have the roof finished in a couple of days. If we get married on Saturday we could leave the next day,' Cleve said.

Leave? So soon? But then why wouldn't he? Goldfinch was his life.

He'd taken time out to come and find her and offer to do the honourable thing. He hadn't bargained on a baby. He hadn't actually bargained on a wedding. He certainly hadn't bargained on fixing a hole in the roof.

He must be desperate to get back to his desk.

'That suits me,' she said.

He turned back to the mayor and asked him if the *municipio* was open on Saturday.

'No, *signor*. But I can perform the ceremony any day, anywhere within my *comune*.'

'This Saturday.'

'Except this Saturday. It is my daughter's birthday.'

'Sunday, then.'

Sunday, too, was a very busy day for the mayor, what with church and lunch involving his entire extended family, but he finally agreed that he could marry them late in the afternoon, just before sunset. They just had to let him know where.

'Any ideas? On the beach?' he suggested.

Miranda shook her head. 'There are some occasions that are not enhanced by the addition of sand.'

'You don't like picnics on the beach?'

'Gritty sandwiches. No, thanks.' Then, apparently able to read his mind, she blushed. 'And it doesn't do anything for designer dresses. Why don't we have the ceremony on the terrace overlooking the sea?'

'I will convert you to beach picnics,' he warned her, before turning back to the mayor. 'We have a date, *signor*. On the terrace at the Villa Rosa just before sunset on Sunday.'

They picked up a bottle of champagne to share with Matt and Gloria when they called to tell him to save the day.

Matt met them at the front door. 'Have you checked your messages?'

Andie's heart did a flip. 'Is there a problem?'

'Come in. You're going to want to be sitting down when you hear what's happened.'

'Is it my parents?' she demanded. 'Has there been an accident? Is Dad sick?'

'Matt,' Cleve said sharply.

'Sorry. Nothing like that. Posy rang.'

'Posy?'

'She knew the house was a mess and wanted to be sure that you were okay. I was working and my mother answered the phone.'

'Oh.' Certain she knew what was coming, she sank onto the nearest chair. 'What did she say?'

'Too much. As you know she called the fire brigade and I had no idea that Cleve being here, the wedding, was a secret. I'm really sorry.'

'What did Gloria actually say?' Cleve persisted.

'She said that Miranda was fine despite the bang on the head and the fire, which understandably freaked Posy out, so Mum told her not to worry because Cleve was taking good care of you. And then, because of course she's met Posy, she said she was looking forward to seeing her at the wedding.'

Head, fire, Cleve, wedding… Not quite the full house.

'Did she mention the baby?'

'I think the explosion from the other end of the phone in response to the word *wedding* warned her that she might have already said too much. She panicked and hung up.'

Well, that was something.

'Ten minutes later your other sister called.'

'Imogen. Please, please tell me that your mother

didn't speak to her.' Imogen would have had the lot out of her in ten seconds flat.

'She'd already called me and explained what had happened so when the phone rang again I picked up. Before she could start I told her that I'd ask you to call her. Her response was that if she doesn't hear from you by seven this evening she'll be on the first plane out of London tomorrow. I'm so sorry,' he repeated.

She shook her head. 'It's not your fault. It's mine. Is your mother okay?'

'She's hiding in the conservatory, too upset to face you.'

'Please tell her not to worry. This is my family drama and I've handled it really badly. I'll tell her myself as soon as I've sorted this out.'

'Thanks. I appreciate that. I'll go and reassure her. Help yourself to the phone.'

When Matt'd gone Cleve folded himself up in front of her, took her hands in his. 'What do you want to do?'

'Fly to Las Vegas?' Her laugh was a little shaky.

'That seems a little extreme. Since the cat appears to be well and truly out of the bag why don't we just call Immi, tell her our news and promise we'll throw a party when we get back?'

'All our news?'

'You're nervous about telling her that we're having a baby?'

That *we* earned him a gazillion brownie points.

'It's a bit embarrassing to have to admit that at my age I wasn't practising safe sex.'

'That wasn't sex,' he said, 'it was first aid. The kiss of life.' For a moment he was deadly serious, then a crease appeared at the corner of his mouth. 'What we did last night was sex.'

Despite everything she laughed. 'I can't argue with that.'

But as he hugged her she tried not to cling too tightly. She was old enough to know that sex didn't mean the same thing to men as it did to women; their emotions did not have to be engaged.

'So,' he said, after a moment, 'do we run or do we put on a brave face and tell the world?'

'There's no point in running. We'll have to face them sooner or later and if I don't phone Immi she'll explode.'

He handed her the phone, she dialled the number but didn't get a chance to speak.

'Andie! What the heck is going on? What bang on the head? What fire? Posy is frantic.'

'She needn't be. I bumped my head on a cupboard. The only damage was to the cupboard. The fire was nothing. The kettle was left on the stove and boiled dry. I threw a damp cloth over it and gave it a squirt with the fire extinguisher.'

'Okay. That's the easy stuff. Now tell me why Cleve Finch is there. No, I can guess why. How? When did that happen?'

'Are you sitting down?'

'Andie!'

'I'm pregnant,' she said, reaching for Cleve's hand.

'What? How long has this been going on? No, wait, it was the weekend you flew him up to pick up the Mayfly! You were a bit weird and teary at the dress fitting…'

'I was not weird.' She glanced at Cleve. 'I was…
tired.'

Immi laughed. 'So, apparently, was he. Jack told me
that Cleve hadn't left until late the following morning
but I didn't think anything of it. I assumed he'd stayed
in the pub but it's obvious now that he was dropping
a heavy hint.'

She didn't bother to answer. Immi's imagination
would be working overtime and Cleve's breakdown
was between the two of them.

'You're really having a baby? When? Hold on, if
I'm right it's…' Andie heard her counting on her fingers '…November?'

'November,' she confirmed.

'I'm going to be an auntie! How brilliant is that? Do
Mum and Dad know?'

'Not yet.'

'You can tell them when we chat tomorrow. Can
you find somewhere?'

The temptation to say no was almost overwhelming
but she'd already messed up big time and her parents
had the right to hear it from her.

'I can get a signal in San Rocco.'

'This is such fabulous news. Hang on… Posy wasn't
fantasising about a wedding, was she?'

'No, but we're getting married here, Immi. Quietly.
Just a quick stand-up-in-front-of-the-mayor on Sunday.
We don't want to wait and I'm not going to get in the
way of your big day. We'll have a party later.'

'Excuse me, twin, but if you think you're getting
married without me there you can think again. Is Cleve
there? Let me talk to him.'

She turned to Cleve. 'I'm afraid she wants to talk to you.'

'I imagine I'll survive.' He took the phone, listened, laughed at something Immi said and then, after several minutes, during which he didn't say more than 'yes' and 'I've got that', he handed back the phone.

'Immi?'

'I've told Cleve that you can get married on the island but only if we're all there. We're a bit scattered so it's going to take a few days to get organised but you are going to have a proper wedding. Not this Sunday— I need more time. Cleve is going to change it to the following weekend but it will be worth waiting for. In the meantime just lie back and enjoy the honeymoon.'

'Aren't you supposed to have those after the wedding?'

'Andie, I hate to be the one to state the obvious but you've already jumped that hurdle. You've waited a long time for this, love. Don't waste another moment.'

'Is that an order?'

'If you need an order...' She didn't bother to complete the sentence. 'And don't fret about the details. That's my job as your chief bridesmaid. I'll get on the 'net and start things rolling.'

'Immi, we don't want a fuss.'

'Tough. It's not every day a girl's dream comes true and when it does it calls for a celebration.'

Aware that Cleve was watching her she managed to hang onto the smile. 'I don't know what to say.'

'Say nothing. No, wait, you can tell Mrs Stark that I love her. I'll see you on our video chat tomorrow.'

She hung up. Looked at Cleve. 'What did she say?'

'That I'm not to marry you until everyone is here.'

'She said a lot more than that.'

'That sums it up.'

She doubted it but she handed him the phone. 'You'd better phone your parents before they hear the news from someone else. I'll go and give Gloria a hug and persuade her to come and have a glass of champagne with us.'

Breaking the news to her parents was an emotional experience but Cleve was at her back and if her father was quiet, her mother said all the right things and her sisters made enough noise to attract the amused attention of people sitting at other tables in the café.

They all promised to be at the wedding, even Posy. She found it difficult to get away from the Royal Ballet during the season but having the ceremony on a Sunday meant she would only miss one performance.

Cleve said he'd fly over to pick them up, but her father stepped in and said if he texted him the details of the flying club he'd get them all to L'Isola dei Fiori for the wedding.

They passed on Gloria's offer of a comfortable room for her parents and grandmother, which was gratefully accepted. Cleve had already booked his parents into a hotel in San Rocco and he was going to join them there for the night before the wedding.

'That wasn't so bad, was it?' Cleve asked as they walked back to the car.

'Dad was quiet.'

'I'll talk to him.'

'Oh?' She'd love to be a fly on the wall for that conversation. 'What will you say?'

'That's probably better left between us.' He tucked her arm beneath his and smiled at her. 'Happier now?'

'Yes. Thank you.'

'Why are you thanking me?'

'For putting up with my family. With the hormones. With the silly superstitions.'

'How are you getting on with the something old, something new stuff?'

'Well, the dress can be either old, or borrowed. Blue is the tricky one because the dress has green and yellow notes.'

'I thought a garter was traditional.'

'Did you?' And just like that the day lost its lustre.

Immi thought that this was her dream come true but the reality was that Cleve had done all this before. That time there had been a glossy ceremony in one of the classiest venues in the county, a bride that any man would have lusted after, but even with everything as perfect as a father's money could make it the marriage hadn't lasted.

This time he'd been guilt-tripped into marriage because of a one-night-stand baby. The wedding would be a handmade affair in an overgrown garden with a handful of guests and instead of an expensive honeymoon in the Maldives, he would be back at his desk the next day.

'Miranda? Are you okay? Do you want to sit down?'

'I can make it to the car,' she said, jacking the smile back into place.

'You're sure?'

She nodded, but the only thing she was sure about was regret that they hadn't gone to the *municipio* in San Rocco when they'd picked up the declarations and the rings and had the mayor say the words over them there and then.

No fancy dress, no photographs, just a couple of witnesses called in from an office. No family turning what was a marriage of convenience into a celebration.

The roof was fixed. Alberto's son, Toni, arrived to cut the grass, remove the weeds from the terrace and cut back some of the shrubs so that the calla lilies had a chance to shine. He'd brought his wife with him and she helped prepare the bedrooms for Andie's sisters, and did what she could with the painted drawing room and the conservatory.

And then, on Thursday, Immi arrived two days ahead of everyone else. Cleve, who had clearly known, had already packed his bag.

'Where are you going?'

'I'm going to leave you two to do whatever women do before a big event. Mostly have fun, I hope.'

'But—'

'In the meantime I'm going to pick up my family and yours.'

'I thought Dad was going to organise that.'

'He asked Immi to make the arrangements. She organised me.' He turned to Immi. 'Look after her.'

'I will. We won't make toffee or chips.' She used a finger to cross her heart.

'What?'

'It's what Dad always used to say when he and Mum went out leaving Portia in charge. No making toffee or chips...' She laughed. 'Maybe we should add a warning about leaving kettles to boil dry on the stove.'

Andie followed him out to the porch. 'How are you getting to the airfield?'

'Immi asked the taxi to wait.' He put down his bag, took her in his arms. 'There are one or two things I have to do. I'll see you on Sunday.'

'But you'll be back on Saturday.'

'I think you'll find that Immi has organised something special for Saturday.'

'A hen party?' She buried her face in his chest. 'Please tell me that you're not going on a stag do with my dad.'

'Your dad, my dad, Matt...' He tucked his hand beneath her chin. 'If we end up in jail will you bail us out?'

'I'll send Immi,' she warned. 'And you will be sorry.'

He laughed, kissed her. Lingered... 'I have to go or I'll miss my slot.'

'Go!' she said, then as he headed for the gate, 'Take care!'

She'd seen him take off hundreds of times but suddenly it was personal. 'Take care...' she whispered as she heard the car pull away.

CHAPTER ELEVEN

IMMI HAD A LIST. The first item on it was 'The Dress'.

'What are you going to wear?'

Andie showed her the kimono. Immi sighed, shook her head. 'What on earth were you thinking?'

'I was thinking simple, elegant.'

'If you were ten centimetres taller and model-girl thin, maybe. You are lovely, darling, but you are not Sofia. This is not a dress for a woman with any kind of a bust.' She opened the trunk and began to lift out dresses. 'Oh! Do you remember this?' She held up a pleated dress in green ombre-dye chiffon. She held it against herself. 'I swanned around in this one imagining I looked like Sophia Loren.'

'Flat chest, mousy brown hair? I don't think so!' They burst out laughing, hugged one another, then turned back to the chest, remembering lovely days, the parties, shedding a tear for Sofia who, older, wiser, they knew must have been lonely in her pink villa by the sea. Who had died far too young.

'She had a dress that would be perfect,' Immi said. 'It was very delicate and must have meant something to Sofia because she wouldn't let Portia wear it.'

'What did it look like?'

She shook her head. 'Wait until you see it. In the meantime,' she said, holding up a jewel-bright gown, 'this is what I'll be wearing.' She looked around. 'Sofia had fabulous costume jewellery to go with these clothes. She had an old safe under the stairs where she kept it.'

Andie opened the box beneath her mirror and held up the key. 'If you are prepared to brave the spiders I think this might be the key.'

'Oh, boy. This is going to be so much fun,' she said. 'Of course, I will need shoes. And underwear. Shopping tomorrow?'

'Is it compulsory?'

'Absolutely, but today we'll lie back and soak up the sun.'

'Shouldn't we be organising food? Doing something practical?'

'It's all taken care of.'

'How?'

'You might be cut off up here but the rest of the island is hooked up to the phone system and the World Wide Web. Dad gave me *carte blanche* with his credit card along with a few pointed comments about how thoughtful daughters ran away to get married.'

'He didn't mean it. He'll burst with pride when he walks you down the aisle.'

'I know. Come on, let's go down to the beach.'

They swam, lazed in the hot pool, went down to the village for supper and sat well into the night reminiscing about their holidays at the villa.

The next morning Portia flew in from the States and hugged her half to death. 'You finally hooked the bad boy?' She shook her head, grinning from ear to ear as she exclaimed over the ring. 'You would never settle for second best.' Then she turned to Immi. 'Have you fixed everything for tomorrow?'

Andie looked from one to the other. 'Tomorrow?'

'We decided that instead of a boring wedding present we're going to take everyone to a spa for a pampering day.'

'Oh…'

Portia grinned. 'It's not as if you'll need a toaster. You've already got two of everything. Have you decided where you'll live?'

She shook her head but Cleve's flat was bigger. And filled with stuff chosen, used by Rachel…

'It hardly matters,' Immi cut in, pointedly. 'You'll be looking for a house, I imagine. Children need a garden.'

'It's all happened so fast,' Andie said, helplessly.

Immi touched her arm, a gesture of reassurance, then swiftly reverted to the wedding details. 'We've decided that we're all going to wear Sofia's dresses,' she said, turning to Portia. 'A kind of tribute to her. You need to choose one.'

'Vintage?' Her eyes lit up. 'Fabulous. What are you wearing, Andie?'

'We haven't decided,' Immi said. 'I've been looking for that dress Sofia wouldn't let you wear. Do you remember? You sulked for hours.'

'I never sulked!' Portia rolled her eyes. 'Okay, I sulked but it was a dream dress.'

'Exactly.'

She sighed. 'You're right. It would be perfect.'

'It's not in any of the trunks we've found.'

'When she rescued it from me she took it into her bedroom.' Portia led the way, then turned at the doorway. 'You're not sleeping in here?' she asked, surprised.

Andie shook her head. 'It didn't feel right.' She saw Immi and Portia exchange a glance and quickly said, 'All I found in Sofia's wardrobe were day clothes.'

Portia crossed to a chest of drawers, sighing as she opened each one, lifting out a scarf, something in oyster satin that slithered through her fingers, lace... 'Posy is going to make a fortune selling this stuff.' Then, as she opened the bottom drawer she reached in and lifted out something wrapped in tissue paper.

'Is that it?' Immi asked.

Portia placed it on the bed, unfolded the tissue, removed satin lavender bags and then shook out an ethereal shimmer of a dress. The simplest long-sleeved shift created from sheer lace into which flowers had been worked and from which tiny beads glistened. At first sight it looked transparent, but beneath the lace there was a nude slip.

For a moment none of them said anything then Andie gathered herself. It was too much... Too bridal. Exactly what she'd wanted to avoid.

'It will be too long,' she objected. 'There's no way to shorten it.'

'Let's see.'

They had her out of her T-shirt and trousers before she could argue and dropped the dress over her head.

It slithered over her body and crumpled gently at her feet but before she could say a word Portia and Immi spoke as one.

'High heels!'

They did a high five, then burst out laughing. 'Come on. Let's go shopping.'

* * *

Next morning they picked up Gloria and all four of them made their way to a hotel overlooking San Rocco that had a luxurious spa. By the time they'd ordered coffee and cake her mother, grandmother, Laura Finch and Posy had arrived.

There were a few tears, exclamations over the ring, an unexpectedly heartfelt hug from Laura, a whispered thank-you and then it was time for facials, massages. They had lunch. The afternoon was all about hair and nails, the bliss of pedicures followed by champagne in the hot tub for everyone but Andie and then afternoon tea.

But all the time, amidst the laughter, there was a little nagging voice that kept repeating Portia's words.

'You would never settle for second best...'

'Andie...'

Portia caught her as they were leaving.

Her sister had been full of life all day but just once or twice she'd caught a look, as if Portia were somewhere else.

'Are you okay, Portia?'

'Fine,' she said, too quickly. 'A bit stressed. Work... I was wondering, are you and Cleve staying on here after tomorrow?'

She shook her head. 'We've been here too long already. We'll be home on Monday.'

'Oh...' She looked surprised, then grinned. 'Honeymoon before the event...' Then, 'If I'm not going to be playing gooseberry I thought I'd ask Posy if I can stay on for a while. Decompress.'

By the time they arrived home Andie was desperate to be alone and, making the excuse that she was tired, went up to her room.

For a while there were the familiar sounds of her sisters squabbling over the bathroom, the murmurs and giggles as they picked over the day and then gradually everything grew quiet with only the now familiar sounds of the old house as it settled and cooled.

Silent but for a tap on her window.

The first time she heard it Andie thought it was a moth, tricked by the light of the moon shining on the glass. The second time it was accompanied by her name whispered softly.

'Miranda…'

Only one person ever called her that.

'Cleve?' She scrambled out of bed and found him leaning on the windowsill. 'What are you doing?'

'Standing on a ladder, talking to the woman I'm going to marry tomorrow. It's damned uncomfortable. Can I come in?'

'Have you been drinking?'

'A glass or two of wine. A brandy…'

'How did you get here?' she demanded. 'You'd better not be driving.'

'It's a lovely night for a walk and I have something important to tell you.'

'Idiot. Get down now, before you fall. No, wait. I'll come and hold the ladder.'

She pulled on a wrap, held her breath on the landing half expecting one of her sisters to appear, then crept downstairs. Cleve was waiting on the doorstep but before she could berate him he'd caught her around the waist and was kissing her senseless.

He tasted of old brandy, delicious, warming, melting all her doubts. 'You do know that if you're here after midnight you'll turn into a pumpkin?' she said, when he finally eased away so that they could breathe.

'I won't stay,' he promised, 'but on the subject of superstitions, I wanted you to know that I've sorted out the troublesome "something blue". You'll have it tomorrow.'

'You walked all the way from San Rocco to tell me that?'

'There isn't a phone but I cannot tell a lie. I had a lift in Matt's taxi. I only walked up from the village.'

She shook her head. 'Come on, I'll drive you back.'

'The walk will clear my head.'

'If you don't put your foot in a rabbit hole and break your ankle,' she said, pulling away in the direction of the garage.

'Wait. It wasn't just the something blue,' he said. 'There's something else.' Now he was serious and her heart, beating much too fast, seemed to stop. 'While I was home I realised that everywhere I turned in my flat there was a reminder of Rachel—the colour of the walls, the sofa, pretty much everything in the kitchen. I want us to have a fresh start so I've put it on the market, fully furnished.'

His flat was so much bigger than hers, it was the obvious place to live but she'd been dreading it. She leaned against his chest and let him hold her while she gathered the breath to whisper, 'Thank you.'

'You might not be so happy when we're squeezed into your little flat while we look for a house.'

'We'll manage.'

'It's nearly twelve. I'd better go.' He kissed her again. 'Until tomorrow.'

* * *

The next morning Immi produced boxes of tiny white solar lights and yards of heart-shaped bunting that she'd brought with her. While she and Posy threaded them through the garden, along the wall and over the terrace, Portia disappeared on some mysterious errand of her own.

Boxes of flowers arrived from a smart florist in San Rocco.

'Immi!'

Imogen held up her hands. 'Not me,' she said. 'All I did was pass on Cleve's instructions.'

Andie took the lid off one of the boxes to reveal a circlet of white daisies with soft yellow centres and a bouquet made of the same flowers with a sprinkling of pale blue *osteospermum*.

In the other were buttonhole flowers. White daisies for everyone except the groom, whose buttonhole matched her bouquet.

'African Daisies…' She touched one of them lightly with a fingertip. 'I was struggling to think of "something blue",' she said. But Cleve had come up with something very special.

'I'm not surprised with the green in that kimono dress,' Immi said. 'I suppose with the *osteospermum* surrounded by the white and yellow you could have just about got away with this, but thankfully that's no longer a problem. You do know it's unlucky to get married in green?'

'Is it?' Andie shook her head. 'I seem to have missed that one.'

'Lucky you. Gran knows dozens of wedding superstitions and she's shared every single one of them, bless her. She's bringing her pearls for you to wear, by the way.'

'That's everything, then. Borrowed dress, new shoes, old pearls and blue daisies.' She looked at Immi. 'How are your wedding arrangements going?'

'Endless. And you've just added the letting out of a bridesmaid's dress to the list.' Immi rolled her eyes. 'I'm beginning to wish I'd opted for running away.'

'I don't think that's quite Stephen's style.'

'No. I think he's making more fuss about this wedding than I am. He sends his apologies that he can't be here, by the way. Things are hectic at the factory and we'll both be taking time off after the wedding.'

She nodded. 'You're here, that's all that matters.'

'Are you okay, Andie?'

'Fine,' she said. She didn't care about not having a lush wedding in a country house, but Cleve would be back at his desk on Monday and she would, presumably, be doing the rounds of the estate agents.

It didn't matter. He'd thought about the flat, remembered that she loved daisies. He'd even found blue ones for her. And last night he'd climbed up to her window like a midnight lover...

'That's better,' Immi said.

'What?'

'You're smiling.'

'Of course I'm smiling. It's my wedding day. Come on, we'd better get these inside where it's cool.'

Crates of champagne arrived and the caterers with the cold buffet packed into cold boxes and then, when it was time to go and get ready, she discovered what Portia had been up to.

Sofia's suite had been transformed. The furniture

gleamed, the bed had been made up with fine lace-edged sheets and pillowcases, the bed frame hung with gauzy drapes. There were candles tucked into tall glass holders in the bedroom and bathroom, and a luscious selection of toiletries arranged on the glass shelves.

'Portia…'

'The clock is ticking. Take a shower or a bath and then we're going to turn you into a princess.'

Posy was on make-up, giving them all the benefit of her theatrical experience. Portia did something complicated with her hair, pinning it up, creating wisps of curls with curling tongs.

They all stepped into the vintage dresses they'd chosen, each a jewel colour and style that perfectly complemented their personalities.

The last thing they did was help her into her dress, dealing with tiny hooks, draping it so that it trailed a little behind, supporting her as she stepped into the highest heels she'd ever worn that just lifted the hem clear of the floor at the front.

Her grandmother arrived with her pearls, exclaiming at how beautiful all the girls looked in Sofia's dresses before turning to Andie.

'Sofia was wearing this dress the night she met Ludo,' she said as she fastened the pearls around her neck. 'She would be so happy that you're wearing it today, my darling.' She handed her the earrings and, once she'd fitted them to her ears, Immi placed the circlet of daisies on her head, pinned it in place, then handed her the bouquet.

There was a round of photograph taking and then Portia said, 'Come on, girls, Dad wants a little father/

daughter time with Andie before he surrenders her to Cleve.'

'Is he here?'

'He's just arrived. Were you worried he might have overslept after his late-night outing?' Portia shook her head.

'Climbing up to your window in the middle of the night.' Immi sighed. 'How romantic is that?'

Posy giggled. 'Oh, bless, she's blushing.'

They left, all of them giggling like schoolgirls. So much for being discreet!

A moment later there was a tap on the door and her father put his head around it. 'I'm told it's safe to come in.'

'I warn you, if you say something nice I'm going to cry all over you.'

'Your mother warned me. I came prepared,' he said, taking a mini pack of tissues from his pocket.

She laughed. 'They've got hearts on them.'

'Immi ordered a box of them for her own wedding.' He took her hands. 'You look beautiful, my dear. Cleve's a lucky man.'

'We're both lucky,' she said.

'Yes. I'm afraid I badly misjudged him.'

'Misjudged him?' She frowned. 'When?'

'Oh, years ago. He had a bit of a reputation back then.'

'A girl at every airfield?'

'You knew?'

'I was eighteen, Dad. Old enough to know that any man who looked like him would be beating girls off with a stick.'

'There was that,' he admitted, 'but when he came to buy his first aircraft I was sure he'd be broke within a year.'

'Cleve?' She frowned. 'No one works harder, is more respected in the business.'

'Not then.' He shrugged. 'He was young and it was all a game.'

'Not like you and Mum giving up all your dreams to save Marlowe Aviation.'

'Maybe that influenced me. Envy… But I could see how taken you were with him and I knew he'd break your heart.'

'Dad?' She tightened her grip on his hands. 'What are you saying?'

'I did what I thought was right for you, Andie. What I still think was right.'

'You warned him off?' For a moment she couldn't be sure which would be worse. Her father's interference or Cleve's capitulation. She let go of her father's hands, took a step back. 'What did you do?'

'It's not important. I just wanted you to know that I'm glad you finally found one another.'

'I'm about to marry him, Dad. I've a right to know what it took to make him walk away the first time.'

'He wouldn't…' He lifted a hand in a gesture of surrender. 'Very well. Cleve had signed a contract to courier goods for a big electronics company, the bank had agreed to loan him the money for a Hornet.'

She knew all that. She'd been at uni then, but he'd always texted her to let her know when he'd be there so that they could snatch a few minutes. The last time they'd met he'd promised to let her know when he was going to pick up the Hornet and they would go out and celebrate the new contract that established Goldfinch as a serious contender in the business, and his new aircraft. A proper date with all that promised.

In the event there had been no text, no date and no more kisses.

She'd assumed that he'd met someone closer to hand. She'd wept on Immi's shoulder, soaked her pillow for a week and then she'd got on with her life because what else was there to do?

Her mouth was dry but she had to know. 'What happened, Dad?'

'Two weeks before the delivery date the banks went into meltdown and they pulled the plug on hundreds of small companies.'

'But...'

'Without the Hornet Cleve wouldn't be able to fulfil the contract. Staring ruin in the face, he came to see me. His parents were prepared to lend him some money to cover his working overdraft but he needed me to accept staged payments for the aircraft.'

'What did you do?'

'I offered him a deal on the understanding that he would stay away from you.'

'Me or the Hornet?'

'You were at university, Andie, doing well. I wanted you in the company, designing for me. I didn't want him tempting you away, not just to his bed, but giving you a chance to fly.'

'He took the deal.'

Of course he did. He might have had a *tendresse* for her but Goldfinch was his life.

'I gave him an hour to decide and to give him his due he took every second of that hour but we both knew that he had no choice. He'd signed the contract on the bank's word. If he was unable to deliver he would have gone under.'

'Did you make him sign an agreement?' she asked. 'Or did you shake hands like gentlemen?'

'Andie…'

'Didn't you call him on it when he broke his word and gave me a job?'

'He was married by then. Settled.' Her father walked to the open French doors and looked out over the bay. 'I watched you sending off application after application, Andie. I saw a light go out of you when no one would even give you an interview.'

It took a moment for what he was saying to sink in.

'Are you saying that you asked Cleve to give me a job?' No, it was worse than that. There hadn't been a job. There had been precious little for her to do for the first couple of months… 'You didn't just ask him to take me on, you paid him…'

She didn't wait for his answer. She tore the circlet of daisies from her head and walked out through the open French doors.

She needed to be alone to process what she'd just heard but the garden was full of people who all turned to look at her and, kicking off the ridiculously high heels, she picked up her skirt and ran for the beach.

Out of the corner of her eye she saw Immi make a move to follow her, saw Portia catch her arm and hold her back.

Andie didn't stop until she was at the edge of the water and it was only Sofia's precious dress that stopped her from wading in so that the sea could wash her clean.

It felt as if her entire life had been a lie. The one thing that she'd clung to, that was hers alone, had been a conspiracy between the two men she loved.

CHAPTER TWELVE

ANDIE HEARD THE SQUEAK of the sand against his shoes as Cleve crossed the beach but didn't turn around, not because she couldn't bear to look at him, but because she was afraid that if she did she would cry.

He'd said there would be tears after bedtime but she wasn't the girl who'd had her heart broken and cried enough tears to flood China. There would be tears but not here, not in front of the man who'd lied to her.

She was a grown woman and she would handle this with dignity. She would send away all the people who loved her, who'd come to see them married. She would forget about the fantasy happy ever after. Because it was a fantasy. Even when she was telling herself that she was marrying to give her baby a father, a proper home, that it was for Cleve, she'd been fooling herself. This wedding was for that eighteen-year-old girl who'd fallen hopelessly in love with a bad-boy flyer...

She'd just needed a few minutes to gather herself, to come to terms with that, but it wasn't going to happen.

'I'm guessing this is more than last-minute cold feet,' he said, making no move to touch her as he reached her side.

'Give the man a coconut.'

'Can we talk about it?'

'Talk?' She heard the sarcasm coming out of her mouth but this wasn't her hormones reacting. This was visceral, gut deep... 'Now you want to talk?'

He sighed. 'I'm guessing your father has said something.'

She turned on him. 'Don't you dare blame him!'

It was a mistake. He'd relaxed in the days they'd spent together, lost the grey, gaunt look as he'd worked in the sun and his eyes were no longer the colour of wet slate but had taken on a little of the blue in the sky, the sea. While, in her head, she wanted to scream at him, her body responded to the memory of his touch, the closeness they'd built between them, sharing not just their bodies but their innermost thoughts.

At least that was what she'd been doing. He'd been selective with what he'd revealed.

'We were just having one of those father and daughter chats,' she said, when she could force down the lump in her throat. 'The kind you see in old movies when he's about to give his daughter away to a man he thought wasn't good enough for her but who, when the chips are down, turned out to be a hero.' She sniffed, blinked. She would not cry. 'Except you're no hero.'

'Miranda—'

'Why do you call me Miranda?' she demanded. 'No one else does that.'

'The first time I saw you, you offered me your hand and said, "I'm Miranda Marlowe, it's my eighteenth birthday and I'm a pilot."'

She swallowed, turned away to hide the sting of tears that would not be denied. The moment was imprinted on her memory.

'You took my hand, kissed my cheek and said, "Happy birthday, Miranda. Great landing. Come and see me when you've got your CPL and I'll give you a job."'

And then she'd been looking into his eyes and the only flying either of them had been thinking about hadn't involved an aircraft.

Cleve turned to look at her. 'If anyone had told me that I'd fall in love at first sight I would have told them they were off their head, but everything changed for me that day.'

'And then Dad made you an offer you couldn't refuse. Me or the Hornet.'

He didn't deny it.

'He was looking out for you, Miranda. I hope to be as good a father to our little girl—'

'And if it's a boy? What will you do then?' she snapped. 'Make sure he knows which side his bread is buttered?'

'If it's a boy we'll call him George and keep Daisy in the bank for next time.'

'Next time? You lied to me, Cleve!'

'Lied?'

'I came to you for a job and you acted as if you remembered your promise which, to be honest, I was sure you'd forgotten ten minutes after you had your hand up my skirt,' she said. 'Or was it ten minutes after you forgot about our first proper date?' She didn't give him time to reply. 'That's the one when you were going to take me out to celebrate buying the Hornet.'

'I didn't forget,' he said. 'I had it all planned. I'd booked the restaurant. I was going to pick you up at your home, bring flowers for your mother, be glowered at by your father, giggled at by your sisters.'

'I didn't want…' She stopped. 'I didn't need any of that.' She shook her head. 'Why didn't you tell me, Cleve? I would have understood. I would have waited.'

There was a moment of silence while they both absorbed that betraying 'waited'. A moment in which his hand reached for hers and, without thinking, she took it.

'I couldn't tell you. That was the deal I made with your father. He knew that if I'd told you why I'd walked away you wouldn't have accepted it.'

'No.'

'Do you want to take a step back? Your dress is about to…'

She used her free hand to lift her hem clear as the sea swirled around her feet.

'What happened to the green and yellow dress?'

'Immi vetoed it. Apparently, I'm not tall enough or skinny enough to carry it off. When my grandmother brought me her pearls she told me that this was the dress Sofia was wearing when King Ludano fell in love with her.'

'I'm not surprised. If I hadn't fallen in love with you six years, eight months and fifteen days ago, I would certainly fall in love with you now.'

'Don't…' She shook her head, pulled away. 'Don't say something you don't mean. We both know you only took me on because Dad offered to pay you.'

'He offered but I didn't take his money.'

She met his gaze head-on.

'Ask him if you don't believe me. Ask Lucy. She'll show you the books.'

'But…' She shook her head. 'There wasn't a job for me, Cleve. It was weeks before I was flying more than a couple of times a week. At the time I was too thrilled to give it any thought but you couldn't possibly have afforded to employ me under those conditions.'

'I hadn't forgotten my promise and I would have kept it even if I'd had to pay you out of my own pocket.'

'That's crazy. If you'd said come back in three months I would have been over the moon…' She moved back a step as the sea began to creep up her ankles. 'How did you explain it to Rachel?'

'I told her the truth. That your father had bailed me out when I was in trouble and I owed him.'

'And she accepted that?'

'Probably not, but she was clever enough not to make a fuss.'

'That's why you bought the new Mayfly, isn't it? Because Dad bailed you out.'

'He was in trouble, but it was more than that. Not only had he given me his trust but despite what he wanted, all the plans he had for you, he had shown how much he loved you by giving you what you wanted most in the world. Your wings.'

Now there were tears…

'Oh, damn!' She sniffed. 'Immi bought a load of special tissues but I left mine behind.'

He produced a freshly ironed linen handkerchief from his pocket and, cradling her face in his hand, wiped away a tear that had spilled onto her cheek, giving her no choice but to look at him.

'I'm going to tell you something now and it's the truth, the whole truth, nothing but the truth. You asked me why I married Rachel.'

'No…' She pulled away from the drugging touch of his hand and began to walk away. She didn't want to hear any of this but he was beside her, blocking her escape, and there was nowhere to go but the sea.

'Your father was right about me, Miranda. I was about as solid as a marshmallow. It wasn't just the girls. I was literally winging it. I still don't know why the bank loaned me the money for that first Mayfly except, as it turns out, they were winging it too. Then I met you.'

She stopped. 'And what? Are you saying that you changed overnight?'

'Pretty much.' He was the one walking now and she was the one keeping up. 'Once I'd got over the frustration, I was glad that Posy had blundered into us that night.' They were running out of beach and he stopped, turned to her. 'You were different, Miranda. The kind of girl a man would take home to meet his mother and hope to hell that she would love you too, because it was that important. I knew how hard your father had worked to save Marlowe Aviation and I wanted to be the kind of man someone like him would accept. Respect.'

He took the hand that wasn't holding her dress out of the wet sand and this time she didn't pull away.

'I took a long hard look at what I was doing and buckled down. No more parties, no more girls; there was only one girl I was interested in.'

'And then there was the bank crash.'

'Without Goldfinch I had nothing to offer you, Miranda. Forget offering you a job, I wouldn't have had one myself.'

'I saw how you stuck with it, Cleve. Grew when other air couriers were going under.'

'And I was ready to ask your father to give me another chance with you.' He was looking at her hand now, the ring he placed on her finger sparkling gold in the lowering sun. 'It was a few days before Christmas. I'd flown the Mayfly back to the factory to have some new electronics fitted and I went up to his office. He knew why I was there, but then, through his office window, I saw you fly in like an angel. An angel with a passenger. Your father was standing next to me and he said, "She's brought the Honourable Freddy home for the holidays."'

'Freddy?'

'The Honourable Frederick Cornwell-Jones. The implication was that you had moved on, found someone worthy of you. That I was history.'

'Wishful thinking,' she said. 'Freddy is a lovely guy and it should have worked. We shared digs at uni, had a lot in common, but he knew all about you and said he'd rather be my best friend than my second-best lover. His parents were going through a very nasty divorce and so, as his best friend, I took him home for Christmas.'

'So while I thought I was doing the right thing, the honourable thing in retiring from the lists, I should have been battering your door down?'

'Instead you went to a New Year's party…' And they'd missed one another by days. 'You said it, Cleve. It wasn't our time.'

'No, but this is. Whether we get married today or not, I'm not going to walk away again. You're named for one Shakespearian heroine but I'm thinking of another one right now. Are you familiar with *Twelfth Night*?'

She nodded. 'We did it at school. Immi and I played the twins.'

'Were you Viola or Sebastian?'

'Viola.'

'Then you'll have learned the speech where she told Olivia what she'd do if she was in love with someone?'

'The willow cabin speech?' She knew it by heart. 'How do you know it?'

'English Lit GCSE,' he said. 'Will you say it for me?'

Pointless to say that she didn't remember it. She had read it over and over in the days, weeks, months she had waited for Cleve to come to her and after a moment to catch her breath she began, softly at first and then, as the words took hold, lifting her voice...

'"*Make me a willow cabin at your gate and call upon my soul within the house. Write loyal cantons of contemned love and sing them loud even in the dead of night. Halloo your name to the reverberate hills and make the babbling gossip of the air cry out 'Olivia!' Oh, you should not rest between the elements of air and earth, but you should pity me.*"'

'I flew to L'Isola dei Fiori with the express intent of telling you that I love you, Miranda, that I'd always loved you. I was going to ask you if we could start again. Spend time together, go on old-fashioned dates, build a relationship that had a future.'

'Then I tossed in the baby bombshell.'

'The baby complicated things because I knew you'd think I was just responding to that, but it meant that we had a shared future and I thought, hoped, that given time I could convince you that that future would be about more than the baby we made.'

Before she could reply, he had gone down on one knee. 'I'm asking you now, Miranda… Will you take pity on me? Be my one true love, my life, the mother of my children, my wife, my mistress, my lover for as long as we both shall live?'

Her heart melting and uncaring about the dress, she knelt in front of him and took his hands in hers.

'You said that Dad had given me what I wanted most in the world but there was something I wanted more. Will you take pity on me, Cleve? Will you be my one true love, my life, the father of my children, my husband, my lover for as long as we both shall live?'

The kiss they shared, sweet, tender, was all the answer they needed. A promise shared.

Neither of them wanted to move but there were anxious people waiting. 'Before we go and put everyone out of their misery,' Cleve said, as he helped her to her feet, 'I have something for you.'

'I have everything I've ever wanted right now.'

'This is something blue.'

'But the flowers…'

He looked confused. 'Flowers? But I asked Immi to get daisies.'

'She did. You can get blue daisies. I thought, when you said you'd got it sorted…'

'Blue daisies?' He shook his head, clearly unconvinced. 'I would have given it to you last night but it needed a fastening. The jeweller delivered it to the hotel this morning.'

He took a small jeweller's box out of his pocket and

opened it. Inside, mounted on a silver fastening, was a pair of old RAF wings.

'These belonged to George Finch, my great-grandfather,' he said, as he took them from the box. 'He was one of The Few and his wings are my most cherished possession.' Fastening them to her dress, he said, 'I cannot think of anything more fitting to show how much I love and honour you.'

Andie, the tears flowing down her cheeks, her hand over her mouth, just shook her head, totally unable to speak.

Cleve did some more mopping with the handkerchief, tucked his arm under hers and then, as they walked back up the path to the garden, he said, 'I'm glad that turned out so well. I was afraid I'd have to go on honeymoon by myself.'

'Honeymoon?'

'We leave at dawn for Capri.'

Fifteen minutes later, all traces of tears removed by clever Posy, the sand washed from her feet by Portia, her father peered nervously around the door.

'Your mother is furious with me. She says I'm not to say another word.'

She took his hand. 'Tell Mum that I'm glad you told me. Everything you did was because you loved me, wanted the best for me. And because you told me, because Cleve and I had a chance to talk about what happened in the past, we are stronger, happier than you can ever imagine.' She slipped her hand beneath his arm. 'And I've a proposition for you.'

'Oh?'

'If we hadn't got married, I'd have come home and asked if I could have a job in the design office. Obviously I can't do that now, but I won't be flying for a while so I thought, maybe, I could set up a drawing board in the Goldfinch office. If you'll have me?'

'I'm giving you away and getting you back all in one day.' He hugged her. 'I couldn't be more happy.'

'Then let's go and grab the future.'

There were so many people waiting on the terrace, her sisters looking gorgeous in their vintage dresses. Her mother, Cleve's parents, Matt. But the only person Andie had eyes for was Cleve, all doubts assuaged as he took a step towards her, taking her hand as her father surrendered her to him, this time for ever.

The mayor said something, they made their responses, exchanged rings, but as Cleve paused in the moment before he kissed her and they both, as one, said, 'I love you,' it was as if they were the only two people in the world.

Each of her sisters gave a reading.

Portia had chosen Sir Philip Sidney's poem 'My True-Love Hath My Heart, and I Have His'. Immi read Shakespeare's 'Shall I Compare Thee to a Summer's Day?' and then Posy read Christina Rossetti's 'A Birthday', by which time even the mayor was wiping his eyes.

As the sun sank below the horizon and the solar lights flickered on around the garden, toasts were drunk, a lavish buffet was enjoyed and the cake, topped with a spray of handmade fondant daisies that matched her bouquet, was cut.

Her father's speech was emotional, Matt's was funny and then, as the strains of 'Fly Me to the Moon' whispered across the terrace, Cleve took Miranda in his arms and they danced as if no one was watching.

EPILOGUE

CLEVE HAD KEPT his promise. He'd been with her and the baby every step of the way. He'd been there for the scans, grinning like a loon when the midwife told them they were going to have a little girl.

He'd shared the antenatal classes, becoming a master at the back rub. He'd sacrificed his running routine to go swimming with her so that she had plenty of exercise. He'd hunted down little treats for her when she was craving her favourite—forbidden—soft cheese.

Together they'd planned and created a nursery in the house they'd bought just off the village green.

'What on earth are you doing?' he asked, when he arrived back from the airfield and found her in the nursery, up a stepladder, fixing something to the ceiling.

'You painted Daisy a bicycle built for two. This is my contribution.'

He looked up at the sleek little aeroplane that looked as if it were swooping across the room.

'You've built her a model aircraft?'

'It's a prototype I'm working on…' she said, wincing a little as he helped her down, kissed her. 'An aero-

plane built for two because for our little girl the sky
is the limit.'

'That stepladder is the limit. You should have waited
until I got home.'

'I just wanted…' She stopped as the pain at the base
of her spine intensified.

He leaned back to take a closer look at her.

'Are you okay?'

'Backache,' she muttered, clinging to him a little
more tightly.

'Come and sit down. I'll get supper.'

She gasped as another pain hit her. 'Actually, when
I said backache…'

He was way ahead of her and two minutes later he
was driving her to the birthing centre as if she were a
piece of the finest Venetian crystal.

Labour was not pretty but he was there with her in
the birthing pool, taking everything she threw at him,
supporting her with a seemingly endless supply of cold
cloths and ice to suck like the hero he was.

Finally, when he'd cut the cord and she was a red-
faced, sweaty mess he kissed her, kissed their baby
and, looking at her as if she was the most beautiful
woman in the world, said, 'I didn't know there was this
much love in the world, Andie. Thank you…'

She laid her hand against his cheek and, half asleep,
said, '"How do I love thee? Let me count the ways…"'

The midwife took away the baby to be weighed,
measured and for all the little tests they did to make
sure she was perfect—as if she could be anything else.

A nurse cleaned Andie up, tucked her up in bed and
brought her a cup of tea. Cleve caught it as she drifted

off and when she woke he was still there, singing softly
to the baby lying in the cradle next to her.

'"*Daisy, Daisy, give me your answer do. I'm half
crazy, all for the love of you...*"'

'She's definitely a Daisy, then?'

'Daisy Marlowe Finch. As sunny and beautiful as
her mother,' he said. 'I've sent a photograph to everyone. They all send their love and can't wait to see you
both.'

She took his hand.

'We're not a *both*,' she said. 'We are a three, a family. Let's go home.'

* * * * *

ONE NIGHT, ONE UNEXPECTED MIRACLE

CAROLINE ANDERSON

For Alison Roberts, Annie O'Neil and
Tina Beckett, three fabulous ladies it was a
privilege to work with.

Love you all! xxx

PROLOGUE

HE COULDN'T TAKE his eyes off her.

He'd had to for a moment while he was tied up with Ryan Walker, the new neonatal cardiac surgeon who'd arrived in the UK just in time for the gala opening of Hope Children's Hospital. Theo Hawkwood, the CEO, had asked him to introduce Ryan to people at the party, but he'd skilfully palmed him off on the head of ICU so now he was free to indulge himself again and, man, was it worth it.

She looked stunning.

What a contrast from her usual scrubs, which hung on her petite body and did a great job of hiding what he now realised was an amazing figure.

From all the time she spent in the gym when she was off duty? It wasn't his thing, he liked the great outdoors, but he'd heard she was constantly either in the gym or in the pool, swimming for an hour at a time, and occasionally when he'd been out running in the early morning he'd seen her leave her house in tracksuit and trainers. Going to the gym, probably, and whatever she did there obviously worked.

Not for him. He hated being trapped in a room filled with pumping music and sweaty bodies. He'd grown up amongst the slopes of the family vineyards in Tuscany, and although the city of Cambridge was set in a flat landscape with barely a wrinkle, it made for good running, so he ran every morning, rain or shine, pushing himself to the limit, and sometimes his route took him past her house as he pounded the footpaths by the river and the bridleways out into the countryside.

Now, though, the only thing pounding was his heart, the heavy thud as he studied her beating in his ears. Her dress was blue, the same astonishingly brilliant blue as her eyes, and it clung to her slender frame like a second skin. It shimmered in the lights, showing every curve and hollow, so that even though the neck was high and the sleeves elbow length—typical Alice, all demure and buttoned up like a Victorian schoolmarm—it left little to the imagination.

She glanced across at him, her eyes locking briefly with his through the crowd, and he lifted his glass to her, feeling the tension that was always between them tighten like an invisible thread that ran across the room and connected them together.

It had been like that since the first day, this *thing* that hovered in the background so that even if he couldn't see her, he knew when she was near him. Was it the same for her? He thought so. He'd caught the odd glimpse, a little flash of something quickly hidden, an inner battle with herself which she always seemed to win.

Like now.

She'd held his eyes for a fraction, then coolly turned away, winning the battle of wills with herself again, but the tension stayed with him like a knot in his chest.

Was she still angry with him? Maybe. She had reason to be, because he'd really pushed it this morning and the tension was tighter now than ever, the verbal sparring that had been business as usual for them since day one for some reason escalating today without warning.

They'd taken it to a whole new level, and he didn't really understand why. When they were operating, they moved like clockwork, reading each other's minds, two halves of a whole, and neither of them ever criticised the other's clinical ability or judgement. But Alice Baxter was his boss, and outside the operating theatre she did things a certain way and expected him to do the same.

Which he didn't. Not always, at least, and sometimes he deliberately didn't just to get a rise out of her. Like today. And he teased her and flirted with her for the same reason. Was that why she'd lost it with him? That he'd gone too far just to ramp up the tension and push her to the limit?

He'd been going to apologise, but then she'd been so cutting, so short with him that he'd gone all macho Italian male on her and then stalked off because it was either that or kiss her, which was so massively unprofessional and out of line that even he, with his cheerful disregard for convention, had backed away.

Yes, he really needed to apologise.

Then someone in the crowd moved, giving him a perfect view of her, and he nearly choked on his prosecco.

The dress was backless.

Well, not entirely, of course, but backless enough to take his breath away and send his heart into overdrive. A fine strand of fabric was held together by a sparkling clasp at the nape of her slender neck, and below it the pale, smooth skin of her back was bracketed by shimmering blue, plunging all the way down to her hips, reuniting to caress the subtle curve of her bottom.

He swallowed. His hands ached to cup that sweet curve, to pull her up against his body, to feel those surprisingly generous breasts against his chest...

Time to put things back on an even keel. He'd flirted outrageously with her this morning, but he didn't want to flirt with her now. Not any more. He wanted more than that, something else entirely, something much, much more serious.

A relationship?

Never going to happen. She was his boss, and his feelings were totally inappropriate.

But not unreciprocated, unless he'd read her wrong? Yes, they wrangled constantly, but under it all was this quiet simmer of emotion, attraction, sensuality—call it what you will, it was there in every moment of every day, unless they were operating. Well, they weren't operating now, and maybe it was time to confront this, to apologise and get things back to normal.

He put his empty glass down on a passing tray and headed across the room.

He was watching her. She could feel it, feel the stroke of his eyes over the bare skin of her back like a caress, and the conversation around her was dead to her ears. All she could think about, all she could feel, was Marco watching her across the room.

She always knew when he was there, could always feel his presence, knew he was coming even before she heard his voice. It was like some sort of sixth sense—a sense she could gladly have done without because it was playing hell with her work life and even creeping into her dreams.

And last night the dreams had been definitely X-rated...

She laughed when the others did, took another gulp of prosecco and nearly choked on the bubbles. What was *wrong* with her tonight? It was all just because of that stupid dream, and she could still feel the touch of his hands on her body—

Ridiculous. Sheer fantasy. There was no way anything

was going to happen between them, even if he did flirt constantly with her.

That was just Marco, and it didn't mean anything. He flirted with every female with a pulse, from the babies up to the great-grandmothers visiting their tiny relatives, and he had them all eating out of the palm of his hand.

He probably didn't even realise he was doing it, it was as natural as breathing—and to be fair it wasn't so much flirting as just breaking the ice and gentle teasing. Unless it was her.

Then there was an undercurrent of sensuality that, try as she might, she couldn't ignore.

Because she didn't *want* to ignore it? Wanted to call him out on it, see if he really meant what he said? But she wouldn't, of course, for all sorts of reasons, not least cowardice. What if she was reading much more into it than was actually there? Although it had certainly been there in her dream.

She sighed crossly, stopped pretending to listen to the conversation she should have been part of and excused herself.

She needed some air. Preferably cold and bracing and strong enough to blow some common sense into her before she did something stupid.

She was his *boss*, for goodness' sake! She couldn't let herself give in to it—which was why she'd ripped his head off earlier when he'd been pushing her buttons, and he'd drawn himself up and gone all Italian male on her and made it even worse, but it had been her fault. She'd started it by overreacting and she ought to apologise—

'Alice.'

Even her name was a caress on his lips. She closed her eyes briefly, annoyed that her radar had failed to warn her that he was coming. Marco Ricci, her unbelievably sexy, unbelievably annoying and insubordinate subordinate. Except that had sexual connotations, and there was no room for any of that in their relationship and she was keeping it that way if it killed her.

Which it might.

She sucked in a breath, plastered a noncommittal smile on her lips and turned to face him.

'Marco. Did you want me?'

Stupid! Stupid, stupid, stupid!

Something flitted through his eyes and was gone, but his lips had twitched and she braced herself for the smart retort.

'Nothing that won't keep. You look beautiful tonight, Alice,' he murmured, his voice like rough silk teasing her nerve endings.

She felt a wash of colour sweep up her throat and she looked away, shocked by the hitch in her heart rate and her body's reaction to that deep, rich, slightly accented voice and the slow caress of his eyes that had left fire in its wake.

She was used to him flirting with her, but he wasn't flirting now. The look in his eyes and the tone of his voice went far beyond that and called to something deep inside her, long repressed, cold and lonely and desperate for attention.

'Thank you,' she muttered, and swallowed hard. 'You don't look so bad yourself.'

Understatement of the century. He was sexy enough in scrubs. In a beautifully cut tux that showed off broad, solid shoulders to perfection, with the sharp contrast of the blinding white dress shirt against olive skin darkened by the shadow of stubble, those dark-lashed eyes simmering with latent heat, he was jaw-droppingly, unsettlingly gorgeous and she felt the impact of it in every yearning cell of her body.

'So—Evie's done a brilliant job organising this,' she added hurriedly, hauling her eyes off him and groping for something uncontroversial. 'I wouldn't have believed the conference hall could be turned into such an amazing ballroom.'

'No,' he said, not taking his eyes from her face. Not that she was looking at him, but she could still feel the steady, searching gaze of those magnetic eyes and her pulse was rocketing.

She was trying to find something to say to fill the yawning void when the music started, and to her surprise he held out his hand to her.

'Come. Dance with me. We've been fighting all day about nothing and it's time to stop.'

'Is that an apology?'

She made herself meet his eyes again, and for a fleeting instant she thought she saw regret. No. Marco never regretted anything, he wasn't made like that. She'd imagined it. Of course it wasn't an apology.

'Yes, it's an apology,' he said softly, his Italian accent suddenly stronger. 'Dance with me, Alice. Life's serious enough. It's time to have some fun.'

Fun? She hadn't let herself have *fun* in years. At least, not the sort of fun she thought he was talking about.

Eyes steady, he took the glass out of her hand, handed it to one of the circulating bar staff and led her to the dance floor, turning her into his arms. She felt the heat of his hand on her bare back, the other still holding hers, curled loosely between them by her shoulder. Normally her head was level with his chest, but she was wearing heels tonight and her eyes were right by his immaculately knotted bow tie. Above it she could see the throb of a pulse beating in his throat, and he tilted his head so his cheek was against her forehead as he drew her closer.

She could smell cologne, just a faint touch of something exotic, something dangerously enticing that seemed to enter her bloodstream and invade every part of her as she swayed to the music. The hand on her back slid down, down to the base of her spine, his fingers splayed against her skin as he eased her closer still.

Too close for her sanity. Close enough to bring back the dream—

She took a step back out of his arms.

'I need some air,' she said breathlessly, and, turning, she made her way quickly off the crowded dance floor and out of the conference hall, her body on fire with a need she'd never felt before, hadn't even known existed.

The lift? She couldn't run downstairs in her heels, so there was no choice, and the lift was standing there waiting...

He watched her retreat for a nanosecond, then followed her, carving his way through the crowd, the white-blonde of her hair easy to pick out when he could find it, but even in those heels she wasn't tall and the room was full and he kept losing her.

The doors. She was heading for the doors, and then the lift. He cut off the corner, went through another set of doors and reached the hallway just as the lift doors started to close.

Good job he was fit. He sprinted across the landing from a standing start, slammed his hand into the gap and pushed the doors open again.

She turned and met his eyes furiously—or desperately?

'What are you doing?' she demanded, but her voice sounded odd, a little frantic.

He hit the button to close the doors. 'What does it look like? I'm following you.'

'Why?'

Her voice was breathless, a slight catch in it, and he smiled a little grimly. 'Because I need to apologise properly. Not just about the fighting, but about this, too.'

He stabbed the button for the ground floor and folded his arms just to stop himself reaching out to her.

'What *this*? I don't understand.'

He sighed again. 'Yes, you do, Alice, because it's just here, between us, all the time,' he told her, waving his hand back and forth between them, 'and it's getting in the way of our work. We need to talk about it.'

'You're imagining it,' she said, but she couldn't hold his eyes, and he unfolded his arms and reached out and turned her head gently to face him.

'Am I?' he murmured. 'Am I really? I don't think so, Alice. I think you want me as much as I want you, and what we have to do is work out how we're going to deal with it, because we have to, one way or the other, because it's getting in the way all the time and it can't go on like this.'

It was there again in his eyes, that flash of something she'd seen just before he'd asked her to dance, briefly pushed aside by regret but back again now, with bells on.

Heat. Smouldering heat in the black depths of his eyes, his pupils flared, his chest rising and falling as he studied her silently, those eyes reeling her in.

'Why would you want me?' she asked, her voice annoyingly breathless again. 'Of all the women in this hospital, why me, Marco?'

His eyebrows shot up. '*Why?* Because you're beautiful and sexy and funny and sharp and clever and— because you keep your distance, button yourself up, bottle up everything that I can see raging inside you, and all I can think about is unbuttoning all those tiny little buttons holding you together and seeing what would happen if I set those feelings free.'

Set them free? The thought terrified her, because he was right, they *were* there, raging inside her, and every day, every minute, every time she saw him, this beautiful, magnificent, tempestuous, arrogant man, she wanted him.

And it was *never* going to happen—

'You're wrong. You don't really want me,' she whispered, but he just laughed and took her hand and pressed it firmly against his chest so she could feel the pounding of his heart.

'Can you feel that, *cara*? Can you feel how I want you? Always,' he murmured, his eyes softening, 'every minute of every day,' and then he lowered his head, his hands cradling her face, just as the lift pinged a warning.

He wrenched his head up and moved away, slid his hand down her arm and threaded his fingers through hers, nodded to the people waiting to go up and walked with her briskly out of the lift, across the central foyer and into the consulting room area.

He pulled his lanyard out of his pocket, swiped the security lock with the magnetic card and opened the doors, then pushed the nearest consulting room door open and ushered her through it.

She heard it click shut, then nothing, just the suspense that swirled around them in the air and robbed her brain of oxygen.

What did he want from her?

A deep, slow sigh cut through the silence and she heard the examination couch creak behind her as he sat on it.

'What do we do, Alice?' he asked, his voice low and, oh, so sexy, unravelling her rigid self-control and leaving her open and vulnerable.

'I don't know. What do you want from me, Marco?'

He laughed softly, and the sound teased her nerve endings and sent shivers of need through her body. 'I have no idea. Well, I have, but that's not going to happen, we both know that.'

Was that regret in his voice? She couldn't tell without looking into his eyes, so she turned and searched them, and then wished she hadn't because the humour, the teasing that seemed to dance almost permanently in them was gone, leaving something far more dangerous to her self-control and peace of mind.

Desire, white-hot and irresistible. She swallowed and took a step back, bumping into the desk and sitting down abruptly on the edge of it before her legs gave out.

'So what do we do?'

He laughed again, a wry huff of sound that unravelled her a little further, then met her eyes again.

'I don't know, but I know we can't go on like this, fighting all the time about nothing and dancing round the elephant in the room. I want you, Alice, and I don't seem to be able to put that on one side, and I don't think you can, either.'

His eyes held her, the need in them so openly expressed she was in no doubt about it. He wasn't toying with her. He really meant it, and his words had so accurately expressed her own feelings that she felt as if he could see into her soul.

He was right. She couldn't put it on one side, couldn't ignore it any longer. Didn't *want* to ignore it any longer.

As if he saw the moment she crumbled, he held out his hand silently, and she stood up, her legs shaking, and walked over to him, taking his hand and letting him draw her up against him, standing between his legs as he was propped on the edge of the couch, his warmth enclosing her.

He raised a hand and traced the line of her jaw, lifting a stray lock of hair away and tucking it back behind her ear. The caress was so tender, so gentle that it made her want to cry. It had been so long since anyone had touched her like that, as if she was something precious and fragile. If ever...

She met his eyes again, and he stared into hers for an age, then drew her nearer, lowered his head and touched his lips to hers.

She moaned softly against his mouth, parting her lips to him, and she felt his hands cradle her cheeks as he deepened the kiss. She met him touch for touch, stroke for stroke, their tongues searching, duelling.

They always duelled, but not like this, not—

'Marco...'

'I want you, Alice,' he groaned softly. 'Tell me you want me, too.'

'No—yes— Marco, I—'

'Alice, you're killing me...'

He kissed her again, his lips coaxing, trailing fire down her throat, over her shoulders, in that delicate, sensitive place behind her ear. She arched her neck to give him better access, his name a sob in her throat. 'Marco...'

'Tell me, Alice,' he said, his voice low, scraping over her senses like gravel and bringing everything to life. 'Tell me you want me. Tell me you want this, too, before I go crazy—'

'Yes.'

'Yes, what?'

'Yes, I want you. *I want you...*'

He muttered something in Italian and his hands reached down, bunching up her dress as his mouth plundered hers and his body rocked against her, pressing her up against him. She could feel his hands on her skin, cradling her bottom, sliding up around her waist as he lifted her easily and turned, settling her on the edge of the examination couch where he had been.

Her legs wrapped around his waist, holding him tightly against her, the pressure building as her fingers found the ends of his bow tie and tugged it undone. She couldn't do the buttons, her fingers were shaking too much, and with a little scream of frustration she ripped his shirt open, her nails raking down his chest in the process.

'*Dio*, Alice—'

He buried his hands in her hair and rocked against her, his body tight against her most intimate places as his mouth took hers again, his tongue searching, delving, and she wanted him closer. Needed him closer. Needed him…

'I want you,' she said, her breath hissing out between her teeth. 'Marco, please, now. I want you—'

He swore softly and pulled away a fraction. 'Don't move.'

She dropped her head back and closed her eyes, the breath shuddering out of her body as he let her go and stepped away, and she clenched her legs together against the raging need and waited. She could hear him doing something, heard the snap of a wallet, the soft rasp of a zip, a slight rustle.

A condom. Of all the tragic ironies. She nearly laughed, only it wasn't funny. He didn't need it—except to protect her and himself from the other unintended consequences of random sex. Nothing else…

She opened her eyes and moaned again, her body throbbing with need as she reached for him, gripping the firm shaft of his erection and sliding her hand down it, unrolling the condom along its length. He swore softly in Italian and eased away the scrap of silk that passed for her underwear, his hips nudging her legs apart again as he slid his fingers deep inside her.

She gasped and tried to clench her legs together to quell the waves of sensation but there was no way because he was there, his body filling her at last, making her sob with need as he thrust into her, slowly at first and then faster, harder, again and again, his hands cradling her bottom and holding her tight against him, rocking as her control splintered into pieces and she convulsed around him.

He caught her cry in his mouth, his body tensing, shuddering with the force of his climax, and then as it passed he let out a long, fractured sigh, dropped his head against her shoulder and cradled her close, his mouth against her ear murmuring soft words she didn't understand.

She couldn't speak, couldn't think, couldn't move. Her body was a seething mass of sensation so intense that even now she could feel the shockwaves rippling through her, and as he finally eased away she couldn't look at him.

What had she done?

She'd *never* felt like that. Never responded like that, so wildly, so spontaneously, so freely it had felt like she was flying.

Not now, though. Not any more.

Now she'd come down to earth with a bump, crippled with self-consciousness, and she slid off the edge of the couch, rescued her underwear from the floor and pulled it on hastily. As she tugged her dress straight with shaking hands, she felt a nail catching on the delicate fabric.

'Cara?'

Gentle fingers caught her chin, lifting her face up so he could read her eyes, and he sighed and drew her back into his arms. 'You're buttoning up again,' he murmured, his voice heavy with regret, and she tried to push him away.

'I have to. I'm your *boss,* Marco! I can't just sleep with you—'

'Who said anything about sleeping? I think we were both wide awake just then. And don't even try and tell me you didn't enjoy it.'

She didn't. She wasn't a liar, and he'd only laugh at her anyway.

'It was a mistake,' she said, knowing instantly that he'd argue, but he didn't. Instead he bent his head and kissed her tenderly, nearly trashing her resolve.

'Yes. It was. You deserved better than a—' He broke off, and she could almost see him rearranging the words in his mouth. 'I should have taken you for dinner, taken you back to my house and made love to you slowly, for hours. Explored every part of you, kissed every inch of your skin, made you come for me again and again and again—'

'It would still have been a mistake,' she said, her insides weeping at the thought of him loving her so thoroughly, so tenderly, so meticulously. 'We can't do this, Marco. I agree we have to find a way to work together without fighting, but this isn't it. This isn't the way. We can't do it again.'

She stood motionless, and after a second or two his arms dropped and he stepped back, glanced down at his ripped shirt with a rueful smile, shrugged and opened the door.

'I'm sorry. Not for doing it. I can't regret that. But if that's what you want it won't happen again, I promise you. Goodnight, Alice.'

And with that he walked out, headed through the door at the end and left her standing there wondering what on earth she'd done, and why it suddenly felt as if, by letting him go, she'd thrown away a chance at happiness that she hadn't even known was there…

CHAPTER ONE

Five weeks later...

'Do you want me to close?'

'What, because you imagine you can do it better than me?'

His eyes crinkled above his mask. 'Because I *know* I can do it better than you,' he said, and she could hear the smile in his voice. It was odd, but since that night five weeks ago their sparring had changed to a mutual and much more gentle teasing, almost as if they'd called a truce and were carefully tiptoeing around each other's feelings. Even his flirting had toned down, which was a shame. She almost missed it, but she knew why he'd done it. It was too dangerous now, after what had happened. It would be fanning the flames of a fire that had to be allowed to die. A fire that hadn't, sadly, burned itself out.

'You're so arrogant,' she said mildly, stepping away and stripping off her gloves. She tried so hard not to smile, but he just chuckled as if he could see it and held out his hand to the scrub nurse.

'Three-oh Prolene, please,' he said, and the nurse placed the suture in his hand and he dropped his eyes and began meticulously drawing the wound edges together, layer by layer.

He was right, he was better than her at suturing, but only by a hair and she had a feeling it was a simple matter of Italian pride that prevented him from failing. And not to be better than her would be failure in his eyes.

She dragged her gaze away. She couldn't watch him, couldn't watch those sensitive, intelligent hands delicately repairing the boy's abdomen. So skilful. So focused. Just as they'd been on her body—

'I'll go and talk to his parents.'

'OK. Just don't take all the credit.'

'Only where it's due.'

She turned away, stripped off her mask and hat and gown and went to change. She would talk to Amil's parents, tell them how it had gone, and then she had things to do, a patient to see, letters to write to parents, some results to review. She couldn't just stand around looking at him simply because he was poetry in motion. Too dangerous. She was trying to keep her distance, and watching him wouldn't help that at all.

And besides, there was something else she had to do. Something pressing. Something she'd never thought she'd need to do, and couldn't quite believe. Couldn't *dare* to believe.

She had to do a pregnancy test, because this morning she'd made herself a coffee and she'd been unable to drink it. She'd sipped it, but it had sat in her stomach like a rock and she'd had to rinse her mouth to get rid of the taste.

Maybe she'd just had too much coffee over the years and her body had started to rebel? But she was hungry, too, and although she was used to that, almost welcomed it because it was a good sign in her case, today she felt a little light-headed and woozy. And her periods, never as regular as clockwork, were an unreliable sign, but even so it had been a while.

So while he was working miracles on the child's skin, she spoke to the boy's parents, went to her locker, got out the test kit she'd bought on the way to work and went to the ladies' loo.

It wouldn't be positive. It couldn't be. Her body didn't do ovulation—couldn't do it, because her ovaries were stupid.

PREGNANT

She stared at the wand for a good five minutes before she moved, her mind in freefall.

She was pregnant with Marco's baby.

How? It *couldn't* have happened. There was no *way* she could have conceived, and besides, he'd used a condom! But one of her nails had snagged her dress as she'd tugged it straight afterwards. Just a tiny jagged edge where she must have caught it on something. When she'd shredded his shirt and raked her nails across that strong, solid expanse of chest? Could that have been enough? And when she'd reached down and touched him right after that, helped him put the condom on, had her nail torn it maybe?

It seemed so unlikely—but what other explanation was there?

None. And, however it had happened, however unbelievable it was, it was definitely Marco's baby, so she'd have to tell him, but how?

She closed her eyes, squeezing them hard against the well of mixed emotions, and pressed her hand over her mouth. How would he react? Would he be angry? She hoped not. Delighted? Unlikely. And then a chilling thought crossed her mind. Would he want her to keep it, or—?

No. She'd seen him with children. There was no way he'd want that. He was an Italian, and children were at the front and centre of their world. They were for her, too, which was why she'd chosen paediatrics, because it was the closest she'd thought she'd ever come to having children.

Until now. And now, totally unexpectedly, right out of the blue, she was having a baby. The thing she'd dreamed of and longed for and tried to put out of her mind ever since she'd been told it might never happen for her *was* happening, but she daren't invest too much of herself in it because she knew there was a distinct possibility it might all go wrong, because it would be considered a high-risk pregnancy.

Pregnancy. A word she'd never thought she'd use in association with herself, certainly not now in her late thirties, and as she sifted through the blizzard of emotions whirling through her, she didn't know how she felt about it.

Thrilled? Shocked? Or just plain terrified?

All of them. And add sick to that.

'How's Amil?'

'Fine. He's in Recovery, looking good. They're moving him to PICU shortly and the anaesthetist is going to keep his pain relief topped up with the epidural so he should feel much better soon. I spoke to the parents again, filled them in a bit more.' He cocked his head on one side. 'How about you? Get your admin done?'

Admin? She hadn't even been in her office. 'Some of it,' she said—which, if you counted finding out if you'd need maternity leave as 'admin', wasn't a lie. 'We need to talk.'

'About a patient? I've got time now.'

'No. Not about a patient. About—us.'

His right eyebrow climbed into his hair. *'Us?'*

She held his eyes silently and with a huge effort, and he shrugged.

'Sure. How about this evening over dinner? I know a nice little Italian restaurant. They do great pasta.'

Pasta. Hunger and nausea warred, and hunger won. 'That sounds good. What time? Do we need to book?'

'No. Seven?'

She nodded. 'I'll meet you there.'

'No. I'll pick you up.'

'You don't know where I live.'

'Yes, I do. I run past your house some mornings, and I've seen you coming out in your gym kit on your way to the hospital.'

He ran past her house? Why had she never seen him? Or had she, maybe, once or twice, and not realised who he was? There were plenty of runners in the morning. She often saw them. He must be one of them.

'So—shall I come for you at ten to seven? The restaurant's not far from you, it'll only take a few minutes to get there on foot.'

'Ten to seven is fine. Now I need to go and make some calls and write a couple of letters. I'll see you later.'

He didn't see much of her for the rest of the day, which was just as well because he didn't know what to think and she'd only distract him. She always distracted him, unless he was operating. Then he was focused, but otherwise…

They should never have done what they did at the gala. Not that he regretted it, not a bit, and things between them had been easier since, in a way. She'd been less on his case about everything, but he wanted more than they'd had that night, much more, and he knew she didn't. She'd made that perfectly clear, and he had to respect that, but the memories were playing hell with his sleep and he kept imagining her with him, sharing his bed, sharing his house—sharing his life? Never going to happen, he'd told himself, and now this.

This wanting to talk to him about 'us'. What 'us'? Was there going to be an 'us'?

It drove him crazy for the rest of the day, so it was a good job he was busy checking on his post-op patients, ending with Amil Khan in PICU, and he spent a long time talking to the boy's parents about his condition going forward. One of Theo Hawkwood's pro bono cases, the boy had Crohn's disease, and so far he hadn't been in remission. Maybe they could turn it round for him at last, and this op to remove a section of badly damaged bowel had at least given him a chance of recovery. And he hadn't needed a stoma, so he wouldn't need a bag, which was good news.

It was after six before he left them, and he ran home, showered rapidly and got to her house a minute late. She opened her door and for once didn't comment on his time-keeping. And she looked—nervous? Why? If she was going to suggest they had an affair, he was more than willing. And they were working better together, so it wasn't that...

'Ready?'

She nodded, and he stepped back and held open the little gate at the end of her path, then fell into step beside her as they walked into the centre and turned down a narrow, cobbled street, and as they walked he told her a little about the restaurant.

'This place is a gem. I found it when I first moved here seventeen years ago, and it's still run by the same family, but the son's taken over and he's every bit as good as his father. I eat here often because the food's healthy and it's delicious and it reminds me of home.'

'I'm surprised we didn't have to book if it's that good.'

'They were expecting me tonight anyway. Here we are.'

He opened the door and held it for her, and as she walked in she hesitated and he nearly bumped into her.

'Are you OK?'

She nodded, her pale hair bobbing brightly in the atmospheric lighting. 'Yes, I'm fine.'

No, she wasn't, but he couldn't work out why and then he didn't have time because the old man was walking towards him with a beaming smile, addressing him by name as he always did, showing them to their table, taking her coat, telling them about the specials.

'Alice?'

'I just want something simple,' she said quickly. 'Something fairly plain and light.'

'My son cooks a wonderful fish linguine,' Renzo said. 'That's light and delicate with a touch of fresh chilli.'

'Just a touch?'

'I can ask him to put less.'

She nodded. 'Thank you. And could I have some iced water, please?'

'I'll have the same. It's a great dish. And a glass of house white, Renzo. *Grazie mille.*'

He watched Renzo walk away, then propped his elbows on the table and searched her eyes, his patience finally at an end. 'So—this "us" you wanted to talk about...'

She wasn't sure she did. Not now, not here where he had friends. And she wasn't sure the restaurant was a great idea for another reason, either. One she hadn't even thought of, stupidly.

'Alice?'

She'd looked down, knotting her hands on the edge of the table, unsure how she felt, but now she made herself look up and meet his searching brown eyes. 'It's about what—happened.'

'The gala.'

She nodded and swallowed. 'I—um—it seems it's had…'

'Had…?'

She dropped her eyes again, unable to hold that searching gaze while she groped for the word. 'Consequences,' she said at last, and held her breath.

He said nothing. Not for at least thirty seconds, maybe even a minute. Then he reached out slowly, tipped up her face with gentle fingers and gave her a slightly bemused smile.

'You're pregnant?' he mouthed.

She nodded. 'Yes. Apparently I am.'

He leant forward, his voice low. 'But—how? I was careful.'

'I know. I'm not sure. I might have broken a nail when I—when I ripped your shirt. Maybe that…'

'Your nail? But…'

She could see him scrolling through what they'd done in those few frantic minutes, and saw the moment the light dawned.

He swore softly in Italian, then took her hands in his and held them firmly. 'I am so sorry. I never meant that to happen, but of course it changes everything.'

'Everything?'

'*Sì*. Because we're definitely an "us" now. I can't walk away from this.'

'But it may not even—'

They were interrupted by the arrival of the steaming, fragrant linguine. Renzo set a plate down in front of Alice, and as he turned away she felt her colour drain.

She pushed back her chair and stumbled to her feet. 'I'm sorry. I can't—I'm really sorry—'

Then she grabbed her bag and ran, not even waiting for

her coat because if she didn't get out it was going to be hideously embarrassing.

She headed home, half running, half stumbling on the cobbles, and as she reached her house and let herself in, the nausea swamped her and she fled for the bathroom.

He knocked on the door, rang the bell, knocked again, and then finally he heard her coming down the stairs.

He'd known she was in because the lights were on up-stairs and they hadn't been before, but when she opened the door she was as white as a sheet and trembling and he was racked with guilt.

'Alice,' he said softly, and stepped inside, closing the door behind him and putting the bag and her coat down on the floor to take her into his arms. 'I'm so sorry. If I'd known I would never have suggested going there. Come on, you need to sit down.'

'Did you bring my coat?'

'Yes. And I brought our food. Renzo put it in boxes for me.'

'I can't—'

'You can. You must. You need carbs, *cara*. Trust me, I grew up surrounded by pregnant women and I know what works.'

He left her on the sofa, arms wrapped round her slen-der frame and looking miserable and strangely afraid, and he headed down the hall towards what had to be the kitchen. He'd never seen her anything but confident, so why was she afraid? Afraid of what? Of him, his reaction? Of being pregnant? Of having a child? Maybe he'd misread it. Maybe she was just unhappy about it. She didn't looked exactly thrilled. And what was it that may not even—what? It was the last thing she'd said before she'd run out, and it was playing on his mind.

May not even be his?

He found bowls, glasses, forks, and headed back, setting the food and water down on the coffee table.

'Come on. Try it, please. Just a little.'

She tasted it suspiciously, refilled the fork and took another cautious mouthful, then another, and he felt a wash of relief.

He picked up his own fork and joined her, but the unanswered question was still there and he had to force himself to eat.

'Better?'

She was, surprisingly. At least the nausea was. The humiliation was another matter. 'Yes. Thank you. And I'm so sorry about the restaurant.'

'No, I'm sorry—'

'Why? You didn't know. I should have thought about it, suggested somewhere else. Here, maybe.'

'Well, we're here now, and we have a baby to talk about. I'm still trying to get my head around that and I guess you are, too. Unless it's not mine?'

She stared at him, horrified that he could think that. 'Of course it's yours!'

'Is it? Because in the restaurant you said, "it may not even—" and then you broke off. What was it, Alice? May not even be mine? Is that what you were going to say?'

'No. Not that. It can only be yours, Marco. There hasn't been anyone else for years. Please believe me. I would never do that to you—to anyone.'

His eyes searched hers, and then he nodded slowly, just once, and she looked away, the tenderness in his eyes unnerving because whatever happened, whatever he said next, she was sure it would just be out of guilt and pity and she didn't want that, so she cut him off before he could start.

'I was going to say it may not even happen. It's very early days, I could lose it.'

A tiny frown flitted through his eyes. 'That's not likely. Many more pregnancies end in a baby than a miscarriage.'

Not necessarily in her case. But she wasn't ready to tell him anything so personal about herself. Not now. Maybe never, because she'd seen what that did to a relationship and she never wanted to see that expression on anyone's face again.

Disgust. Revulsion. And a rapid retraction of his proposal. And she hadn't dated anyone since—

'Alice?'

No. She wouldn't tell him. She sucked in a breath and met his eyes. 'Sorry. I'm just a pessimist. I can't believe it's happened. I never thought I'd ever be pregnant, especially not right after landing the job of my dreams, so I know it seems wrong but you'll have to forgive me for not being ecstatic about it. To be honest, I have no idea how I feel. I'm still getting over the shock.'

He gave a soft laugh. 'It wasn't exactly in my plans, either, but a baby's a baby, Alice. They're pretty harmless. I should know, I'm the oldest of eight, and I spent half my childhood changing nappies and pushing prams around the vineyards with a trail of small people following after me. There were times when I felt like a cross between the Pied Piper and Mary Poppins.'

That made her smile. 'I didn't realise you had such a large family. You've never talked about them before.'

'I don't. I love them, of course I do, but I don't see them very often. I disappointed them a long time ago—I was engaged to a lovely girl from a good family, and I couldn't give her what she needed, which was to stay at home near her family and have babies, rather than follow me around from one strange place to another while I did my rotations in England, so I ended it for both our sakes because I felt we were in love with the idea rather than each other. And then my family accused me of leading her on and breaking her heart because I'd been so selfish and uncaring and put myself first as usual, so I don't go back unless I have to. And I have to, in three weeks, because my little sister's getting married and I need to be there.'

'That's the long weekend you booked off?'

'Yes.' He was looking at her thoughtfully suddenly, and then he said, 'I told them I'd be bringing someone, mostly to defuse my mother's matchmaking efforts because despite the fiasco she *still* wants to see me married to someone she considers suitable, and a wedding is the perfect matchmaking opportunity, so I need a plus one or she'll be a nightmare. Why don't you come with me? It'll be fun.'

That shocked her. 'To your sister's wedding? I don't know any of them.'

'I know, but you need to, because they'll be a part of our child's life—'

'Why? And there *is* no child yet.'

He frowned. 'Why? Because they're my *family*, Alice, and they'll want to be part of their grandchild's life.'

'Marco, they haven't *got* a grandchild yet! There's nothing to tell them. They don't need to know about the baby. Not for ages, maybe never if it goes wrong—'

'No, they don't. I agree. At this stage I'd rather they didn't. But it might help you get to know more about me if you met them, and anyway it's beautiful there. It'll be cool, but it's the end of the olive harvest and it'll be a huge celebration. My parents do seriously good weddings. And it'll give us time away from work to get to know each other.

And whatever happens between us I think that's important, if we're having a child together.'

Having a child together? That sounded weird. So out of left field that she could hardly get her head round it.

'Can I think about it? This is all a bit sudden.'

'Yes, of course. If you decide not to come, I can always make an excuse. So—that's my family. What about yours?'

She relaxed a fraction. 'Oh, I have three brothers. I'm number three in the family, but we're all close together in age and we love each other to bits. One's a doctor, one's a vet, the other one a dentist. We're pretty competitive.'

'Are you winning?'

She laughed. 'Sort of. The vet and the dentist have their own practices, but the doctor's a mere specialist registrar at the moment, so, yes, I'm winning as far as the doctors go but I would say we're pretty equal. Except they're all married with children, but at least it takes the heat off me,' she said rashly without filtering her words, but he pounced on it.

'Why aren't you married?'

She blinked. 'Why aren't you?'

'Because it's not on my agenda, which I think was part of the reason it went wrong before. I'd just qualified as a registrar and I had my paeds training to complete. I needed all my focus, needed to be able to follow my career wherever it took me, and to a certain extent that's still true.'

'So you understand, then, why I'm single.'

He smiled wryly. 'Yeah, I guess I do.' He got to his feet, picked up the plates and took them through to the kitchen. She could hear him rinsing them, loading them into the dishwasher, then the tap running again, and he was back.

'I should go. You need an early night, but I'll see you in the morning. Make sure you eat before you get up. Toast, crackers, slivers of apple—'

'Marco, I'll be fine,' she said without any confidence if today was anything to go by, and got to her feet. 'Look—I don't want this all round the hospital. You know how people love a good juicy story.'

'Don't worry, I won't talk about it. I don't talk about private stuff, not at work, and especially not this.'

No, he didn't. Tonight was the first time either of them had talked about their families, and it helped to explain a little of how at ease he was with the children.

He'd be a brilliant father—

'Goodnight, Alice,' he said softly, and bending down, he touched a gentle, tender kiss to her lips and let himself out.

A brilliant father, an amazing lover and a good husband. And she was getting horribly ahead of herself, and it was so unlikely to happen. Even if she got through the pregnancy without incident, which wasn't likely, she'd still have to tell him about her condition, and then she'd see *that look* on his face and it would tear her apart.

She switched off the lights and went up to bed.

CHAPTER TWO

'MORNING.'

Alice swallowed a wave of nausea and looked up from her desk.

'Do you *ever* knock?'

He went back out of the door, knocked, walked in again and smiled mischievously. 'Good morning. There, is that better?'

She put her pen down and leant back with a sigh, stifling the urge to smile. 'You're supposed to wait for an answer. I assume you want something? And shut the door, please.'

He peered closer, and frowned. 'Are you OK?'

'Yes, I'm fine,' she lied. 'Thank you for last night—for looking after me—I appreciated it, but I'm fine now. So, what did you want?'

He shrugged as if he didn't believe her, but he let it pass. 'Just an update for you. I've checked the post-ops from yesterday, spent a few minutes with Amil and his parents in PICU—the boy with Crohn's?''

'I do know who Amil is. How is he today?'

'OK. He's had a reasonable night, apparently, which is excellent news, and we should be able to move him out of there later onto a ward. Hopefully the surgery will have done the trick for now and once he's on the mend we can hand him over to gastroenterology and see if they can get him a bit more settled on a new drug regime. So, boss lady, what's on the agenda for today?'

She swallowed another wave of nausea and looked down at the file of notes on her desk.

'Daisy Lawrence. She was diagnosed with malrotation of the gut as a toddler because she was having lots of stomach cramps without any other symptoms, but it wasn't considered severe enough for surgery at the time and they adopted a watch and wait policy, but she's flared up again, they've got private medical insurance and they wanted a second opinion so they chose us.'

He perched on the corner of her desk beside her and studied the notes. 'So what are we doing? X-rays, MRI, CT?'

'I'm not sure. I think we'll start with a follow-through contrast scan to see what's going on in there, so I've booked that with the imaging suite for this morning, and we'll review the results and see where we go from there, but I think we need to go and meet them and examine her and talk it through.'

'Are they here?'

She shook her head. 'I don't believe so. They're not due until nine. I was just going through her notes again.'

'So—have you had breakfast?' he asked, and she swallowed again and shook her head.

'I couldn't—'

'Well, isn't it a good job you have me to feed you?' he said, passing her a small packet of salty wholewheat crackers.

She eyed them with suspicion. Food? Really—?

'Eat them,' he instructed gently, and she tore the bag open reluctantly and tried one.

Surprisingly edible. She had another.

'OK?'

She nodded. 'Yes—thanks.' She took a sip of water and had another one while he flicked through the notes.

'Apparently watermelon is good if you feel sick,' he told her without looking up. 'Just a little piece. I've put some in the fridge in the staffroom where you keep your lunch. And you need carbs.'

'I don't eat carbs.'

He looked up and met her eyes. 'I noticed. That's why you're feeling sick, because your blood sugar is low because you're on one of these crazy celebrity diets where your body's in a permanently ketogenic state. It's bad for you.'

'It isn't. A ketogenic diet means I maintain a healthy weight and keep my blood sugar and cholesterol under control,' she said, feeling a little flicker of panic because he was getting too close to the truth and she didn't want to tell him, or at least not yet.

'Why on earth do you need to do that? You're not overweight, you're under if anything, and you spend your free time in the gym.'

'How do you know that? You're never in there.'

'No. I don't do gyms, but our colleagues use them, and they talk.'

She hated the idea of people talking about her. Speculating?

'So I keep fit—and I'm not underweight, my BMI is nineteen point five.'

'That's borderline underweight.' He frowned, his voice softening. 'Alice, is food a problem for you? Do you have an eating disorder?'

She stared at him, stunned. 'No! Of course I don't have an eating disorder! I've told you, I'm just keeping healthy—'

'Then why don't you eat cake if it's someone's birthday? Why do you always say no to snacks and biscuits? They won't kill you occasionally if you make an exception to avoid hurting someone's feelings.'

She sighed and gave up. 'Because I have insulin resistance,' she said flatly, giving him a symptom rather than a diagnosis just to get him off her back, but she could see it wasn't working. He frowned, looked thoughtful and tipped his head on one side.

'I just don't buy it. The only way you have insulin resistance is if you're borderline diabetic and have metabolic syndrome, which you haven't because you're much too thin for that, or you've got a hormonal imbalance or something like PCOS…'

He trailed to a halt, frowned again and searched her face, and she could hear the cogs turning as the frown softened into concern.

'Is that it? Is that why you were so surprised that you were pregnant, because you have PCOS?'

'That's a bit of a quantum leap, isn't it, from insulin resistance to polycystic ovaries?' she said, flannelling furiously because she wasn't ready to have this conversation. Wouldn't *ever* be ready to have it—

'Not for a doctor. And I know I'm a paediatric surgeon, but I'm still a doctor and I haven't forgotten everything I learned in med school. So is this why you were surprised you're pregnant, and why you're so convinced you could lose the baby, because of the risk of high blood pressure, pre-eclampsia, gestational diabetes, miscarriage—is there anything else? I'm sure there must be other things you're torturing yourself with.'

'So what if I have got it?' she asked, suddenly sick of not telling him and wanting to get the revulsion over, but there was no revulsion, to her surprise. Instead he shrugged away from the desk, put his arms round her and hugged her, tutting softly.

'Oh, Alice. Is this why you're not married? Why you're so defensive? Because some idiot didn't want a wife who couldn't be sure of giving him children?'

She eased out of his arms, her emotions all over the place, and if she stayed there with her head against him, she'd lose it and blub all over him. 'No. I'm not married because he didn't want a wife who was fat and hairy and had more testosterone than he did.'

He sat back on the edge of the desk, his eyes wide. 'But that's not you! You're not fat, and I can't believe you ever were because you're far too well controlled. Besides, most people don't have all those symptoms, if any. It's rubbish.'

'You don't have to tell me that, I know, but he didn't and once he'd researched it—which he did there and then on his phone, the minute I told him—he didn't hang around long enough for me to put him right,' she said, grabbing her pager like a lifeline as it bleeped.

'Daisy's here,' she said, sliding her chair back, and she stood up, picked up the notes and headed for the door, pausing to look over her shoulder. 'Well, are you coming, or are you going to stay here all day making annoying comments and quizzing me about my medical history?'

He rolled his eyes. 'Yes, of course I'm coming.' He straightened up, grabbed the bag of savoury crackers and followed her.

Polycystic ovary syndrome.

He never would have guessed if he hadn't pushed her, but now so much of her defensive behaviour made sense, especially in the light of some ignorant—

His thoughts lapsed into Italian, because he had a better grasp of the language he'd need to sum up someone that ignorant and cruel. No matter. He, whoever he was, was in the past, and now was for them. He'd look after her, take care of her and the baby, go to all her antenatal appointments with her and support her in any way she'd let him.

Assuming she'd let him, which was a big assumption.

He fell into step beside her. 'So, how old is Daisy?'

'Four. She's seeing us first and then being admitted to the assessment unit until we have a better idea of what's going on, and if and when we'll need to operate. She's coming in without breakfast ready for the contrast scan, so I don't want to keep her hanging about long because it's a slow process and she'll be hungry.'

'OK, so we'll go from there. Do you want me in on the consult?'

She stopped and turned to face him. 'Yes, because if she needs surgery, I'll want you in on it, and you're good with the children. And besides, I value your opinion.'

He resisted the overwhelming urge to smirk, restricting himself to a slight smile and a tiny shake of the head. 'Did that nearly kill you?'

She looked away, but not before he saw her mouth twitch. 'Don't be ridiculous. Your ego's showing again.'

'Oh, dear. Me and my ego. We're always in trouble.'

He swiped his lanyard, held the door open for her and followed her through to the consulting room waiting area.

A couple were sitting there, a small girl with long blonde hair cuddled on the woman's knee, and he thought they looked uncomfortable, strained. With worry?

'Mr and Mrs Lawrence?' Alice said. They got to their feet and she held out her hand to them. 'Welcome to Hope Hospital. I'm Alice Baxter, the senior gastro-intestinal surgeon, and this is my colleague Marco Ricci. And you must be Daisy,' she said, bobbing down to the child's level. 'Hi, Daisy. You can call me Alice, if you like.'

'I'm Olive, and this is Dan,' Mrs Lawrence said, and smiled down encouragingly at Daisy. 'Daisy, say hello.'

But Daisy had obviously had enough of doctors, and she turned her face into her mother and hid, so Alice straightened up and smiled at her parents. 'Shall we go on through to the consulting room and talk through what we're planning to do today? And if it's all right, I'd like us to have a look at Daisy.'

She ushered them into the room, and Marco scooped up Daisy's forgotten teddy and followed them into the very room where he'd accidentally got Alice pregnant just over five weeks ago.

Was that really all it was? Thirty-eight days?

Trying not to look at the couch, he let Alice do the talking, taking the opportunity to sit on the floor and prop his back against the wall. Daisy was looking withdrawn and wary, so he hid the teddy behind his back and brought it out in surprising places. Under his other arm, behind his legs, upside down and sideways, and all the time Daisy watched him, warily at first, and then with a glimmer of anticipation.

And then finally she giggled, and he felt as if the sun had come out.

'Does your teddy have a name?' he asked her softly, and she nodded and moved a little nearer him—but not too near.

'He's called Wuzzle.'

'Wuzzle? What a lovely name. Hello, Wuzzle. Nice to meet you. I'm Marco. So, Wuzzle, what can you tell me about Daisy?'

'She's my best friend,' he said, pretending to be a ventriloquist and making Daisy giggle again.

'And what else can you tell me, Wuzzle?'

'She's got a sore tummy.'

He put the teddy down and looked at Daisy. 'Is that right, Daisy? Do you have a sore tummy?'

Daisy nodded and sat down facing him. 'Sometimes, especially when I've had my dinner.'

'Oh, no. That's a pity. So do you just have a little bit of dinner then?' he asked, because she was a skinny, lanky little thing and it could have been because she'd had a growth spurt or because her appetite was off. Especially if she was afraid to eat. And she was pale and wan. Worryingly so.

She nodded. 'If I eat too much, my tummy hurts.'

'OK, Daisy, I have an idea. Will you let me and Alice try and find out what's wrong with your tummy?' he asked gently. 'Because we can't have you hurting, can we, when you eat?'

She shook her head. 'Wuzzle's tummy hurts, too.'

'Does it? Can you show me where?'

Daisy pressed her fingers gently onto Wuzzle's soft, furry body, around about what would be his epigastric region if he wasn't a teddy bear. 'Here,' she said, and pressed again to the right. 'And here.'

'Is that the same place as your tummy?'

She nodded, and snuggled Wuzzle tight against her chest.

'OK. Daisy, do you mind if I have a little feel of your tummy now? See if I can feel anything wrong? Would that be OK?'

She nodded again, her brown eyes soft and wounded, and he felt his heart wrench for her.

'Come on, then, poppet. Let's help you up onto the bed and I can have a look at both of you, OK?'

He stood up, pulled Daisy to her feet, handed Wuzzle to her and lifted them easily onto the couch. The couch where he and Alice had made not only love, but a baby. Amazing...

'Now, let's have a look at Wuzzle first, shall we?'

Alice's eyes strayed to him, to his gentle, careful hands examining first the teddy and then little Daisy, with just the same thoroughness and attention to detail he'd brought to their lovemaking right there on the edge of that couch.

Did he realise it was the same room?

'He's so good with her,' Olive said quietly, and she nodded.

'Yes, he is.' Good with everything...

She turned away from Marco and gave the Lawrences her undivided attention. 'Has anybody explained to you what malrotation of the gut is, exactly?'

Daisy's mother nodded. 'Something to do with the way she formed as an embryo, they said, and I've worried ever since that it was something I ate or did—'

'No. It was nothing you did. There's no evidence to suggest anything of the sort. What happens is that the cells that become the gut migrate up into the umbilical cord at about ten weeks of pregnancy, and then at around eleven weeks they migrate back down again, and coil into the area that becomes the abdomen. And sometimes, about once in every five hundred babies, they coil the wrong way, because our bodies aren't symmetrical inside.

'The liver is on the right, the spleen and pancreas and stomach on the left, and the small intestine starts at the bottom of the stomach and curls around past the liver, picking up the bile and pancreatic ducts, and then this great tangle of small intestine wriggles around inside and joins the large bowel down on the right, where we get appendicitis.

'In children with malrotation it coils the other way, so that join in the gut can end up near their stomach or even on the other side, so diagnosing appendicitis is difficult, and that's often when asymptomatic malrotation is diagnosed.

'The problem arises when the part that is trying to be the right way round gets twisted somehow in a bit of a conflict of interests with the other bit, and that twisting process can lead to what's known as a volvulus, which means the blood supply to that part is kinked and cut off by the twisting, and that's a life-threatening emergency.

'Daisy is *not* at that stage, but she may be approaching it, because she could have bands of fibrous tissue called Ladd's bands holding her intestines in the wrong place. That's what our tests today are going to look for, to find out exactly how her gut is coiled inside her, and where the pinch points or twists might lie so we can rearrange her gut to relieve that, if it's what's causing her pain. Does that make sense?'

They nodded, but she noticed they didn't offer each other any support or interact in any way, which seemed odd.

'Is there anything else we can tell you before we admit her and she goes down for her scan?'

They shook their heads, again not conferring.

'OK, that's good. Feel free to ask, though, at any time, because I know it's a lot to take in. So, Dr Marco, what's the verdict?' she asked lightly, turning to face the examination couch again. 'Do Daisy and Wuzzle need to have some pictures taken?'

He turned his head and smiled. 'Yes, I think they do. I think we need to find out why they've got tummy ache. So, Dr Alice, how are we going to take the pictures?'

'Well, Daisy, after you've been checked in by a nurse we'll take you downstairs, and a lady there will give you a special drink, and then we'll take pictures of the drink all through the morning as it moves through your tummy. It's called a follow-through contrast scan, and it's very good at showing us where things aren't working quite like they should be. Is that OK?'

'Will Wuzzle have some to drink, too?'

'I'm sure he can. Would you like strawberry, blackcurrant or chocolate flavour?'

Daisy tipped her head to one side and contorted her little face thoughtfully. 'Chocolate,' she said in the end, sounding a little bit triumphant as if she'd just made an important decision, and Alice stifled a smile.

'Chocolate it is, then,' she said, and on the way to the admissions unit she managed to get a few words with Marco.

'So?' she murmured softly, trying to concentrate on Daisy and not the warmth she could feel radiating from his body, the scent that was uniquely him.

'There's a firm mass in the upper right quadrant—it could be the start of a volvulus or simply the adhesions restraining the midgut. If her gut's only just beginning to twist it could explain why it's been intermittent, but I don't think she's far off having a full-on volvulus, so I think we may need to operate tomorrow, if not today. Her abdomen was a little tense and it's definitely sore.'

'And Wuzzle?'

He smiled, his eyes softening and threatening to melt her insides. 'I think Wuzzle might need to have a few stitches and a little plaster on his tummy,' he said in a low murmur, and Alice felt the warm drift of his breath against her skin and a ripple of need went through her. It would be so easy to lean against him, just to feel that warmth, that strength, that solid wall of muscle.

She moved away a fraction and smiled up at him.

'That sounds like your department,' she murmured,

and he chuckled softly, sending that enticing drift of air over her again, and she took herself out of range for the sake of her sanity.

He paused as Alice opened the door to the admissions unit and ushered the Lawrences through, and Daisy turned and looked at him, her little face worried.

'Aren't you coming with me?' she asked him, her chin wobbling, so he walked back towards her and crouched down.

'I can't. I have to go and see a little boy who had an operation yesterday and make sure he's comfy and happy and that everything's going well, but then I'll come back and see you if you like.'

'Promise?'

He glanced up at Alice, and she nodded.

'Yes. I promise. Alice will ask them to tell me when you're ready, and I'll go downstairs with you when you have the pictures taken of your tummy, but Mummy and Daddy will be there, too. Nobody's going to leave you alone, poppet. It's OK.'

She nodded, then gave him a little hug, Wuzzle brushing up against his face. 'OK,' she said, and he eased away and stood up, a lump in his throat for some reason.

'I'll be as quick as I can,' he promised, and he waved goodbye to Daisy and left them to go up and check on Amil, the child with Crohn's in PICU.

Evie, the ICU receptionist, resident baby-cuddler and organiser of miracles, including the opening gala, was at her post in the reception area outside the unit, and she looked up and smiled at him and he paused, glad to see her there because, if the hospital grapevine was correct, she and Ryan Walker had just got engaged after a whirlwind romance.

He leant on the desk and grinned at her. 'Hi, Evie. I gather congratulations are in order. That's fabulous news.'

Evie smiled with every part of her face. 'It is, isn't it? And Ryan and I are hoping to adopt baby Grace.'

'Really? Oh, that's amazing. How is she?'

'Oh, she's wonderful—she's doing so well I can't believe she's the same tiny newborn we found by the bins. She's so strong now, I'm really proud of her. It's all down to Ryan's surgery on her poor little heart, of course—'

'That's not what I've heard, I reckon it was all the love you gave her,' he said with a smile. He hesitated, then leant closer. 'Have you seen the Khans today? They've found Amil's illness very distressing. Can you keep an eye on them? They're struggling a bit.'

'Of course. I was talking to them earlier. They seem better today. Yesterday was hard for them.'

'I'm sure. I'm just going to see him now. Thanks, Evie.'

Amil was doing well, to Marco's relief.

He was propped up slightly and seemed to be pain-free, thanks to the epidural, and his notes showed a steady heart rate and blood pressure.

His mother was sitting with him, reading him a story, and although the strain still showed in her face, her eyes were more relaxed and she smiled up at him.

'How's it going?' he asked, and the boy's eyes filled.

'It doesn't hurt. That's the first time in so long.'

Courtesy of the epidural. 'Good. That's what we want. Now we just need to give your gut time to mend, and then we can start you on food and see how that goes, but you're getting food through your drip in your arm, so your body's getting all the food and water it needs, which means there's no hurry. Mind if I have a look at your tummy?'

'No.'

There was no bleeding under the transparent dressing, and his wound looked good. Neat sutures, so with luck he'd heal with hardly any scarring. He felt a flicker of satisfaction and covered Amil up again.

'OK, I'm happy. If you carry on like this, we should be able to move you down to HDU on the ward soon. Anything either of you want to ask me?'

They both shook their heads, so he left them to it and went back out into Reception.

'How is he?' Evie asked.

'He's doing well, and you're right, his mum looks much happier. So, what are you up to now? I'm sure Theo's got you planning something else amazing after the success of the gala.'

'Oh, all sorts of things. I had an idea, though. I was watching something about PAT dogs—Pets As Therapy?—and I suggested to Theo that maybe we could introduce it here, give it a try and see if the children benefit. It sounds such an amazing idea.'

'It is. I know a lady with a PAT dog. Her name's Alana, and she's got a soppy labradoodle—a Labrador poodle cross—called Doodle. He's the gentlest dog I've ever met, and he's just lovely and he smiles with his whole face. I could ask her if she'd be interested in coming here so we could trial the idea. I can think of lots of children who'd benefit from an ice breaker like that, and she's had people who tell the dog things they'd never tell a person. It can be a way of helping them to acknowledge their fears, and she's had great success with him, which doesn't surprise me, he just loves everyone unconditionally. He's gorgeous. Do you want me to talk to Theo before I speak to her, or will you?'

'Oh, I can if you like. I've got a meeting with him this afternoon to discuss the arrangements for Halloween and the Guy Fawkes firework display, so I could tack it onto that, if you don't mind? I'm sure he'll say yes.'

Marco nodded. 'That would be great. Let me know what he says, and then if he gives us the go-ahead, I'll talk to Alana. Right, I have to go. Daisy and Wuzzle are having a follow-through contrast scan and Daisy says they need me.'

Evie's lips twitched. 'Wuzzle?'

'Her teddy.' He pulled a sad face. 'He might need stitches too. They may be up here, possibly today, maybe tomorrow. I'll let you know. You may have to look after Wuzzle.'

She smiled. 'I'm sure I can manage that.'

His pager bleeped, and he glanced at it. 'OK, Daisy's ready. I need to go. Let me know how it goes with Theo.'

The follow-through scan showed several areas that were minor pinch points, and one loop that was clearly a borderline volvulus. Anything could tip it over the edge and cut off the circulation, and there were Ladd's bands, which were holding the gut in the wrong position and making it all much worse. And Alice was worried.

'I think you're right. I think we need to operate as soon as we can, preferably today. She's been starved, she's not critical, she's reasonably well. I don't want to wait for this to turn into a crisis in the middle of the night so we need to get her on a drip, drain her gut and upper bowel with a nasogastric tube and then operate as soon as she's ready.'

'Are you OK with that?' Marco asked her, his voice low.

'Of course I am. Why not?'

He shrugged, but his concern was written all over his face, and she resisted the urge to give in and let him look after her, because she was only pregnant, for goodness' sake, not ill! But she did need to eat, and soon, or she would be.

'Can we take this conversation to the cafeteria? I didn't get round to making lunch today.'

'Of course. And then you need a nap while I talk to them and prep Daisy for the op.'

'I can't nap in the middle of the day!' she protested, but he just raised an eyebrow, opened the door of her office for her and fell in beside her.

'So, what are you going to eat, if you can't eat carbs?'

'I don't know. I'll see what they've got. Something high calorie and not too smelly, like avocado or cold salmon or something harmless.'

'Hmm. I tell you what. We'll get Daisy sorted, and then tomorrow night I'm cooking you dinner.'

She felt a flicker of panic. 'No, Marco. You don't know what makes me feel queasy, you don't know what I can eat—'

'Alice, I'm not stupid. Trust me.'

Could she? She wanted to, because the thought of prepping food made her stomach churn, but she had to eat.

And judging by the options available in the cafeteria, that could be awkward. She helped herself from the salad bar, added a portion of cold salmon and a cup of mint tea and picked her way through it while Marco ate his way steadily through a mountain of food.

Oddly, it didn't affect her, mostly because he'd chosen things that didn't smell. Because of her?

'Are you OK with what I'm eating?'

'Yes, I'm fine, but I'm guessing it wasn't your first choice.'

His mouth twitched. 'Don't worry about me. So, how are you going to fit this nap in?'

She rolled her eyes and put down her fork. 'Marco, I'm a busy doctor. I don't have time for a little nap in the middle of the day! I have too much to do.'

'So delegate to me. I can talk to parents, examine patients, write letters—even if you sign them. I can review results, order tests—use me, Alice. Make time for yourself, even if it's just half an hour at lunchtime after you eat. Please.'

She closed her eyes, just the thought of a nap so appealing she could have cried. 'Marco, really, I'll be fine. I don't need a nap, and I don't need you clucking over me like a mother hen. I want to talk about Daisy and her management.'

He shrugged, stuffed another forkful of food into his mouth and gestured to her to go on. Nothing said 'Suit yourself' louder than that did, and she realised that getting him to back down was going to be a fight she'd probably lose.

But nevertheless, the fact that he so obviously cared and wanted to look after her left a warm feeling inside. A feeling she wasn't sure she'd ever felt before, and it nearly made her cry…

CHAPTER THREE

SHE WENT WITH Marco to see Daisy, and while he was busy
ordering blood tests and discussing her transfer to the surgical unit with the ward staff in the admissions unit, Alice
took Daisy's mother into the office to talk to her.

Her father was nowhere to be seen, and Alice asked
Olive if she wanted to contact him so they could discuss
the results and what they were going to do for Daisy together, but she gave an awkward smile and shook her head.

'No, it's OK, Dan's busy, he had things to get on with,'
she said, and it sounded as if she was being evasive.

'We can wait for him if you like?' she offered, but again
Olive shook her head.

'We've got our own business and—well, it takes a lot
of time, especially since he's on his own now. We worked
together building the business for over ten years before
Daisy came along, and ever since it's been—I don't know.
Because of her illness I haven't felt happy leaving her with
anyone so I don't help him any longer and to be honest
it's probably easier that way. He can't handle Daisy being
ill, being in pain, so he leaves her to me largely. It doesn't
mean he doesn't love her, but we just tend to do our own
thing now.'

That was an unexpected outpouring of honesty, and
Alice reached out and touched her hand. 'I'm sorry, I didn't

realise that. Well, I'm sure you can pass on anything I tell you, and if he wants to talk to me I'll be more than happy to go through it again. I'm always here for you both, so's Marco.' She sat back and pulled up Daisy's scan results on the tablet. 'So, this is what we found out this morning.'

She showed Olive the scan results, explained what they were going to do and how it would help Daisy, and then discussed the method they'd use to operate.

'Ideally we'd like to do it with keyhole surgery, and we'll remove the appendix because it's in the wrong place and that could make it hard to diagnose appendicitis.'

'Is she likely to get it?'

Alice shook her head. 'No more likely than anyone else, but if she gets abdominal pain in the future it eliminates it as a possibility. I have to warn you, though, that we may need to revert to open surgery if we can't get what we consider to be proper and sufficient access to the bits we're worried about.'

'So who's going to operate?'

'Both of us—me and Marco.'

'Is he good?'

She thought of their banter over Amil's sutures, and smiled. 'Yes. He's very good. Better than that, actually. He's excellent, and I trust him absolutely.'

Olive's face crumpled slightly. 'I can't believe she needs an operation, but she's been getting more and more uncomfortable and miserable, and sometimes she wakes up in the night crying with the pain. Dan can't cope with it, he just gets up and goes to the office and leaves me with her, as if I can cope with it any better, but I'm her mother, I can't walk out when she hurts just because it's too upsetting—'

She broke down in tears, worn out with the strain of it as so many parents were, but she was coping alone without her husband's support, and Alice put an arm round her and comforted her while she cried.

How could Dan have abandoned her to deal with this alone? Busy or not, she couldn't imagine Marco walking out and leaving his child, but then Olive hadn't probably expected that, either, and you couldn't know until you were tested how you'd behave. Still, ten years together before Daisy came along was surely long enough to know each other—unless it hadn't been a surprise? Maybe Dan had always avoided anything difficult?

She'd only known Marco a few months but she thought she knew him better than that. Was she deluding herself? After all, what did she really know of him outside work? Nothing. Well, a little about his family now, but not much. Maybe he'd behave just like Dan? Except he'd made it perfectly clear the moment she'd told him she was having a baby that he was in it for the long haul, so he clearly wasn't one to avoid tackling difficult issues.

Although the chronic illness of a much-loved child would be a challenge to anyone, and it was easy to make assumptions about how he'd behave. She wasn't even sure what she'd be like if Daisy was hers.

Agonised by every pang the child had, she realised. And not all parents had a support network. Theo Hawkwood, their own CEO and a former paediatric surgeon, was facing this alone with Ivy, his little daughter, and without the help of his beloved late wife, Hope. Ivy had been unwell for a few weeks now, with progressive pain and weakness in her legs, and so far, despite the cumulative brains of the highly talented, hand-picked staff within Theo's own Hope Hospital, nobody seemed to be able to work out what was wrong with her, hence waiting for the world-renowned American diagnostician Madison Archer to arrive, and you could tell he was worried, just like any other parent.

Just like Olive—and probably, although he wasn't here to show it, her husband Dan. Worried, and coping the only way they knew how.

The tears had subsided now, and Olive straightened up and blew her nose.

'I'm sorry—I don't know what came over me.'

'I do, and it's a perfectly normal reaction. Why don't you go and get a cup of tea or coffee and have a little break, and Marco and I will get the consent forms ready and everything lined up so we can operate as soon as Daisy's been prepped for surgery. It'll be a few hours yet, probably not until four, but we don't really want to leave her overnight because we could end up having to do it as an emergency on a much sicker little girl, and nobody wants that.'

'No, of course not. I'll go and get a coffee and ring Dan and talk to him, get him to come back.'

'OK. If you want to talk to me again, just ask anyone to page me and they can get hold of me. And please don't worry, Olive. We're here for you and Dan, as well as Daisy.'

Olive nodded and dredged up a wobbly smile. 'Thank you.'

'My pleasure.'

She showed Olive out of her office, went back to the admissions unit and found Marco.

'Have you had that nap yet?' he asked, and she rolled her eyes.

'No, I haven't. I've been talking to Olive Lawrence. She's going to get hold of her husband and talk to him.' She lowered her voice. 'He doesn't do Daisy's sickness, apparently. Can't cope with it.'

Marco scowled and made a disgusted noise, and she didn't need a psychology degree to work out what he was thinking.

'So, what's the plan?' he asked. 'Are we going ahead?'

'I think so. I sent her off to get a coffee, and when she comes back we'll get the NG tube in and the drip up.'

'I've done the drip,' he said. 'She was in pain again, so I've written her up for some IV pain relief. I think we need to get on with it before this escalates.'

She nodded. 'OK. I can send someone down to find her mother. She'll be in the café in the main reception area, trying to get hold of Dan. She needs to be here for the NG tube. It's bound to make Daisy gag and she'll need her mummy to hold her hand while it's done.'

'I agree. Everything's ready when you are. Just give me a call when you've seen the parents and I'll come straight back. I want to be there for her when they do the tube.'

'Where are you going?'

'Just to check on Amil again, and I've got a couple of discharge letters to write and I need to chase up Daisy's bloods. I'll be in your office.'

'OK.'

Why on earth had he said he wanted to be there?

It wasn't necessary, the nurses knew exactly what they were doing and they were brilliant at putting children at their ease, but Daisy had latched onto him after the game with Wuzzle and he didn't want anything getting in the way of her going into Theatre as soon as possible.

Which was how he ended up volunteering to have an NG tube inserted, to show a frightened little girl that it was harmless.

She was on the general surgical ward now, settled into her new bed, and he found himself parked in the chair beside the bed, subjecting himself to having a tube passed up his nose and down into his stomach.

Why had he suggested it?

'OK, Marco?'

He summoned up a grin. 'Yeah, go ahead, I'm fine.'

'Here, have Wuzzle,' Daisy said, holding him out. 'He wants to cuddle you.'

'Thank you, Daisy.'

He took the little bear, snuggled him against his chest and then he winked at Daisy, picked up the paper cup of water with a straw in it and waited while the nurse slid the nasogastric tube carefully up his nose. It made his eye stream—just the one, on the side of the tube—and then it hit the back of his throat and made him gag slightly, so he took a suck of the water to stifle his gag reflex and help him swallow it down, his eyes still on Daisy.

He gave her another wink as the nurse finished, then slowly pulled it out himself, wiped his nose and grinned at Daisy. 'See? Easy. What's that, Wuzzle?' He held the bear to his ear, nodded and then said, 'Wuzzle says it's OK and not to worry, he'll cuddle you, too.'

She didn't look convinced. 'Did it hurt?'

'No. It tickles. That's why I coughed. If you drink the water, it helps a lot. Then you just swallow and down it goes, easy-peasy. It feels a bit funny but it's OK.'

'Will you put it in?' she asked, and he nodded and handed Wuzzle back to her.

'Sure, if you want me to.'

'I do.'

'OK. Mum, if you sit her on your lap and hold her hand, that would be good. So, first I have to measure it, from the tip of your nose to your ear, and then down to your tummy—like that, and then I mark it so I know how far it has to go, because everybody's different and my tube was much longer and fatter because I'm bigger than you. So, there, it's marked, and now I just have to dip the end of the tube into this slippery stuff to help it slide down nice and easily, and in it goes. OK, Daisy? You're doing really well. Nice and still for me—good girl! Have a little drink, that's it, and swallow—and that's lovely. Keep drinking— good girl! It's in! There.'

He grinned at Daisy and gave her a high five while the nurse taped the tube to her cheek, tucked it behind her ear and attached a large syringe to the port to withdraw her stomach contents before she taped it to Daisy's gown so it didn't move.

Marco turned round to talk to Alice, and found she'd gone.

Because watching had triggered her gag reflex? Very likely. How he'd stifled his he had no idea, but it had done the trick and Daisy was all tubed up and ready to go.

'You're a brave girl, Daisy. Well done,' he said gently, and her mother's eyes filled.

'Thank you. Thank you so much for doing that.'

'My pleasure.' Well, that was a lie, but, hey. 'I'll bring you the consent form for the surgery, and then I'll talk you and Daisy through it.'

'Alice tells me you'll both be in Theatre. She speaks very highly of you.'

He chuckled. 'You're not supposed to tell me that. She say's my ego's big enough for both of us.'

Olive smiled sadly. 'I don't think you've got an ego, Marco. I think you're amazing. Thank you.'

'It's all part of the job,' he said softly, and went to get the forms.

It was a long operation, and for a while Alice wasn't sure they'd be able to recoil the gut into a safe position without open surgery.

'It doesn't want to go,' she said, and Marco took the other instruments and moved the bowel carefully to one side.

'There's another adhesion. Can you reach it?'

And then it moved, slowly but surely, allowing them to work the coils into a better position. The section of bowel that had been slightly darker instantly pinked up, and she sighed with relief.

'Brilliant. Well done.'

'So much praise today. My head's going to fall off under its own weight at this rate.'

'Praise?'

'Yes, from Olive, and from you, apparently,' he said, carefully manoeuvring the last coil into position. 'She said you spoke highly of me. That was after you bolted.'

She could feel herself colouring. 'Sorry. I had to.'

'I guessed that. I could have done with bolting, too. I don't know why I volunteered.'

'Because you're a nice man,' she said, realising it was true. There weren't many people who'd do that, they'd leave it to the nurses to talk the children round, and if necessary do it with sedation. Not Marco. Oh, no. He had to have it done to show her how easy it was. Except it wasn't, because however you looked at it, it was unpleasant.

'Did Dan show up in the end?'

'No,' he said, and his eyes over the mask were disapproving.

'Not everyone can cope with it, Marco.'

'I know that, and I don't know that I could. I just know you try. You do it even if it hurts you, because if it hurts you and scares you, you can be sure it hurts and scares the child far more. You can't escape that by running away. OK, I think we're done. Are you happy?'

'For now,' she said. 'We might need to go back in if it doesn't resolve or if it moves again, but I think we've done all we can for now and I don't want to open her up and slow her recovery unnecessarily.'

'No, I agree. I'll close, you go and talk to Olive and then go home. It's nearly eight and I bet you haven't eaten.'

'I have. I had something earlier, but I've got admin to do. Come and find me when you're done.'

'OK.'

She went out, and to her surprise found Dan there with Olive. They both leapt to their feet as she emerged, and she smiled at them encouragingly.

'She's fine, we've sorted it out, her bowel is looking much happier now and we managed to do it without open surgery, so assuming it all settles down in the next day or two and we don't have to go back in, her recovery time should be much quicker. Marco's just closing, then they'll take her through to Recovery and then back to the ward. She'll be in the high dependency unit on the ward, but don't be alarmed. It's just because they'll be checking on her every half hour or so and it keeps the rest of the ward quieter for the children who need less intervention in the night.'

'Oh. That makes sense. Thank you so much.'

'Yes, thank you,' Dan chipped in, looking uncomfortable. 'I'm sorry I wasn't here earlier, I find it really hard to see her like that.'

'You don't need to apologise to me,' she said gently. 'It is hard and not everyone can do it, but Daisy could do with all the support she can get, and so could both of you.'

He nodded, but he didn't look convinced, just worried, stressed and unsupported, like Olive.

Was their marriage under strain because of Daisy's condition? It sounded like it.

'Look, she'll be a while yet. Why don't you go down to the cafeteria and get yourselves something to eat and drink? It could be a long night if you're going to sit up with her, although she'll be sedated and have pain relief so you could go back to your family suite after you've seen her, if you'd rather, and we'll contact you if we need you. But in the meantime take advantage of the fact that you can't do anything else and look after yourselves, OK? Because it's tough being the parents of a sick child, and you need to cut yourselves some slack.'

They nodded, and she walked back across the link to the central building where her office was, shut the door and sat down with a tired sigh.

She was exhausted.

The pregnancy? It was ridiculous, in gestational terms she was only seven and a half weeks pregnant. How could she be so tired? Maybe Marco was right, maybe she needed a few more carbs in her diet. Or a nap, but that was never going to happen. She pulled open the drawer, took out the last of the little wholewheat crackers he'd given her this morning and ate a couple, then leant back and shut her eyes.

Just for a moment...

She was asleep.

He watched her for a moment, surprised by the surge of tenderness and—no, surely not love. He didn't know her well enough to love her. But he suddenly realised he wanted to, to know her well enough, and to love her. Was it possible? Would she let him get that close, let him into her heart? And could he let her into his? Did he want to?

Yes—and that surprised him. He'd broken up with Francesca because he'd known in his heart of hearts he didn't love her enough, any more than she loved him, and since the ensuing emotional fallout with his family he'd always kept his emotional distance from the women in his life, wary of causing any more heartache and so held something back, but suddenly—because of the baby she was carrying?—he wanted a much greater closeness with Alice, a deeper intimacy, an intimacy of their hearts and minds, not just their bodies.

The physical side he could have with anyone, although probably not as good as it had been with Alice, but to have that special closeness, that meeting of souls bonded together by their love for each other and their child—could he have that with Alice? Would she let him that close to her?

Even the thought of it put a lump in his throat, a tight knot of longing in his chest, and he took a long, slow breath in and blew it out, calming his body, slowing his heart. There was no hurry, no urgency. He'd work at it slowly, take it day by day, and prove to her that she could trust him. And maybe then...

He crossed to her side, laid his hand gently on her shoulder and shook it slightly.

'Alice? Alice, wake up,' he murmured.

She straightened, sucking in a breath and blinking at him.

'Oh—sorry. I must have dozed off. What's the time?'

'Half past nine.'

'Really? Gosh. How's Daisy?'

'She's fine, so's Amil. They're both settled for the night, everyone else is fine so you don't need to worry. Go home, Alice. You're exhausted, and you need your sleep.'

'I can't go home. Someone needs to be here.'

'Yes—me. I've told Daisy's parents I'll be here all night in an on-call room, so you don't need to do anything.'

'But what if she has to go back into Theatre?'

'I'll call you, but she won't. She's fine, she's looking good. She's nice and drowsy and she's comfortable, and she doesn't need you, and she doesn't need me, so go home now and get some decent rest, and I'll see you in the morning, OK?'

She nodded tiredly, stretched, yawned and got to her feet, reaching for her coat.

'Are you sure you don't need me?'

That nearly made him laugh. Need her? He'd always needed her. Ever since he'd met her he'd needed her, and since the gala it had been far worse, tormenting him day and night. Once had been nothing like enough, but that wasn't what she meant, so he stuck to the script.

'No, I don't need you,' he said firmly. 'I can cope with a sleeping child. It's not like there aren't dozens of staff here to help me. Go on. Shoo.'

She nodded, walked over to him and went up on tiptoe and kissed his cheek.

'Thank you,' she murmured, and then left the room.

He closed his eyes, ran the last twenty-four hours through his mind and shook his head.

It seemed incredible, but it was only this time yesterday that he'd found out he was going to be a father, and it had changed his life.

It had been a long, long day. Time for one last check of his little charges, and then bed. And hopefully, tonight, he'd sleep.

'Don't forget I'm cooking for you tonight.'

Alice tilted her head and frowned at him. 'You are? When did I say yes to that?'

He smiled. 'Yesterday.'

'I didn't say yes!'

He smiled again. 'Not in so many words, but I took it as read.'

'Well, you don't need to be so presumptuous. I might have plans.'

'Do you have plans?'

Damn. She couldn't lie to him. 'No. I don't have plans.'

His mouth twitched but he managed not to laugh out loud at her, to her relief. 'Well, you do now. I've got my car here. We'll go when we finish. Oh, and I got you these.'

He handed her a small packet of pills.

'Folic acid?' She felt a twinge of worry, and he must have read her mind because he shook his head.

'You'll be fine. You have a very good diet full of folic acid, if the fridge here is anything to go by. Lots of dark leafy greens, any carbs I've ever seen you eat have been wholegrains—really, Alice, you'll be fine, but you should be taking them, just to be sure. And if you take multi-vitamins, nothing with vitamin A. Too much—'

'Is potentially harmful. I know.' She frowned down at them, glanced back up at him and smiled ruefully. 'Thank you, Marco. It was very thoughtful of you.' Like everything he was doing for her now.

He grunted. 'Don't thank me. It's my baby, too.'

As if she could forget. And that's what this was all about, of course. Making sure the baby was OK. The fact that he had to take care of her to ensure its safety was just a by-product, and she swallowed down the little pang of regret that it wasn't just for her. Or at least she didn't think so. 'How are Daisy and Amil?' she asked, getting back onto safer ground.

'Doing well. Daisy was a bit sore this morning so I upped her pain relief, Amil is making very good progress. I think we can discharge Tyler and Abbie today, too. Oh, and Ivy Hawkwood's not doing so well. I saw Evie up at PICU—we were talking about introducing a PAT dog to see how the children got on with it, and she was going to discuss it with Theo but apparently he had to cut their meeting short and go home. I think he's possibly talking about admitting her for further tests.'

'Oh, no. I wonder what's wrong with her? Have they ruled out a brain or spinal tumour?'

'I don't know what they've done, but he must be worried sick. Whatever it is it seems to come and go so a tumour's unlikely, but she's only five. That's very young for something like MS but from what Evie said the symptoms seem to fit.'

'Gosh. Poor little Ivy. Oh, Marco, I hope it's nothing awful. He's lost his wife. He doesn't need to lose his daughter. That would be too sad.'

'Tell me about it. So—have you had breakfast?'

She laughed and shook her head slowly. 'You don't give up, do you? Yes, I've had breakfast. I had scrambled eggs on wilted spinach. And I've brought some lunch and other snacks. I seem to be able to eat avocado and just about anything with salt on it, for some reason. And, yes, I'm resisting the urge to overdo the salt in case I get high blood pressure, before you ask. Right, shall we do some work or is there anything else you need to nag me about before we start?'

He bit his lips, his eyes sparkling with laughter, and she had the sudden and almost irresistible urge to kiss him.

She checked on Daisy herself, and found her snuggled up to Wuzzle, her mother by her side as usual.

'Hello, Daisy,' she said softly, sending a smile to Olive. 'How are you feeling today?'

'A bit sore, but so is Wuzzle and Marco says he'll get better soon, too. See.'

She held the teddy out, and Alice saw four tiny, bright blue sutures scattered around his abdomen, in just the same place as Daisy's. Marco again, going the extra mile to comfort a child.

'Marco says he can have his stitches out tomorrow, but I might have to wait a little longer.'

'I think teddies get better quicker,' Alice said, not sure about going along with this fiction but backing Marco regardless, because it seemed to make Daisy happy and that was all that mattered.

'Can I have a look at your tummy, too?' she asked, and Daisy lifted her arms up so Alice could turn back the covers. Perfect little sutures, beautifully done—of course—but her abdomen seemed a little tense and that worried Alice.

'Does this hurt?' she asked, pressing gently and then letting go suddenly, and she got her answer in a flicker of pain across Daisy's little face.

'A bit,' she said bravely.

Alice covered her again, scanned the chart at the foot of the bed and frowned. She seemed to be on quite a lot of pain relief, and it wasn't working. Would they need to go in again?

'Is something wrong?' Olive asked, and Alice shook her head.

'No, I don't think so. Daisy, may I borrow Mummy for a minute? I want to ask her a few things.'

'OK,' she said, and Alice wasn't sure if it was the light or if she was looking slightly flushed.

They moved away from the bed, and Olive immediately asked again if something was wrong.

'It could be. Has she eaten anything yet?'

Olive shook her head. 'No. She tried but she retched. All she's had is a little water and she didn't really want that.'

'OK. Well, her abdomen's tense, and she's got what we

call rebound tenderness, a pain brought on when you release the pressure suddenly. That could indicate peritonitis or a twisted bowel. Either would explain why she can't eat. I want to run a few more tests, and depending on what we find we may have to take her back to Theatre because there may be something else going on that we missed.'

Olive's face crumpled, and Alice led her round the corner out of Daisy's line of sight.

'It's just a possibility at this stage, and it was always a possibility. We hoped we wouldn't have to take her back in, and maybe we won't, but in the meantime why don't you go and get a coffee and we can keep her company and set up the tests. I want some more bloods and another X-ray before we make a decision.'

Olive nodded and went back to Daisy to pick up her bag and explain where she was going, and Alice paged Marco.

She was requesting the tests when he appeared at her side and she filled him in.

'Rebound tenderness? That's new, she didn't have it earlier.'

'It's only slight—but she's on quite a bit of pain relief.'

'I know. How are her obs?'

'OK, stable. No raised temperature, but she's looking a little flushed.'

'She looked pale as I walked past an hour ago. She seemed to be asleep. What are you thinking?'

'Peritonitis or volvulus. According to Olive she's only had drinks, and when they tried to get her to eat something for breakfast she retched. I think we're going to have to go back in.'

He swore softly in Italian, then sighed. 'I didn't want to do this.'

'Neither did I. Let's run the tests and see. Another contrast scan should give us the answer.'

* * *

It did. For some reason, or no reason at all, the gut had twisted on itself and she had a volvulus, cutting off the blood supply to almost all her midgut.

They took her straight to Theatre, made a midline incision and Alice reached in, carefully eased the gut out and turned the tangled mass back anticlockwise to free it. Immediately the little coils began to pink up, but not all of it seemed to be free to move.

'There must be another adhesion,' Marco murmured. 'How did we miss it?'

'Here—right down here, by the rectum. It's not a Ladd's band, it looks more like post-infection adhesions. Look, you can see scarring on the surface of the bowel. Poor little thing. She's obviously been in more pain than anyone had realised.'

She freed the adhesions carefully, and then the gut relaxed and slithered easily into a more natural and open position.

She felt her shoulders drop, and she saw Marco's sag with relief as well.

'Good,' she said. 'That's better.'

'Yes. It was a little resistant yesterday, but I thought we'd got it in the end. Obviously not all of it.'

'No, but it was really hard to see. I wish we'd done this yesterday so she didn't have to go through it twice, but I really thought we'd got it all. Still, it's done now,' she said, and stepped back, straightening her shoulders briefly.

He met her eyes. 'Are you OK?'

'Yes, I'm fine. Would you like to close?'

He smiled at her, his eyes creasing over his mask. 'If you like. Or you could close and I could put the sutures in Wuzzle.'

She smiled back at him and shook her head slowly.

'Have I ever told you what a softie you are?' she murmured, and she was rewarded with a low, sexy chuckle that sent tiny shivers up her spine. 'Go on, you close, and do Wuzzle,' she told him. 'I've got a ton of admin to do and I haven't had time for lunch yet.'

'Don't forget I'm feeding you tonight.'

'Only if Daisy's OK. Otherwise I'll stay.'

'She'll be fine. I'll come and find you when she's in Recovery.'

'Do that. I'll talk to Olive—and Dan, if he's around.'

Marco growled under his breath, and Alice just shrugged and left him to it. Dan would do what Dan would do, and it was Olive's problem, not theirs. All they could do was support the family as well as they could, and get Daisy better, and hopefully she was now on the road to recovery and a much, much brighter future.

CHAPTER FOUR

THEIR DINNER WAS postponed and Marco stayed in the hospital again overnight, but Daisy was doing well in PICU after her second operation and the next day they felt they could relax a little, so they rescheduled for seven.

Alice rang the bell right on the dot, and he opened the front door and she stepped inside and looked around curiously.

'Wow, what a fabulous house! I love all the period features.'

'Thank you. I like it. It was a bit of a run-down mess when I got it, but I've had a lot of work done over the last fourteen years, bits here and there, and now I can just enjoy it. Come on through to the kitchen.'

She followed him, taking the original encaustic floor tiles in the entrance hall with the intricate border pattern round the edges, the mahogany banister rail that curved gracefully upwards, the cherubs supporting the plaster arch spanning the hall—a much grander version of her own more simple arch—and then they walked through into the kitchen and time-travelled forward about a hundred and fifty years.

'Wow!' she said, craning her neck to look at the skylights where the room had been extended at the side, the double doors out of the end of the dining area, the acres of gleaming integrated appliances to the right set in a wall of cupboards, and jutting out as a divider between the two parts of the room was a pale granite worktop over base units painted a soft, muted grey.

How had he possibly afforded a house like this smack in the middle of Cambridge? Family money? Maybe. He'd said they did good weddings and everyone knew weddings didn't come cheap.

She ran her fingers over the granite and sighed. 'Oh, Marco, I love this room.'

He laughed softly. 'I love it, too, but it's a bit of a self-indulgence, rather like the rest of the house.'

'Well, why not, if you like it? It's not that big.'

'It's bigger than it looks. It has five bedrooms—well, no, not really. It has a loft conversion with an en suite and a fantastic view, which I use for guests, and I have one as a study and another as a dressing room, and then there's my room and another spare but, yes, it is ridiculous, before you say it.'

She bit her lip but the laughter bubbled out anyway. 'I wasn't going to be so rude, but I thought mine was outrageously expensive, and it's nothing like as big or as gorgeous as this.'

'It wasn't always gorgeous. I've had it a long time, and it was a bargain,' he said, taking things out of the fridge. 'And anyway, I've rented it out to bring in an income for a lot of the time and put the money back into doing it up. It's an investment.'

He'd turned towards the hob and placed a pan on it, and she stared at his back, slightly shocked by that last throwaway comment. 'It's your *home*, Marco.'

He shrugged. 'It can be both. And, yes, it's definitely my home. It's good to be back in Cambridge again, I'm enjoying it. I'm looking forward to the summer. The garden's beautiful, and it takes a lot of work but it's relaxing. It's my detox for the mind.'

'I thought that was running?' she said, settling herself on a high stool on the other side of the granite peninsula so she could watch him as he worked.

'That, too,' he said with a grin. 'Can I get you a drink?'

He put the food down in front of her with a twinge of concern. He'd found the recipe on the internet, ordered the ingredients and had them delivered to the hospital and spent the last half-hour throwing it together.

It was a sort of minced chicken and sautéd *cavolo nero* stir fry with an Italian twist, and just because he was starving he'd cooked some pasta for himself to serve with it, but he wondered if it might be too much for her delicate stomach.

'Wow, this is tasty,' she said, to his relief, and bit by bit, while they talked about this and that and not a lot, she ate it all. Then finally she pushed her plate away and smiled at him.

'OK?'

She gave a little laugh. 'More than OK, Marco. It was delicious. Thank you. I didn't realise how hungry I was. I've got so used to it, but it doesn't normally make me feel ill.'

'I guess that's because you're not normally pregnant,' he said drily as he gathered up the plates. 'Come and sit down, I'll put the kettle on and we can have tea. Peppermint would be my guess?'

She laughed again. 'I'm sorry, I'm a bit predictable. Do you know what I'd really like, though, while the kettle boils? A guided tour of your house.'

He frowned for a second, his mind running over the state he'd left the bedroom in, the bathroom—and then he shrugged. 'I can't guarantee it's tidy. I haven't been here for two days and my cleaning team haven't been.'

'You have a *team*?' she asked, her eyes widening.

'Not like that. A couple. They come once a week for an hour and run the vacuum cleaner over and dust and clean the bathroom and kitchen, change the sheets, that sort of thing. I don't make a lot of mess so they rotate the rooms.'

He could hear her mind working and frowned. 'What?'

She shrugged. 'It would never occur to me.'

'What, to have a clean and tidy house?'

'No, to pay someone to do it. My grandmother still cleans her own house and she's eighty-seven.'

He felt his eyes widen, then thought of his own grandmother, his mother's mother, much the same age, still fiercely independent. Maybe they weren't so different, but he was pretty sure his sisters didn't know one end of the vacuum cleaner from the other. One of the benefits, or not, of a privileged upbringing.

He took her upstairs—tidy, to his relief, as it hadn't been a foregone conclusion—and showed her first the guest suite in the attic, then the main floor, with his study that was a little chaotic but a practical room, the spare room, and then finally his room with a balcony and a wonderful view through French doors over the garden.

He turned off the light and switched on the outside lights on the balcony, and they lit up the first part of the garden so she could see it through the sparkle of the falling rain.

'Oh, that's gorgeous! How long is it?'

He shrugged. 'I don't know, I've never measured it. There are several "rooms" that you have to pass through to get to the end, and each one has its own identity. I'll show you at the weekend, if you like—assuming you're not busy and it isn't pouring with rain.'

He switched off the outside light and turned, and she was just there, inches from him in the shadowed room, lit only by the light spilling from the landing. And the bed, his ridiculously self-indulgent super-king-size bed, was just *there*.

For a moment he stood there, so tempted to reach out and touch her, to draw her into his arms, to kiss her slowly, tenderly, lingering over every sip and nibble, and she looked up and met his eyes in the dim light and he was lost.

He reached for her at the same moment she reached for him, taking her in his arms and touching his lips to hers—just lightly, nothing too intense, nothing hasty like before, but slow, tender, lingering...

He felt the tension between them tighten, felt it in her body as if it was his own, felt the need, the yearning—and then she stepped back out of his arms and turned and headed for the door, and the moment was gone.

'I expect the kettle's boiled now,' she said, and he wasn't sure if he'd imagined it, or if her voice sounded just a little bit strained.

He made them both tea with fresh peppermint, fragrant and delicate, and she sipped it gratefully, her hands cradling the mug as she blew on it and tried not to think about that vast bed just above them in his bedroom.

If she hadn't pulled away they might well have been lying in it now, making love the way he'd told her she deserved on the night of the gala, when they'd finally given up fighting it in the consulting room and all but torn each other's clothes off in their haste. Well, she had, anyway.

His kiss tonight couldn't have been more different.

Why had he kissed her like that, so gently, so delicately, almost soothingly? Except it hadn't soothed her at all but, oddly, it had wound the tension inside her even tighter.

She'd told herself he was only being so caring because of the baby, but his kiss hadn't felt like that at all—instead, the tenderness of it had been so unexpected, so loving, almost as if he cherished her—her, not the baby—and that had confused her completely, when frankly she was confused enough.

'So, you've got a day-case list tomorrow morning,' she said to break the silence that seemed to be stretching to eternity.

'Yes, I have. I need to be in early to go over the notes.'

'Anything interesting?'

'Not really, I don't think. All pretty routine stuff. A couple of endoscopies, that sort of thing. Nothing exciting, which is good because I want to be on hand for Daisy.'

'Yes, I'm still worried about her. I'm much happier now than I was, but still. I might go back to the hospital and spend the night there, just in case.'

'There's no need. I can go in if necessary, but I don't think it will be, and I've left instructions for them to ring me if they're concerned. I've left my stuff in the on-call room I used for the last two nights just in case, so it might as well be me.'

She didn't argue. Frankly, although she'd eaten everything he'd given her and felt better for it, she knew the morning would be less than lovely.

She drained her cup and put it down on the coffee table.

'That was delicious. Thank you—not just for the supper, but for looking after me, and for taking the nights. I know I'm a bit ungracious when you nag me to eat and rest, but feeling like this doesn't come easily and I could never have cooked that for myself.'

'You're not ungracious, and you're very welcome.'

'You're a liar. I have been less than grateful.'

'Your independent streak a mile wide?'

She laughed softly and chose not to answer that one. 'I ought to go.'

His eyes met hers over the coffee table as they both stood up. 'You could always stay,' he said softly, his eyes curiously tender, and for a second she dithered, the memory of their kiss tempting her almost beyond reason, but then common sense cut in again and she shook her head. The last thing she needed was an audience first thing in the morning when she was at her worst.

'I don't think that's such a good idea. And anyway, you've got an early start tomorrow and mornings aren't good for me at the moment. I wouldn't want to put you off your breakfast.'

'That's not likely,' he said with an understanding smile. 'But whatever. It's your choice. Have you got your car here, or do you want me to drive you home?'

'No, but I can walk, it's not far.'

'But it's raining, and I don't like the idea of you walking around the city at night alone.'

She nearly laughed at that. 'Marco, I'm thirty-seven! I'm not stupid.'

'No, but you are a woman and that makes you vulnerable, and I'd never forgive myself if something happened to you, so if it's all the same with you, I will take you home.'

She smiled then and gave in, knowing she was never going to win the argument and not really wanting to, anyway, as it was raining. 'Thank you. I'd love a lift, I haven't got my mac. It was dry when I left home.'

He showed her out to the car, drove the short distance to her house and pulled up outside. It would have been so easy to reach out to him again, to lean over and kiss that firm, mobile mouth that showed every flicker of his feelings.

Not a good idea, because then she'd let herself fall in love with him and she didn't know him well enough yet.

She had to trust him before she could dare to let that happen, and she wasn't quite there yet.

She reached for the door handle instead, and he got out of his side, came round to her and walked her to the door, then as she put her key in the lock and opened the door she turned back to thank him and his hand cupped her cheek.

'Goodnight, *tesoro*,' he murmured. 'Sleep well.'

His mouth brushed hers, the lightest, sweetest touch that sent fire searing through her body, and then before she could change her mind he got back into the car and raised his hand in farewell as he drove away.

She swallowed her disappointment and told herself it was probably just as well. They had to forge a friendship that would last throughout their baby's childhood and beyond, and a messy affair could compromise that. Ignoring the wails of regret from her body and her heart, she went inside, closed the door and went to bed alone.

It was strange, how simple and somehow cramped her house seemed to be after spending time in Marco's.

It felt—unfriendly? Surely not. She loved it, she'd chosen everything in it, and she liked it. But oddly, after last night at his, this morning it felt empty and soulless, and she realised she felt lonely.

She'd *never* felt lonely in her life! Well, only once or twice, if you didn't count the time after she'd revealed her diagnosis to the man who'd trashed her already fragile body confidence. She'd certainly felt lonely then, but somehow grateful for it, because she wasn't going to say or do anything to hurt herself, and being lonely wasn't a bad thing in comparison to the hurt he'd inflicted.

But Marco had never hurt her, never said anything cruel or unkind or other than gently teasing. Could she let herself fall in love with him? Did she dare?

Maybe…

And if she did, would they end up living in his beautiful home? She could almost picture it, picture their baby on the floor in the relaxed living space beyond the kitchen, lying on a mat and kicking her legs.

Her legs? Or his?

Her hand slid down and lay over her abdomen, still board-flat, of course, at this stage. Flatter even than usual, with her loss of appetite. Without Marco she'd be fading away, she realised, and she made herself eat breakfast although it was the last thing she wanted to do.

It worked, of course. She had scrambled egg again, with avocado this time and a good scrunch of salt over the top, and by the time she reached the hospital she was feeling almost human. She was missing her exercise routine, but for now she didn't feel up to it and anyway, she was busy and worried about Daisy.

She found Marco at the little girl's bedside in PICU, carefully examining Wuzzle. He was listening to the teddy's heart with his stethoscope, and then Daisy's, and then he put the stethoscope on Daisy and let her listen to his own heart.

And she smiled, which made Alice's eyes well up.

'Morning, all,' she said brightly, and as he turned his head and looked at her, Daisy pulled a strange face.

'Your heart just went faster,' Daisy said innocently, her voice drowsy from medication.

Did it? That was interesting…

'That must be because Alice crept up on us and made me jump.'

Daisy giggled sleepily, and he retrieved his stethoscope and slung it round his neck, throwing Alice a wry grin.

'Have you come to check up on me?'

'No, I've come to see how Daisy is.'

'Daisy's doing well, aren't you, Daisy?' he asked her, and the little girl nodded.

'I'm a bit sore and a bit thirsty, but Marco says I can have little drinks now and I'll be better soon and my tummy won't hurt any more then.'

'We hope not,' Alice said with a smile. 'That's why we had to operate on you again, to make you better, even if it doesn't feel like it now. How's Wuzzle doing?'

'He's getting better, too. He slept all night.'

'Oh, that's really good. I am pleased.' Her eyes flicked back to Marco and for some reason her heart tumbled in her chest.

'So, shall we get on with the rest of the day?' she asked briskly. 'I thought you had day cases?'

'I do, but they're not here yet, it's only seven-thirty.'

Was it really? She hadn't even looked at her watch, not since she'd woken up and run to the bathroom, but thinking about it Evie wasn't at her post in ICU reception yet.

'Don't you need to read the notes?'

'Done it. I'm super-efficient, Alice. Firing on all cylinders.'

'So I can see,' she said drily, but she couldn't stop the smile. 'That must be why your heart's revving up.'

His mouth quirked and he kissed his fingertip and pressed it to the tip of Daisy's nose.

'Byebye, *piccolo*. I'll see you later, OK? And remember, only tiny sips of water.'

She nodded, and Marco joined Alice and they walked towards her office. 'Any sign of her parents this morning?' she asked, because it worried her that they hadn't been at Daisy's bedside.

'Yes, her mother was there, she went off to have breakfast, and her father's going to pop in later. I got the feeling she wasn't happy but he has no choice, she says. If he doesn't work, the company will fold and there are a lot of people relying on him. She seems very understanding but she's finding it tough, doing it all alone.'

'Of course she is. And I don't think Daisy's happy. I think she wants to see much more of her father.'

'I think they both do. So, how are you today?' he asked as he shut the door of her office behind them, and she laughed.

'Thoroughly average, thank you. I'm struggling to understand how people can have more than one child.'

'Because women definitely aren't the weaker sex,' he said drily. 'Men would never do it twice. On the subject of children, by the way, Ivy's been admitted for further tests. She's in a little family suite so Theo can keep an eye on her, and Madison Archer is due to arrive soon.'

'Ah, yes, the American diagnostician he managed to collar.'

'Yup. I think he's pinning a lot of hope on her, so let's hope she lives up to his expectations. From what he was saying last night, it's all pretty vague and he has no idea what on earth can be wrong with her.'

'Last night?'

He grinned ruefully. 'Yeah. I spent the night here in the end. I wanted to be close to Daisy, just in case—you know.'

'I do. I wish I'd known, I spent half the night worrying.'

'You don't need to worry.'

She rolled her eyes. 'Marco, that's like telling me I don't need to breathe. I can't help it.'

The grin widened into a wry smile. 'No, me, too. Anyway, so Theo and I chatted about Ivy for a while, and then we talked about the PAT dog I told you about, and I'm going to contact Alana and ask if she and Doodle can come in soon and visit Ivy. And I thought maybe Daisy would benefit, as well. She's going to be here for another couple of weeks, I would think.'

'Yes, she will. I'm not letting her go until she's entirely right and eating normally. Ditto Amil Khan. He might like to meet the dog, too. I take it Doodle is civilised?'

Marco laughed, his eyes crinkling. 'Civilised? Yes, he's civilised. He's immensely gentle, and utterly lovely. He's like the softest teddy bear you've ever felt, and he's warm and cuddly and he has the biggest, daftest eyes in the world. He's just a sweetheart.'

'Have you talked to his owner yet?'

'No. I wanted to get the OK from Theo first, but I'll ring her this morning.'

'What, in between your day cases and all your other duties?'

'That's the one,' he said with a cheeky grin, and waggling his fingers at her he left her to deal with the mountain of admin that was waiting for her.

She didn't mind. It meant she could sit quietly in her office, sipping chilled water and nibbling on bland, salty snacks that she wouldn't normally touch but which seemed to be the only thing that kept her going, but she found herself unable to concentrate.

Daisy was clearly missing her father, didn't see nearly enough of him. Was this what was in store for their child, to feel cheated on a daily basis because his or her parents weren't together?

But apart from that one night, and Marco's constant nagging to her to eat or rest, there was nothing between them. No, that wasn't quite true. He'd kissed her yesterday in his bedroom, and asked her to stay, and she'd said no and he'd kissed her again when he'd taken her home. If she'd stayed, they would have made love, but would it have made a difference? Would it have brought them closer to a real, potentially lasting relationship, or stirred up the embers and set light to them again, just when it was all under control?

She had no idea, and there was a bit of her about a mile wide that was reluctant to put it to the test. Being torn apart once by someone she'd thought loved her was enough. She wasn't going to let it happen again, and it was much, much too soon to take anything for granted with Marco.

She had another sip of water, put him out of her mind and turned her attention to the day.

Three hours later, by which time she'd seen three new outpatients and tackled a heap of admin, she had a call from Marco.

'Come down to main reception. There's someone I want you to meet.'

She glanced at her watch. She was about to go for lunch anyway, so she could go that way. 'OK. Going to give me any clues?'

'Nope.'

She rolled her eyes, told him she'd be there in two minutes and made her way down to the glass-fronted circular reception area in the centre of the hospital. As she came out of the lift, she could see Marco standing with a young blonde woman on the far side of a group of sofas, and she made her way towards them, her curiosity piqued.

'Marco.'

He glanced across at her and smiled, and as she took the last few steps something pale gold and fluffy wafted across the floor by the sofa. Another step further and the waving fluff attached itself to the tail of an even fluffier body as the dog—at least she assumed it was a dog!—got to its feet and turned a hapless, tongue-lolling smile in her direction.

'Oh—you have to be Doodle!' she said with a laugh, and walking round the end of the sofa she stooped and fondled the softest head she'd ever felt. 'Oh, you soft, soft thing,' she crooned, staring down into melting brown doggy eyes that begged her to pour out her worries.

'Oh, he's so sweet,' she said, straightening up and meeting the smiling eyes of the blonde woman on the other end of the lead. 'Hi. You must be Alana. I'm Alice.'

She shook hands, her left hand still fondling Doodle's ears, and then she felt a weight settle against her left leg as Doodle sat down at her side, one surprisingly heavy foot resting on hers as if to anchor her there. She was more than happy to be anchored.

'Oh, Marco, you were absolutely right, he's gorgeous! Has Theo met him yet?'

Marco shook his head. 'No, not yet. He's just making a phone call and he's coming down—ah, here he is. If Doodle passes his test, he's going up to see Ivy.'

Alice smiled and gave Doodle one last fondle. 'I can't see how he could possibly fail. He's the most gorgeous thing I've ever met.'

Marco arched a brow and his mouth twitched. 'I could take offence at that,' he said lightly, and she chuckled.

'Seriously? The dog's way cuter. Right, I have to go for lunch. Lovely to meet you, Alana. I hope it goes well and you can join the team. I'm sure Daisy would adore Doodle—he's just like her teddy, Wuzzle, only even cuddlier, and the poor little thing could do with all the friends she can get.'

'Well, she'll certainly have a friend in Doodle,' Alana promised, and Alice left them just as Theo joined the group.

She headed towards the cafeteria, and a quick glance

over her shoulder showed Theo crouching down, the dog sitting up with his paws on Theo's shoulders, nose to nose.

She had to smile. It looked like love at first sight, and never mind Ivy, Theo could do with some love in his life right now and a therapy session with Doodle might be just the ticket for both of them.

'So how did it go with Doodle?'

Marco perched a hip on the corner of her desk and smiled a little sadly. 'Ivy adored him. Theo said it was the first time she'd really smiled in weeks, and he was pretty choked.'

She tutted softly. 'Oh, poor Ivy. So I take it Theo was convinced?'

'Yes, absolutely. He's going to ask if she can come every day for a short while and he's making a very generous donation to the Pets As Therapy charity, which, knowing Theo, doesn't surprise me, so I'm pretty sure we'll be seeing a lot more of her soon.'

'Won't Doodle get fed up with all that cuddling?' she asked, but Marco just laughed.

'I doubt it. He lives for cuddles and he just adores children.'

'How come Alana's got time?'

He shrugged. 'She's got a grooming business and she trains dogs, so a lot of her work is in the evenings, and she has staff to do the grooming so she can do the thing she loves, which is working with children. She's never said anything, but I get the impression children aren't on the cards for her. I think she might have had cancer as a teenager, which is how she got involved with this, so she's been doing it for years now—maybe ten? Doodle's her second dog. Her old dog's retired now from the cuddling, but she was a sweetie, too.'

Alice tipped her head on one side and tried to stifle a pang of what felt remarkably like jealousy. 'It sounds as if you know her quite well.'

He shook his head. 'No, not really. I met her when I was working locally a few years ago, and I bump into her every now and again out walking the dogs in the morning.'

'And she gave you her number?'

He peered closely at her and laughed. 'Are you jealous, Alice?'

She felt herself colour slightly. 'No, of course I'm not, don't be ridiculous. It just seemed—odd, that's all.'

'Not odd. I know her name, I know she has a grooming parlour, I know where it is, I looked it up and got her number. It's not rocket science, Alice. Or subterfuge. She's just an acquaintance.'

And now she felt stupid. 'Sorry. I wasn't quizzing you, it just seemed as if you knew her rather better than that,' she said, making it even worse, and giving up, she grabbed the open file on her desk, slapped it shut and stood up. 'Right, I need to review some test results and do a ward round. Are you coming, or are you going to sit there all day and do nothing?'

He got lazily to his feet, tipped up her chin and laughed softly into her face as he stooped and dropped a kiss on her lips.

'God forbid I should pause for a minute. I only started work at five this morning,' he said drily, and opened the door for her in a display of courtesy that made her feel even more grumpy and ungracious.

Which just annoyed her even more.

CHAPTER FIVE

ALICE THOUGHT THE weekend would never come.

She'd been struggling with the early mornings and the relentless routine, made harder by the fact that, until it was blindingly obvious, she had no intention of telling anyone about the baby. It was hard to find time to eat, never mind rest, and because no one knew about the baby she found herself putting on an act, pasting on a cheerful face when she just wanted to crawl into a corner and sleep for a week.

And then, finally, it was the weekend. Daisy was improving, so was Amil, none of the other patients were a worry, so when Saturday morning dawned she took it easy, giving herself the luxury of surfacing slowly and gently. She ate a small but nutritious breakfast, surprised herself by keeping it down and decided to go for a walk.

Not a run. She didn't feel up to that, and she certainly didn't want to work out in the gym at the hospital, but she needed to do something, and getting out in the late October sunshine was exactly what she needed.

It was a glorious day, and she strolled down to the river and along the Backs behind King's College Chapel and the colleges that bracketed it. She hardly ever took time to do this, to study the stunningly beautiful architecture of the old university buildings, or to walk beside the river and watch the ducks swimming along without a care in the world. She found a café not far away and had a peppermint tea out in the sunshine on the deck overlooking the river in the company of the dog walkers, the only ones rash enough to brave the great outdoors this late in the year.

Then she turned and walked back towards her house, her feet straying off course and leading her past Marco's house. She hesitated opposite it, wondering if it would be rude to knock on the door, but then she heard the rhythmic thud of feet on the path behind her. She stepped to one side, but the feet slowed and came to a halt.

'Buon giorno.'

She turned and found a heaving, muscular chest just inches from her face, the damp T-shirt clinging lovingly to it as it rose and fell with every breath. The chest she'd raked her nails down—

'Good morning,' she said, hauling her eyes up to his. 'Had a good run?'

'Long one. I've been out into the country—about twenty-five K or so? I don't know. Longer than usual, but it was such a beautiful day I just kept going.' He cocked his head on one side. 'Fancy a coffee?'

She recoiled slightly at that, and he must have seen because he grimaced in a smiley way.

'Sorry. Peppermint tea, then?'

'Don't you need to shower?'

He laughed and took a step back. 'Was that a hint? I can shower quickly, *bella*. Give me five minutes. Come on, because it's such a lovely day, and I want to show you my garden.'

He didn't wait for an answer, just jogged across the road, unlocked his front door and stood holding it while he waited for her. She shrugged, shook her head laughingly in despair and followed him in.

* * *

He showered quickly, as he'd promised, although he would happily have stood there for several more minutes being pounded by the deluge of hot water streaming over his aching muscles. Still, at least he'd washed the sweat off.

He towelled himself roughly dry, pulled on clean jeans and a sweater and went down to the kitchen. Alice was perched on a stool at the breakfast bar, flicking through a recipe book. Looking at the pictures, he imagined, since it was Italian and he knew she didn't speak a word of his mother tongue.

'Seen anything interesting?' he asked, and she glanced up, a fleeting expression on her face that vanished before he could analyse it.

'Not really.' She shut the book and swivelled round to look out of the wall of glass at the end of the room. 'Your garden looks lovely.'

'It is. Peppermint tea?'

'Please.'

She'd boiled the kettle already, he realised, and nipped some shoots off the pot of mint on the windowsill. He rinsed them under the tap, put them into mugs and poured the boiling water over them. The fresh, clean scent rose in the steam, and he slid a mug across the worktop towards Alice.

'Here you go. So—have you had any more thoughts about my sister's wedding?' he asked, propping himself up against the granite and blowing the steam off his mug.

She turned her head to look at him, then picked up her mug and swivelled back towards the garden again.

'Not really. Tell me more about it. How dressy is it? How formal? How many people?'

He laughed gruffly and put the mug down. 'I have no idea. Two hundred?'

'Two hundred?' she said, glancing back at him, her eyes widening.

He shrugged. 'Maybe more. At least half of them will be family in one way or another, then some business contacts, neighbours, family friends, and their own friends. There'll be a lot of people there.'

'So where would we stay?'

'At my family house or somewhere on the estate. Where else?'

'I have no idea, that's why I'm asking.' She swivelled back to face him, her eyes a little wary. 'Will they be expecting us to share a room?'

He shook his head. 'No, not if I tell them we aren't together, and I don't want to invite any unnecessary speculation about our relationship at this point—and I certainly don't think they need to know about the baby yet.'

'No. No, absolutely not. So—um—the dress code?'

He shrugged. 'The usual—I'll be wearing a suit, of course, probably a tux. You could wear the dress you wore for the gala, so long as you cover it with a jacket or a wrap or something for the ceremony. And you'll need something for the night before. We'll have a dinner just for family, but it'll be quite dressy. Then the next day there'll be a civil ceremony in the town hall in the morning, followed by a religious ceremony in the church on the estate and then an endless round of eating and drinking and dancing until everyone gives up and goes to bed in the small hours. Then the following day it'll all start again, with a huge lunch for everyone before they set off home.'

She looked thoughtful, and not in a good way.

'That sounds pretty full-on,' she said, and he laughed.

'It's an Italian wedding. They are full-on. The wedding itself is on Sunday, the family dinner on Saturday, and we'd fly back on Monday afternoon.'

'Monday? But what about work?'

'We're booked off until Tuesday.'

'We? I haven't said yes yet!'

'You didn't need to. We have no new patients booked in, there's a short day-case list on the Tuesday and otherwise nothing apart from the usual routine, and we'll get back on Monday afternoon in time for a quick ward round and a catch-up. We won't need more than usual weekend cover, and we'll be back in on Tuesday to do any discharges. You've got an outpatients' list, and I've got the day cases.'

'You've got it all worked out, haven't you?'

'Yes, of course. For me, at least, because I was always going.'

She looked away again, turning her attention back to the peppermint tea so he couldn't read her eyes.

'So—if I come, do I really need to be there for the night before?' she asked after a slight pause.

'Yes,' he said firmly. 'It's remote, and we'll travel together. It's easier that way than trying to get there under your own steam. If you prefer, you could miss the dinner and eat in your room, but it's pretty pointless. Nobody bites.'

'Marco, I don't speak a word of Italian.'

He shrugged. 'That's fine. They all speak English, some better than others but enough to get by. You won't be isolated. And anyway, I'll be there. I won't throw you to the wolves, Alice.'

Wolves? Wrong choice of word, probably because it didn't seem to reassure her at all, so he put his mug down again, let the subject drop and headed for the doors at the end. 'Come and see the garden,' he suggested, and she slid off the stool, put her mug down beside his and followed him out.

* * *

He was right, it was a beautiful garden.

The first part close to the house was designed for overflow from the house and to bring the outside in, and although they weren't in flower she could see small hedges of lavender edging the paving, and behind them, some still in bloom, were roses.

She reached over to smell one and her foot brushed the lavender below and released a soft wave of scent from the foliage. It must be heavenly in the summer, she thought, and wondered if she'd be there to see it.

Not if she kept holding him at arm's length, but he'd just been so emphatic about telling his family they weren't together in order to avoid unnecessary speculation, and he clearly didn't want to mention anything about the baby.

She followed him up the garden, her hand sliding down protectively over her abdomen, her fingers splayed low over where the baby—their baby—was lying.

Was it really only six weeks tonight since the gala? How her life had changed. Not on the outside. The baby was tiny still; at this stage it was barely recognisable as a human foetus, hardly the size of a kidney bean—but not too small to make its presence felt in multiple tiny changes to her body. Yet nobody looking at her would know the fundamental nature of what was brewing, the earthquake that would shake up her life and change everything, with the baby at its epicentre.

It would change Marco's life, too, of course, which was one reason he wanted her to go to the wedding, to meet his family, the baby's grandparents and uncles and aunts and cousins. Hundreds of them, by the sound of it.

Was she going to go?

Maybe. There was a massive part of her that was curious about his family, about the place he'd grown up, the people he'd shared his early life with. She'd get to meet the people who were related to her baby. That was a plus point.

The other plus point, of course, was that she'd get to spend time with him away from the hospital, time out from reality when she could maybe see if they might have a future. Because they would have a future together, tied together for ever by their child, whether they were living as a couple or not. He'd be a part of her life for the next twenty years, at least, and she wasn't sure how that felt.

Exciting? Challenging? Terrifying?

She was so used to living alone, so used to making her own decisions, dictating her own timetable, choosing her hobbies, her food, her colour schemes, what she watched on the TV—all that would change if she was in a relationship. Did she want it to change?

Or did she want to be like Olive Lawrence, struggling to bring up a child with a largely absent and remote father figure lurking in the background?

Not that she could imagine Marco lurking.

No. He'd be at the centre of his child's life, playing a full and active role, and constantly underfoot—

'So, what do you think of it?'

She realised they'd reached the end of the garden, and she hadn't heard a word he'd said to her. She looked up and met his eyes, and he sighed softly and cupped her face in his hands and feathered the lightest kiss across her lips, a soft frown puckering his brow.

'Don't look so troubled, Alice. Is it the wedding?'

She shrugged. 'I don't know. The wedding, the baby— all of it. I'm afraid I'll lose it, worried about what the future will bring—it's all the unknowns, really.'

He tsked gently, and folded her into his arms, cradling her head against his broad, solid chest. She could hear his heart beating under her ear, thought of Daisy listening to it and laughing when it speeded up.

Had that really been because of her?

'Come to the wedding with me,' he urged softly. 'It will give us some time away from all of this, time just to be together, get to know each other away from work. Neutral territory.'

She eased out of his arms with a little laugh. 'Hardly that. It's your family home! I'll be like a fish out of water.'

'Nonsense. It'll be fine, *carissima*, believe me. Besides,' he went on, his eyes twinkling with mischief, 'I need you there to protect me from all the single women who'll be gathering round me like a school of piranhas.'

That made her laugh again, properly this time. 'You really do have a massive ego,' she teased, but he shook his head, the laughter fading from his eyes.

'No. They're after my status, my family's money. They don't care about me, they don't know me. It's all about what they can get for themselves.'

She frowned. 'That's horrible.'

'It is. But it's the reality.'

'Does your family really have that much money and status?' she asked, slightly shocked, and he gave a wry laugh and turned back towards the house. His ridiculously extravagant and beautiful house.

'Yes. Sadly. It doesn't interest me, not in the slightest, but it's there, and it's one of the reasons I needed to get away and just be myself, be a doctor, heal kids, because that's who I am.'

'And they didn't understand?'

'No. They didn't. Well, except my grandmother, my mother's mother. Nonna understands—not that she approves of the way I did it, but at least she can see why and she's hugely proud of me now. She's the only one who is. I think you'll like her.'

'She'll be there?'

'Yes, of course. Her granddaughter's wedding? She wouldn't miss it for the world. And I have to say she and my baby sister Annalisa, the bride, are the only two reasons I'm going, because I can't bear to hurt either of them.'

He opened the door for her, and they went back into the kitchen.

'Come, I'll show you where I grew up,' he said, and led her up the stairs to his study. He pulled up a chair, turned on the laptop and with a few keystrokes went onto a website.

'This is where I lived,' he said, and clicked through the gallery of photos—a beautiful, classic Tuscan stone house set high on a hill with stunning views all around it.

She felt her jaw sagging. 'It's huge!'

'It's a *castello*—an ancient castle. Parts of it are probably over twelve hundred years old, but nobody's sure and it's been extended so many times, a bit on here, another bit on there. It's been in the family for over five hundred years, and everyone's put their mark on it. It's surrounded by a sprinkling of small villas and farmhouses, which have been turned into guest accommodation to supplement the estate. We grow grapes to make our own wine, olives for oil, there are chestnut woods that are harvested, sheep that are milked for cheese-making, and we do tourism. Tours of the cantina—the winery—and tours of the estate and surrounding area. It's a big family business.'

'And they wanted you to be part of it?'

'They wanted me to run it.'

'But you're a doctor!'

'I know, but I'm also the firstborn son. It's my *duty* to

stay and carry on the family tradition. That's more important.'

She sat back and stared at him. 'Seriously? They thought that was more important than following your heart?'

'Yes. All except Nonna.' He closed the computer and turned to face her, his eyes a little bleak. 'So you understand why I had to leave.'

'Of course I understand! Oh, Marco—don't they realise what you'd have been giving up? How many children would have suffered if you'd given in to them?'

He shrugged. 'There are other doctors who could have done my job. They have no other firstborn son.'

'But it's not like it's the monarchy! Don't they have any other sons or daughters who want to carry the torch?'

He laughed. 'Yes, of course. Two of my brothers and one of my sisters are heavily involved. That's not the point. It was *my* job, *me* who was meant to do it. Not my brother Gio, who's a Master of Wine and a first-class sommelier. He has a nose for wine like nobody I've ever met, but he's not good enough for them, and neither is Raffaello, who has a first-class business brain and has done a huge amount for the family business. It should have been me, despite the fact that I don't really like wine and couldn't give a damn about business or earning money.'

'That sounds—I don't know. Medieval! It's awful!'

He shook his head, his laughter weary this time. 'No, it's not awful, they're just so steeped in tradition that they don't know how to escape from it. It's worked for generations, and then I come along and spoil it.'

He leant forward and took her hands. 'Please come with me. I love it there, and I love them, but they suffocate me. Come with me and let me show you what is so much a part of me that even I can't deny it completely. And meet my *nonna*. She'll love you, Alice. She's a proud, strong woman, so much like you, but she's getting old now and she won't last for ever. I really want her to meet the mother of my child.'

Because she might not live long enough to see the baby? It was a plea from the heart and she couldn't refuse him that.

She nodded. 'OK. I'll come with you and meet your grandmother and see where you grew up. You obviously love it, and it might help me to understand more about the father of my child if I know what moulded you.'

For a moment he didn't reply, then he bowed his head slightly in acknowledgement. 'Thank you,' he murmured. His hands, still holding hers, squeezed gently, and he leant forward and touched his lips to hers.

It was a fleeting kiss, or meant to be, but she ended up in his arms and only a massive effort of will made her able to ease away before it escalated into something more.

'I need to go, Marco,' she said, but she couldn't hold his searching eyes, and after a moment he sighed and stood up, freeing her from her trance.

'Me, too. I want to go back to the hospital and check on Amil and Daisy, and one of my patients I should have discharged before the weekend who I wasn't happy enough to let go. But—maybe later? Can I cook you dinner?'

She was so tempted—ludicrously tempted—but she shook her head. 'I've got food in the fridge that needs eating,' she said, which was a lame excuse but the best she could come up with at such short notice, and it seemed to satisfy him. Maybe he was just being kind, following through on his promise to be there for her and help her through her pregnancy?

They went back downstairs, and he reached for the door and opened it.

'Take care, Alice. I'll see you tomorrow, maybe.'

'Maybe. I've got a lot of things to do.'

He nodded, his eyes somehow withdrawing, and his smile, when it came, didn't quite reach them.

'I'll see you on Monday, then,' he said, and she nodded and stepped out into the sunshine, but it had lost its magic, the light fading with the light in his eyes, and she felt a weight in her chest that was probably common sense but felt oddly like disappointment.

His phone rang at six the next morning, and he reached for it, blinking his eyes open as he scanned the screen.

Alice? At this time of the morning?

'Alice? Are you OK?'

'No.' Her voice had a slight shake in it, and he threw off the bedclothes and reached for his clothes. 'I—I've had a bleed. Nothing much, just a few spots, but—'

She broke off, and he rammed a hand through his hair and sucked in a deep breath. 'OK. Where are you?'

'Where? Um—I'm at home.'

'Stay there. Unlock the front door and go and lie down on the sofa. I'm on my way.'

He cut off the call, threw on his clothes and was there in five minutes, grateful that the streets were deserted. Her door was unlocked and he pushed it open and called her name.

'In here,' she said, and he went into the sitting room and found her curled up at one end of the sofa, a blanket over her and her face streaked with tears.

'Oh, Alice...'

He gathered her up into his arms, his heart aching as she sobbed into his chest. Not for long. She only gave herself that luxury for a moment before she pushed him away and sniffed, her hands scrubbing the tears from her cheeks.

'So—what happened?'

'Nothing dramatic. I woke up, went to the loo and there were these spots of blood.'

'Anything since?'

She shook her head. 'I don't think so. I can't feel anything.'

'No pain anywhere?'

Again she shook her head. 'No. No pain, nothing. And I think I must still be pregnant because I still feel horribly sick, but I'm afraid to eat in case I need to go to Theatre.'

He frowned. 'It's a long time since I did any obstetrics, but I would think that's unlikely today. Maybe if you go on to miscarry they might need to do a D&C, but not just for a slight bleed. It would have to be a lot worse, I think. Mind if I have a feel of your abdomen, just to check it's not an ectopic or anything like that?'

She shook her head and rolled to her back, and he pressed very lightly, very carefully over her slender abdomen, pushing gently to see if it caused any pain, but she said there was none, to his relief.

'I think that rules out an ectopic,' he said, 'but I do think you need to go in.'

She nodded. 'Yes, that makes sense. So maybe I should try and eat something first.'

'What can I get you?'

She shrugged. 'I don't know. Cold water? There's some in the fridge. And maybe some fruit. There are some slices of mango in there, too.'

'OK.' He left her and went into the kitchen, put the kettle on, took the mango and water back to her and sat down by her feet. 'Have you done another pregnancy test?'

She shook her head. 'No. I've got one—I bought a double pack last week because it was all they had in the supermarket I went to, so there's one left over, but I didn't think about doing a test when I was in the bathroom. I just wanted to talk to you—'

Her voice cracked and he reached out and rested a hand gently on her hip. 'Don't be scared, Alice. I'm here. I'm not going anywhere. Well, maybe in the kitchen to have a coffee,' he said with a wry smile, and she smiled back.

'Thank you.'

'What for?'

'All sorts of things, but most specifically never drinking coffee in front of me. I know you miss it, and I do appreciate it.'

He laughed softly and got to his feet. 'It's not much of a sacrifice, *cara.*'

He went back to the kitchen, spooned ground coffee into a cafetière and took it, a mug and the kettle out into her garden to make it, closing the door behind him to stop the smell filtering in.

And while he waited for it to brew, he checked on the local NHS trust website for advice on threatened miscarriage in the first trimester.

Bingo. There was an early pregnancy assessment unit in Cambridge, which opened at eight-thirty on Sundays. Good.

He poured and drank his coffee, rinsed his mouth so he didn't breathe coffee fumes all over her and went back and told her about the clinic. 'I think you should go and see someone there,' he said, and she nodded.

'Will you come with me?' she asked, as if she'd seriously doubted that he would, and he frowned in disbelief.

'Alice, of course I'll come with you. This is my baby, too, and I'm as concerned as you are. Of course I'll come. I wouldn't dream of letting you go alone.'

Her shoulders drooped, as if she'd been afraid he'd leave

her to it, and he knelt down beside her and put his arms around her, letting his head rest against hers.

'Don't be afraid, Alice,' he murmured. 'Lots of women have bleeding in the first trimester and go on to have a normal pregnancy.'

'And lots don't.'

'Shh. Let's cross that bridge when we get to it, hmm? If we do. And in the meantime, you need to eat.'

'I can't. I tried. The mango's too flavoured.'

'So what do you fancy?'

'Scrambled egg and avocado.'

He felt his eyebrow twitch and schooled his expression. 'With lots of salt, I imagine?'

Her smile was weak. 'How did you guess?'

It was delicious.

Well, delicious for something that hardly tasted of anything except salt, but that was fine by her. She sat up and ate it, sipped the cup of hot water he'd brought her and then went upstairs to wash and dress and pack a bag to take to the hospital, just in case. She was conscious all the time of his presence in the house, the sound of his movements, his voice on the phone, the sound of water running in the kitchen as he rinsed the plates, the clatter of the dishwasher being loaded.

She smiled to herself, wondering how he managed to be so domesticated and yet still needed a cleaning team to keep his house in order. Although she could do with a visit from them. She'd hardly done anything this last week because she'd felt so tired, and the house was beginning to look a little unkempt.

She zipped on her boots, straightened up and her hand slid down, coming to rest over her baby.

'Please be all right,' she whispered, her heart suddenly

flip-flopping at the thought that it might all go wrong. Might have *gone* wrong, and then she'd have lost not only the baby, but Marco, and all her dreams for the future…

She heard his tread on the stairs, a gentle tap on her bedroom door.

'Alice?'

She opened it and stepped straight into his arms, resting her head against his heart. It was beating strongly, the rhythm steady, solid, comforting.

Would her baby have a heartbeat?

Please, let my baby be all right…

'Come on, *tesoro*,' he murmured. 'Don't worry. We'll do this together. I won't leave you, I promise.'

She straightened up, and he slid his hand down her arm and threaded his fingers through hers, and she felt his strength seeping into her, giving her the courage to do this, to go to the hospital and find out if they still had a baby.

What happened after that she couldn't worry about now, but for now she had him, and that was enough.

CHAPTER SIX

THEY WERE AT the hospital before the clinic opened, but they were second in the queue and she was called in almost immediately.

'Want me to come?'

She felt a flicker of alarm. 'Please.'

He took her hand, as if he could read that she needed the comfort of his touch, and all through her examination he was either beside her or she could feel his presence.

She was asked a whole raft of questions, most of which Marco had already asked her, including whether or not she'd had a positive pregnancy test and when her last period had been, and then the nurse took her blood pressure.

'It's a little high. Is that normal for you?'

'I have PCOS,' Alice told her. 'It's not normally high, though. I keep it controlled with diet and exercise, but that's gone out of the window a bit in the last week with the pregnancy sickness.'

'OK. It could just be worry, then, but that's what you're here for so let's try and give you some answers. Do you mind if I examine you?'

'No, of course not,' she said, lying down on the couch and wishing Marco was there to hold her hand, not seated on the other side of the curtain out of reach.

The examination was gentle but thorough and brought an element of good news, which was a relief.

'Well, your cervix is tightly closed, you don't appear to have any significant bleeding at the moment and there's no abdominal tenderness, so that's all good, but I do want you to have an ultrasound scan to see if we can find out a bit more about what's going on,' the nurse said, stripping off her gloves and helping her off the couch. 'Once you've had that done, depending on what they find you'll have blood tests and we'll arrange a follow-up or admit you, but let's start with the scan and see what that comes up with. You'll need a transvaginal scan, so you'll have to make sure you have an empty bladder, and while you're doing that, if you could get me a urine sample I'll do a quick pregnancy test on it while you wait.'

Alice nodded, tugged her clothes straight and went back to Marco, who was sitting quietly, his eyes watchful.

'OK?' he asked softly, and she nodded.

She was shown to a toilet, armed with a little pot for her urine sample, and when she came back she was sent back out to the waiting room. A couple of minutes later the nurse emerged with the news that the test was positive, which showed she still had pregnancy hormones in her body, and although she knew that didn't necessarily mean the baby was still alive, it gave her some hope.

Until she saw that tiny heart beating with her own eyes she wouldn't dare believe it, though, and it was an agonising ten more minutes before she was called through for her scan.

'Do you want me with you?' Marco asked as she stood up, and she nodded.

'Yes—definitely. Unless…'

'No. I want to be there.'

'Then come—please?'

She undressed and lay down under a blanket, and he sat beside her and took her hand, his eyes fixed on hers as the sonographer inserted the probe. An image popped up on the screen and she turned her head to see it, hanging onto him for dear life. Her grip on his fingers must have been painful, but she couldn't let go, couldn't relax so much as a hair until—

The image settled, and as a fast, rhythmic whoosh, whoosh, whoosh filled the room, she felt his grip tighten.

'Is that—?' Marco asked, and she held her breath.

'That's your baby's heartbeat,' the sonographer told them with a smile, and the blurry little image blurred even more. 'It sounds good and strong. Look, this is the baby's head, and here's its heart—can you see it beating?'

Alice blinked hard to clear her vision, and there it was, a tiny bean of a thing, fatter at the head end, with a dark, pulsating blob in the centre, beating in time to the whooshing sound that filled the room.

'Oh…'

Was that her, or him? Both, she thought, staring at the screen, her heart swelling with love as she watched that bravely beating heart inside their tiny baby.

Marco removed his hand and fiddled with his phone for a second, and she realised he was recording it, filming the grainy little image, recording the sound of their baby's heartbeat as it filled the room with hope.

The sonographer took a few measurements, and smiled again. 'So, that's all looking good, spot on for eight weeks—did you say eight weeks today since your last period?'

'Something like that. Six weeks yesterday is the only possible time it was conceived,' she said, feeling a little numb as she realised how much had happened deep inside her body in those six short weeks. Lying there watching her baby's heart pumping was like an out of body experience, and she felt strangely light-headed, as if she was floating...

'These little things here are the arm buds, one each side, so, and down here we have the leg buds—oh, and it's doing a little wiggle for you! How about that. Do you want a photo?'

'Yes,' they said in unison, and then a little while later, after a few more measurements had been taken, the sonographer said, 'Right, you're all done,' and the image vanished from the screen.

'Wow,' Marco said softly, breaking the breathless silence, and for the second time she adjusted her clothes and sat up, her body shaking all over as she slid off the couch to her feet.

'I'm still pregnant,' she said unsteadily, looking up into his eyes, and to her horror and embarrassment, she burst into tears.

'Oh, Alice,' he murmured, and then his arms wrapped her tight against his chest, his lips pressed to her temple, and she could feel the thudding of his heart through his chest wall. 'It's OK, *amore mio*, it's all right. Our baby's OK.'

She could hear his voice cracking, and she tilted her head back and stared up into his eyes. His lashes were clumped together with tears, and as he bent his head and kissed her, she felt one fall on her cheek and mingle with her own...

'Better now?'

'Much better.'

Because she'd said she felt light-headed he'd got her a fruit tea and a banana in the café at the hospital, and they were still sitting there, armed with a follow-up appointment and the knowledge that their baby was still alive and seemed to be doing well, to her relief and his, too, she was sure of that now. She gave him a rueful smile. 'Thank you so much for coming with me.'

That seemed to shock him. 'Did you really imagine I'd let you do it alone, Alice? This is *my* baby, too. Of course I'm here.'

Her eyes welled again, and she nodded once more and looked down at her hands, twisting in her lap. 'I thought…'

'I know.' He reached out and took her hands, wrapping them in his and resting his head against hers. 'Come on, let's get out of here and take you home.'

He drove to his house, and as he cut the engine she turned and looked at him in surprise.

'This is your house.'

'Yes. I thought it would be better. I'll take you home if you'd rather, but I don't really want to leave you alone. I thought you could lie on the sofa and watch the birds in the garden while I work, and I can cook you lunch, if you like? I've got stuff in the fridge.'

She searched his eyes, not sure what she was looking for, but there was tenderness there in those rich brown depths and she nodded.

'That sounds nice. Thanks.'

'Don't keep thanking me, Alice. It's fine.'

It was fine, she realised as she followed him in. She didn't want to be alone, and she didn't want to be in her own house, she realised. It was nice enough, but Marco's house was more than that, it felt like a home, and hers had never felt as homely as his. Maybe because she'd moved in and started work and hadn't really had time to claim it, but Marco's taste and personality were stamped all over this house, and she loved it.

He settled her on the sofa, pampering her with plumped-up cushions and the softest, snuggliest throw tucked around her.

Not that it was cold in his house, but she felt chilled inside. Shock? Maybe, but that was slowly receding, leaving a sense of wonder.

'Can I see the recording?' she asked when he came back in with a glass of mint tea for her, and he sat down beside her, perching on the edge of the sofa, and turned it on so they could both watch it again.

Her finger reached out and hovered over the screen. 'It's so tiny.'

'It's a long time to the beginning of June.'

'It is. Just think, Daisy Lawrence was only three weeks older than this when her gut coiled the wrong way, but looking at it, how tiny and unformed it all is, it seems incredible that things don't go wrong more frequently. How can something so complex as a human being be so perfect so very often?'

'I have no idea. Life is a miracle, Alice. It never ceases to amaze me. Just listen to that.'

He played it again, the sound of their baby's heart filling the room, and she felt her eyes well with tears again.

'I never thought I'd ever hear that, my baby's heart beating. I could listen to it all day,' she said softly, and he handed her the phone and stood up, bending to drop a gentle kiss on her cheek.

'Be my guest. I'll go and see what I can find for lunch.'

She watched it over and over again, until the sound of their baby's heart became a part of her, a sub-rhythm playing quietly in the background as she fell asleep.

She was sleeping.

Good. She'd looked exhausted, racked with worry, and it wasn't over yet. Things could still go wrong, and he hadn't really registered until she'd told him she was bleeding just how much he cared, how very much the baby and Alice meant to him.

Far more than he'd imagined. Far more than was sensible, given her reluctance to let him into her life.

He retrieved his phone from the floor and left her to sleep, going back to the kitchen and turning down the oven. Lunch would keep, and a little longer in the oven wouldn't hurt it. He had plenty to do.

With one last look back at her, he went upstairs into his study, turned on his computer and settled down to work.

Her phone woke her, the sound penetrating her sleep and dragging her out of a strange and surreal dream in which she and Marco were walking along pushing a pram.

She groped in her bag, came up with the phone and glanced at the screen. Her mother.

She struggled into a sitting position and tapped the screen. 'Hi, Mum. How are you?'

'I'm fine, we're all fine. I just wondered how you are. I haven't heard anything from you for ages and I thought it was time to touch base, that's all.'

'Oh. Yes, I'm sorry, I've been ridiculously busy.' She shifted herself more upright, propping herself up against the back of the sofa and staring out at the garden. The sun was shining, and she could see the last of the roses blooming bravely behind the little lavender hedge. They'd be in flower again when the baby was born, she thought, and then realised she needed to tell her mother—or at least some of it.

'Mum, there's something I need to tell you,' she said abruptly, cutting off her mother's ramblings about what her father had been up to in the garden. 'I'm having a baby.'

The gasp was followed by silence, and then a tiny sob.

'Oh, Alice! David! David, come here! Alice is pregnant! So, come on, tell us all about it. Who's the father? Is it that gorgeous Italian guy you're working with?'

How on earth had her mother worked that out? Alice knew she'd been all over the hospital website looking at the profiles of the staff, and she'd been fixated on Marco since day one. Rather like she had herself.

'Yes, it is, but don't get over-excited, Mum, I've got a long way to go,' she said, suddenly regretting telling her because she was going to misunderstand and jump to the conclusion it was all sunshine and roses and it might not be—there might not even be a baby if it all went wrong, which it still might.

What was she thinking? She shouldn't have told her yet, especially when Marco was still—no, not distant, he'd never been distant, and if he was, she only had herself to blame, because she'd been holding him at arm's length, she realised, but he'd been amazing today. It was just the cosy, sentimental dream she'd been woken from which had made her blurt it out, and now her mother was in a tizzy of excitement and it was way too soon for that.

'Mum, stop it! Listen. There isn't going to be a wedding or anything like that. We're not—together,' she said, for want of a better way to put it. 'Marco and I are just col-leagues, friends, maybe, and he's going to be part of the baby's life but it was an accident, really, I never intended this to happen, but it has, and I thought you should know. I had a scan today, and—oh, his phone's gone. I was going to play you the recording of its heartbeat—'

'Here,' Marco said, appearing beside her and handing her the phone. He pressed the button to start it playing, and walked out into the kitchen, closing the door behind him.

She stared at the door, because there was something

about the way he'd closed it. Not hard, not loud, just—significant.

'Oh, darling, that's amazing,' her mother was saying tearfully as the recording came to an end, and Alice dragged her eyes off the door and answered a few more questions—how many weeks was she, when was it due, how was she feeling, was there anything she needed?

Only Marco, and from the way he'd shut that door it didn't look like that was happening any time soon. She answered the questions, said goodbye, hung up and got carefully to her feet.

Not together?

Dio, how could she say that after today? They'd waited together for news, held hands, gasped, cried—how was that *not together*?

He'd come down when he'd heard her voice, thinking he'd dish up their lunch as she was awake, but he'd never expected to hear that. Who was she talking to? Her mother, he thought. He might have heard her say that as he'd got to the bottom of the stairs. Right before she'd said they weren't *together*, just colleagues or maybe friends.

Colleagues? Friends? Maybe?

He felt gutted. Angry and frustrated and hurt and—just plain gutted that he meant so little to her, after all they'd been through this past week. He'd thought they'd made some progress when she'd agreed to go with him to the wedding, but apparently not.

Damn. He wished he hadn't asked her now, wished he hadn't booked their flights last night, but that was ridiculous, because a thousand things could happen in the fortnight before the wedding, including, although he hoped not with all his heart, her losing the baby. The baby that, after the initial shock, had suddenly made him realise just how much he wanted to be a father. How much he wanted a family—but it seemed he might be alone in that.

'Oh, Alice, what do you want from me?' he sighed, propping his hands on the edge of the worktop and dropping his head forward, staring at the floor as if it held any answers.

It didn't.

His own head did, but none that he wanted to hear. He'd been going to ask her to move in with him, to live here with him in this house so he could look after her and they could start to build a life together—and not just because of the baby. Because he wanted her, needed her.

Loved her?

No, it was too soon for that, but he had his answer now, anyway, and without the humiliation of having to ask her and have it thrown back in his face, because it seemed that whatever Alice wanted from him, it wasn't togetherness.

He heard the door open and he straightened up as she came in.

'Your phone,' she said, handing it to him with a searching glance. 'Thanks for that. I was telling my parents about it. They're ridiculously over-excited.'

'Was that really wise, until you're sure your pregnancy's secure?' he said, probably not as tactfully as he could have put it but the truth, for all that, and she sucked in a breath and stepped back.

'I just—I wanted to tell them. It seemed like the right thing to do. You think I shouldn't have told them? Do you still think I'm going to lose it?'

The look on her face ripped a hole in his heart, and if he could have swallowed the words, he would have done. 'I have no idea, Alice,' he said heavily. 'I sincerely hope not. As for telling them, they're your parents, not mine, only you can be the judge of that. Look, I need to go to the hospital. There's a chicken casserole in the oven keeping hot. Help yourself. I won't be long.'

'Is everything OK?'

'Yes, it's fine, I just want to check on Daisy and Amil and look over some paperwork before tomorrow's list. Help yourself to anything you need, and ring me if anything changes. I'll see you later.'

He almost kissed her goodbye, but thought better of it, pulling back into himself before he gave her the ammunition to hurt him any further.

She ate some of the casserole, but without any enthusiasm because she was worried now.

Worried that she might still lose the baby, which Marco seemed to think was a possibility.

Worried that she'd got her parents all excited, and then might have to snatch that happiness away.

Worried also that for some reason she'd lost the closeness she and Marco had had today at the hospital, because it seemed that somehow she had, but she didn't know why or how.

Why was he so cross that she'd told her parents? Or maybe he wasn't cross, but he was certainly something. Distant, at the very least, but only since her phone call and it had been like throwing a switch. Anyone would think she'd told *his* parents, but she wouldn't ever do that because it wasn't her place to tell them and, anyway, he had enough problems with them, by all accounts. But surely she could tell her own parents whatever she liked? Even if it *was* a little too soon, under the circumstances...

She pushed her plate away, barely touched, and gathered her things together. She had a sudden and desperate need to be back in her own home, not his, because she was done dreaming about happy ever after and letting herself get carried away with roses and lavender and ridiculous non-sense when she had no idea what he really felt or wanted.

She knew what she wanted—her life back on an even keel, without this emotional wringer she was putting herself through with Marco.

She didn't need him, she could do this alone. She was happy—more than happy—for him to be part of the baby's life, if there still was a baby in the end, but she didn't need him in hers, not if it meant this endless turmoil. She'd be fine. Really. Why not? Lots of women did it on their own.

She swiped away the tears that she hadn't even known were falling, and sitting down at the breakfast bar she scrawled a note.

Gone home, feeling much better. Thank you for looking after me. I'm fine now.
A

She hesitated, then didn't put an *x*, just left the note on the worktop where he'd find it, but as she got to her feet she heard the scrape of a key in the lock and Marco walked in.

He looked at her, looked at the coat over her arm and the note on the worktop and frowned.

'Where are you going?'

'Home. I thought I'd cluttered up your life enough today,' she said, and he swore softly and walked up to her, tilting her face up so he could see the tears that were welling again, to her disgust.

'Oh, Alice,' he murmured, and wiped them away with a gentle stroke of his thumbs. 'I'm sorry. I shouldn't have said that about the baby—'

'No, you're right, it is a possibility, and maybe it was too soon to tell my parents, but you didn't need to be so angry about it—'

'I wasn't angry!'

'Well, it certainly felt like it from where I was standing.'

He shook his head slowly, his eyes puzzled. 'No. I was never angry. Hurt, maybe. I thought we were getting somewhere today, getting closer, and then…'

'Then you heard me tell my mother we were just friends,' she said, realising what it was about the phone call that had upset him. Of course…

'*Colleagues*,' he said bluntly. 'How could you do that, Alice? How could you dismiss how close we were today?' He let out his breath on a soft huff and looked away. 'I was going to talk to you about us, about our relationship, see what we could build together so we have a strong foundation before the baby comes.'

He looked back at her, his eyes weary now. 'At the very least I thought we could be friends—good friends, close friends. Maybe more—much more. I know it's too soon to talk about what form the future's going to take for us, but we will have one, Alice, we'll have to, for the baby's sake, and maybe even for ours. We have to work towards that, and we have to do it together. I can't do it alone.'

She stared at him, feeling like her strings had been cut, and all the hurt and anger and worry drained away and left her exhausted and confused.

'I thought—I don't know what I thought. Marco, I'm sorry, I didn't mean to hurt you. It's just been a really difficult day, and I can't think straight. I need to go to bed, I'm so tired.'

'Then stay here, with me. At least for tonight.'

'I can't. It's not fair on you—'

He cupped her shoulders gently. 'What's not fair on me? Alice, I *want* you to stay. Let me look after you, please? You had a threatened miscarriage today and it brought it home to me how much I want our baby, how much I want to be part of its life, and part of yours. I don't know on what basis, but I do want to be part of it. Don't shut the door on that, Alice, please. There's far too much at stake.'

She stared up into his face, trying to read his eyes, but the light was behind him. 'You want to be part of my life?'

'Yes. Definitely. I will be, whatever happens. And who knows? We may end up together, we may not. I hope we do, but it's too soon yet, we need time before we can say that for sure. The last thing we need is to leap into marriage and end up with a hideous divorce and the baby caught in the middle. That's what could have happened with Francesca, and I won't let it happen to us. We need to take it steady, wait until we're sure. And in the meantime, you need to let me look after you, especially today.'

She gave a shaky sigh and rested her head against his chest, and he gathered her into his arms and held her, his thumb stroking her back rhythmically.

'I didn't mean it,' she said, and then tilted her head back so he could see her. 'About us just being colleagues. I was just trying to defuse the situation, because I didn't want my mother to start jumping to conclusions and telling all her friends there was going to be a wedding—and my phone hasn't stopped ringing. I've had to turn it off because my brothers have all been on the phone trying to talk to me and I just don't want to talk to them yet. I wish I hadn't told her—'

'No, you should have. She's your mother, Alice. A woman needs her mother at this time, it's what happens, all part of being a family. I'd like to meet them.'

'Would you?' She rested her head against his chest again. 'Be careful what you wish for, Marco. They can be pretty full-on.'

She heard the low chuckle deep in his chest. 'Oh, Alice. I have seven siblings to your three. Don't tell me about full-on. I know exactly how it is.' He eased away from her and turned her towards the sitting room. 'Come and sit down and put your feet up—unless you want to go to bed already? That's fine with me.'

She tipped her head on one side and smiled at him wryly. 'I don't believe I've said I'll stay,' she murmured, but he just smiled back.

'You didn't need to. So what's it to be? Sofa or bed?'

'Bed, I think—but I haven't got any things here.'

'Yes, you have. Your hospital bag was still in my car. I've brought it in.'

'You have? Wasn't that jumping the gun a bit?'

His smile had some of the old familiar Marco in it. 'I can be very persuasive,' he said softly, and she chuckled tiredly.

'Come on, then, show me where I'm sleeping.'

They went upstairs, and to her surprise he pushed open his bedroom door.

'Oh. Your room?'

'Why not? My bed's the size of a football pitch, and I won't intrude on your privacy, if that's what you're worrying about, but I do want to be near you, just in case. Or I can sleep next door if you really want to, but this way you have the en suite bathroom, and it's more comfortable.'

She hesitated, but his bed looked so inviting, and there was a gorgeous view of the sunset through the floor-length windows. She could lie in bed and watch it set, and it might be nice to have him near...

She told him so, and he hugged her gently.

'Thank you. I'll be much happier near you, too. Did you eat any of that casserole?'

She shook her head. 'Only a little. I didn't feel hungry—too wound up, I think.'

'Maybe later. You have a nap now, and call me if you

want anything. I'll just be in my study up here and I'll leave the door open. The bathroom's through here.'

He pushed open a door she hadn't even noticed, and she nodded and turned to him with a smile.

'Thank you, Marco.'

'What, for pointing out the bathroom?'

She laughed, then her smile faded and she reached up and touched his face. 'No. For everything. For looking after me, for being there for me today when it could have all gone hideously wrong, for standing by me, for wanting to share my life—for all of it, really.'

He stared at her for a long time, then his face softened into a tender smile.

'Oh, Alice. Come here.'

He pulled her gently into his arms, held her for a long, lingering moment and then let her go. 'Go on, get ready for bed. I'll make you a drink. Peppermint tea?'

She shook her head. 'Just hot water would be lovely. Thank you.'

He closed the door, and she undressed and pulled on her pyjamas and crawled into his bed—not the side with the book and clock on the bedside table, because that was obviously where he usually slept, but the other side, furthest from the door.

She'd meant to watch the sunset, but as she snuggled down between sheets made of the softest cotton and breathed in the scent of him, it was as if she was cradled in his arms, and she drifted off to sleep in seconds, the sunset forgotten.

She'd gone to sleep.

He stood and stared down at her, the paleness of her hair against his pillow, and she looked so right there he felt a lump in his throat.

Did they stand a chance? *Dio,* he hoped so, because bit by tiny bit she was edging into his heart and carving out her own little niche.

He went back down to the kitchen, put the casserole into the fridge and made a heap of pasta with pesto, grated a ton of *parmigiano* cheese over it and ate it at his desk with a fork while he sat and worked his way through his emails. Then he used the other bathroom, turned off all the lights except the one on the landing, and slid quietly into bed beside her.

For a while he lay there watching her sleep and wondering where their relationship was going, and then he gave up trying to second-guess the future and closed his eyes, content to listen to the soft sound of her breathing as his body relaxed and sleep claimed him, too.

He woke her with a kiss, and she hauled herself out of a beautiful dream and realised it wasn't a dream at all, she really was in his bed. Had she spent the night in his arms? Maybe…

'Morning, *tesoro,*' he murmured. 'How are you?'

'I'm OK,' she said, realising she was. 'I feel much better.'

'Good. I've put you some hot water and crackers here, and there's an avocado and some eggs on the side in the kitchen. I have to go. I've got a day-case list at nine and I've got a ton of stuff to do before then.'

'What time is it?'

'Only half past six. I'll see you later. Don't rush,' he said, and stooped and kissed her again, just a fleeting touch of his lips before he left, but it left a warm feeling inside her, and she found herself smiling.

She didn't dawdle, because she had a lot to do herself, but she sipped the hot water and ate a couple of crackers before she headed for the bathroom. She had a quick shower without washing her hair because she had no idea if he had a hairdryer, then went down to the kitchen, made some breakfast and walked home to pick up her car.

By the time she arrived at the hospital he was already occupied with pre-op checks on his day-case patients, so she did a quick ward round to see how her patients were.

Daisy and Amil were side by side in the ward now, and Alice was pleased to see that they were eating at last. Tiny amounts, carefully controlled and still supplemented by the TPN drip, but a huge improvement on five or six days ago.

There was no sign of either set of parents, though, which troubled her.

'Are you OK to be at work?'

She turned at the softly murmured words and met Marco's searching eyes.

'Yes. I'm fine.'

'Sure?'

She nodded. 'Perfectly. I wouldn't be here if I wasn't, I'm not silly.'

He gave a nod and walked off, and she finished what she was doing and went back down to Reception. Maybe Olive was in the café, having breakfast?

She was, and Alice walked over to her with a smile.

'Mind if I join you?'

'No, not at all.' She pulled her coffee towards her, and Alice felt a little wave of revulsion.

Too late. She sat down, put it out of her mind and concentrated on the core business.

'I'm sorry I haven't been around over the weekend. How do you feel Daisy's been?'

'Much better. She seems a lot more comfortable. I've spent quite a bit of time with her, and Dan came in yesterday so I took the chance to go home and do some washing and have a bit of a tidy up.'

'How's he coping?' she asked, and Olive shrugged.

'I don't know. We don't really talk about it. He comes, he stays a while, he leaves. I don't think he's enjoying it, but that's not what it's about, is it? But at least he's making the effort.'

'He does find it hard, doesn't he?'

Olive sighed and stirred her coffee, sending another wave of the aroma towards Alice. 'Yes, he does. I won't lie to you, things aren't great between us, but since her operation he's not really talked much at all. Men are like that, aren't they? Trying to understand them is all guesswork, and I think a lot of the time I get it wrong.'

Oh, how true. She thought of her conversation with Marco after she'd talked to her parents, and she smiled. 'At least he's trying now. And she's getting better steadily, so hopefully that'll continue and you'll be able to take her home soon without any more symptoms. That's what we're aiming for, that she should be able to live a normal life and you won't have to worry about her being in pain whenever she eats.'

'Oh, I hope so. Maybe then he'll want to spend more time with us—maybe even have another child. Who knows? I haven't dared think about it because of Daisy needing so much of my attention, but—maybe now? I don't know, though. Dan might not want it. He might just be waiting for Daisy to be better before he leaves me.'

'Really?' That shocked her. 'Do you think that's a possibility, Olive?'

'I don't know. I hope not, because I do still love him, but he's got so distant…'

Like Marco, tenderness one minute, distant the next—

only he hadn't been, not really, and all it had taken was a simple conversation to sort it out.

'I think you need to talk.'

'We do, but I'm putting it off because I'm afraid of the answer,' Olive confessed. 'At least this way I can pretend.'

'I don't think it's fooling Daisy,' she said gently, reaching out and touching Olive's hand.

'I know. I need to talk to him, because I can't live like this and it's cruel to leave her with so many doubts. It's just finding a way.'

Alice squeezed Olive's hand. 'I hope you can find it, and I hope it goes well. I'm always around if you need to talk.'

She got up with a smile, and left Olive to finish her coffee while she headed up to her office to check on her day's schedule. It wasn't quite eight, but she knew they had a busy week ahead and she didn't want Marco to feel he had to manage all of it alone.

Assuming the baby stayed where it was and everything continued to settle down. She had her follow-up on Thursday, to check the hormone levels in her blood hadn't fallen and that everything was resolving. Would he want to come?

Yes, of course. He'd been there for her yesterday, every inch of the way.

She put it out of her mind, went into her office, turned on her computer and while it was booting up she checked her phone, and there was a message from Marco.

I thought you might want this. M x

He'd attached the video of the scan, and she saved it without playing it. Time enough for that when she was at home. For now, she had other priorities, none of which involved listening to her baby's heartbeat.

* * *

She ran into him later, while she was on her lunch break, and her heart gave a curious little thump.

'I thought you were in Theatre?'

He shook his head. 'I've done my list. Everyone's in Recovery or back on the ward. How about you? You seem to be hanging around without a job. Why don't you go home? You should be resting.'

'Marco, I'm fine. I've done my outpatients, done my admin, checked on Daisy and Amil, spoken to both sets of parents—well, more or less. I spoke to Olive.'

His brow creased. 'Ah. I was going to talk to you about them. Dan doesn't seem to be around. He was here yesterday, but not for that long, and she'd gone home, so I spent some time with Daisy just having a chat.'

'And?' she asked, because she could see there was more.

'And she's not happy. She thinks they're both sad, and it's making her sad. Oh, and Alana's coming tomorrow. I thought she could see Daisy and Amil, if you're OK with that? It might cheer them both up.'

'Yes, of course. I think it's a great idea.'

'Good. I'll send her an email confirming. And go home. I've got this.'

He made an expansive gesture to indicate the hospital, and to be fair to him she *was* tired.

'OK. But just today—just in case…'

He nodded his understanding, and his expression softened.

'Call me if you need to.'

She didn't.

Need to, or call him.

She cooked herself something nutritious and relatively odourless for supper, had an early night and was fine the next day. Whatever had happened at the weekend seemed to be behind her, and her follow-up at the end of Thursday would answer any further questions, so she put it out of her mind for now, and got on with her job.

It involved the monthly meeting of the clinical leads, another pile of letters to write, and a batch of cases to consider, and she called Marco in to discuss them and they decided who would be the best placed to operate on them.

Some were allocated to her, some—mostly the day cases—to him, and others would need their joint expertise.

And it kept her busy enough to take her mind off the baby. For now.

The hospital was filled with excitement when she went in the next morning, because it was Halloween and there were pumpkins with battery-powered tea lights lining the entrance to the hospital, and a stall in the foyer selling fairy cakes with black and orange icing.

There was more Halloween stuff around the entrance to the ward, pumpkin-shaped cut-outs stuck to the windows, and the children who were well enough were planning a 'Trick or Treat' raid on all the staff.

Tough for the children like Daisy and Amil who weren't allowed sweets, but to Alice's surprise—or not, really, knowing her as she did—Evie had made all the children like Daisy and Amil a plaited bracelet of black and orange bands. But it didn't matter about the sweets in the end, because the kitchen staff had excelled themselves.

The children's lunches were a feast of ghostly delights—even Daisy and Amil could have some of the things they'd prepared, and lunchtime was an adventure.

And then of course there was Marco dressed as Count Dracula, with fake blood running down his chin and surgical gloves with paper talons stuck on the end.

'Don't you have anything useful to do today?' she asked, but he just laughed.

'Yes. Of course. But this is just as important.'

'As operating?'

'You can talk.'

'I'm on my lunch break,' she pointed out.

'What, eating the kids' mock pumpkins and googly eyeballs?'

'What's wrong with that? Eyeballs are highly nutritious.'

He snorted softly, then shook his head. 'I need to get on. I have kids to scare.'

'Yeah, right,' she said, because there was nothing scary about Marco and they all knew it.

But he winked at her, bared his fangs and wandered off, and she turned away and swallowed a sudden lump in her throat, because he was going to make a brilliant father for their baby, and he'd be an amazing life partner—if only it all worked out.

CHAPTER SEVEN

'You have to see this.'

Alice looked up from her desk. 'See what? I'm writing a discharge letter.'

'Daisy and Doodle. And Wuzzle.'

Wuzzle? She got up, trying to stifle her smile. 'I meant to ask—how is Wuzzle?'

His mouth softened into a grin. 'He's much better, thank you. He had his stitches out this morning.'

She felt her mouth twitch. 'Did he?'

'Yes, he did. And he's telling Doodle all about it.'

He was. Daisy was sitting propped up in bed, Alana in a chair on one side of her, and Doodle, the soppy great thing, was lying on Daisy's bed staring attentively up at her and Wuzzle as she talked, his tail waving softly.

'And now I'm *all* better,' Daisy said in a high, squeaky voice, and then giggled.

Doodle's plume of a tail waved a bit harder, and he rested his head on Daisy's thigh and sighed, his eyes still fixed on her face.

'Oh, Wuzzle. I think Doodle's tired, don't you?' she said, and the tail waved again. She tucked Wuzzle in between Doodle's paws, and Doodle looked down at him, rested his head beside Wuzzle and sighed again.

Alice heard a soft click, and realised Marco had taken a photo. 'For Olive,' he said softly, and she nodded.

'She'll like that.'

Daisy heard their voices and looked up. 'Wuzzle and Doodle have made friends,' she said, her face brighter than Alice had ever seen it.

'That's lovely. Doodle's very nice, isn't he? And I hear Wuzzle's all better now.'

'He is—and I'm nearly all better. I had toast this morning.'

'Did you? And were you all right?'

She nodded. 'Yes. It was very nice. It had chocolate spread on it, but not much. Jenny said I could only have a little bit. And then I had some chicken and rice for lunch, and ice cream. It was yummy.'

'That's great news, Daisy,' Alice said, glad that Jenny, the nurse assigned to Daisy, had managed to find something that the little girl dared to eat. She'd become afraid of food because it had caused her pain in the past, and it was a relief to know that she was starting to enjoy it again.

Alana looked at her watch and got to her feet. 'Right, Daisy, I think Doodle and I have to go and see another little girl somewhere else, but I'll come again tomorrow, if you like?'

Daisy nodded enthusiastically, and gave Doodle a lovely gentle cuddle before he hopped off the bed, had a little shake and trotted off by Alana's side.

'Do you know where Mummy is?' Daisy asked, but Alice shook her head.

'No, I don't. Marco?'

He shook his head. 'No, but I'll call her, *bellissima*. Don't worry, she'll be here soon.'

'Where's Amil?'

'He's gone to have some pictures taken of his insides. He shouldn't be long. And I'll come back soon, I promise.'

They walked away together, and Alice gave him a searching look. 'Pictures?' she said, and he nodded.

'Yes, a follow-through contrast scan, and also a lactose intolerance test. But now I need to send this picture to Olive and find out where the hell they are.'

His mouth was set in a grim line, and Alice knew he was tamping down his anger at the couple, although Olive was almost always at Daisy's side.

'I've got my follow-up appointment in an hour,' she murmured, and his eyes snapped up to hers.

'I know.'

'Did you want to come?'

'Yes. Can I? I don't know.'

'Don't worry if you can't.'

'I can,' he said decisively. 'I'll come back later if necessary. Let me have a quick word with Jenny, and I'll be back with you. Don't go without me.'

They had a longer wait this time, but the scan showed the baby's heart was still beating strongly and her blood pressure was down, which was all good news, so the nurse took some blood for comparison of the pregnancy hormone levels.

'We'll get the results back to you in the next day or so,' the nurse she'd seen before told her, 'and in the meantime if there's any more bleeding or you're worried about anything, just call us, but so far it's looking positive so we're hopeful.'

So was Alice, but Marco seemed preoccupied. It was only after they'd returned to the car and he was heading back to the hospital that he spoke.

'So, that's good news.'

'It is. It's looking more and more likely that we're going to have a baby, so I'm glad I told my parents. Are you still cross about that?'

He frowned. 'I'm not cross, Alice. I thought maybe it was a bit hasty, under the circumstances, but only because I was worried. Anyway, you seem to be all right now, which is good, but I don't think we should tell my parents yet, because I don't want either of us put under that much pressure. If you think your mother's over-eager to get you married and settled down, wait till you meet mine.'

Which she would, of course, in just over a week. 'Marco, do you think I should go to the wedding? Do you think it'll be safe for me to fly?'

He frowned. 'I don't know. It's a good point. If you've only had a very little spotting, and it's finished, and the baby's looking fine and your hormone levels are good and nothing else changes, I don't see why not, but if you'd rather we could drive—although that would probably be more tiring for you.'

She nodded. 'It's a long way to Italy.'

'Not that far. Well, it is, it's just over a thousand miles. I have driven it, but not just for the weekend. It takes about sixteen or seventeen hours non-stop.'

'Do you do it in one?'

'I have done. Another option is the train, but that's twelve hours at the least, so again a lot of sitting. Flying is certainly the fastest and least tiring way.'

She nodded. 'Can I see how I feel nearer the time?'

'Sure. I don't want you to go if you're not happy with it. I heard from Olive, by the way,' he added grimly. 'She and Dan were "talking", as she put it. She didn't sound happy.'

Alice dropped her head back against the headrest and sighed. 'Oh, no. I was afraid it might come to this. I have a horrible feeling they're heading for divorce, from what she said on Monday.'

'Well, I hope not, for Daisy's sake. I want to shake that man.'

'Get in the queue,' she said drily as he turned into the hospital and parked the car. 'Are you going back in?'

'Yes, I have work to do. All that time prancing around as Count Dracula yesterday, as you would say.'

She laughed softly. 'I didn't say a word.'

'You didn't need to.' He turned his head and searched her eyes in the gloom. 'What are you doing about eating this evening?'

'I don't know. Nothing yet. I need to go shopping.'

'I have food in my fridge.'

She hesitated, probably for too long because he shrugged.

'It was just an idea, but I might be a bit late anyway. Don't worry if you'd rather not,' he said, which made it sound as if he was regretting asking her, so she let him off the hook.

'Actually, I'd probably be better buying some food, cooking something simple fairly soon and having an early night, but thank you for the offer. And thank you for taking me to the hospital.'

'You're welcome.'

She reached for the door handle but he stopped her with a hand on her shoulder.

'I'm glad it was good news about the baby,' he said softly. 'I've been worrying about you both.'

She turned back and smiled at him. 'I know you have, and I have, too, but it looks like we can stop worrying now. Don't work too late.'

And with that she got out of the car and walked towards

her own, and she heard him close his door, heard the plink of the central locking as he walked away.

'*Ciao, bellissima,*' he said over his shoulder. 'See you tomorrow. Sleep well.'

'Goodnight, Marco. Thanks again.'

He lifted his hand but kept walking, and she suddenly felt ridiculously alone. Why had she turned down his invitation? What did it matter if he was late? She could have had a nap and gone round later, done a bit more towards working at this relationship that they were going to need instead of saying no yet again. Was that any way to get closer to him?

She got into her car, dropped her head down on the steering wheel and gave a stifled scream, then wondered how Olive and Dan were getting on.

Not well, judging by the sound of it. Why were relationships so difficult?

Her follow-up results gave her the all clear on Monday, and she phoned them and asked about flying and was told she was probably at no more risk than she would have been without the very minor bleed, but that it had to be her decision.

They didn't say *don't*, which in a way she'd been hoping for.

An excuse to get out of the wedding? Probably.

Still, there was the rest of the week to get through before then, and her first and most pressing problem was Daisy.

She was refusing to eat again, and there was little sign of Dan, either.

And then things came to a head when Marco walked into the room, his face like thunder.

'Can I have a word?'

'Sure.' She pushed back her chair and turned to face him. 'What's wrong?

'Daisy. The Christmas trees have been put up, and the kids are all talking about writing letters to Santa. I said it was a bit early, but Daisy wanted me to help her write hers, so she told me what she wanted to say and I put the dots for the letters and she wrote over them.'

'And?' she asked, because there was obviously an 'and'.

'She asked Santa to make her mummy and daddy happy again.'

She felt her chest clench. 'Oh, Marco. That's so sad.'

'I know. I struggled a bit,' he said, and his eyes were glittering now with unshed tears. 'She's been so brave, and she's just run out of being able to cope. And Alana told me she told Doodle that she thinks her daddy doesn't love her any more.'

'Oh, no! Oh, Marco, that's dreadful! Oh, *poor* little Daisy.'

She felt her eyes fill, and she looked away, sniffing hard. 'Here.'

He was holding out a tissue, and she grabbed it and blew her nose. 'Sorry. That just got to me.'

'Don't worry. It got to me, too. At least you can blame it on your hormones. I just wanted to hit something, so I hit the wall. Better than Dan, but still not a good idea.'

It wasn't. She could see the bruise coming out on the side of his hand, and she didn't fancy the wall's chances, either.

'You need to take care of your hands. You can't work with broken fingers.'

'Tell me about it. Don't worry, they're not broken, they're just bruised. I've iced them and put arnica and ibuprofen gel on.'

'Well, at least it wasn't Dan.'

'No. That's why I'm talking to you, because someone has to address this and I don't think it should be me. I wouldn't trust myself.'

She sighed. 'Do you know if they're around today?'

'Olive is. She wasn't there when Daisy told Doodle that, she'd gone to get a coffee, otherwise I don't think Daisy would have said it. Will you talk to them?'

She nodded. 'Yes, of course I will. I'll have to ask Olive if she can contact Dan and get him to come in. I don't have his contact details. He seemed reluctant to leave them.'

'I wonder why,' Marco said drily, and opened the door. 'Let me know how it goes.'

As expected, was the answer to that.

She called them both into her office later that afternoon, closed the door and turned to them.

'We're worried about Daisy. She's stopped eating again, and we don't think it's because she's sore.' She hesitated, then went on, 'I realise things are difficult with you both, and I don't wish to interfere, but you should know that Daisy's dictated a letter to Santa, the gist of which is that she wants you all to be a happy family again, and she told Doodle, the therapy dog, that she doesn't think you love her any more, Dan.'

Dan sucked in his breath, his face racked with guilt and grief, and Alice felt a pang of regret for having to tell them. 'I'm sorry. I know that's hard to take, but I didn't feel we could sit on it. Perhaps I can leave it with you?'

They nodded, and Alice could see that Dan was on the verge of tears.

'Why don't you stay here for a little while? I'll put the engaged sign on the door, and you can stay for as long as you want. Or, if you've still got a family suite, you could take yourselves up there and make a cup of tea and sit and chat. That might be better.'

They nodded again, both of them seemingly bereft of words, and Alice squeezed Olive's shoulder and ushered them out, watching them go with a heavy heart.

'How was it?' Marco asked softly, coming up behind her.

'Grim. He looked gutted.'

'I expect he was. He's her father, after all. He can't feel nothing for her, even if that's what comes over.'

'So why did you want to hit him?'

'I didn't. That's why I hit the wall.'

They both looked down at his hand, and she frowned and picked it up and looked at it, turning it over, prodding it gently.

'Ouch.'

'Sorry. Marco, are you sure you haven't got a fracture?'

'Not entirely, but I'll live. It'll make me more circumspect in future.'

She laughed at that. 'I doubt it. Will you be able to operate tomorrow?'

'I don't know. I'll tell you when I find out. We've got another complex case coming in, so I hope so. Can we discuss it?'

He was an idiot.

He knew that, but the following day he had a baby with gastro-oesophageal reflux disease who was coming in for repair to his diaphragm and a fundoplication, using the top of the stomach to strengthen the sphincter at the base of the oesophagus. And he would need both hands in good working order to do it, or else he'd have to ask Alice, which he didn't want to do. Not after he'd been such an idiot.

He didn't really know why he'd hit the wall. Because

he was mad with Dan? Or because he was mad with himself, because he'd allowed himself to get so emotionally involved with Alice and the child she was carrying? Their baby. His baby, her baby. And he might end up like Dan, marginalised in the child's affections, pushed out by the failure of an already fragile relationship with its mother, so that the baby ended up losing that closeness with both parents that was every child's birthright.

Or should be.

His father had withdrawn from him when he'd told him he was going into medicine and not the family business. Not physically, because they had still been living in the same house, eating in the same room, sharing the space. But the closeness between father and son had gone, and it had never come back.

And that *hurt. Dio*, how it hurt. It had hurt him then, and it still hurt him now, sixteen, seventeen years later. Almost half his life.

So he knew how little Daisy felt, and he was desperate that his own child would *never* feel that pain, and to ensure that he would have to focus harder on his relationship with Alice and make it work. But how?

He would have to woo her. He hadn't really done it, he realised, hadn't pulled out all the stops and done his best to convince her that they should be together, partly because he'd concentrated on making sure she and the baby were all right rather than exploring their own relationship. And it hadn't been enough to gain her trust, he realised, remembering how hurt she must have been by her previous relationship.

More hurt than he'd appreciated when she'd told him? Probably, because every time he made an approach, every time he kissed her or offered to feed her, she either gave in with slight reluctance or pulled away, but always he could sense this fight in her, the need to keep herself apart from him as if she daren't trust him completely.

And he wanted her to trust him, wanted her to feel that he would never do anything to hurt her. He wanted her to get to know him, wanted to get to know her—the real her, not the façade that she put on to protect herself, convince everyone that she was fine, that she didn't need anything or anyone, which was blatantly not true.

They had the wedding—assuming that she was still all right, which looked probable. He would whisk her away, lavish affection on her, spoil her, pamper her—make love to her, maybe, in the way he should have done in the one chance he'd had, only he'd blown it.

Well, not this time.

This time, he'd make sure she knew just how much he cared, just how much he wanted her. Because he did want her, the crazy, stubborn, complicated woman that she was, and not just for the baby.

He wanted Alice Baxter for herself, and he was going to have to up his game if he was going to stand a chance of getting her. But in the meantime he'd take the pressure off, stop cornering her for a kiss, bribing her with food and all the other things he'd been doing, because they clearly weren't working and might even be doing the opposite. No, he'd stand back for a little while and let Alice make the first move. If she did. And then at least he might know where he stood.

To her huge relief, Olive and Dan seemed to have come to an understanding, and over the next few days Daisy started eating again, but only a tiny bit. Gradually, though, she was increasing the amount, and for the first time since it had all blown up, Alice felt that Daisy was now stable enough that she might be able to go away at the weekend for the wedding with Marco.

And if the worst came to the worst, the hospital was staffed with excellent surgeons, many of whom could take over. Theo Hawkwood, for a start, although he was more and more preoccupied with Ivy.

Alice had lost count of the number of tests Ivy was supposed to have had, and there had been multi-disciplinary meetings with anyone who had anything to offer being asked to attend and discuss her case.

Madison Archer, the American diagnostician Theo had taken on, had finally arrived and was slowly and methodically working through all the test results, and Theo was pinning his hopes on her.

Poor Theo. He'd been haunting the hospital, spending most of his time either engaged in research or sleeping at Ivy's bedside, and so far they'd all come up with nothing.

She pitied Madison. That was a lot of responsibility, and a huge weight on her shoulders, brilliant though she might be.

Still, nothing Alice could do, it was way out of her field and Marco's so they hadn't been involved in the MDT meetings, but it seemed as if nothing much apart from decorating the hospital for Christmas was going to happen in the next week if the buzz in the wards was to be believed.

Starting with the huge Christmas trees Evie had ordered all the way from Scandinavia. They'd arrived on Friday morning, and by the time she left the hospital that evening they were safely up and held in place by guy ropes, and a cherry picker had arrived in time for the trees to be decorated over the weekend.

Not that they'd be there, because it was the weekend of the wedding and they'd be in Italy.

Her heart thumped, and she felt a quiver of unease.

What would his family make of her? She'd have to shore up her defences and make certain she didn't give away anything that she felt for Marco in front of his family.

Or in front of him, come to that, because for the last week he hadn't asked her to eat with him, offered to cook for her—he wasn't being unfriendly, and their working relationship was fine, but it was as if in some way he'd withdrawn from her, and she felt it like a cold draught around her heart.

She packed on Friday night as soon as she got home, because they were leaving first thing in the morning. Marco was picking her up at seven in a taxi and they were taking the train to Stansted and flying into Pisa, and she managed to get everything she'd need into a cabin bag.

Well, she hoped it was everything. A simple LBD that wouldn't crease for the dinner on Saturday, the blue dress she'd worn for the gala—complete with tiny plucks which she'd pulled through to the other side and didn't show—and a jacket to cover it for the ceremony, one pair of heels and some ballet flats. Minimal toiletries and make-up, thin pyjamas, changes of underwear and the clothes she stood up in. Her passport, purse and phone were in the neat little clutch she'd use for the wedding, and there was room for it to fit in her case.

That would do. It wasn't as if she was an important guest.

She was at the door when the taxi pulled up outside, and she was halfway down the path with her bag when he took it from her and told her off for carrying it.

'It doesn't weigh anything, Marco,' she said, but he just arched a brow.

'Where's the rest?'

'There is no rest. That's it.'

His eyebrow climbed into his hair, and he blew out his breath and shook his head. 'If you say so.'

He handed it to the taxi driver, held the door for her and got in on the other side, and they pulled away.

'OK?'

She nodded, although she wasn't sure. The butterflies were having a field day in her stomach at the prospect of meeting his family, and she just hoped her breakfast would stay put.

She looked—no, not nervous. A little uncertain?

He was waiting all the way to the airport for her to say she'd left something vital behind, but she didn't, and although she looked a little pale on take-off and landing, the flight was smooth and mercifully short and they were out of passport control in record time.

'So, welcome to Italy,' he said with a smile as their feet hit the paving outside the airport building just four and a half hours after he'd picked her up. 'Now we need the car.'

He rang the number, and two minutes later a car glided to a halt outside the front of the airport terminal. He loaded the luggage, tipped the driver and got behind the wheel.

'That was easy,' she said, sounding surprised, but he just grinned.

'I've used the firm before. They're good.'

'I thought you didn't come home?'

'I don't—not often—but I've been to the odd wedding and I've met up with Raffaello and Gio a couple of times.'

'Are they the ones you're closest to?'

He nodded. 'Not in age, maybe, but in other ways. You'll meet them soon.'

'Are we going straight to your home?' she asked, and he nodded.

'Yes. We'll be there in time for lunch—unless you'd rather go somewhere else on the way? How are you feeling?'

'OK. I could probably do with eating something fairly soon.'

'So—food first?'

'Please.'

'OK.'

He pulled out of the airport, up the ramp onto the main road and headed south east towards home. There was a trattoria in a little hill town just off the road which he'd used before. It was full of charm, had a lovely view across the valley and served good, honest Italian food, and it would be perfect.

Alice settled back against the comfortable leather seat of the obviously expensive hire car. Strange, that he'd hired a car like this and yet they'd flown with a budget airline. Because it was the most direct route? It certainly hadn't taken long, and the seats had been fine for her, although she thought Marco would have been a bit cramped. But then he didn't really do ostentatious. So—why the car? To impress his family?

No. He'd given up doing that years ago. To impress her, then? He ought to know she wasn't impressed by things like that.

'Are you OK? Is the seat comfortable?'

'It's lovely—it's great.'

'I was hoping it would be. The country roads are a bit rough in places, especially where we're going, and I didn't want you to be jostled about.'

Well, that answered that question, and not at all in the way she'd expected. He was doing what he always did, looking after her, and she was too busy looking for ulterior motives to realise it. How stupid of her. It was time she learned to trust him.

'I'm not jostled at all. It's lovely. Thank you.'

'You're welcome.'

She rested her head back and studied her surroundings. As they left the city outskirts the buildings gradually gave way to open countryside, a chequerboard of neat fields interspersed with avenues of Lombardy poplars snaking along the valley bottom and climbing the hills at each side.

Some of the fields had olive trees planted in them with geometric precision, others had vines, gnarled and twisted, the leaves in glorious autumn colours.

It was a beautifully sunny day, and as they left the valley bottom and climbed through an avenue of poplars to a small cluster of buildings perched on a hill-top, she could see for miles.

'It's beautiful,' she said softly, and he reached out and took her hand and squeezed it.

'It is. I'm glad you can see that. I love it.'

'Maybe you should come back more often.'

He flashed her a smile. 'Maybe I should. Maybe we should. We'll see. Right, let's get lunch.'

They left the little hill town an hour later after a light but delicious meal, and headed back down to the valley bottom, picking up the main road again for half an hour until he turned off through huge stone gateposts with a pretty gate lodge at one side.

'Here we are. Castello di Ricci, the seat of the family empire,' he said drily, and as they headed along the neat gravel drive she noticed his face had fallen into that set, unreadable expression she was all too familiar with.

She reached out and laid her hand over his on the steering wheel. 'Hey. It'll be OK.'

He flashed her a smile. 'Yeah. It will. Are you OK?'

She nodded, not entirely sure, but she wasn't going to do anything to make his life more awkward and she could see he definitely had mixed feelings.

Would his family greet him coolly? She hoped not. The thought of her family being anything other than delighted to see her was chilling. Did he face that every time?

Apparently not.

They pulled up in a gravelled courtyard at the foot of a broad sweep of steps that rose to a massive door, and as she got out of the car she could see a welcoming committee at the top of the steps.

A man almost identical to Marco ran down the steps and hugged and kissed him, followed by others—a sister, maybe, who flew down the steps and hurled herself into his arms, another brother, who hugged him and slapped his back, and then his parents, his mother beaming, his father more reserved. They shook hands, but his father still hugged him, though, so clearly he didn't hate him that much.

And then they all turned their attention to her and the babble of Italian fell silent.

'This is Alice—she's a friend of mine, and she's also my boss, so please don't tell her too much about me,' he said in English with a slightly strained smile, and one by one they greeted her as he introduced them, first his mother Sofia, then his father Riccardo, his brother Gio, then Annalisa, the bride and the sister who'd thrown herself at him.

And then it was the turn of the younger man who'd been the first to reach him. He hugged her, kissed her cheeks and grinned at her. 'You're his boss? I don't envy you. Marco's never been good at doing what he's told. I'm Raffaello, by the way. It's a pleasure to meet you. Welcome to Castello di Ricci.'

CHAPTER EIGHT

ALICE WAS STUNNED by the warmth of the welcome they gave her, but she was well aware that there was a lot of curiosity mixed in with the warmth.

His boss? She'd nearly laughed at that, although technically it was true, but not in any real sense. Both hugely well qualified, they were professional equals, and it would never occur to her to tell him what to do—well, only with the admin, she thought with a smile. Professionally, at any rate, they were always on the same page.

Sofia said something to Raffaello, and he picked up her luggage, beckoned to Marco and led them up the steps and into the house.

If you could call it a house. It was huge, a cavernous entrance hall with stone stairs rising from either side, and a pair of doors leading through to a beautiful courtyard open to the elements, with a covered walkway all around the outside with doors leading off it.

She'd seen photos of it on the website Marco had shown her, but it was even more beautiful and striking in real life. They followed Raffaello through a set of doors and up a huge stone spiral staircase, the treads worn away by the passage of feet over the centuries, and halfway along a winding corridor he opened a door and ushered her in.

It was a beautiful bedroom—not huge, but with a glo-

rious view over the valley beyond, and Raffaello opened
another door and showed her the en suite shower room.

'I hope you'll be OK in here. It's not big, I'm afraid,
but it should have everything you need. We'll leave you
to freshen up after the journey. Marco, you're with me.'

Marco nodded, his face showing the tiniest flicker of
relief, and with a promise to be back in a moment, he left
the room with his brother and closed the door, and she
crossed to the window and stared down into the garden.

It was beautiful. There was a rose terrace below, some
of the roses still in bloom, and to the right of it a huge
marquee, in readiness for the wedding tomorrow, with
people bustling in and out carrying flowers and chairs
and table linen.

She watched them for a moment, saw Sofia going into
the marquee, presumably to supervise, and she took a step
back from the window and turned to look at her room.

Everything screamed quality. It wasn't ostentatious,
but it certainly wasn't cheap. She fingered the curtains,
all hand-made with heavy linings, the fabric exquisite.
And a glance showed that the en suite shower room was
lined with honey-coloured travertine, the stone cool and
smooth to the touch.

The contrast to her own family home couldn't have been
much starker, and it made her acutely aware of just how out
of her league he was. Her parents had struggled to fund
all four of them through expensive clinical degrees, and
there certainly hadn't been enough left over for luxuries.
She couldn't even make a wild stab at the sum of his family's fortune, and she was sure she didn't know the half of
it. What on earth did he see in her?

Although he'd always protested that the family money
meant nothing to him, and he'd certainly left it all behind,

even though he loved them, so maybe it really didn't matter to him.

She opened her case and shook out her clothes, hung them in the wardrobe and put her wash things in the bathroom. Not that she needed to have brought much apart from her make-up, because it was fully equipped with everything she might want, right down to a new toothbrush just in case.

Such attention to detail.

There was a tap on the door, and she opened it to find Marco standing there, hands thrust in the pockets of his jeans, his eyes warm.

'OK?' he asked, and she nodded.

'Yes. It's lovely. Come in.'

He stepped inside, closed the door and smiled at her. 'Sorry, they're a bit much. I thought I'd tell you I'm next door, through that wall.'

He jerked his thumb in the direction of the room, and she nodded. 'Sharing with your brother. Is that OK? I feel a bit guilty. You should have been in here.'

'Well, *you're* not sharing with my brother,' he said, laughter flitting through his eyes, and she smiled at that and relaxed a little.

'No. You're right, I'm not. I was a bit worried they might have put us in together.'

'No. I told my mother not to, just to avoid it. I thought it would be simpler.'

She nodded. 'Yes. It's better this way if you're trying to convince them we're just friends. Marco, can I have a guided tour? It's just occurred to me that I have no idea of the geography of this place and I don't want to get lost. You know, if I want something from my room or if there's a fire in the night.'

He frowned. 'There won't be, but if there was then you

come to me and tell me. I'm not going to abandon you, Alice. You won't get lost.'

'I'd still like a guided tour,' she told him, and he smiled.

'I knew you would. That's partly why I'm here. Put a sweater on and I'll take you for a walk in the gardens, and then we can go for a drive and I'll show you the estate.'

He gave her a whistle-stop tour of the house, or the parts of it that she needed to know about, like the kitchen, the more casual sitting and dining rooms, the formal rooms they'd use tonight, the cloakrooms, and then he took her out into the garden and led her down the terrace steps and into the rose garden.

'Oh, it's so lovely,' she murmured, pausing to sniff the air. 'Just smell that. Heavenly. It must be amazing in the summer. I bet it takes a lot of looking after.'

He gave a short, wry laugh. 'Undoubtedly. I think they have several gardeners, but then there's all the grass to cut around all the holiday lets, and the shrubs and hedges to clip—it's a lot of work. Here, this is my favourite bit of the garden,' he said, leading her into the rose bower.

It was made of fine black metal hoops linked together with wires to form a semi-circular arched walkway smothered with climbing roses that made a beautiful, scented tunnel. The gravel path was sprinkled with the palest pink rose petals, adding to the romance, and she slowed to a halt and breathed in.

'Oh, Marco—it's beautiful,' she murmured, and he turned her gently into his arms.

'It is. Just made for kissing,' he replied, his voice husky to his ears.

'You know, I think you could be right,' she whispered, a slow smile playing around her mouth.

She looked up and met his eyes, and he couldn't be sure

but he thought there was a yearning in them, a flicker of the real Alice. Would she pull away this time? Please, no.

He cupped her cheeks gently in his hands, bent his head and touched his lips to hers, and she sighed softly and parted them for him. He deepened the kiss, taunting, tempting her, drawing her in, and she met him touch for touch, sipping, tasting, pulling away and tracing his lips with her tongue, nipping them lightly and making him groan.

'Alice...'

Her fingers tunnelled through his hair, drawing his head down to give her better access, and he let her take the lead, driven slightly crazy by her touch. A little nip, a soothing lick, a tormenting little flick of her tongue leading to a full-on duel with his.

As if by mutual consent their hands stayed where they were, hers in his hair, his cradling her cheeks, a small gap between them that he ached to close, but he didn't. Couldn't, because at any moment someone could come along and if he touched her, if his body felt the soft, yielding pressure of hers, he'd lose what tiny fragments were left of his self-control.

Then finally she eased away and settled back on her heels, staring up at him. Her eyes were soft, almost luminous, and her lips were moist and pink and utterly irresistible—

'I think we should stop while we can,' she said, her voice unsteady. 'Someone might catch us.'

'I know,' he said wryly, and his smile felt a little out of kilter, just like his world, tilted on its axis a little bit too far, so he felt out of balance.

He lifted a hand and traced the line of her cheek, her throat, his finger pausing in the hollow at the base. He could feel the beat of her heart, steady, a little fast but slowing gradually, like his, as he came down from the en-chanted high he'd shared with her.

So much for him wooing her. It seemed as if it was the other way round, but he was more than happy with that.

'We should go and find the others. I want to introduce you to my grandmother.'

He turned and she fell into step beside him. 'Tell me more about her.'

'There's nothing much to tell. She's my mother's mother, and the bedrock of my childhood, and the person I love more than anyone else in the world.'

She stopped and put her head to one side and frowned softly. 'That's not nothing, Marco.'

'No. It's not, but it's not complicated. Maybe that's what I meant by nothing much. Come, we'll go and find her.'

He bent his head and kissed her again, just lightly, and then something thudded into his thigh, and he heard a laugh as he stepped back.

'Tut, tut, Marco. Kissing the *boss* under the roses. You old romantic. Juno, come here.'

He fended the dog off with a low growl of frustration as it bounced around, and he turned to his brother with a pithy comment he really hoped Alice wouldn't understand, but his brother was still laughing and Marco looked down at Alice and kissed her again, just fleetingly, on the cheek.

'Ignore Raffe. He's an idiot.'

'I take it you don't speak Italian, Alice,' Raffaello said in English so she could understand, walking towards them with the dog now firmly glued to his side, held there by greed and the hope of the treat in his master's hand find-ing its way into his mouth.

'No, luckily I don't,' she said with a smile. 'Is this Juno?'

Juno wagged his tail, but his eyes were still on Raffa-ello and that treat. 'Yes, this is Juno. He's technically my parents' dog, but since he's slept on my bed since he was a puppy I think he qualifies as mine now. He lives with me, anyway, in my villa.'

'You don't live here?' she asked.

'No. I'm a little too old to want to live with my parents. It—uh—'

'Cramps your style?' Marco suggested drily.

'Something like that. I've been sent to find you, by the way. Mamma would like you both to join us all for an *aperitivo* before dinner.'

He nodded. 'What time and where?'

'In the *salotto* at seven. If you want anything to eat or drink before then, go and help yourselves in the kitchen. Otherwise she suggested you should just amuse yourselves because she's busy with the wedding. But you're already doing that,' he added with an impish grin that hadn't changed since his childhood.

'Thank you, Raffe. You can go now,' he said pointedly.

His brother chuckled, patted his leg to get the dog's attention and walked away whistling softly, and Marco turned back to Alice with an apologetic smile.

'I'm sorry about that.'

'That he saw us kissing? Will he tell everyone?'

He shook his head. 'No. I've told him not to, and he of all people knows just how hard it is to keep any privacy in this family. Don't worry, it won't get out, and if it does, it might just keep my mother in check a bit and stop her introducing me to all the single women. Come on, let's go and find Nonna.'

Dinner that evening was formal but noisy, with all seven of Marco's brothers and sisters there, the older ones with their husbands and wives, and of course Marco's parents and his grandmother, his beloved *nonna* with her wise eyes and gentle smile who'd greeted Alice so sweetly a little earlier. Almost as if she'd known...

There were no children there, because tomorrow would be a long enough day for them, she guessed, but this evening was all about Annalisa, and she could feel the love of the family surrounding the young bride, the youngest of his sisters.

She found it difficult with all of them speaking Italian unless they were talking directly to her, so Marco had translated some of it and there was a vague attempt to speak in English, but she still felt a little isolated and out of the loop.

After all, she wasn't his girlfriend—he'd made that clear to everyone—and they had no idea that another Ricci grandchild was making its presence felt in subtle ways. Even so, they were lovely to her, and to Marco, and there didn't seem to be any sign of his family being angry or disappointed or distant, as he'd implied. Maybe they'd all got over it, or maybe he'd read more into it than was there, because all she could see from any of them was great affection for him, and his father's eyes hardly ever left him.

She was seated between Marco and Raffaello, which was a relief in one way, a worry in another. Could she trust him not to say something revealing about her relationship with Marco?

Yes, she realised. It was there in his eyes, the flicker of laughter dancing in them as he asked her innocently about working with his brother. 'So what's it like, being his boss?' he asked, and she laughed.

'Impossible. Do I really have to explain to you?' she said. 'He's exasperating at times, but mostly I can forgive him because he's a brilliant doctor and a highly skilled surgeon, and he's great with the little ones.'

'He's always been good with babies—he's had a lot of

practice. He'll be a good father,' he added, his eyes sending her a clear message.

She felt her smile falter and looked away, unable to hold those searching, all-seeing eyes so very like his brother's. 'I'm sure he will one day,' she said, and picked up her glass, but it was empty.

'Here, have some more water,' Raffe said quietly, and she could tell just from the way that he said it that he knew. And if he knew, was it because Marco had told him, or because he'd worked it out?

She wasn't drinking alcohol, and the wine was flowing freely, so in the end she'd let someone fill her glass and taken a sip, but no more, although she lifted it to her lips a few times. Had he noticed that?

And there was a shellfish dish, which she avoided, and unpasteurised cheeses and a dessert with raw egg.

Was it obvious? She hoped not, but she was also avoiding any carbohydrates, and so hopefully anyone watching her would think she was on some ridiculous diet out of vanity and not necessity, although she wasn't sure his grandmother was fooled, either, but then maybe he'd already told her, too?

Then finally they all got to their feet and the party broke up, and Marco escorted her to her room, went in with her and gave her a long, gentle hug.

'I'm sorry, it was a bit chaotic. I thought it might be. Are you OK? Was Raffe looking after you?'

'Yes, he was. It was OK,' she lied. 'I was a bit worried they'd notice what I was eating and jump to conclusions. Had you told Raffe?'

'No, I haven't told anyone—why? Did he say something?'

'No, I just got the feeling he knew. I might be wrong.'

'I hope so. If anyone says anything I'll just tell them

you're really picky and you have a medical condition that means you have to restrict certain foods as well. At least it won't be a lie.'

'I don't think pregnancy is a *medical* condition,' she pointed out wryly, but he just hugged her closer, and she rested her head on his chest and sighed.

'They're all very elegant,' she said uncertainly, wondering if she'd let him down. She'd been conscious of her simple dress all evening, but he shook his head.

'They should be, they all spend a fortune on their clothes, but I thought you looked lovely this evening. Your dress was perfect, and the dress you had for the gala is stunning. I hope you brought it?'

'Yes, I brought it. I didn't have a lot to choose from.'

'You didn't need any other choice.'

He tilted her chin, stared down into her eyes for a moment and then slowly, giving her time to back away, he kissed her.

Not like he had in the rose bower, but a simple, tender kiss, more affectionate than anything else that instead of lighting a fire inside her simply made her feel—cherished? And then he let her go, took a step back and gave her a slightly crooked smile.

'I need to go back down. My family will wonder what we're up to and we don't want to fuel the fire.'

'No. What time do I need to get up in the morning?'

'Whenever you're ready. There's plenty of time. The civil wedding's at two-thirty at the town hall, and then we'll all come back here for the religious ceremony in the *chiesa*, the little church here in the *castello*, and then we'll have drinks and canapés, and then speeches and then finally we'll sit down to dinner, which will take hours, and that'll be followed by dancing well into the night.'

'Gosh. That sounds exhausting!'

He laughed. 'It will be, but it's fun. Are you wearing heels?'

'Yes, but not too high. Not the ones I wore for the gala. I can't stand all day in them and there's usually a lot of standing around at weddings.'

'Good plan,' he said. 'Although if I know my sisters they'll kick off their shoes and dance in bare feet.'

She laughed, relieved that it wouldn't be unrelenting formality. 'I might join them.'

He smiled, told her to sleep well and knock on his door if she needed anything, and then he left her and went back to his family, and she washed and changed into her pyjamas, crawled under the covers and played the evening back in her mind.

She'd felt like an outsider—which of course she was. She got the feeling that his family didn't really understand why she was here, not if she really was just his boss, and she wasn't sure, either, apart from the obvious of meeting the family of her unborn baby, Nonna most especially. Maybe that was all he really wanted, for her to meet them and get to know them, and them her, so that when they finally broke the news it wouldn't be so totally out of the blue.

How would they react? She honestly wasn't sure. Not unlike her family, she didn't suppose. She'd had all of her brothers and their wives on the phone quizzing her endlessly, and she'd had to stop answering their calls. She guessed that was how Marco's family would be, and she could quite see why he didn't want to tell them. They'd be all over it.

She slid her hand down over her tummy, and realised there was a tiny bump. Not noticeable, she was sure, but there for all that. And suddenly it felt more real, more so even than when they'd seen the scan and heard the baby's heartbeat.

She really was going to be a mother, and he was going to be a father—the father Raffaello had said he should be.

And that, at the end of the day, was what mattered. Not his family, not her family, but her, and Marco, and their baby. And somehow, given time, she hoped they'd find a way to make it work.

The wedding was wonderful, and the weather for mid-November couldn't have been kinder.

Annalisa looked beautiful in her pure white lace gown, her tumbling rich brown hair clipped back under a long veil of incredibly delicate antique lace. Her groom, who'd met her at the doors of the little town hall, had given her a bouquet of deep red roses trailing with ivy, and when the short ceremony was over they'd been bused back to the Castello di Ricci for the church service and then they'd gathered in the enclosed courtyard for prosecco and cana-pés before moving to the marquee for dinner.

It wasn't like an English wedding, with a top table, but everyone was mixed up together and the bride and groom circulated between courses, bringing a lovely informality to what could have been a very stuffy occasion.

And the food was wonderful. Even though she had to be careful what she ate, to her relief Alice found there was plenty of choice, and then after the meal was finally over the tables were cleared and the dancing started.

'Come,' Marco said, his voice warm, and he led her to the dance floor and turned her into his arms.

She'd kicked off her shoes and taken off her jacket, and he laid a warm, firm hand against the bare skin of her back and eased her closer, his other hand cradling hers by her shoulder, and he rested his forehead against hers as they swayed together to the music.

This was how it had all started, she thought, him dancing with her in this dress, wearing his tux instead of the suit he wore today, but with her eyes closed it was the same, and she felt the slow burn of need start to kindle.

He shifted his head, bringing her even closer so her cheek was on his chest and his body was against hers, and she felt the change in him, felt the shift in his breathing, the heat of his breath against her skin as he groaned softly.

He wanted her. She could feel it in the tension in his muscles, hear it in the beat of his heart and the sound of his breath against her ear.

Then he lifted his head and searched her eyes, and he broke away from her slightly.

'Let's get out of here. I need some fresh air.'

They detoured back to their table to pick up her shoes and jacket, and went out into the garden, cutting across the terrace and down the steps to the rose bower.

He stopped in the middle, as he'd done the afternoon before, only this time they were bathed in the silvery light of the moon seeping through the canopy of roses as he cradled her face in his hands, his eyes glittering in the darkness. 'I want you, Alice,' he breathed, and then his mouth found hers.

This was no tender kiss, no affectionate peck or gentle graze. This was the plundering, needy kiss of a man who wanted her, a man who needed her just as much as she needed him, and she went up on tiptoe to meet him, to search his mouth, her tongue exploring, duelling with his, her hands sliding round under his jacket to press against the warmth of his back and hold him closer. She felt the strong columns of muscle that bracketed his spine, felt them tense, slid her hands lower and felt his buttocks tighten as he rocked against her.

'Alice—'

'Make love to me, Marco,' she murmured, and he held her motionless for a moment, then broke away.

'Not here,' he said gruffly, and took her hand and led her away from the rose terrace, going into the house by a different door, cutting through corridors and passageways she'd never been in, until at last they were in her room.

He turned the heavy iron key in the door but left the light off and the curtains open, so that all they had was the moonlight.

'Now I'm going to do what I should have done before,' he said softly, and taking her in his arms, he kissed her again, the promise sending tiny shockwaves of anticipation through her.

He kissed her gently this time, building the heat slowly until she wanted to scream, and then he stepped away, stripped off his jacket, his tie, his shirt, laying them meticulously on the chair as he heeled off his shoes and peeled away the rest of his clothes.

She'd never seen him naked, but she saw him now, his skin silvered in the moonlight, and it took her breath away. His body was powerful, his limbs long and lean and taut, his chest and abdomen defined by a scatter of hair that arrowed down. Her eyes followed it and fluttered shut on a trembling sigh.

'I need you,' she said, her breath sobbing, but his lips touched hers to silence her, then as he drew away he murmured something in Italian, his voice soothing.

She felt his hands on her again, turning her, finding the button studded with crystals that held the dress together at the nape of her neck. He eased it undone and turned her round again to face him but she kept her eyes closed as he drew the shoulders down, peeling away the sleeves so that the dress slithered off her, leaving her standing only in tiny silky shorts.

She had a ridiculous urge to cross her arms over her breasts, but then she felt his hands cup them and her breath shuddered out on a fragile sigh.

Alice felt him move closer, felt the brush of his thighs, the solid, heavy press of his erection against her belly, the slight rasp of hair as his chest came into contact with hers and his arms closed around her.

She felt one hand slide up her back, felt him thread his fingers into her hair and tug it gently down so that she arched her neck to him. His mouth—hot, soft, gently biting—teased the skin of her throat, his breath drifting over her skin and setting fire to it, his other hand finding a breast and cradling it.

He groaned and said something she couldn't understand, his breath hot against her skin, and his mouth moved on, finding her nipple, but he'd had to move away to do that and she'd lost contact with him.

'Marco—'

She heard the rustle of bedclothes and he lifted her easily and laid her on the bed, coming down beside her and pulling the covers over them to keep her warm.

He touched her everywhere, his mouth following his hands, tormenting every inch of her skin, from the soles of her feet to the delicate skin behind her ear and everything in between, taking her to the brink time and time again until finally she broke and begged him.

'Please, Marco—I need you... Please—'

And then at last he was there, burying himself deep inside her, his mouth on hers, his tongue thrusting in time with his body as the tension tightened until she thought she would die.

And then it rolled through her like the crash of thunder, wave after wave of sensation as the tension broke and shattered into a million pieces, and he caught her scream in his mouth and sobbed her name as his body went rigid. And then he slumped against her, his chest heaving.

'Alice, *tesoro*…'

His mouth found hers again, raining tender kisses on her lips, her eyes, her cheeks, then back to her mouth again for one last, tender caress before he lifted his head and stared down at her, his eyes glittering in the moonlight.

'Oh, Marco,' she whispered, tears flooding her eyes, and he bent his head and kissed them away.

'Don't cry, *tesoro*,' he murmured tenderly.

'I'm not,' she said, and tried to laugh, but she could still feel the aftershocks echoing through their bodies, and the tears fell anyway.

He rolled to his side, taking her with him, and as she settled against him, her head on his shoulder, she touched her lips to his skin.

'I love you,' she said silently, and he might have understood because his arms tightened slightly around her and his lips pressed gently to her forehead.

'Go to sleep, *amore mio*,' he murmured, and she snuggled closer and let her eyes drift shut.

'I won't ask where you've been.'

Marco stubbed his toe on the end of the bed and swore. 'Good. It's none of your business.'

'No, it isn't. Just a head's up, though. They know she's pregnant.'

Marco found the bedside light and turned it on.

'What are you talking about?'

'Alice, *figlio mio*.'

'I realise that. What on earth makes them think she's pregnant?'

Raffaello laughed. 'She hasn't drunk any alcohol, she's been avoiding all sorts of food—'

'She doesn't drink, and she has a medical condition. She has to be very careful with her diet. It has nothing to do with being pregnant.'

'You're a lousy liar.'

'I'm not lying!'

His brother propped himself up on his pillows and folded his arms. 'Maybe, maybe not. It may be that she does have a medical condition, but she's also pregnant. I guess you didn't want them to know?'

Marco gave up trying to deny it, sat down on the other bed and met his brother's eyes. 'No. I didn't. It's very early, she's had a threatened miscarriage, her medical condition makes it a high-risk pregnancy—and anyway, we're not together, as I keep telling you.'

Raffe laughed at him. 'Well, that's not how it looked in the rose bower, or last night when you were dancing, and it was no surprise to anyone when the two of you slipped out of the marquee and vanished. That looked pretty together, to me.'

Marco shook his head. 'We're not. Or we haven't been, not since—well, whatever. Not really. We're working on it, but tonight was the first time since then, and it's really early days, so say what the hell you like to me but please don't tease her about it.'

His brother frowned. 'You really love her, don't you?'

He hesitated, then nodded, the admission torn from him. 'Yes. Yes, I love her, and I want us to be together, but she's wary, and independent, and she doesn't trust easily, and she won't marry me just because she's pregnant.'

'Have you asked her?'

'No, of course I haven't asked her! We're not that close.'

'You got her pregnant. That's pretty close.'

'That was an accident! A one-off. We got carried away, that's all.'

'I'm not surprised, if she was wearing anything like that dress. It's very revealing, by the way. Nice neat little bump.'

He felt his blood run cold. 'Bump?' He knew she had a bump, he'd felt it last night when he'd made love to her, but—did it show?

'Ah, come on, man! She's stick thin, there's nowhere to hide it, and it may be early, but it didn't go unnoticed.'

He swore and met Raffe's eyes. 'They're going to be all over us tomorrow, aren't they?'

'Absolutely. That's why I'm telling you, just so you're forewarned.'

'Forewarned? I wish I thought that would help. The women in this family could teach the Mafia a thing or two when it comes to interrogation.'

'You could always sneak off early without talking to any of them.'

He snorted, although the idea had already crossed his mind. 'No. I haven't said goodbye to Annalisa and Matteo and, anyway, if we run away it'll only fuel the fire. We'll just deny it.'

Raffe laughed. 'Like that'll work.' He glanced at his watch, punched his pillows and lay down again. 'Put that light out and go to sleep. It's five-thirty and I've only been in bed two hours.'

Marco undressed—well, the little he'd bothered to put on to go from one room to the other—and got into bed, but he couldn't sleep. Not now, not with the knowledge of what was waiting for them. Although maybe if they were together, his family wouldn't say anything in front of her. Surely not even they would be so crass?

He'd talk to her in the morning, work out what they were going to say.

CHAPTER NINE

THE DAYLIGHT WOKE her gently, and she turned towards Marco with a smile and found he was gone.

Back to his room, so that Raffaello wouldn't realise where he'd been all night? Or in case someone else came to find them in the morning and found his bed untouched?

Whatever, he was gone, and the sheets were cold. She rolled to his side of the bed and breathed in the scent of him, reviving the images of the night. She wanted him, wished he was still there to make love to her again.

Not that he hadn't already. She felt herself smile, and she pulled his pillow into her arms and hugged it.

It had been amazing. Their first time, right after the gala, had been shocking in its intensity, pure and unadulterated hot sex, but this time—both times—it had felt completely different. He'd drawn every nuance out of their lovemaking, and while it had still been hot, still intense, it had been so tender, so gentle, so—*loving*.

And the things he'd said—she hadn't understood the words, but from the way he'd said them, the way he'd touched her, she'd understood the meaning. Or hoped she had.

Had he had a change of heart? Or had she simply misunderstood what he'd felt for her all along? He'd been amazing ever since she'd told him she was pregnant, done all manner of things to make her life easier, tried to take the load off her at work, gone with her to the hospital a fortnight ago when she'd had the scare, held her hand through all the tests, gone with her again—what more could he have done?

Told me he loves me?

He hadn't, hadn't even hinted at it until last night. Sure, he'd been affectionate, but never passionate. Why? Because she'd pushed him away? Or had he pushed her?

She'd been so adamant that she wasn't going to be in a relationship with him simply because she was pregnant, but then although he'd talked about them maybe being together, he'd done nothing to move their relationship forward since then—or had he? Had the times he'd fed her, the times he'd kissed her, been a gentle attempt to strengthen the bond between them and move it on into something deeper and more meaningful?

She'd just assumed all that care and attention was because of the baby. She'd pushed him away so many times in so many little ways, but only because she didn't want him to be with her just because she was pregnant. He had to want her for herself, and how could she know that if he didn't tell her?

But maybe he'd tried. Maybe that was how he'd told her that he cared, in all those endlessly thoughtful gestures, the little kindnesses he'd shown her day after day?

She sighed, defeated by the endless circle of her thoughts, and throwing back the bedclothes she got out of bed and went to the bathroom. She needed something to eat soon to stave off the nausea before it got out of hand, and there wouldn't be anyone in the kitchen so early, so she showered quickly, pulled on the clothes she'd travelled in and sent him a text, hoping it would get through.

I need to eat. I'm going down to raid the kitchen. See you soon?

She hesitated, then added an *x* and pressed 'send', then let herself out and crept quietly along the corridor and down the stairs, her ballet flats soundless on the old stone.

She wasn't going to be first in the kitchen, she realised as she approached the door. There were people in there talking and laughing, although it was barely eight o'clock and the music had been playing until at least three in the morning. Still, she needed to eat and she was sure they wouldn't mind.

She'd opened the door and was about to step inside when she heard the sound of running feet and Marco appeared, a little dishevelled, his jeans and sweater tugged on, his feet still bare, his voice urgent.

'Alice, wait—'

'Auguri!'

She stopped dead in the doorway, shocked by the sudden eruption of noise from the women in the room, all smiling and laughing and gathering round them, drawing them in. Marco was at her back, his hands on her shoulders giving them a gentle squeeze, and she could feel the tension coming off him as she heard his name called a dozen times, with laughter and evident happiness.

She turned her head. 'What are they saying?' she said to him, and he shook his head.

'It means congratulations. They know about the baby,' he said softly, so softly that she barely heard it over the clamour of voices.

'Congratulations,' his mother said in English, coming over to hug them both. 'I wait so long for Marco to find someone he really loves, and now he is having a baby with you. I am so happy.'

'Thank you,' she said, because it seemed pointless to deny it, and then everyone was hugging them.

Until Sofia said, 'We need to plan the wedding,' and she felt the words like a bucket of cold water flung over her head.

'Wedding?' She shook her head dumbly, forced into a corner and unable to know what to say or how to respond, but Marco said something in rapid-fire Italian and his mother stepped back and looked from him to her as if she was waiting for her response.

But she had no idea what Marco had just told them, so she said the first thing that came into her head. 'No, you don't understand, we don't have any plans—'

'But the baby—it is Marco's baby, yes?'

She couldn't deny it, couldn't lie to them, so she nodded. 'Yes, of course, but we aren't—he isn't—'

She turned to him in desperation, but his eyes were fixed across the room, and she followed the direction of his gaze and saw a young woman who'd been at the wedding, one of the guests. She'd been seated near Raffaello and Alice thought she'd seen them dancing, but she was staring at Marco now, a million emotions written all over her face, and then with a shake of her head she put a hand over her mouth and slipped past them out of the room, tears in her eyes.

His head turned, his eyes on her, and she could feel the tension in him like a steel cable about to snap. '*Scusi*,' he said, and pushing past her he followed the girl out, leaving her alone with the women.

No way. She turned and followed them, catching up with Marco in the courtyard. 'Marco, wait. What's going on? Who is she? Why's she crying?'

He stopped and turned to her, his face ravaged by an emotion she didn't understand. 'It's Francesca. The girl I was engaged to. I'm sorry, I have to go to her. I'll come and find you.'

And everything fell into place.

His reluctance to come here for the wedding, the tension she'd felt in him when they'd arrived, his wariness about anyone knowing—all of it, because despite what he'd told her he still loved Francesca, and now it seemed she still loved him.

He wasn't free. His heart was definitely taken, and not by her. She watched him go, sprinting across the courtyard after the woman he loved, and all her hopes crumbled to dust.

She should have known better than to believe in fairy tales. Of course he didn't love her. She drew in a breath, gathered herself together and made her way back up the stairs to her room, the need to get away overwhelming her. His family was in meltdown, Francesca was heartbroken—she had to pack and get out of here before she did any more harm or caused any more grief—

'Alice?'

She turned. Raffaello was standing in the doorway in jeans and a sweater. Unlike Marco he had shoes on, but he'd obviously got straight out of bed. Because Marco had called him?

'They know,' she said, her voice trembling. 'The women. They think we're getting married, and Francesca was upset—'

'Francesca?'

'Yes. He still loves her—he must. He ran after her—I don't know. Raffaello, I need to get to the airport. Will you take me? Please? I should never have come here and I need to go now, before Marco comes back. I can't deal with him, not now.'

'You can't go, Alice, not without talking to him—'

'I can. I have to. I can't talk about this, not here, not now. I just want to go home.'

'I have to tell him—'

'No! Please, Raffaello, no. Don't tell him. Please—just help me. If you can't take me, then please call me a taxi or find someone who can, because I need to go home.'

He looked up at the ceiling, closed his eyes, breathed out and nodded. 'OK. I'll help you. I think you're wrong, but I'll help you to get home. You can talk to him later. Are you ready to go?'

'Yes. I'm all packed.'

'Do you have your ticket?'

She shook her head. 'No, but we weren't going until tonight. I want to go now. I need to—'

'No matter. We can buy a ticket but we need to hurry, there's a flight leaving soon. They might have a seat.'

He dived back into his room, came back with a jacket on and car keys in his hand, and he lifted her case and took her out the way Marco had brought her back in the night before, down the back stairs and out of the side door.

His car was there, and he started the engine and headed down the drive as she was still fastening her seat belt.

It was fast, of course, a sleek, low sports car with rock hard suspension, probably ridiculously expensive, but he treated it like a hire car, or maybe worse.

It took less than an hour to the airport, and he dropped her off to park the car. By the time he reappeared she was trying to negotiate a seat on the next flight.

He took over, his rapid Italian getting her a ticket for a flight that left in less than an hour.

She was reaching for her purse when he pulled out his wallet, paid for the ticket and handed it to her. 'Here. Have it on me, and get moving. That's the last call for your flight.

You get home safely and try not to worry. I'll talk to him, and to Francesca. Don't worry, Alice. It'll be all right.'

Would it? She doubted it. Numb, she boarded the plane and stared out of the window as the ground fell away beneath them.

All right? She couldn't think of any way that it would be all right, any of it, ever again.

Had he got it wrong all this time? Did Cesca still love him?

He rapped on the door. 'Francesca, it's me. I need to talk to you.'

The door opened and Francesca stood there, tears streaking her face.

'Oh, Cesca, I'm sorry,' he said, but she shook her head and hugged him.

'No. No, I'm sorry. Sorry you still can't commit to anyone, still can't let yourself be happy, can't let yourself be the man I know you are inside. I thought you'd finally found someone you could love, someone who loved you, too, but I saw Alice's face today, the way she loves you, the sorrow in her eyes when you didn't acknowledge that.'

She looked up at him, her eyes searching. 'You looked so good together last night, so happy, and I thought, Finally!, and then today—was it all a lie, the way you were with her last night?'

He shook his head, confused by her words. 'No. It wasn't a lie, Cesca, none of it. I do love her, and, yes, we are having a baby.'

'So why didn't you tell them all that instead of yelling at them to leave her alone and saying it was none of their business? Why not commit to her? Doesn't she deserve that?'

He rammed a hand through his hair. 'Of course she does, but it's not like that, we're honestly not together.'

'You were last night and clearly you have been at some point in the past,' she said, in much the same way Raffaello had in the early hours of the morning. 'It's so obvious she loves you—'

'She doesn't trust me, Cesca. She's been badly hurt, but we're getting there, and I'm hopeful, and she's happy for me to be part of the baby's life, if it gets to that point—'

'If?'

He turned to face her, meeting her troubled eyes. 'She's not… She has a condition that makes any pregnancy high risk, and she's already had a bleed two weeks ago. It's all OK, but whether it stays that way, I don't know, but she thinks I only want her for the baby, and it's not true.'

'No, of course it's not true. I know that, but then I know you. You need to be a husband and father, deep down inside you're aching for it, you always have been, but you've always put yourself last and your career first for the sake of other people's children, but you're having your own now, Marco! Surely this time that's more important? Please, don't let this go wrong for you both. I so want you to be happy.'

Another tear ran down Francesca's cheek, and he reached out and wiped it gently away. 'Oh, Cesca, don't cry for me, I'm not worth it.'

'Of course you are! You're a good man, and last night I thought you were finally getting somewhere for the first time since I sent you away.'

'You didn't send me away.'

'Yes, I did, and they all blamed you, and I feel guilty for that.'

He shrugged. 'They had to blame someone, why not me? I was already the black sheep for leaving to follow my dream, it was just another nail in the same coffin. And anyway it wasn't right between us. I would have gone sooner or later.'

She nodded, but her eyes were troubled. 'Marco, there's something you don't know. Raffe and I—after you left, we…'

He frowned at her, stunned as her meaning sank in. 'You and Raffe? But—why didn't he tell me? He would have done, I know that.'

'I asked him not to. We became friends while you and I were still engaged, while you were in England. I was unhappy because I knew you didn't want to settle down in Italy, at least until you'd finished your training, so I told you I wouldn't move to England with you and you ended it, and suddenly my feelings for him crystallised. He was my first lover, Marco—my only lover. It didn't last long, I think because he felt guilty that he might somehow have caused our break-up, but we've been seeing each other again in the last couple of months—nothing serious, not yet, but last night we danced and we talked and—he wants to talk to you today, to tell you about us, ask your blessing—'

'My blessing? Francesca, of course you have my blessing! You and Raffe would be *perfect* together. He's everything I was supposed to be, everything you wanted. How could I possibly mind if you found happiness with each other?'

Her eyes filled with hope. 'Are you sure?'

'Of course I'm sure! Cesca, I need to talk to Alice, to explain why you were crying. When I saw that look on your face I thought you weren't over us, I thought I'd got it wrong when we split up. I would never have guessed this in a million years. I need to explain to her—'

'She's not here,' she told him, looking up from her phone. 'She's with Raffe. He's taking her to the airport.'

'What?'

'He's just sent me a text. He said not to tell you. She doesn't want to talk to you and she doesn't want you to follow her.'

'But I have to!'

'You won't catch them. You know how Raffe drives, and there's an early flight. You won't get there in time, Marco, and you don't want to make a scene at the airport.'

He sat down on her bed and dropped his head into his hands, stunned. Alice was leaving him, just when everything was starting to look so good for them. Last night, in bed, she'd been so loving, so tender with him, and he'd finally thought they were getting somewhere, but now— now she was running away from him again. How could it all have gone so wrong?

He felt the bed dip, felt the warmth of Francesca's arm around him, and he straightened up and looked despairingly into her eyes.

'What can I do, Cesca? I love her more than I've ever loved anyone. I'd do anything for her, but she doesn't want to know.'

'Have you asked her?'

'What?'

'Have you asked her? Asked her to marry you?'

He shook his head. 'No. It's too soon.'

'How can it be too soon? She's having your baby! Marco, have you even told her that you love her?'

He let his breath out on a long sigh. 'No. Well, yes. Last night, in her room, but in Italian. I don't know if she understood, but I instinctively said it in Italian because it's the language of my heart, but that was stupid, wasn't it?'

She laughed softly. 'Probably, but communication has never been your strong point. You've never really talked about your feelings. You're just like your father.'

'My father? My father doesn't even *like* me.'

'Of course he does. He loves you to bits, Marco, and he's so proud of you. He's got the profile picture of you from the Hope Hospital website as the screensaver on his phone!'

Really?

He turned back to her, took her hands in his. 'Cesca, I have to go. I need to make this right. I'll send her a text, tell her to wait for me at the airport—'

'No, Marco. Let her go, catch the next flight, and talk to her at home, in private.'

He sighed harshly, angry with himself for not going straight back to Alice in the middle of the night when Raffe had told him they all knew, asking her then to marry him, telling her—in English, for heaven's sake!—that he loved her. 'Yes, you're right. I need to do this privately, and face to face. She deserves what I never gave you either—the truth about how I really feel.'

'In English, though!' Cesca told him, laughing gently at him. 'And don't stop saying it until you're sure she's understood.'

She got to her feet and pulled him up. 'Come on, you need to get your shoes on and come into the kitchen, have some breakfast and get on your way. And you need to say goodbye to Annalisa before you go.'

'And Raffe. I need to talk to him—give him my blessing. I hope you find happiness together, Cesca. I've been so worried about you.'

'No more worried than I've been about you. I did love you, you know, just not enough to fight for you. If I'd loved you enough to last a lifetime, I would have followed you anywhere in the world.'

'Would you follow Raffaello?'

She smiled, her eyes filled with love. 'Yes. I would follow him to hell and back, Marco.'

'Does he know that?'

She smiled again. 'Not yet. But he will, as soon as he gets back. So—first things first. Let's get some breakfast.'

Alice let herself into her house, dropped her bag on the floor, ran upstairs, stripped off her clothes and stepped into the shower, standing motionless under the steady stream of hot water.

She felt numb, numb and empty, reamed out inside, but as the water warmed her the feeling came back, and pain swamped her. Her chest heaved, then heaved again, and she slumped against the wall and sobbed her heart out.

She should never have trusted him! It had taken so long for her to give in, and as soon as she had, as soon as she'd decided she could trust him, he'd betrayed that trust, because he was still in love with another woman and everything he'd said and done to and for her was all about the baby.

'You're a fool,' she told herself. 'A stupid, stupid fool.'

And then she straightened up, pulled herself together, washed her hair, her body... Her hands lingered over the slight swelling low down in her abdomen, over the fullness of her breasts. Her body was changing. It wouldn't be long before everyone would know.

Well, she could deal with that. She'd dealt with worse. Working with Marco would be worse, but maybe it wouldn't come to that. Maybe he'd change his mind and go back to Italy, to Francesca who obviously still loved him. And from the way he'd run after her, it was obvious he still loved her, too.

So much for all those tender endearments in the night.

She gritted her teeth, washed herself properly and then towelled herself dry, pulled on clean clothes, did her hair, her make-up, and went to work.

There were people there who needed her, vulnerable sick children. She'd had enough time out, and look where it had got her. Time to get back to reality.

'So, you're all better, Daisy. I'm so pleased. Would you like to go home soon?'

The little girl nodded, her eyes bright with excitement.

'Can I? Can I really?'

'Yes, I think you can.' She turned to Olive. 'Is that OK with you? She can go either today or tomorrow morning, whichever suits you better.'

'Today would be wonderful! Dan's taking some time off work, so he's only going to be doing the mornings, and—oh, here he is. Dan, Daisy can come home today!'

'Oh, that's fantastic,' he said, hugging his daughter in a way that left no doubt in anyone's mind how much he loved her. 'That's fantastic,' he said again, and Alice could hear his voice was choked.

Her own would be, too, because all she could think of was her baby and how Marco would feel every time he said goodbye and flew back to Francesca without his child. How she would feel every time it was his turn to have the child for Christmas, or a birthday, or some other celebration.

She blinked away the tears and got back to business.

'Right, if you're all happy about that I'll go and write your discharge letter and then you're free to go.'

'Can I say goodbye to Marco?'

Marco. 'Daisy, I'm sorry, he's not here today, but I'll come down to see you off. I'll be about an hour, that's all.'

She went to her office and the first thing she saw was Marco's stethoscope lying on the desk. The stethoscope Daisy had been listening to his heart with when it had speeded up. Because she'd arrived on the scene?

Nonsense. It was nothing to do with it, and if it was, it was all about sexual attraction and nothing to do with loving her. He didn't love her. If he'd loved her he wouldn't have abandoned her like that with his entire family and gone to Francesca.

She put the stethoscope in a drawer out of sight, put him out of her mind and turned on her computer. Twenty minutes later she'd written the discharge letter, sent a copy to file, another to Daisy's GP and tucked a hard copy into an envelope for the Lawrences, and checked her emails.

Dozens of them. She deleted a lot, read others, replied to a few, left some for later and went to see Daisy off.

She wasn't at home, but he could see through the letterbox that she'd arrived because her flight bag was on the floor in the hall.

Her car was missing, too. Had she gone to work?

Probably.

He logged into the hospital site and checked the emails to see if there were any sent by her, and found two he'd been copied into by default. Right. So she was there. Good.

He drove to the hospital, parked his car at the front and walked between the huge, sparkling Christmas trees and into the foyer, and there she was, talking to Dan and Olive Lawrence. It looked like Daisy was going home, and she'd seen him, so he had no choice but to talk to her, to say goodbye.

Not what he'd planned, but at least he'd found Alice, and he wasn't letting her walk away from him this time.

'It's Marco!'

Alice felt her heart thud, and then he strode through the doors and walked up to her. She'd never seen him look so deadly serious and determined, and she swallowed.

'Did you want me?' she asked as he reached them, and something flashed in his eyes.

'Yes, I want you, but we can talk about that in a minute,' he said, his voice laced with hidden meaning. 'We need to say goodbye to Daisy first.'

He crouched down and held out his arms, and Daisy threw herself at him and hugged him hard. 'I thought you weren't coming to say goodbye to me,' she said, and he hugged her back and then let go and straightened up.

'Of course I've come to say goodbye. I'm so glad you're better, Daisy, you and Wuzzle.'

She held Wuzzle up to him, and he kissed the teddy goodbye and handed him back before shaking hands with Dan and Olive.

'Thank you,' Dan said. 'Thank you both for everything you've done for Daisy, and for us. I just—there aren't words—'

'You don't need to thank us,' Alice told them, hugging them both with a huge lump in her throat. 'Seeing you together with Daisy well is all the thanks we need. And you'll be back in Outpatients in January for Daisy's check-up, so have a wonderful Christmas together, and we'll see you soon.'

She watched them walk out through the doors, then, her heart in her mouth, she turned to Marco.

'Not here,' he said. 'My house, now.'

'But I'm at work—'

'Not any more, Alice. Not today. You're not on the rota, neither am I, and we need to talk. My car's just here.'

'I can't—'

'Yes, you can, Alice, because this won't wait and I'm not going to let you run away again. There are things I need to say to you, things I should have said long ago, and I'm not waiting any longer.'

'I have emails—'

'Of course you do. You'll always have emails, and patients, and results and admin and meetings, but not now. Not today. Today, we talk.'

She opened her mouth, shut it and nodded, because he was right, those things would always be there, and if nothing else they needed to clear the air so they could both move on with their lives.

Swallowing back tears, she followed him out to his car in a silence that wasn't broken until they'd walked through his front door.

'So,' she said when they reached the sofa by the garden doors, 'you wanted to talk, so talk.'

She wasn't going to make it easy, but that didn't surprise him. Nothing about Alice was ever easy. Nevertheless, he wasn't going to let her off the hook so he put the ball back in her court.

'Why did you run away this morning?'

Her eyes flicked away. 'I didn't run—'

'You ran. Raffe said you couldn't get away fast enough and you wouldn't let him tell me where you were, wouldn't talk to me yourself, just wanted to get home. Why?'

'Why? You heard them, Marco! All those women, clamouring for some idealistic happy-ever-after when all the time you were still in love with Francesca—'

'No! I'm not in love with her! I've never been in love with her. I love her, sure, but I've *never* been in love with her and she's never loved me, not the way she loves Raffe and he loves her.'

She turned her head and stared at him. 'Raffe? Francesca and Raffaello?'

'That's exactly what I thought, but they're perfect for each other. He's the son I should have been, the husband she needs, and she's the woman he wants. Apparently they had an affair years ago, right after I broke up with her, but just briefly, and now they've been seeing each other again, but they didn't know how to tell me. They're getting married, Alice. He proposed to her right after I left.'

'So—why was she crying?'

'Because she was sad for me, because even though everything between us looked right the night before, this morning we denied that we were together, and she thought it was because I was still running away from commitment, that after all this time I still wasn't letting myself be happy, still putting medicine first before my personal life. I didn't talk to her at the wedding—I think she was keeping out of my way, and this morning—well, you saw what happened this morning.'

She was silent for a minute, and then she looked back at him. 'Why did they all jump to conclusions about us?'

'Because they could see how we felt about each other! We didn't exactly keep it secret, and they could all see that you're pregnant. They could see how much I love you, Alice, and they could see that you love me. And you do love me, don't you?'

It wasn't really a question, and she didn't answer it, at least not in so many words. Instead she turned it round.

'You don't love me, Marco. You're only saying it now because you're afraid if you don't, you won't be with the mother of your child. I saw you with Daisy today. You love children, and I watched the way you said goodbye to her. How much harder would it be if it was your own child you were saying goodbye to, over and over again, because you couldn't be together as a family? So of course you're telling me you love me, because you want to be near your child and that's the only way you can achieve it.'

He sat down on the sofa, and pulled her down beside

him. She sat stiffly on the edge, keeping herself contained, buttoned up as only Alice could, and it made his heart ache.

'Why do you believe you're so unlovable, Alice?' he asked softly. 'Why is it so hard to believe that I love you with all my heart? You're the light in my darkness, the sun to brighten my day, the reason I wake up in the mornings, the person I long for at night. *Ti amo, carissima mia.* I love you. I will always love you, as long as my heart's beating, as long as I'm breathing, and nothing you can say will change that.'

She sucked in her breath, glanced at him quickly and looked away again.

'You're just saying that. It's just words, Marco, pretty words to fool me. I'm not going to stop you having access to your baby—'

'This is *not* about our baby,' he said, cutting her off. 'This is about you, and me, and what we feel. When you had that bleed, my first thought was for you. That you should be safe, not bleed to death, not lose the baby that meant so much to you, the baby you'd never thought you'd have. It was never about the baby for me, Alice. It's *never* been about the baby. It's *always* been about you.'

'You're just saying that,' she said again, but he could hear something in her voice, something unbearably sad that told him she wanted to believe him, desperately wanted to believe him, but simply couldn't.

'No,' he said, sliding off the edge of the sofa onto his knees and taking her hands in his, waiting for her eyes to meet his.

'Look at me, *tesoro*. Do I look as if I'm just saying this? I. Love. You. *Ti amo*, Alice. *Sei l'amore della mia vita.* You're the love of my life, the only woman I've ever, ever loved like this, so much that it hurts. *Mi vuoi sposare?*

Will you marry me, Alice? Marry me, and make me the happiest man alive?'

'What if I lose the baby? You won't want me then.'

He shook his head and sighed in exasperation. 'Of course I will, and I will *cry* with you, *bella,* but I'll still love you, and I'll still be there for you, because I can't help myself from loving you. I told you that last night—said all of this, but I did it wrong, I said it in Italian, instinctively, because it means more to me than it does in English. If I speak in Italian it comes from my heart, and I wanted to tell you these things from my heart, not my brain, not in translation, but from my soul, *amore mio. Ti amo,* Alice. Now and for ever. I love you.'

He stared into her eyes, willing her to believe him, willing her to dare to trust him, and then slowly, bit by bit, he saw the hope dawn in their depths, the blue, always bright, turn brilliant ultramarine as the sun slanted in and caught the tears that shimmered in her eyes.

'Oh, Marco,' she said, and then she slid to her knees and cradled his face in her hands. 'I love you, too, so much. I thought you were just—I don't know. I was so confused, but I couldn't believe that you loved me that much, that anyone could love me that much.'

His hands came up and cupped her face. 'Why? What's not to love, Alice? You're beautiful in every way—the care you give the children entrusted to us by their parents is incredible, their lives so infinitely precious to you. I've seen you cry when they hurt, laugh when they're happy, grieve when they die. I've seen you take the load off colleagues to give them time to be with their families, I've heard you talking to your mother, your concern for your family, concern for everyone but yourself.

'You always put yourself last, try not to be a burden,

deny yourself happiness—you didn't even stay and fight for me when I went after Francesca!'

'No, because I thought you still loved her. I thought I'd lost you—no, that I'd never really had you. You'd never told me you loved me, never asked me to be with you, to be part of your life—'

'That's not true. I've asked you to stay over, I've asked you to come for a meal so I can cook for you—I've done it countless times—'

'To keep the baby safe.'

'No! To keep you safe, to make you happy, to care for you the way you care for everyone. But every time, or almost every time, you say no and push me away. I'm a proud man, Alice. I wasn't going to grovel, but it didn't stop me loving you, and it never will. My heart belongs to you.'

She smiled tenderly up at him, her hand sliding down to rest right in the centre of his chest. 'Then I'd better take care of it, and you'd better take care of mine, Marco, because although I didn't dare to believe you would really want it, it's been yours ever since we met. I love you. I love you so much. And, yes, please.'

He frowned, not entirely certain... 'Yes?'

'Yes, I'll marry you, but only if you promise to teach me enough Italian that I can understand when you tell me something that really, really matters.'

He closed his eyes, squeezing the lids tightly shut to hold back the tears of joy, but then he gave up and opened them and stared down at her. His lover. His friend. And soon to be his wife.

'Lesson one,' he said. '*Baciami*. It means kiss me.'

'*Baciami,*' she repeated, and he smiled.

'I thought you'd never ask,' he murmured.

She laughed softly, the sound like music in his ears, and lifting her face to his she met him halfway...

EPILOGUE

Christmas, one year later...

'*Buon Natale*, Mamma.'

Alice opened her eyes and saw Marco standing over her with a smile, their baby Sophia snuggled in his arms.

'Merry Christmas, my darlings,' she said with a smile, and reached up for a kiss from both of them.

'Your baby wants her *mamma*,' he said, and perched on the edge of the bed as she wriggled up and leant against the pillows. He handed Sophia over so she could feed her, and stayed there as the baby suckled, the tenderness in his eyes filling her heart with happiness as it did every day.

'Is anyone else awake?'

He chuckled. 'Absolutely. Our parents are up, and some of the children, and Raffe and Francesca will be here soon. You've had a lie-in. It's nearly eight.'

'Eight? I need to get up! My family—'

'Are fine. All the parents are in the kitchen with Annalisa and Matteo and the baby, and I could hear children running round in the courtyard. Here, give me Sophia so you can get up—and Sophia and I will go and change that nappy, won't we, *bellissima*?'

'Hmm. Sometimes I think you love her more than me,' she teased, but he turned and shook his head.

'No, *bella mia. Sei l'amore della mia vita.*'

She chuckled. 'I'm not convinced I *am* the love of your life, but you can spend today trying to convince me, if you like.'

He snorted softly, chivvied her into the shower and took the baby away so she could get dressed in peace. Twenty minutes later she found them all in the kitchen—Marco's parents Sofia and Riccardo, his beloved Nonna, who was bouncing Sophia on her knee, Raffe and Francesca, married now for six months and expecting their first baby in April, Annalisa and Matteo with their brand-new baby Giorgio, her parents, her brothers and their wives and the children, all gathered together to celebrate not only Christmas but their first wedding anniversary.

Their wedding had been a quiet celebration in Cambridge the previous year, followed by Christmas with his family and hers, and now they were all back together again, gathered round the huge kitchen table that was piled with the traditional pastries and little tarts, the air sweet with the scent of toasted *panettone* and freshly brewed coffee and the trill of excited little voices.

'Alice, look!' they chorused, and her nephews and nieces almost fell over themselves to show her what they were eating.

'Cappuccino, *bella mia,*' Marco said, putting the coffee down in front of her and stealing a kiss before handing her the baby. 'I'll make you some scrambled eggs.'

'Thank you,' she said, knowing his family understood now how important it was to her to keep her body balanced, because little Sophia had opened her eyes to a love she'd never hoped to experience, and they both wanted another child.

But for now she wasn't pregnant, and the coffee smelt

amazing so she was going to enjoy it while she had the chance.

'*Buon Natale,* everyone,' she said, and raised her cup to them. 'Merry Christmas!'

* * * * *

FROM PASSION TO PREGNANCY

TINA BECKETT

To my babies.

You may not be little anymore, but you will always hold my heart in your hands!

PROLOGUE

Two THINGS CAME to mind as Sara Moreira stood behind
the bride-to-be.

One: she was grateful her boyfriend hadn't waited
until her wedding day to ghost her. Instead, he had left
in the middle of the night. No response to her texts. No
returned calls. He'd just disappeared into the ether.

And two: Dr. Sebastian Texeira looked as gorgeous in
a tux as he did in a lab coat.

More than gorgeous. Even when he slid a finger behind his bow-tie and tugged as if his collar were ten times
too tight. Something he'd done repeatedly during the
wedding, looking none too happy with the proceedings.

Why was she even noticing that? Wasn't she supposed
to be knee deep in her own woes, not worrying about
someone else's problems?

Her tummy tightened as she took in the broad chest
and narrow hips. Wow, evidently her devastation hadn't
reached the more primal regions of her brain.

Dr. Texeira's glance shifted with shocking swiftness
and—*yikes!*—caught her staring. The second time he'd
done that. His mouth kicked up to one side, sending her
errant stomach diving feet first into a dark pool.

What was wrong with her?

This was his sister's wedding, for heaven's sake. She needed to keep her eyes to herself.

Besides, this man was way out of her league. Even further than the guy she'd imagined herself in love with. The man she'd cried bitter tears over a month ago.

Or had that just been wounded pride?

"Up here, please?"

Sara's attention snapped back to the minister. He'd asked something and was staring right at her.

Céus. Was she supposed to be doing something? Straightening the bride's train? Vacuuming the red carpet that covered the dusty ground of her dad's ranch? Lying down and dying of embarrassment?

The last option was a definite possibility.

A sense of hysteria began building in her chest before Dr. Texeira snagged her gaze once more, lifting his right hand and waggling his little finger. The glitter of a diamond band appeared. What the…?

Oh…ring! She was supposed to give Natália the groom's ring.

But where was it? Her mind went blank in an instant.

A few giggles came from behind her. Oh, Lord, she couldn't believe this was happening.

The good doctor came over to her. "Here." He reached for the bouquet she held. Tied to one of the ribbons was the errant ring. With a few quick twists, he teased it free of the knot.

"Give me your hand," he murmured.

She jerked it back in a rush.

"I'm just going to give it to you."

"Oh." Feeling like a fool, she opened her hand, and the sizzle of cool fingers brushing across her palm made her suck down a couple of breaths. She handed the ring over to Natália as if it were coated with poison.

It might as well be.

She looked back across the aisle to where he had retreated.

Okay, the man was now watching her with open amusement. Her lower lip jutted slightly, then froze when his gaze dropped to her mouth.

Mini-frissons of heat overtook each of her limbs.

Was she getting heatstroke?

What had her father been thinking, inviting members of his cancer care team to have their wedding at the ranch?

Dr. Texeira had been part of that team. And Sara had spent the better part of last year at his hospital during her dad's treatment.

And now Antônio Moreira was well again. *Graças a Deus.* She could feel his presence in the small group of people seated behind the wedding party.

Once they'd left São Paulo and returned home, she'd never expected to see the hunky doctor again. But here he was. And her thoughts were not the kind she should be having at a friend's wedding.

He'd looked at her mouth. She was almost sure of it. Except when she gathered the courage to glance through her lashes, she found him staring straight ahead.

She'd imagined it.

Just like she'd imagined him leaning toward her and...

"You may now kiss the bride." The minister's proclamation whipped that thought from her head and sent it spinning away.

The pair at the front of the makeshift chapel turned toward each other, their happiness almost palpable as they came together for a long, long, *long*—she counted down the seconds—kiss that had her attention sliding back toward the best man.

She gulped.

Not her imagination. He was definitely looking at her. Then the bride and groom broke apart and swept down the aisle, leaving them behind. Dr. Texeira pivoted, his shiny black shoes unscathed by the red dust that covered every inch of the ranch. He held his right arm toward her.

Oh! She was supposed to go down with him.

She settled her hand in the crook of his arm, trying to calm her rattled nerves. "Nice wedding, huh?"

"Yes. *Great.*"

Hmm, that word didn't ring true. In fact, she was pretty sure he was lying, which was odd considering the fact that it was his sister who had gotten married.

She frowned. "Is everything okay?"

"Hmm. I just see someone I'd rather avoid." He glanced down at her. "Mind cutting through that section of chairs on our way to the reception?"

Maybe he was ghosting someone too.

Without waiting for a response, he towed her between the rows of organza-draped seating to their right.

"I think we're supposed to be following the bride and groom."

"Humor me for a second. We'll get there." Only there wasn't a trace of humor in his voice.

Who exactly was he trying to evade? When they reached her dad's huge barn, which had been converted into a reception hall for the big event, she led him to one of the side entrances. The massive sliding door stood open, and a drape of gauzy fabric had been interwoven with twinkle lights, a slight breeze making them wink in and out like stars against the growing dusk. "We can sneak in this way, if you want."

"Perfect, thank you."

Thinking he was just going to abandon her there at

the door, she was shocked when he cupped her elbow and ducked through the curtains, eyeing their surroundings before moving toward the table set aside for the wedding party. The same frothy organza that graced the chairs and all the entrances had been tossed over it. Placed on a wooden platform lined with more tiny glimmering lights, Sara had to go up three steps to reach it. Natália and Adam were already seated. The bride glowed with happiness, while the groom gave Sebastian a pointed look. "I wondered if you were taking off before the toasts."

"No."

The answer was short and curt, and he cut around the table and went to Natália, whispering something in her ear. She gave a quick shrug and glanced out at the guests. "There was nothing I could do. They insisted."

When Sara peered out at the tables, which were filling with guests, she saw a lot of strangers, so Natália could have been talking about anyone.

Just then, a small group with stringed instruments began playing, a fiddler stepping forward to set up a lively melody that drowned out Sebastian's response. And, of course, there were only two more chairs at the table. One for Sebastian. And one for her. Right next to each other. There were even little printed cards with their names on them.

Unfortunately, those seats had been placed next to the groom, so she didn't even have the luxury of turning and engaging Natália in conversation for the entire evening.

Did it matter? It shouldn't.

She should just sit back and enjoy Sebastian's company.

Except he made her just a little nervous. Because he was a city man like her ex?

Big deal. It was one night. She'd survived much worse.

He sat down next to her, his arm brushing her bare shoulder as he did. A shiver went through her.

Yep. Nervous.

One of her dad's rugged ranch workers, looking out of place in formalwear, brought a tray with four champagne flutes. His hands gave him away. Gnarly with calluses he grinned at Sara as he moved down the table and handed her a glass. "You look great."

"So do you, Carlos."

He then turned to Sebastian, his tray outstretched. Sara was unable to suppress a smile when the doctor took the proffered drink with a frown.

"You don't like champagne?" she asked after Carlos move away.

"I was hoping for something a whole lot stronger."

He had to lean close to make himself heard, and his shoulder bumped hers again. This time she went with it, not even attempting to put any distance between them. Instead, she focused on that point of contact and allowed herself a tiny forbidden thrill. He'd never know.

"Something stronger? At a wedding?"

"Especially at a wedding." The wry humor behind those words came through loud and clear.

"Drink enough of that stuff and it will probably have the same effect."

"So would cough syrup."

This time she laughed. "Okay, so champagne really isn't your thing. If you want something fast and to the point, you can always head to the Casa de Cachaça afterwards. I can show you where it's at."

Why had she said that? Maybe because he was so obviously unhappy about someone in attendance. And his "especially at a wedding" comment resonated with her.

Boy, did it ever.

At least her ex hadn't shown up tonight.

She scanned the guests again. Maybe Sebastian had an ex who had. Could that have been what he and Natália had been discussing a few minutes ago?

"*Cachaça* sounds like a good choice." Sebastian set his fancy flute beside the plate. "In that case, I'd better hold off on those so I can drive us there."

Us? An even bigger and more forbidden thrill cut through her belly. Well, she *had* just offered to show him where it was. He must have taken that to mean that she would be drinking with him.

If she was going to correct him, now was the time. Instead, she set her own glass down next to his.

Didn't she deserve to drown her sorrows? She had always been about playing the good girl, and look where that had gotten her: abandoned and forgotten. Couldn't she, for one night, do something daring? Something a little out of character?

She didn't have to work in the morning. And if she was honest, having a man like Sebastian take an interest in her was highly flattering.

Not that he had. Not really.

The sound of spoons clinking against glasses began to filter up to their table, growing in volume until it almost drowned out the music. Right on cue, Natália and Adam turned to each other and kissed. Murmured to each other.

She glanced at Sebastian. Not even a hint at a smile. Wow, something really was wrong.

Just then an older gentleman at one of the center tables stood and lifted his glass high, sweeping it from side to side as if trying to gain everyone's attention. The music stuttered, then faded to nothing.

The guest gave a toothy grin, staring up at them. "I'd like choo propose a toast. To my darrrrling girl and her new husband."

The voice slurred its way through the words, and the woman next to him tugged on his sleeve, urging him to sit down. Sebastian's hands curled into fists on the table, and he turned to Adam and Natália. Her friend seemed frozen in time.

"Do you want me to ask him to leave?"

Adam nodded at him, but Natália laid a hand on his arm. "No. It's okay. Mom will get him back under control. If she can't…"

The groom leaned over and kissed her cheek. "Just say the word, and I'll take care of it." He then glanced at Sebastian. "Can you propose your toast now, to get everyone pointed in the right direction? Then we'll get the dancing started. Hopefully that will circumvent any more problems."

"Sure thing." Picking up his own glass, he made a tall and imposing figure as he went to stand behind Adam and Natália's chairs. "Can I have everyone's attention, please?"

The whole barn went silent. He waited a second or two longer, and Sara was pretty sure he leveled a glare at the man who'd made the previous toast.

"I've known these two people for a very long time." A couple of chuckles came from the tables below. "And while in all those years I never dreamed this would happen, I'm happy for them. Genuinely happy."

His gaze softened, and he put a hand on Natália's

shoulder. Tears gathered in her eyes as she mouthed, "Thank you."

Sebastian continued. "And while I gave them a hard time of it for a while, I can't think of two people more deserving of happiness. May you have many years of it." He raised his glass. "To my sister and my best friend. Cheers."

Sara remembered to grab her champagne just in time to take a sip along with everyone else. Adam stood, and he and Sebastian embraced.

Then the groom held out his hand to Natália. "Dance with me."

They made their way down to the floor where thick wooden planks had been fitted together to form a dance area. The music started back up, taking on a slower, more intimate tone that was perfect for the couple's first journey around the room. Adam swept his new bride into his arms and smiled down at her.

It was beautiful. *They* were beautiful.

Her dad had made the right decision in having the wedding here, despite her earlier reservations. Sebastian sat back down, and only then did she realize he'd never lifted his glass to his mouth after giving his toast. Had he not meant what he'd said?

Struggling to find something to say, she settled for, "Nice job."

He gave that wry smile that jerked at her tummy muscles. "Would you believe I wrote the words on my palm so I wouldn't forget them?"

"No."

She'd seen those hands, and there was nothing on them except a light, masculine dusting of hair. Neither had there been anything on them when his fingers had brushed her palm in a way that had shattered her composure.

His smile widened. "Well, I probably should have. I think that concludes my duties as best man. I am more than ready for that *cachaça*. Do you want to stay for the rest of the reception?"

She had a feeling his real motivation in wanting to leave was to avoid the toast maker from a few minutes ago. The same man he'd been trying to evade earlier? It had to be his father. Or stepfather, if she was reading the signs correctly.

Did she want to stay? He was obviously giving her an out.

She should take it and run.

And do what? Sit here all by herself while the happy couple—and everyone else—celebrated all around her?

No. She deserved a little bit of fun too, especially after all she had been through in the last several weeks.

"I'm not really interested in staying. Besides, I need to show you where the place is, remember?"

He studied her for a minute. "Are you sure? I probably won't be in any condition to drive you home afterward."

"Don't worry about me. I'm a big girl, and this is a very small town."

"Let me tell Adam I'm leaving, then. I'll be back in a minute."

She had a feeling he wanted to make sure his friend could handle things with the older man, if they got out of hand.

A minute later, he was back beside her chair. "Okay, he cut me loose."

They ducked out of the same entrance they'd come in at. By now, it was dark, the lights from the barn spilling out onto the ground. When they reached the parking area, he stopped in front of a sleek silver sports car.

"Are you sure you want to ride with me?"

There was something loaded about that question. The memory of his shoulder pressed tight against hers rolled through her mind, along with a warm, prickly sense of need.

This was a man who could help her forget the ache of loss in a way that no amount of champagne or Brazil's famed sugarcane alcohol, *cachaça*, ever could. If she dared to let him.

And suddenly she realized that's exactly what she wanted. To forget. For a few hours. Or an entire night. Whichever one he was offering.

"I'm very sure. I'll ride with you."

He paused for a second, then leaned down and brushed his lips across hers, the briefest of touches that left her trembling and wanting more. So much more.

When he opened the passenger side door, he murmured, "Buckle up, Sara, because if I'm reading this correctly, things could get very, very bumpy before the night is over."

She sank into the plush leather seat and clicked her seat belt into place, yanking it tight. "Is that a promise?"

"It is now." His fingers feathered across her cheek and were gone. "And I never go back on my word."

It was all a blur.

Sebastian Texeira's arm stretched to the side and found…nothing. Sitting up, he scrubbed his fingers through his hair and glanced at the pillow on the bed next to him.

She was gone. Not even the indentation of her head remained. Should he be relieved or upset?

He wasn't sure of anything right now.

Deep purple curtains hid the view outside. And the same gaudy color was splashed with a generous hand throughout the room.

Damn. A motel.

But it had been the closest place to the bar. Not an accident, obviously.

He groaned and fell back against his own pillow. He hadn't even had the decency to take her to a respectable place?

The motels in his country were all used for the same thing. Cheap encounters at a cheap price. Normally the place where affairs took place.

The type of place his dad would have holed up for a few hours.

His father had been the reason he'd been hell bent on getting away from the wedding as soon as possible. He'd had no desire to talk to his parents. And that toast his dad had given had been cringe-worthy.

What he hadn't expected was for Sara Moreira to offer to go with him. Or to climb into the taxi beside him as he'd headed for this place. Which meant his car was still at the liquor joint.

He swallowed and closed his eyes. Except as soon as he did, images of the frantic press of mouths and bodies moving deep into the night flashed behind his eyelids. He snapped them back open.

He lifted the purple bedspread and peered underneath. Still naked. Damn.

Where were his clothes? He scanned the room.

There. On the dresser. His formalwear was neatly stacked and folded.

Relief was beginning to outweigh regret and the throbbing in his head. It was easier this way. She obviously didn't want to be found here with him. And that was fine with him. He'd rather her dad not find out about this at all. Although Antônio Moreira was no longer his patient, it could still prove to be awkward.

Climbing out of bed and stalking toward the bathroom, he showered quickly, using the tiny bottles of products he found on the counter. They were untouched, the seals intact until he opened them. She'd left in a hurry, evidently.

He finished and toweled off, his nerves beginning to settle as he padded back into the bedroom.

It was okay. Yes, he'd had a few too many drinks. Yes, he'd shared a couple of hours at a motel with a beautiful woman.

That this was not his normal behavior didn't matter. What was done was done.

The shock of his sister and his best friend deciding they were "in love" had still not worn off, almost a year later. He'd kept thinking it was just a phase, that they would get over it. They hadn't. And as of yesterday they'd sealed the deal. They were married.

He shook off the thoughts, snagging his clothes from the dresser and jerking them on. He should have at least thought to bring along some jeans to change into.

Grabbing his wallet from the heart-shaped nightstand, his lip curled in disgust at the gaudy furnishings, an over-the-top nod to what the room was designed for, from the cheerful wicker basket of condoms on the dresser to the…

His gaze jerked back.

Condoms.

And three torn Cellophane wrappers.

He blew out a breath. At least they'd been protected. Both he and Sara were free and clear. And that's the way he intended to keep it.

No weddings or rings in his future—he was strictly

a best man kind of guy. Although as he'd held that ring
over Sara's hand, he'd had the weirdest sense of déjà vu.
Only here in the motel room, there was no 'déjà' and no
'vu'. There was only him.

No wife. No children.

And "for as long as he alone shall live", that was exactly the way it was going to stay.

CHAPTER ONE

Four weeks later

"WE'VE FINALLY HAD someone respond to our request for a nurse. It looks like your mobile screening unit is a go after all. We still need to discuss the start-up costs, though."

The slums of Brazil weren't the most desirable place to work, and yet Sebastian had hoped for more than just one taker so he could choose the most qualified individual. Especially since the memo had been sent out to hospitals in various states of the country.

He sat back in the chair and regarded Paulo Celeste, the hospital administrator. "The costs are all listed in the dossier. I know we have a couple of ambulances that are out of commission. If we could use one of those, it would cut costs tremendously. I'm donating my time, of course, so that will help as well."

His trip to *gaúcho* country had brought more than just a wedding and a night in a motel, it had once again emphasized the need for screening services in areas where medical facilities were few and far between. Even in the state of São Paulo, there were rural locations that were difficult to access. And then there were the *favelas*. Hospital Santa Coração had a clinic in the slum down the hill, which was run by Lucas Carvalho. But if the mobile unit was up and running, they could go into some of the other areas as well.

The hospital administrator opened a folder on his desk. "So basically a portable ultrasound machine and some blood draw equipment?" The man peered a little closer. "And, of course, the nurse. She is willing to settle for the stipend listed as long as we provide her with lodging. Check and make sure there's a place available in the hospital housing division."

"Okay. And if there's not?"

The administrator made a sound in his throat. "We can't afford to rent her an apartment in the city." He shuffled through a stack of files on the right-hand side of his desk. "She's from a little hospital in Rio Grande do Sul. No local relatives. Her father was a patient here a while back, and she's anxious to do an *estágio* in oncology. With the hiring freeze it's a little tricky…but if there are no units in the hospital you could always consider housing her yourself." The man gave him a sly smile.

"I don't think so." That was all he needed. He'd just hope there was something available. "The hospital bigwigs would probably frown on that kind of arrangement."

"I *am* the bigwig, but yes. It was a joke. Professionalism is the key, especially in this kind of situation."

"Of course."

Wait. He flipped through his own mental file drawer. Rio Grande do Sul—wasn't that where his sister's wedding had taken place a month ago?

"Who was the patient?"

"I'd have to check. The daughter's name is Sara Moreira."

A stream of shock zipped up his spine. He knew exactly who that was.

Tall with legs that wouldn't quit, and expressive eyes that reflected every single second...

Deus, it couldn't be.

She was applying for the job?

"Does she know who the request came from?"

Paulo's head tilted. "It came from Marcos Pinheiro, since he's the head of oncology. Why?"

What was he supposed to say? "Oh, remember that whole *professionalism is key* thing? It's already gone way beyond that."

And boy had it. Several times. In multiple positions.

He swallowed hard. That was probably the dumbest move he'd ever made. And if he admitted to it here and now, his project was dead in the water. She hadn't been a nurse at his hospital at the time, so there had been no problem. Right?

When Paulo started to hand him the file, he waved it away. "I know who she is."

He wanted to tell the man, hell, no, he didn't want her. Standing next to her at that wedding had made something in his gut churn to life, just like when he'd worked her father's case. After a few drinks, things had gotten out of hand, and the rest was history. A crazy sensual history he was better off forgetting.

But if he said he wasn't willing to accept this particular nurse, he would have to explain why, and that could make for a very awkward conversation. It could also mean the death knell for this project, since no one else had responded to their request. Was he looking a gift horse in the mouth here?

He'd certainly enjoyed kissing that mouth.

He took a deep breath, hoping he wasn't making a huge mistake. "I can give her a try and see if she works out."

The administrator shook his head. "We'd need to be

able to offer her three months, minimum, and six months is what she prefers. She wants the experience, Sebastian. She can't get it in less time than that. Take it or leave it."

In other words, his pet project was resting on the answer to this one question.

The question was could he keep his hands to himself for that long? Yes. Some mistakes did not bear repeating, no matter how pleasurable they had been at the time.

"Sure. Why not."

He could handle six months of anything. After all, he'd lived in a household that had been pure hell during the time Natália had been undergoing her cancer treatments. He'd never told his sister what he'd found out about their father. And seeing the jerk at her wedding had made a slow boil start up in his gut. It had been part of the reason he'd dragged Sara to the bar that night. To avoid having to interact with the louse that had cheated on his mother and made her cry, who had said terrible things about his sister when she'd been ill.

The folder slid back to Sebastian's side of the desk. "Take this down to Human Resources, then, and tell them that I'm okaying the transfer." The man tapped his pencil on the paper in front of him. "But I'm keeping six months as the maximum, and I'm holding you to these figures. So, keep the costs down as much as you can."

Time for a little last-minute haggling. "I want to be up and running in a week or two."

"A week or two? The ambulance needs to be painted at the very least. I don't want anyone mistaking it for an emergency vehicle, especially if you're taking it into the *favelas*." His lips tightened. "And no narcotics of any kind are to be carried onboard, understood?"

The *favelas* could be dangerous places on a good day,

and if someone thought that they could find drugs inside it would be a recipe for a disaster.

"Understood. I'll make arrangements for the painting." He wasn't going to tell the administrator he already had a body shop lined up. A friend of a friend who was giving him a huge discount on the job.

"If this goes well, it will be great PR for the hospital. So make sure everything runs smoothly. No snafus, got it?"

"I understand." And if there were snafus with Sara? What if she expected to take up where they'd left off at the motel, once she found out she'd be working with him? Although the fact that she'd disappeared before he'd woken up made him think she wouldn't. There'd been no sexy good mornings. No breakfasts in bed. Just an empty motel room.

There would be no snafus. Sebastian would do everything in his power to make sure they were able to work together. As long as she was okay with keeping things purely professional.

And if she wasn't?

Then she might very well make his life difficult. Or at least his job.

So he had to make sure that didn't happen.

No matter how hard it became. At least for the next six months.

Sara was elated. Even though part of her had been dreading this trip for the last week.

Would she run into Sebastian? It had been five and a half weeks since they'd found themselves at that motel together. But they'd both had far too much to drink. He probably didn't even remember that night. Not that she'd waited around to find out.

What did it matter? She had the job! Carrying her small suitcase up the walkway toward the huge modern hospital, she felt like she was coming home. She'd spent almost a year of her life at this place while her dad had undergone treatment—first chemo, and then surgery to replace part of his femur with an internal prosthesis, a surgery she hadn't even known existed before they'd come here. That was when she'd realized how insulated her little world was.

Her dad's care had been first class. His doctors had saved his life. And Natália, the neonatal doctor who had shared her personal story of surviving the same type of cancer, had infused him with the will to try. Sara really believed that. The two had become fast friends over the course of their time there. And if she had to face Natália's brother at her new post, well, she would grit her teeth and bear it. He hadn't tried to contact her since that night, but that was understandable, since she'd been the one to sneak out at the crack of dawn.

Her stomach gave a twinge of nerves, the butterflies she'd felt for the last week developing wings of steel as they flapped around her belly. Her dad was worried about her being this far away from home, but at twenty-six it was well past time she found her own wings and flew away. Even if they were waging war inside her at the moment.

She was pretty sure that in the big city men made love to women and then went on about their lives—wasn't that how things were depicted on television? Thank God she'd never told her father what had happened that night. He would have been firmly against her coming here if he'd known, and it might tarnish his perception of Sebastian. Instead, Sara had simply told him that she'd spent the night with a friend after having one too many drinks.

And she had.

Pushing a buzzer at the entrance, she gave her name to the person who answered. The glass door promptly clicked open and she pushed through it, wiping Sebastian Texeira from her thoughts. At least for now.

The service entrance was well lit, the marble fittings she remembered being in the main corridor were echoed even here. Employees were treated well. You could tell by the care put into the details. They probably had to attract and keep the best talent in the country, so they treated them right. And now she was here. Among the best of the best. A place she'd never thought she'd be. The fact that it was only temporary made her determined to get as much as she could out of the experience. Maybe she would learn something she could introduce to her own hospital back home.

She swung into the door marked "Administration", where she was supposed to meet some of the members of her team. As soon as she entered the room, however, she stopped, her heart stumbling for a beat or two. Sitting in a beige leather chair, one ankle propped on his knee, was the person she had just shoved from her mind. The wings in her belly turned into chainsaws, slashing at her innards and turning them to mush.

"What are you—?" She tried again. "I'm sorry. I'm supposed to meet someone here."

A someone who isn't you.

His long legs uncurled as he stood upright. And he was much taller than she remembered, her neck having to tilt to look into his face, unusual for her. Of course, when you were horizontal, differences in heights didn't— *Stop it!*

"I'm assuming that person is me."

"Excuse me?" Shock streamed through her, washing

away the saws, the wings and anything else that might still be cruising around inside her.

"Not who you were expecting?" His lips thinned, face turning grim. Other than that, not a hint of emotion flickered through those dark eyes. No "Hello, nice to see you again," or "How have you been?"

So that's how he wanted to play this. He was going to pretend he didn't know her. Or maybe he wasn't pretending. Maybe it had meant so little to him that he could just lock it away and hurl the key out into the universe. Something she should be doing as well. Maybe people here in São Paulo were like the hospital: cold and clinical. Wiped clean of anything that didn't belong. Where she came from things were very different. She'd been a willing participant in his little game, so she was going to have to live with the consequences.

She'd wanted this job, had practically gotten down on her knees and begged her little clinic for the opportunity to come once she'd seen the ad go up on the staff bulletin board. So she'd better get over it or she was going to ruin everything.

"You're in charge of the screening program?"

"I am. Partly because of your father."

Her brow furrowed. "I don't understand."

"He made me realize that not everyone recognizes symptoms of illness before they're advanced. I want to help change that by going into the poorer communities and working with people who wouldn't normally come to the hospital."

Her dad had made that happen?

And what about what had happened between her and Sebastian? Should she bring it up?

Why? So he could sit there and wonder if she was hung up on what had happened over the course of a few hours?

No way. If he could act like it hadn't happened, then she damn well could too.

"I'm grateful for this opportunity."

"That's good. Staff at Hospital Santa Coração are already stretched thin. I couldn't ask anyone to take this on pro bono."

"I wasn't aware this was an unpaid position. My understanding was that the *estágio* brought in a stipend. They quoted me a figure." How was she going to support herself if she didn't get paid?

"You're right. It does. You were the only one to apply for the position…" He nodded toward another man in the room that she'd just noticed. That person's eyes were studiously fixed on some document in front of him. "Did you want me to say no?"

He could have. He could have turned her down flat.

She swallowed. He'd said she was the only one who'd applied for the position. So, was she the only one who had raised her hand when he'd been looking for a sleeping partner at the wedding as well? The thought made her feel physically ill.

Doing her best to choke back the sensation, she drew herself up to her full height. "I guess you said yes."

"And so did you." His voice was soft as he said it, his glance studying her in a way that made her tummy ripple.

"Yes, and so did I. I actually thought I'd be working with Dr. Pinheiro, though." So what if they'd slept together? It wasn't like she'd had any expectations of that night other than what had happened.

But a motel? She'd never in her life set foot in one of those establishments and if anyone she knew found out…

They hadn't. She'd crept out early in the morning, while it had still been dark and had asked the desk to call her a taxi, unable to look anyone in the eye. But she'd made it. And the experience had changed her in a way she didn't quite understand.

She'd gotten over her ex-boyfriend once and for all.

"Marcos is the head of oncology. He signs all the request forms for the department. But this project is all mine."

That made her swallow. She would be working with him? Only with him? If she had known that ahead of time, she might not have applied.

The other man looked up finally. "Sorry, I wasn't trying to ignore you. Dr. Texeira has found you a studio apartment in the hospital. Is that okay? Or would you prefer to make other arrangements?"

Like maybe get on the first plane out of here?

"The apartment will be fine, thank you. It doesn't make sense to try to look for something else. I won't have to worry about transportation to or from the hospital this way."

Besides, the rents in many parts of the city were so high she wouldn't be able to afford it on what she'd be making. And although it was comparable to her salary in Rio Grande do Sul, the amount wouldn't go nearly as far here. A thought occurred. Would she have to travel to get to wherever they were going to do the screenings?

"Is there a metro that goes from here to the screening site?"

"No. We have a mobile unit. We'll leave from the hospital together."

"Leave? Together?" Okay, the way she'd separated the words gave them an entirely different meaning from his simple statement.

If he'd heard it, he ignored it, because he didn't hesitate with his answer. "The hospital is converting an old ambulance for us. We'll go to where our patients are, instead of waiting for them to come to us."

The reality of the situation was creating a buzzing noise in her head. She had been told what the job opportunity was and had jumped at the chance. But then again, she hadn't known at the time who she would be working with. And if what he was saying was true, they would be working together much more closely than she'd been expecting.

She'd assumed they would bump into each other periodically. Had even steeled herself for that possibility.

Get a grip, Sara! If it were any other doctor you wouldn't have batted an eyelid.

But it wasn't. It was Sebastian, a man she'd made passionate love with. Surely the hospital didn't approve of workplace romances.

The incident had happened before she knew she was coming here, so that didn't count, right? And since it was never going to happen again, it was a moot point.

And it *was* never going to happen again, even if Sebastian wanted it to. Although right now he looked all business. It didn't matter. He might be able to play loose and easy with relationships, but Sara really wasn't built that way, as was obvious from the way she kept obsessing over the same topic.

"Like you said, that will make it easy, then. I take it you live close by."

He gave a half-smile. "Close enough."

And what was that supposed to mean? She had no idea, but the sooner she got away from him the better. "Well, I guess I have some paperwork to fill out?"

"Yes." He scooped up a file that was on a nearby table. "I have it right here. We can go over it together."

Perfect. That was all she needed, to have to sit next

to him and have him go over things. But she'd better get used to it if she was going to take the job. Because if what he'd told her was true, she was going to be sitting next to him day after day.

Until either the job was done. Or she was.

CHAPTER TWO

THE VEHICLE WAS PERFECT. But not too perfect, given where they'd be working.

Once an ambulance, but now painted a cool silver to reflect the fierce Brazilian heat, it was fully outfitted and ready to go. The hospital's name was not emblazoned on the side, for fear that it would be a target for thieves who were looking for illegal drugs. In fact, there were little nicks in the paintwork and a dent marred one side. A picture of two hands, palms outstretched, was painted in muted colors. Nestled inside them were the words "Mãos Abertos." The name was fitting since the hospital saw it as opening their hands to those in need. Below the hands was a mobile number that would ring through to a special cellphone that Sebastian would carry. Word would get around quickly about what the old ambulance did, and hopefully it would become a symbol of hope.

"What do you think?" he asked Sara, who stood a few yards away.

"It doesn't look like a normal ambulance."

"The hospital didn't want it to. Besides, I'm hoping to take away some of the stigma—the fear of the unknown that comes with emergency vehicles."

Like the time his teenaged sister had been hauled off to the hospital in a flurry of red lights and sirens, while he'd been left at home with his ailing grandmother, wondering if he would ever see her again. Her cancer diagnosis had devastated everyone. But she'd pulled through, thank God. It was one of the reasons Sebastian had gone into oncology.

To help people like his sister. He'd always felt that if she'd been diagnosed earlier maybe she wouldn't have had to have an internal prosthesis in her arm. It was another reason why this mobile unit was his heart's desire.

"So what will we do, exactly?"

"We'll do things never attempted before." Only when her teeth came down on her bottom lip did he realize how that sounded. He was doing his best to keep his cool, but failing miserably. He cleared his throat. "We'll do screenings and teach people what to look for in themselves. We'll check for enlarged thyroids, breast lumps, do pap smears, look for skin cancers. If we find something suspicious, we'll refer them for testing."

"To Santa Coração?"

That was one of the sticking points. Their hospital wasn't part of the public sector, so the administrator would probably balk at them sending dozens of people their way. But Sebastian was already building relationships outside his hospital. Lucas Carvalho, who ran a free clinic inside one of the larger *favelas*, worked with a public hospital as well as Santa Coração. Lucas had agreed to partner with him and use the mobile unit as a springboard to expand his clinic's reach. It was the perfect way to get started. Hopefully as time went on, Lucas could use this as a means to garner donations and grants from outside agencies, since he and his wife traveled with relief groups quite a bit.

"The sister hospital Dr. Carvalho works with is called

Tres Corações. They're willing to take up to fifty patients a month."

"Fifty?" Her eyes widened. "You think we'll refer that many people?"

"Probably not. It depends on how many are willing to be screened. The whole 'ignorance is bliss' attitude is the scourge of most health-care professionals."

"Ignorance is death." Her voice was soft, maybe remembering what Sebastian had once told her father when he'd tried to refuse treatment. Thank God the man had changed his mind—all thanks to his sister's willingness to be vulnerable and share her own story with him. It was exactly what Sebastian was hoping would happen with this unit.

Sara pulled her hair over one of her shoulders, catching the long dark waves together in one hand, the ends sliding over the curve of her breast. It was something he'd seen her do at Natália's wedding as well—he'd been fascinated by the way she'd kept twisting those silky locks. It had taken his mind off his best friend marrying Sebastian's sister, something he still had trouble wrapping his head around.

She twisted the rope of hair tighter. Nervous habit? He wasn't sure, but with her crisp white shirt and dark skirt she was the epitome of a professional nurse, but not quite what he was looking to put forth when they ventured into the neighborhoods. But he wasn't quite sure how to broach the subject without appearing to be dictating what she should and shouldn't wear. It was just that climbing in and out of the back of the ambulance was going to be difficult enough as it was, and it was Sebastian's hope to appear casual and approachable—engender trust where there was normally suspicion.

His gaze traveled down to her feet, where a hole at the

toe of each shoe allowed a glimpse of pink sparkly polish, something that didn't quite fit in with the rest of her attire. She'd had the same sparkly polish on at the wedding. He'd kissed each of those gorgeous toes of hers...

Her hair not being pinned up was another of those little idiosyncrasies. Maybe that's what was with his continued fascination with it. His eyes traveled back up her bare legs.

He definitely didn't want men ogling them as she got in and out of the truck.

Like he'd ogled them that night? And was still ogling them?

No, he was simply trying to decide how to best bring up the subject of their attire.

He'd worn jeans and a dark T-shirt today.

Her fingers twisted the rope of hair yet again and a corresponding knot in his throat formed and then squeezed shut. He swallowed to loosen it. "Do you want to see inside the vehicle?"

Time to get this show on the road and Sara out of his thoughts.

She nodded, moving around to the back with him. When he opened the doors and pulled down the steps he'd had installed for their patients, her brows went up.

"Maybe this isn't the best thing to wear out on runs." She released her hair, the locks tumbling free as her palms ran down the smooth line of her skirt.

Okay, here was his chance. "I think the more casual we are the better, if that's okay. I want people to see us as allies rather than as authority figures. It's why we put a few dents and dings in our vehicle."

She seemed to think about that for a second. "That makes sense. I *guess*."

Her slight hesitation over that last word made him frown. "I'm not sure I follow."

"Will people take us seriously?"

Professionalism was one of the things impressed upon students in medical school, and it was probably the same in the nursing sector. But he'd seen from Lucas's own practice in the *favela* that his friend had fit in and become a fixture in that community. He almost always wore simple, even slightly tattered jeans. Maybe it wasn't his clothing that did it, though. Lucas had been born in that very same *favela*. But Sebastian thought it went deeper than that, and he hoped to be able to build on Lucas's success. Maybe they could be an example to other doctors who would then give their time and talents in other communities. Sebastian had taken a trip into the Amazon several years ago and had worked with a medical missionary who'd traveled to villages providing free health care. It had impacted him deeply.

Almost as deeply as his sister's cancer journey.

And his parents' simmering anger toward each other. And how he'd always felt the need to shield Natália from it.

He guessed he'd done something right, since she'd fallen in love and gotten married. Too bad he'd been the one to see all the ugliness first-hand. It had soured him on relationships and made him suspicious anytime a woman started wandering a little closer than he wanted.

Like Sara?

Totally different situation.

"I would hope so." He climbed the metal steps that led into the back of the truck. "We also have a ramp we can use for people who have trouble climbing stairs. Do you want me to slide it out?"

Her pink lips curved, activating a dimple in her right

cheek. "I grew up on a ranch, remember? I'm actually a tomboy at heart, so wearing jeans will be a welcome relief. I can manage."

Okay, so much for wondering if she was going to be upset about not wearing scrubs or skirts. When her dad was being treated at the hospital, she'd always worn sleek tops and fashionable slacks. And at the wedding she'd looked like every man's dream.

And she'd been his for a single heady night.

As for tomboy, he wasn't sure he'd ever seen her in jeans. But now that he thought about it, the description might not be so off the mark. It was there in the loose-limbed way she walked. In the slight twang to her words. Maybe she'd felt she had to dress to match the hospital's fancy decor.

Sara put her first foot on the bottom step, the narrow skirt tightening and exposing a pale knee. Her skin was fairer than that of most of the women he knew, maybe because Rio Grande do Sul had a large contingent of people with German ancestry. Her hair was dark, though.

"Okay, so a handrail might be useful for women who come for screening wearing skirts or dresses." She paused.

He got the hint, reaching a hand toward her. Her fingers wrapped around his, and she made short work of the other three steps, coming to stand within inches of him. He released his grip in a hurry. "Point taken. I'll have one installed."

Anything to avoid having to touch her each time she went up or down those steps. Something about the way she stood in front of him...

An image flashed through his head of a woman straddling his hips, laughing down into his face at something he'd said, his words slurring slightly due to the amount of alcohol he'd consumed. The sensation of being squeezed. Soft hands with a firm grip, just like hers had been a second ago.

His brain went on hyperdrive.

What was wrong with *him*?

Then, almost without volition, the words came out. "Why did you leave that night?"

Something in her eyes flashed, and she suddenly grabbed for the metal edge of the ambulance's door opening.

Afraid she might fall out of the back—or turn and flee—he wrapped an arm around her waist and turned them both ninety degrees, the narrow aisle providing precious little room between their bodies. But it also meant she couldn't run away.

"I have no idea what you're talking about." Her face had gone white.

Maybe she didn't even remember the events of that night. Except something about the way those words had shot out of her mouth said she did. Along with her horrified expression. A stab of regret speared through his gut. He remembered most of it. But her leaving without saying goodbye bothered him somehow. Had he done something awful?

His jaws clamped together for several tense seconds while he tried to figure out what to say to make this right. He came up empty.

"I think you know exactly what I'm talking about. Are you okay?" Realizing his arm was still around her, he let it drop to his side.

Right on cue, her chin went up as if daring him to say anything further. "I'm fine. My father doesn't know, though, so I'd prefer you not to discuss it with him or anyone else. We both agreed it was one night. No strings. No regrets."

So why was he feeling a whole lot of that right now?

That warning about not discussing it was completely unnecessary, though. He wasn't about to go trumpeting it to her father, or to anyone else for that matter. "I would rather keep it that way as well."

His head was reeling, still trying to blot out the more explicit images from that night. As drunk as he'd been, he should remember a whole lot less than he did.

"You still didn't answer the question. Why did you leave?"

"Um—because I wanted to. I would just as soon forget it ever happened."

Maybe he really had done something horrible at the end? Passed out on her? Thrown up? Been unable to perform?

No. He could remember each of those performances in stunning detail. Three encores, to be exact. And nothing horrific in any of those memories.

And could there be a more self-centered list of things to be worried about? He didn't think so—except for one glaring issue.

"We used…" he forced himself to spit the word out, changing the term at the last second "…protection. So we're covered, right?"

"You don't remember?"

He wasn't sure what she was asking. *Merda!* He did not want to be having this conversation.

"Yes, but we'd both had a lot to drink. I wanted to make sure." And if that wasn't the lamest excuse ever.

"We're good. There's nothing to be worried about."

But he was, for some unfathomable reason. He tried to find the cause—decided to settle for the truth. "I wasn't that thrilled that my sister was getting married." He shrugged. "I never saw it coming, actually, and when she fell in love with my best friend, I was... Well, I acted like a jerk."

"Do tell." The dryness of the words made him laugh.

"Shocking, I know."

Her dimple appeared again. "Not so much."

He took a deep breath, the urge to reach up and touch her sliding through him. He forced it back. "I'm sorry I dragged you along on my little joy ride of misery. Believe it or not, I don't normally drink. Or seduce wedding guests."

Mainly because his father had done a lot of that. His parents had battled relentlessly all during his sister's illness. He'd finally realized they didn't love each other—his dad's dalliances proved that beyond a shadow of a doubt. They had simply been staying together for their children—more specifically for Natália, because of her illness. It was one reason Sebastian had basically sworn off marriage and children. What if it didn't last? Would he follow his parents' example and stay in a miserable marriage because of any offspring he might have? They'd already been expecting him when they'd got married. He knew that for a fact. Sebastian, like most children, was attuned to whether his parents loved and respected each other—or when they didn't.

"You didn't have to seduce me. I wanted to go. Even though, I've never..." her smile faded "...spent the night at a motel with someone I barely know."

A few more curse words tumbled around in his head. Had she been a virgin?

Before he could ask, she shook her head. "No, not because of that. I just don't normally go to motels. Especially not with a stranger."

Neither did he.

They knew each other in a superficial way because of her father, but for all intents and purposes she was right.

"Hell, Sara, I'm sorry. I have no idea what—"

She stopped his words with a raised hand. "Don't. It's over and done with. Let's just do our jobs and keep the past where it belongs—in the past."

Much easier said than done. And if the flashes of memory kept replaying in his head every time they worked together?

Well, he would just do what she'd suggested and put it behind him. Except Sara was standing in front of him looking too beautiful for words. A shaft of sunlight ventured in through the open door and touched the hair over her left shoulder, infusing the strands with gold. The sight tugged at something inside him.

"You're right. I'll try not to mention it again. Or even think about it." Those last words came out rough-edged, and he knew they were a lie. He'd already been thinking about it. And his body was torturing him with whether or not they might be able to do any of those things again.

No. They couldn't.

"Neither will I." Her voice was soft. Almost a whisper. As if she sensed the turmoil that was chewing up his gut and was answering it with some of her own.

Not good. Because his gaze slid to her lips. Came back up to her eyes, where he saw it. The slightest shimmer of heat beneath the cool brown irises.

"We'll put it behind us."

"Absolutely."

"Starting right now."

"Yes." The tip of her tongue peeked out, moistening her lips before darting back in. He wanted to follow it. Find it.

No, this was not good. Only it had been. Far too good.

He gave a pained groan.

"Sara?" His palms came up and cupped her cheeks, relishing the cool softness of her skin against his.

"Yes."

There was no question mark after that single word. No "Yes? What do you want?" It was more like she'd breathed, "Kiss me. It's what we both want."

It had been what they'd both wanted on that fateful night.

He wanted it to happen again, his body already responding to the stimuli of having her this close. And it was too much.

Tilting her face, he met her halfway, his mouth covering hers in a way that muttered, *Home. Finally.*

Even though it wasn't. It was merely a stopping place.

But, damn, the burst of steam that zipped through his veins erased that notion in a split second. He suddenly didn't care about stopping places or anything else. Instead, he shifted so that the angle was perfect.

And it was. Her lips were warm and giving and the tongue that had played peek-a-boo with his senses a second ago was back, coaxing him to sneak away with her, luring him just like those sirens of old. Without hesitation he ducked inside, finding heat and wetness that shoved his body further down a forbidden road, a growing pressure behind his zipper impossible to ignore.

Sara's hands went behind his back and slid upward until they curved around his shoulders, her body coming into full contact with his.

Maybe she felt the same sudden urgency that he did.

It was only when one of his hands left her face to pull the door next to him shut, only to have it bounce off something with a loud *clang,* that he realized how far gone he was. How far gone they both were.

Their lips came apart at exactly the same time, Sara being the first to come to her senses, uncurling her arms and pushing at his chest.

He released her and tried to take a step back, but his butt hit the metal counter behind him, stopping him from retreating any further.

Her mouth was pink and moist, lips still parted as she drew in several breaths.

He glanced to the side to see what had happened with the door and realized the metal steps had stopped it from closing.

Graças a Deus. Because otherwise…

What exactly would he have done? Tossed her onto that counter and made love to her? In the hospital parking garage?

What the hell had he been thinking?

He hadn't been. That was the problem. Just like the night of the wedding. He'd been operating off pure lust.

Gripping that very same metal counter, he tried to get his bearings. Saying he was sorry was going to be met with angry words. But what else could he do?

"I take it that wasn't what you meant by 'putting this behind us'." She tossed her hair back over her shoulder.

"Not exactly. No."

"So what do we do? I worked hard to get this *estágio,* and I'm not going to let a little thing like this make me run home with my tail tucked between my legs."

A little thing like this? This was pretty damn huge in his book. He never mixed work with personal stuff. Ever. It was just the shock of being alone with her again. But it stopped right here.

"I would never ask you to go home. You're here, and so am I. This project can't go forward without both of us, so we are going to have to figure this thing out. Fast."

"And how do you propose we do that?"

"By making sure we are alone as little as humanly possible."

She blinked. "Isn't that a little unrealistic? We'll be driving around together in this thing—alone—in order to do our jobs."

Maybe, but right now it was the only way. Because his head was still wrapped around the taste of her, the scent of her hair, the sounds of her breathing as they'd been fused together. "If you can think of a better option, I'm all ears."

And mouth. And raging hormones.

She bit her lip. "I can't."

Neither could he. He was appalled that his body had responded with an immediacy that had yanked him from that fully-in-control-but-fake-as-hell persona he liked to cloak himself in. It had exposed the true Sebastian Texeira. And he didn't like it. At all.

"We can still do this. We have to do this. Otherwise I might as well turn this mobile center back over to the hospital and forget I ever asked for the funds to try."

"Which means there would be no reason for me to stay in São Paulo." Her eyes sought his. "The hospital wouldn't keep me on?"

"I could talk to them and ask—"

"No. I want to do this. I need to do this."

"Why?" He wasn't quite sure what had driven her to come here. She'd probably made more money in Rio Grande do Sul.

"When my dad was sick, I realized how isolated my

little hospital was. Doing things the same way as they'd been doing them for decades. I want to make a difference."

"I'm sure you already have."

She shrugged. "Maybe, but I saw the effect you, Natália and Adam had on my father. I want to be a part of something like that. To take back new ideas and ways of doing things." She motioned around the inside of the truck. "This is exactly what I've been looking for. And I'm not going to let an embarrassing lapse in judgment stand in the way of that. Neither one of us should, if you're as serious as I think you are about doing this."

"I am."

"Then let's focus on that, okay?"

She was right. He knew she was.

The only thing left was to get his body to agree to forget this "lapse in judgment", as she'd put it, had ever happened.

Only he knew that was going to be almost impossible.

So he was just going to have to pull that cloak tighter and pretend. And hope to God that Sara never saw the truth.

CHAPTER THREE

SIX WEEKS.

That time frame rattled around in her head over and over as she sat in the cab of the truck beside Sebastian.

Stress. A change of jobs.

Working with a man she'd slept with.

Slept. With.

Those two words linked arms with the other two words and began to dance a little jig in her stomach. Right beside the butterflies that had never left.

Six weeks.

She couldn't be. They'd used protection. All three times.

Oh, God.

"Have you ever visited a *favela*?"

The question slid past her before turning in a smooth circle and coming back at her. "I'm sorry?"

He glanced at her with a frown. "I asked if you'd ever been to a *favela*."

"Yes." She blinked back the growing fear. "I think all cities have some kind of slum. There was one a few miles from our house. It was fairly safe—run by a group of women who decided to fight back against the image that all *favelas* are dangerous, drug-infested places. They had to give the okay for anyone new to move in."

"This one is not like that. It has had—and still does

have—a drug presence. You'll need to be on the lookout for any unusual activity."

She was. Only that unusual activity wasn't happening outside the windows of the mobile unit. It was happening deep inside her body. And there was a sense of panic that said the unthinkable could very well be reality.

But it couldn't. It was—while not impossible, it was highly unlikely.

Except hadn't she read recently about a spate of condom tamperings across the country? A fad where kids dared each other to go into stores unnoticed and stab pinholes in packages? It had caused an uptick in unwanted pregnancies. And STDs.

Deus. STDs. An even stronger spurt of alarm went through her.

Surely she was safe. The condoms had been provided by the motel. There were quality control checks. There had to be.

At a *motel*?

Those establishments were gorgeous on the outside with their high walls, beautiful signs and manicured landscapes. But the elegant facade hid what really went on behind the entry gate. Sex. Lots of it. Mostly between people who weren't married—or who were, but not to each other.

It's okay. You're overreacting. It's an easy thing to check.

Except she had to endure the entire work day before she could get to a *farmácia* to buy a pregnancy test.

She realized he was waiting for a response. "Don't worry. I'll make sure I'm aware of my surroundings. Aren't we going to your friend's clinic?"

"No. We may at some point, but Lucas has already set up a couple of appointments at people's homes. One of them is an elderly lady who rarely leaves her house and can't make it to the clinic. The other appointment concerns a child."

"A child? We're doing screening on a kid?"

"Yes. He's evidently had a lump in his neck that's been there for a while."

"An infection?"

He glanced her way again. "We can hope so."

A reminder that there were more important things out there than her churning stomach right now. She would do well to remember that.

They reached the entrance to the *favela,* and Sara smoothed her palms over her dark-washed jeans. It seemed so strange to not have on her normal scrubs or business attire. It felt like she was simply going out to visit friends. Only none of her friends lived in a neighborhood like this one.

Ramshackle homes made of plywood boards hastily nailed together to form a box were scattered around. Some of the "nicer" places were constructed of bare clay bricks. None of them had seen the business end of a spackle float or a paintbrush. Roofs were either blue tarps held down by more of the same crude bricks or clay tiles. The roads were the same red clay. It could have been a neighborhood on the red planet, it was that foreign-looking to Sara.

He thrust a piece of paper at her. "Does your cellphone have GPS?"

"Yes." She glanced at the address and then reached into her purse for her phone. Then she made short work of punching the address in and waiting as the service pinpointed their location and looked for the destination.

"In thirty meters, turn right onto Viscaya, then turn left."

The neutral computer voice did more to calm her nerves than anything else that had happened today. The voice wasn't worried. About anything.

She shouldn't worry either. It was just an upset in her hormonal system. That was all. She relaxed back against the seat. She was here to do a job. A role she was comfortable with. Or at least should be.

Sebastian concentrated on navigating through the narrow streets, their truck seeming huge compared to the bicycles and motorcycles parked at odd angles. For the first time she was glad they'd played down the appearance of their vehicle.

"Have you been to many of these?" she asked.

He didn't seem like the type of person who popped in and out of a slum on a daily basis.

What about a motel? How many of those had he been to?

This is ridiculous. Stop it already!

"I've been to a few. And I've covered for Lucas at his clinic several times when he was on vacation."

"And you've never had a problem?"

"No. Despite the drug problem, *favelas* have a kind of internal code on who is and isn't welcome." His hands tightened on the wheel. "I guarantee if we came in here with a police car, the reception would be very different."

She swallowed. He must have sensed the trickle of fear that went through her because he continued. "Lucas has made sure people know who we are. They've already had eyes on us, but no one has given us any grief."

"They have? I haven't noticed anyone."

"And you probably won't." Up went his brows. "Are you sorry you came to São Paulo yet?"

Was she? Actually, she wasn't. "No, I'm just trying to be aware of my surroundings, like you asked me to be."

"Great."

"So whose house are we going to first?"

Neither of them had mentioned what had happened a week ago in the back of this very vehicle. As the hospital finished outfitting the mobile unit, Sara had unpacked and tried to get settled, dreading having to actually go out with him and receive patients. But it was either that or admit defeat, and she wasn't one who gave up. Not easily anyway.

Her phone gave another set of instructions, listing the next street as their destination.

"We're going to the shut-in's place first. She has a lump in her breast."

That surprised her. Not the part about the lump but about them tackling that kind of screening. "I don't remember seeing a mammogram machine back there."

Not that she remembered seeing much of anything outside Sebastian's face and the feel of his mouth on hers.

And that was a very inappropriate thought.

"We don't, but we have portable ultrasound equipment."

"You can tell from that?"

He gazed at the row of houses, slowing down slightly. Some of them had numbers painted on them in crude lettering, but some of them didn't. "I can't tell if something is malignant, not with any certainty. But I can tell by the way it registers on the ultrasound what kind of lump it is. We want to see a fluid-filled pocket rather than a solid mass. It won't be definitive, but without being able to force anyone to go to the hospital for check-ups, it's the best we can do. It has a pretty good track record."

"How old is the patient?"

He nudged a couple of files toward her. "She should be in here somewhere."

"Name?"

"Talita Moises. I think she's seventy-eight."

Flipping through the names on the tabs, she found the patient without much difficulty. But when she opened it, there were no neat, computer-generated forms inside. Instead there was a wrinkled piece of paper that looked like it had been torn from a notebook. The patient's name, age and complaint were scribbled on it. "We're not going to keep actual records?"

"Yes. But we'll only do up paperwork for patients we actually treat. Some of them might refuse to be seen. I have a micro recorder that I'll use to take notes. I'll have it transcribed later."

Was that going to be part of her duties? A lot of times nurses acted almost like secretaries, entering diagnoses and listing findings.

"Um, okay."

"You won't have to do that, if that's what you're worried about."

"No, not worried at all. I'll do whatever you need me to do."

Including carrying his child?

The thought entered her head unbidden and her face became a scorching hot mess.

He glanced sideways at her. "Are you okay?"

"Hot flash."

One side of his mouth tilted. "A little young for that, aren't you?"

When this man was around, she wouldn't put anything past her body. She'd had sex with him, for heaven's sake. Something she was still having trouble accepting. She'd only slept with her boyfriend after months of dating.

"We live in Brazil. I think everyone is subject to them from time to time."

His grin tipped higher. "Indeed."

With that, he shut the engine off. "I'll get the equipment."

"I'll go up and ring the bell."

"No. You won't. We don't go up to any doors unaccompanied. We do everything together."

Yes. They had.

She gulped. *Céus.* She'd better stop with all the double meanings. "Is that really necessary?"

"It is. You never know who is going to open that door."

"And you would do what, if some crazed drug dealer appeared brandishing a gun?"

"I would try to talk my way out of the situation."

"And you don't think I could do that?"

His fingers covered hers for a second, the warm grip slightly tighter than necessary. "Yes, I think you could do that. It's just safer—for both of us—if we stick together."

Sara was all for staying safe. Which was why she'd handed him a second condom when the time had come. And a third.

Why? Why are you insisting on thinking about this?

"Okay. I'll help you carry the equipment, then."

As they both climbed into the back of the truck, Sara took the opportunity to look around this time. A metal counter along one wall held an assortment of containers that were wedged into holders so they wouldn't spill all over the place. The standard tongue depressors, rubbing alcohol and cotton balls were all neatly tucked away. And it looked like beneath the counter there was a— She fingered the metal edge of whatever it was.

"Yes, it's an exam table, in case we need to look at someone or draw blood."

"There's barely room in here for us as it is. How are we going to work around something like that?"

"It's gurney sized. It'll be a tight fit, but we'll manage."

Damn. Her brain wasn't even going to try to tackle that one. "Okay, and the ultrasound machine?"

"Right inside that blue box."

A tackle box thing was clamped to the wall, a wooden peg supporting the machine's handle. "Wow."

Sara was seriously impressed. "How many things can we screen for?"

"A lot. Especially if we can draw blood from our patients. We have a mini-fridge just beneath the legs of the pull-out exam table where we can store samples until we get them back to the lab for testing."

A spurt of pride went through her, erasing all the little quivers of fear she'd had ever since she'd climbed back into the truck with him. They could actually make a difference here. Just like she'd hoped. All she had to do was keep her mind focused on that fact, and off a certain handsome doctor. Not an easy task. But she could do it. She knew she could.

"What do you want me to take?"

"I'll take the sonogram machine and laptop so we can view the images, if you'll reach under that cabinet and grab the red soft sided bag. It has the lubricant for the wand and some other items we might need."

She wrapped her fingers around the handle on the only cabinet in the place when he stopped her. "Here's the key."

She took it, noticing the lock. "I thought you said we weren't carrying anything with narcotics in it."

"We're not carrying much of anything, but there are syringes in there for blood collection. Sometimes it's better to keep temptation behind lock and key."

Yes. It was. Too bad she hadn't thought of that the

night of Natália's wedding. She could have locked her heart up and thrown away the key.

Although her heart hadn't been involved in that little encounter, right?

No, just parts of her body. She hoped nothing more than those pleasure centers had been activated that night.

Carrying that thought with her as they hauled their equipment up the dirt walkway, she asked, "Is she not mobile enough to come out to the truck?"

"I don't know. But I didn't want to take any chances. The only thing Lucas left me was that piece of paper, which is sometimes all the information he has."

He raised his hands and clapped three times. Doorbells were reserved for people in wealthier areas. In poor neighborhoods—actually, even at Sara's dad's house because of the migrant workers they often hired—they still gave that staccato series of claps to announce their presence. Even though they'd had a doorbell ever since she could remember.

The door opened and a tall gangly boy with dark eyes appeared. *"Quem é?"*

"We're here to see Dona Talita Moises. Lucas Carvalho sent us. Is she home?"

"Sim. Minha avó está por aqui." He motioned them inside, instead of calling his grandmother to the entrance, which surprised Sara. Maybe they weren't as wary of strangers here as Sebastian claimed.

They went into a living room, and then she immediately saw why they'd been summoned inside. A frail woman with a shock of gray hair sat on a stained floral chair. She wore a blue checked house dress, and unless one of her legs was tucked beneath her... It wasn't. It was missing. She swallowed, remembering her father's cancer and what could have happened if they hadn't been able to get him in for an appointment at Hospital Santa Coração. He could have been sitting on a chair very much like this one.

No, he wouldn't have been. Because he would have refused treatment. A die-hard cowboy whose entire existence was measured in how many kilometers he'd ridden that day, he'd somehow had the notion that his life wouldn't mean anything if he couldn't ride his horse or work his cattle. But people had survived much worse than that and found ways to make their lives count.

Sebastian was already introducing himself and Sara to the woman. Talita Moises' shrewd eyes took in their appearance, making her very glad that she was wearing clothing that didn't scream money. Not that she had that many expensive pieces, but even the little she did have were far beyond the means of this household.

She reached out to shake the woman's hand, finding Ms. Moises' grip tight and unyielding. So much so that she couldn't simply pull away from her. Instead the woman studied her. "You are his wife?"

Her brain stumbled over the question for a second before realizing that—

"No!" The denial bounced around the room with such force that Sebastian's head cranked around to look at her. She softened her voice. "I'm a nurse. I just started at the—at this job." She wasn't sure if Sebastian wanted the name of the hospital announced to everyone, since it could be seen as a symbol of the chasm between this community and neighborhoods that were able to afford the insurance necessary to go to a place like Santa Coração.

The woman grunted a sound that could have been an affirmation or a protest, she wasn't sure which. But at least she'd released her death grip on Sara's hand. For some reason the woman made her nervous, and it had nothing to do with where she lived.

"Lucas Carvalho spoke with you about us coming?"

She nodded and then motioned her grandson to make himself scarce. He left the room, the snapping of his flip flops across the tile floor the only sound for a minute or two. And then it too was gone.

Sebastian sat across from her. "How can we help?"

"Well, I found a…I found a bump on…" Her hand made a circling motion over her left breast. "I've already lost my leg. I'm not sure I want to lose anything else."

"No one said anything about losing something. We're just here to check on it, if you're okay with that."

The woman's head gave a snapping nod. "I have diabetes. Maybe that's what's causing it."

Sara didn't want to tell her that it was doubtful that blood sugar issues had caused a lump in her breast. But the loss of her leg? Probably. It could also complicate surgery, if it came to that.

"Have you been undergoing any treatment?"

Talita's laugh came across like the sound of crumpling tinfoil. "Gave myself a shot in the leg every night. Except it didn't do much good. One of them is still gone."

Sara was out of her depth here. She had no idea what to say or do. Was the woman saying she no longer even tried to control her blood sugar levels?

Maybe this hadn't been the right move after all. What exactly did she think she was doing by coming to São Paulo?

It's your first case. Don't judge everything by just one patient.

That last phrase had been pounded into her head during nursing school. But it was hard not to. In a hospital setting she could slip into a familiar role that everyone expected her to play—and she played it well. So well that stepping outside that box made it hard to breathe—to think, let alone come up with some kind of comforting words.

Because if the woman did have cancer, could it even be treated?

Unlike her own chaotic thoughts, Sebastian went through a calm series of questions that had to be second nature to him. Or maybe he was just inured to the heartbreak of a cancer diagnosis. Somehow, she didn't think so, though.

Sebastian cared.

For his patients, at least. The women he slept with? Well, that was another matter. Big city men were no different than men where she came from except people tended to make a bigger deal out of things, since the pool of available dates was much smaller.

Maybe that was why her ex had been able to slip away without a twinge of conscience. He was from one of the larger cities up north, but had come down to help her father with several cattle auctions. Once those were done? *Poof!* Just like a genie retreating back to its bottle.

Her parents' marriage, on the other hand, had been rock solid. No hint that they'd had to settle for whomever had been available.

That was because they'd fallen in love.

Something Sara had once hoped to do. But right now she was resigned to being alone.

Her hand went to her stomach when it gave an odd twist. Oh, God, if she was pregnant, she wasn't going to be alone for long.

Really? She would be more alone than ever, because there would be no one to share her burden.

Her dad would. But Sebastian?

"Sara, could you help Ms. Moises strip out of her blouse and bra, please?"

And just like that, she was back on duty. Maybe Sebastian had sensed her unease and misread the cause of it. Whatever it was, she was just glad to have something to do that didn't involve thinking about everything that could go wrong but probably wouldn't.

Besides, this woman's life was far more important than anything she was currently worried about. "Of course."

"I'll get set up over in the corner and then bring the machine over on the portable gurney. Let me know when you're ready for me."

Thank goodness the grandmother had shooed her grandson to his own room and told him to stay there for an hour or until she called. "Let's get this over with," she grunted.

It was as if the woman was resigned to her fate. Kind of like Sara had been moments earlier. But who would take care of Talita's grandson if she gave up? "What's your grandson's name? He seems like a nice boy."

"His name is Jorge. And yes. He is." The woman sighed as she unbuttoned her blouse and dropped it from her shoulders. "His mother—my daughter—died of a drug overdose five years ago. So I've been doing my best to raise him. But really he helps me more than I help him."

"I very much doubt that. Does he go to school?"

"He's in his fifth year. His grades are some of the highest in his class." The pride in her voice was evident.

"Thanks to your help, I'll bet."

Ms. Moises reached around to unhook her bra, but hesitated, her hand going to her left breast. "There's a hole…"

A hole. Oh, Lord.

That was bad. If it *was* cancer and had broken through the skin…

"Wait right here for a minute, okay? I want to see if the doctor needs anything."

What Sara really wanted was to warn him that he probably was not going to need the ultrasound machine after all. She went over to where he was arranging the equipment.

Careful to keep her voice low, she said, "Whatever it is has turned into an open wound."

A soft curse met her ears. Before he could say anything, she hurried to finish. "I—I want to let her maintain as much of her dignity as possible."

"Agreed. Good job, by the way." His gaze softened. "Okay. I'm going to need you to go back to the truck and get me some gauze. We may need to transport her."

"She's raising her grandson. I doubt she'll let us take her anywhere."

He gave her a sharp look. "You suggest we just leave her here?"

Sara wasn't sure what she was suggesting. "No, I'm just not sure—"

"Go get the gauze, and I'll talk to her."

Her sense of nausea increased tenfold. She was already screwing this up and she hadn't even been on the job for a week yet. Then his hand landed on her shoulder. "You're doing fine."

She sucked down a calming breath and glanced into his face. "Thank you."

By the time she got back with gauze, saline solution and some antibiotic ointment that they had on the truck, Sebastian was on a stool in front of their patient. On his face was a look of fierce concentration. The woman's bra had not come off yet. Maybe Sebastian had been waiting for her return, since a male doctor normally had someone there with him when examining a patient.

She threw a small protective cover on the table next to the woman's chair and then set the items she'd brought on top of it.

"Okay, are you ready?"

Talita nodded, the thin set of her lips showing just how tense she was.

Sara snapped on gloves and then helped the woman peel the bra away. "I'm going to go slowly, if that's okay. I don't want to damage your skin."

"I think the damage has already been done." Talita looked up at them. "I'm not worried about me. I'm worried about Jorge. If I die…"

Her voice trailed away, but it was obvious what she had been going to say. It was exactly the same thing that Sara had thought.

"Let's not worry about that now," said Sebastian. He nodded at Sara to go ahead.

Carefully she eased the layers away to reveal a hole the size of a small coin on the outer edge of her breast, right where her arm would lie. It could be due to infection. Or, worse, cancer.

Sebastian shoved his hands into his own set of gloves and examined the wound, palpating the tissue around the area. He didn't say anything, but Sara could almost see the wheels turning as he tried to sort through possibilities. "I want to go ahead and set up the ultrasound, but I want to disinfect the skin and cover the wand so there's no transfer. We'll also change into new gloves."

Transfer. So he did suspect there was at least some kind of bacteria inside the tissue, or else he was going with an abundance of caution. She could only imagine what would happen if their mobile center became contaminated by MRSA or one of the other multi-drug-resistant bacteria. While he prepped the patient for the procedure, he asked Sara to set up the machine. Thank goodness she had done a pretty long stint inside the maternity ward at her hospital, so she at least knew the basics of getting it ready. She calibrated it to the tissue depth that Sebastian shot off to her, and laid the components on the sterile pad, ready for Sebastian to use.

Fifteen minutes later, he ran the transponder over the woman's breast while Sara did her best to engage her in conversation, hoping to keep her mind off what was happening. She learned that Talita had become a widow at the young age of nineteen and had been left to raise her and her husband's only child—a daughter named Marisa. She had worked three jobs to try to support them but, having been raised in a *favela* herself, she'd found it almost impossible to rise up out of the narrow streets. And now she was raising her grandson all by herself.

Sebastian interrupted them. "Did you have any kind of procedure done on your breasts?"

"Procedure? Like what?"

"Breast augmentation, maybe?"

"Aug—what?"

"Did you have them enlarged?"

The woman's eyes grew wide. "No, of course not. I could never afford such a thing."

"I could have sworn…" His brows were pulled together. "Did you ever have anything injected into them?"

"No, I haven't—" Suddenly her teeth bit her lip for several seconds. "Many years ago when I was a young woman there was this party some girls talked about. I was very self-conscious about how slowly I was developing…I was very small back then, even after having my daughter.

"A priestess—a *Mãe-de-Santo*—said there was a safe and easy way to make them grow. She could do it right there inside her house. I went along with it because some of my friends were going to have it done. She gave us each a large shot. One on each side. I don't know what it was—other than it really hurt. But she was right. It instantly made us bigger."

Sebastian shot a quick glance her way. "Silicone."

She'd injected silicone into her breasts? And someone had told her it was safe?

Sara knew that what appeared safe and easy wasn't always. In fact, it was something she was having to learn all over again.

"You think the silicone had something to do with this?"

"I've seen a couple of cases of sclerosing lipogranuloma that mimicked cancer."

"Sclerosing lipogranuloma? I've never even heard of it."

Talita tilted her head. "I don't have cancer, then?"

"I don't think so. I want to get you into a clinic where we can check for sure, but silicone—or another substance—injected directly into tissues can sometimes cause a bad reaction. Kind of like globs of fat that turn into lumps. They can sometimes get infected."

"But that was so long ago."

"It sometimes takes decades before the reaction is enough to be noticeable. And it doesn't happen to everyone."

Sebastian put down the transponder wand and set about bandaging her up. "I want to check to be sure. It might still require surgery."

"No. No surgery."

Sara touched her arm. "Jorge needs you. You said it yourself."

"Would they lop them off? Like my leg?"

Sebastian nodded to Sara to help her get dressed. "It depends on how widespread the problem is. You could eventually develop more of these. Or none. But if you get them taken care of, you can live a long life. Finish raising your grandson. I think you both deserve that."

The woman rubbed a palm across her eyes with a forced casualness that belied far deeper emotions. It was as if Sebastian had just given her back her life. And maybe he had. At the very least, he'd replaced fear with hope. Just like he'd done with Sara's dad.

And glancing over at this enigmatic surgeon, she couldn't help but wonder if he had done the same for her, only in reverse. What had started out as hope for a new job, a new beginning, and a chance to help people like her dad was slowly being swallowed up by fear. The very real fear that Sebastian Texeira might have unintentionally changed her life forever—and the fear of his reaction if it ended up being true.

CHAPTER FOUR

HIS NEW NURSE was late to work. Already.

Not a good omen for their future work relationship. He and Sara were supposed to spend one day a week out in their mobile clinic. The rest of the time she did work in the oncology ward at the hospital, which was where she was supposed to be today.

Had she decided it was all too much for her and thrown in the towel? Leaving without so much as a goodbye? She'd done that very thing after they'd spent the night together. It hadn't seemed like her back then, it didn't seem like her today. Then again, people had surprised him before.

Like his dad with his philandering. Or Sebastian's playboy best friend settling down and marrying Natália.

Could she have left?

Her first day spent in the mobile unit had been a kind of trial by fire with Talita Moises and the little boy with a swelling in his neck. The swelling had turned out to be an inflamed lymph node. All in all, he thought everything had gone well. To an oncologist, any day that brought news of survival was a good day. They had connected Ms. Moises with the doctors at Lucas Carvalho's hospital and things were underway for scheduling surgery. One that might not mean the removal of her breasts. Even if it did, she would live.

Definitely a good day.

So where was Sara?

A niggle of worry settled in his gut.

Just as he was getting ready to check to make sure he'd read the schedule correctly, she came hurrying around the corner, her fingers fiddling with her hair, which was in a high ponytail. Relief warred with irritation. She was due at work and she was worried about how her hair looked?

She stopped directly in front of him, her eyes not quite meeting his. "Sorry. I know I'm late."

"You are." He wasn't about to admit he'd been envisioning her scrambling to catch the first flight home. "Most people around here will tell you that I'm a stickler for punctuality."

"Something came up."

"An emergency?"

"Yes. No." Her face was flushed, beads of perspiration lining her upper lip.

His relief morphed into genuine concern. "Is everything okay?"

She still wasn't looking at him. "No, it's not."

"Your father?"

Although Antônio Moreira's cancer treatments were over, something could always go wrong. Or there were accidents. And since he was a cowboy, there were any number of things that could happen.

"He's fine." Brown eyes met his with a jolt before closing. Reopening. "Is there someplace we can go to talk?"

"Are you quitting the hospital?" Maybe he'd been right after all.

"I'm not sure. I just really need... I really would like to talk to you."

"Let's go to my office." If she had a problem with him, he should be sending her down to Human Resources or to the hospital administrator, but he wanted to hash this out face to face. Why would she quit? She'd only just gotten there, and even though they'd almost kissed in the back of the mobile unit, she'd given no indication that it made a difference. So what was going on?

He led her down a short hallway, opened the door to his office and motioned her inside. Rather than taking a seat behind the desk, he stood in front of it, resting his right hip against the solid surface, suddenly sure he needed the extra support. "So what's this all about? Does it have something to do with your reasons for being late?"

"Yes. I was… I haven't been feeling…" She stopped, her hands squeezed together in front of her. "I'm—I'm pregnant."

There was silence in the room for about five seconds before a slurry of something ugly oozed through his head. She was pregnant? He could have sworn she wasn't the kind of girl who slept around, but maybe he was wrong. Or, worse, maybe sex with him had been an effort to make a boyfriend jealous.

"Does the father know?"

She blinked a couple of times before her gaze hardened, lips thinning dangerously. "He does now."

He tried to process that and failed. "And he wants you to quit, is that it?"

"I don't know. I haven't asked him yet." Her chin went up. "Do you want me to quit?"

"I'm not the one you should be asking. But I'll certainly understand if…" His words faded away as a little thought in the back of his head appeared out of nowhere. He stared at her, willing her to be a mirage—for this whole meeting to be some kind of sick joke.

"You'll certainly understand if what?" Her face was stiff, quiet—almost as if a sculptor had carved a gorgeous image and then encased it in a block of ice.

The hatching thought grew into an adult-sized idea within a few more seconds. "What exactly are you trying to say, Sara?"

"Haven't you figured it out yet?" Her hands were still clasped, knuckles white. "I am pregnant. And you—you are the father."

Father. *Father?*

Uh, no. That isn't right. Can't be right.

Nausea roiled through his gut, spinning in all directions until he was no longer sure what was what. He gripped the desk beside him. "I'm the what?"

"You heard me. I'm pregnant." She licked her lips. "And there hasn't been anyone else. Not since that night."

"Are you sure?"

Her brows went up. "Am I sure there hasn't been anyone else? Pretty damned sure. I think that's something I would remember."

"What's that supposed to mean?" He didn't know why he even asked that question, so he squelched anything that might have followed. But they'd used—

"But that's not possible. I sure as hell found the evidence of protection in that room."

She opened her purse and pulled out a pink stick. "I have some evidence too."

A pregnancy test. On the little readout was a pink plus sign as plain as day. "It could be a false positive."

"Would you like me to show you the other five tests? I can go get them from the apartment."

"*Santa Maria.* No, that won't be necessary."

"One of the condoms must have failed. Or something. Maybe we were one of the victims of whoever has been going around stabbing holes in condom packages. I take it you didn't inspect it before using it."

No, he hadn't inspected it. At the time he'd just been happy that his memories would include safe sex.

Only no one who played with fire was ever truly safe. And Sara was fire. And, at the moment, ice.

"I'm pregnant. I'll do a test here at the hospital as well, if you want, but I really didn't come here to tell you that."

"Are you kidding me? The words 'I'm pregnant' just happened to fall out of your mouth and land on the floor?"

"Oh, I meant to say it. The other thing is this. I'm clean. I've only been with one other man in my life— and he didn't stick around for long."

The pain of those words tore at him, erasing some of his horror. But sticking around wasn't always the best thing that someone could do.

His father, for example.

Yeah, he'd stuck around, but he'd gotten some on the side as well.

She licked her lips. "Are you clean? If there's any doubt, I need to know now."

He laughed. As if dropping a bombshell like being pregnant wasn't enough, now she wanted to know if he'd shot anything besides his sperm into that condom? But if anyone should understand it should be him. In medical school they'd stressed that STDs needed to be reported and partners traced, if at all possible. Sara was trying to do the responsible thing.

So the pregnancy angle was just a little sidebar to the real issue? Would she have even told him about the baby if she hadn't been worried about whether or not he'd given her something?

He didn't even want to think about that.

But pregnant?

Dammit. Lightning really could strike twice. He'd been an unplanned child. And now he'd repeated history with Sara.

"I'm clean. I get tested once a year at the hospital because I work with immunocompromised individuals." He jerked his shoulder to the side to make it crack. The sharp sound was followed by a quick rush of endorphins. An old *futebol* injury had turned into a bad habit. One he couldn't seem to break.

"I should know that. Sorry."

His brain tried to make sense of things, but right now that subway train was rushing past at speeds that caused his head to swim. "You're sure. You're pregnant."

"Do you want to say it a couple more times?" She heaved in a deep breath and then let it out so fast that it sent tendrils of her hair flying to the sides. "Listen, I know this is a shock. It is to me too. But I couldn't live with myself if I didn't at least inform you."

"Inform me." His thoughts wavered. So she'd planned on telling him even without the STD angle. Although… "Are you thinking of terminating?"

"No! I wasn't. I'm not." She paused. "I'm sorry if that makes you unhappy. My dad once told me I was an unplanned pregnancy, and I ended up being the only child they could have. I just can't. I won't. So I'm asking you again. Do you want me to quit my job?"

His parents' bitter marriage came to the forefront of his mind. His folks had stayed together because of him and, later, Natália. They'd as much as admitted it on several occasions. He'd sworn that was never ever going to happen to him. And yet here stood a woman who told him she was expecting a child.

Because of him.

Suddenly he was faced with a horrible decision that really wasn't a decision at all. He knew what he had to do.

"No, Sara, I don't want you to quit. I…" Words suddenly rose up from the abyss, unbidden. Maybe it was an old protective streak left over from when his sister had been sick. Whatever it was, they tore out of his mouth before he could stop them. "I'll help support you. And the baby, of course."

Support her? As in with money?

Sara's chest burned as she stared at him in disbelief. Oh, hell, no.

"Are you kidding me, Sebastian? I don't want your money. I'm insulted you would even say that to me."

"Then why did you come? Do you want a proposal?"

The muscles in her abdomen tightened until she could barely breathe. "What is wrong with you? When I get married, it's going to be because I love someone. Not because I'm pregnant with his child."

A cord of tension appeared in his jaw.

"I'm trying my best to do the responsible thing here. If I fathered a child, I certainly want to help take care of it."

"If?" A chill went through her. "You did. And the responsible thing would be to sit down and calmly work through where we go from here, as far as this job goes. If my being here will make it too awkward for you, then I'll move back to Rio Grande do Sul."

And take the baby with her. She left the words unsaid, but they hung in the air nonetheless. Only it wasn't just her baby. It was his too. And her conscience wouldn't let her just keep working with him without telling him the truth. She could have. It would have been so easy. When her condition became evident, he would just assume that the baby was someone else's. He probably wouldn't even have asked. In the end, she couldn't bring herself to be that dishonest.

"Why even tell me? Why not just leave and not look back?"

"Is that what you wish I had done?"

He turned away, going to stand by a large window at the back of his office. From where she stood she could see several apartment buildings fanned out into the distance. A sky-high office with a gorgeous view. This man was so far out of her league it wasn't even funny.

And they'd made a baby together. Tears gathered behind her eyes.

"No. It isn't what I wish you'd done."

He wished it hadn't happened at all. He didn't say it, but he might as well have.

"Don't worry, I'm not asking for anything. I don't *want* anything. I just thought you deserved to know."

He turned around to face her, putting his hands on his desk and looking across it at her. "It's my child too, Sara. If you're keeping it, I'm serious. I'll assume responsibility for it." His cool clinical tone dashed away any urge to cry.

Her heart became a chunk of granite, continuing to pulse and push blood through her system but refusing to feel. "Please, don't think you have to do that. Lots of women raise children on their own. It happens all the time nowadays."

"It's my child too." The repeated phrase was a little softer this time. A little less clinical. "Don't try to keep me out of its life."

That took her aback. Far from telling her to get away from him or, worse, just throwing money at her to assuage his guilt, he was saying he wanted to be a part of the baby's life. Marriage or no marriage.

"No, of course not. I just assumed you wouldn't want anything to do with it."

He gave a rough snort. "You don't know me very well, then. I practically raised my little sister because our parents—let's just say they weren't exactly the doting type. My dad cheated, and Natália's cancer diagnosis ended up being the only glue that held them together."

That shocked her into silence for several seconds.

"I'm sorry. I had no idea." Why was he even telling her this? Her parents' marriage had been the exact opposite. They had loved her with an all-encompassing type of love. And they *were* the doting type. They doted on her. And on each other. She couldn't imagine anything sadder than to grow up in a home devoid of that kind of love.

Sara wasn't so sure her parents' kind of love existed any more. Her runaway boyfriend was a case in point.

"It's not something I talk a lot about. I'm not even sure why I told you, except to say that I don't want any child of mine to go through life not knowing that he or she is loved."

"He or she will be. By me. And by my father."

"But not by me, is that it?"

"I won't try to keep you out of his or her life." That would be making one mistake into an even bigger one. She just wanted to make sure that's what Sebastian wanted to do. She couldn't bear the thought of him being a part-time dad and then at some point down the road deciding it wasn't for him and walking out of his child's life. Like her boyfriend had done to her. No, if he was going to do that, he could just forget about it. "But think carefully about it. Because once you decide, there will be no going back. It wouldn't be fair to the baby."

"I don't need to think about it."

She shook her head, a steely determination she hadn't

known she possessed coming to the fore. Or maybe her maternal instincts were already kicking in. Whatever it was, she felt a fierce protective drive that wouldn't be denied. "Oh, but I insist. Take a couple of weeks. Or, better yet, a month. Think about it. Weigh the pros and cons of all that will be involved in a lifetime of parenting. And then get back to me with whatever you decide."

He came around the desk and took her by the shoulders. "I don't need a month, Sara. Or even a day. I am telling you right now. I want to be involved in this child's life."

"Are you sure?" Suddenly she was backpedaling like crazy.

They stared at each other for several seconds, and then Sebastian's grip softened, his gaze dropping to her mouth before coming back up.

"I've never been more sure of anything in my life."

A shiver went through her.

Céus! What did she think she was doing, handing down ultimatums? He was a city man, well versed in the comings and goings of relationships, just like her ex. To him, she probably seemed like a country bumpkin. And right now, unlike what she'd just told him, she did indeed want to go back in time. To six weeks ago and a certain wedding, actually. If she could, she might have made another choice. And she certainly would have brought her own damn protection.

Except what was done was done. Whether she liked it or not.

And now she was going to just have to stand back and accept the consequences.

Lucas Carvalho's clinic was in the heart of the Favela do São João. The addition of the tiny healthcare post had added a measure of hope to a desperate population. And, actually, Lucas had named the clinic to reflect that: The Star of Hope Clinic. Joined by Adam Cordeiro, Sebastian had driven here to meet up and get some inside information on the residents and hopefully figure out the biggest areas of need. Adam was already donating a couple of hours a week to the staffing of the clinic. They were scheduled to go out and get drinks together after the meeting.

To tell his friends or not to tell them. That was the question. He was still on shaky ground where Adam was concerned. His sister seemed happy, though, and that was all that mattered. Or it should be.

Adam parked the car in front of the whitewashed little building. The red dirt of the favela—splashed up by rainfall and street traffic—stained the bottom half of the clinic. Even so, with its flower-filled planters that hung beneath each window, the building was cleaner than most of the others in the neighborhood. The greenery and the cheery hand-lettered sign had to be the work of Lucas's wife.

Adam turned to him, pausing with his hand on the door latch. "Just so I'm sure, is everything okay between us?"

Sebastian had been silent for most of the trip from the hospital, and he knew he hadn't been acting quite like himself for the past several months. Time to make amends, if he could. "Yeah, it's all good. Sorry about being such an ass about everything."

"I would have wondered about you if you hadn't gotten in my face. I never saw myself as good enough for Natália."

"You're perfect for her." He sent his friend a forced

grin. "But I know where to find you if that silver perfection ever tarnishes."

"Not going to happen, bro. I'm pretty crazy about the woman. Someday you'll meet the right one and understand exactly what I'm talking about."

Hardly. But that made his decision. He wouldn't say anything about Sara's announcement. Not yet. Not until he absolutely had to. "Like you said, 'Not going to happen, bro.'"

Adam rolled his eyes and stepped out of the car. "I seem to remember saying almost the exact same thing. And now look at me."

Lucas met them at the door. Great. Another happily married friend to contend with.

And if Sara had said she wanted a proposal, would he have given her one? He didn't think so. It would have been for all the wrong reasons. Just like his parents.

"I heard you got Dona Talita worked into the schedule at Tres Corações," he said. "I appreciate that."

Lucas stood aside to let them through the door. "Not a problem. She'll have surgery in a couple of weeks and a follow-up with an endocrinologist to get her blood sugar level back on track. I appreciate you making her a priority. She wouldn't have gone on her own."

"Sara Moreira, the nurse working with me in the mobile clinic, had a lot to do with it."

"Well, whatever the reason, it's great news."

The inside of Lucas's clinic was just as simple as the outside. White plaster walls and white tiles were all easy to disinfect. The space had been divided into three small areas: a spartan waiting room with plastic chairs lining the walls, a small but efficient exam room, and a tiny office that he could see from the waiting area. It contained just a basic metal desk. From what he understood, Lucas took the laptop that held all his patient information with him when he left the building to keep anyone from having a reason to break in and steal anything. Actually, his friend had made it so there was very little to steal. Some cotton balls and tongue depressors maybe, but he kept most of his equipment in tubs that he loaded in and out of his van whenever he was here.

If only Sebastian could load and unload his problems like that. Just tuck them out of sight until he was ready to deal with them again. Only he didn't feel like he would ever be ready to deal with a certain unexpected "problem".

And he damned himself for even thinking of it as a problem. It just hadn't been planned, the way he liked to do with most of his life. A product of having to care for his sister and act as referee for his parents' arguments. He was an expert at compartmentalizing.

Only how did you compartmentalize a child?

Or his or her mother?

You didn't. At least not in a way he was accustomed to.

"Is the clinic open today?"

Lucas shook his head. "Not today. Sophia has finally convinced me that I need to take a day or two off each month to 'recharge my batteries', as she put it."

"A day or two a month? I should say so. That's where I come in, I assume."

"Yes, if you have time." He pulled three of the white chairs from their spots along the wall and dragged them to the center. He motioned them to sit. "Adam is already working two hours a week. I don't want you to feel like you need to be at the clinic itself, since I know you're going to be putting the hours in with the mobile clinic. If I could just plan it so that the clinic is closed on the day the mobile unit is here, that would be great. I can send you cases, if you want, like I did the last time."

"That works for me. In between patients, then, I could park by the clinic and if someone has a need they can just stop by. That way it'll be easy to find me."

Adam glanced his way. "Maybe you should have a key to the clinic and just meet patients in here?"

"I'd rather keep things as simple as possible, actually. I'll email you information on any patients I see, just like I did with my first two. It will make your record-keeping easier, I think. And I'll know where everything is inside the truck."

"How are things going with Sara, by the way?" Adam asked. "You two getting along? You seemed to be making eyes at each other at the wedding. Or was that just my imagination?"

Great, he'd been hoping no one had noticed.

"Your imagination. There were no 'eyes'. Or anything else involved. Sara and I have only been working together for a week. We'll see how it goes in a few more. But hopefully any possible issues have been resolved."

Except for one.

The bombshell she'd dropped earlier in the day still seemed unreal, like it had happened to a different Sebastian in an alternate universe. He didn't do things like get drunk and get women pregnant.

Only he hadn't set out to get her pregnant. Even drunk, a little part of his head had tried to do the right thing by protecting them both.

Instead, he'd failed.

Lucas glanced at him. "What issues?"

"Just a little lovers' spat." Adam said it with a grin, but the words hit Sebastian just the wrong way.

"We are not lovers." The words came out half growled.

"Whoa." Lucas's brows shot up. "I'm pretty sure Adam was kidding."

"Sorry." He popped his shoulder joint and sighed. "It's been stressful trying to get the hospital administration fully on board with the mobile unit. If you knew how many hoops I've had to jump through to get this up and running, you'd be buying me a drink—or five."

"If that's what you need, you got it." Adam slapped him on the back.

No, it wasn't what he needed. What he needed was a way out of his predicament. One that had both him and Sara coming out of it unscathed. Once she started showing, and people started asking questions…

Talk about hoops. Somehow he didn't think Paulo Celeste would approve of Sara suddenly expecting his child right after going to work for the hospital.

Dammit, he hadn't even thought about that. Until now. Surely it was no one's business.

But people were curious. They were bound to ask. And the truth would come out, even if he didn't want it to.

He hadn't technically broken hospital policy that he knew of, since Sara hadn't been working for the hospital when she'd gotten pregnant. And if he'd known about it before she'd come to Santa Coração, he would have vetoed them hiring her. But he hadn't known. Neither had she.

Or so she said. What if that's why she'd wanted to come to the hospital? Because she'd already known about the pregnancy?

No, she'd been genuinely shocked.

"Drinking's what got me into this mess."

"What mess?" Both men were now staring at him. It was then that he realized the words hadn't gone with the conversation at hand. Talk about letting the cat out of the bag. They were going to find out. Better that it came from him than from the hospital grapevine. And maybe they could give him some advice on how to handle things.

"Sara's pregnant."

"Sara?" Lucas frowned. "As in your new nurse, Sara?"

"Yep."

"Wow, she didn't reveal this at her interview? It's going to be pretty damned difficult to replace her, isn't it, when she goes on maternity leave? When is she due?"

Sebastian did some quick mental calculations and came up blank. "Subtract six weeks from nine months."

"Six weeks." Adam planted his elbows on his knees and leaned forward. "That's back when Natália and I got married, so let's see… Do not even tell me."

It was now or never. "I think I just did. We'd both had a little too much to drink and things got—out of control."

How lame did that sound?

Lucas's gaze sharpened. "*You're* the father?"

"It would seem that way."

Adam shook his head, patent disbelief on his face. "What was it you said to me in the car a few minutes ago? 'Not going to happen'?"

"It's not. We're not. It was an accident."

"Is she going to keep it?"

Lucas's question was innocent enough, but it raised the hair on the back of his neck. Hadn't he asked her the same thing, though?

"Yes, she's going to keep it."

"Well, congratulations. I think."

"Yes," said Adam. "Congratulations. Sometimes things don't go as planned. I'm proof positive of that. But they tend to work out the way they were supposed to."

Not for his mom and dad. Not for Natália either, in getting cancer. But there was no way he could say that.

"We'll see."

"Are you going to keep working with her?"

Sebastian gave a shrug. "What else can I do? If we tell anyone, things could get messy. Worst-case scenario is that she'd be asked to leave the project."

"Because of that? Even if she is, surely there are other jobs at the hospital."

"We're currently on a hiring freeze, according to the hospital administrator. Unless someone quits, we can't hire any additional personnel, because of the economy tanking. Sara was already the exception to the rule. I imagine the other local hospitals are in the same spot."

"I know Tres Corações is. Damn, that puts you in kind of a touchy situation, though, doesn't it?" Lucas propped a foot on his knee.

"Touchy is how he got into this."

"Oh, you're a funny, funny guy, Adam." He knew his friend was trying to lighten the atmosphere, but right now there was nothing anyone could say or do to make this any easier. In truth, Sebastian held both his future and Sara's in the palm of his hand. He'd spoken the truth. If he let Paulo know, the man might start worrying about corporate sponsors and turn sour on the whole Mãos Abertas project. Sara would probably then be let go because of a lack of other job positions, and Sebastian himself might receive an unwelcome lecture on maintaining professional appearances.

And with the mobile clinic being an experiment, he could very well sink its chances for continuing into the future. All because of a single error in judgment.

Sara was going to pay for it, and so was he. But he would be damned if all of the patients who'd stood to be helped by this endeavor would pay.

So he would just have to do his best to keep this thing under wraps. Starting with Adam and Lucas.

Then, he somehow had to convince Sara to keep her pregnancy a secret for the next several months. Or else ask her to go back to Rio Grande do Sul before anyone at the hospital got wind of the situation.

Even if she hated him for it.

CHAPTER FIVE

"I ALREADY TOLD YOU. I'm not planning on telling anyone. At least not right away."

When Sebastian had called her into his office this morning, she'd expected him to maybe try to get her to agree to let him support her again.

Not a chance. He'd obviously seen the error of his ways and had decided on a different tack. Just shove his future child under a rug to keep the scandal from messing with his stellar reputation.

She should be glad and take that as evidence that he'd never gotten anyone else pregnant. Until she'd come along.

Instead, an oppressive weight of exhaustion came over her. Probably due to the early changes in her body from her pregnancy. She thought of something.

"I won't deny this baby prenatal care. And I'm not sure how you can keep it a secret if I'm seeing an obstetrician."

The pencil he'd picked up from his desk tilted back and forth between his thumb and index finger, the speed increasing. "I'm not asking you to not get medical care, I just…" His glance went beyond her as if he was thinking things through.

So he hadn't thought about that angle either. "Natália is a neonatologist, maybe she can help."

"In other words, you're willing to share the news with your sister as long as it benefits you." Her voice was flat. So he could dictate who knew and who didn't? To hell with that.

He shifted in his chair, the pencil in his hand going still. "This situation isn't easy for anyone."

"'Anyone' being?"

"Why are you so angry?" The pencil dropped onto the desk.

"I'm not. You just went from not caring if anyone knew to keeping it a complete secret."

Up went his brows. "I never planned on sending out birth announcements, so I don't know where you got that idea."

He'd started out by asking to be a part of this child's life. If that wasn't sending out an announcement, she didn't know what was. Or had he forgotten about that?

Since she couldn't think of a witty response, she clamped her jaws shut and willed them to stay that way. He stared at her for a few seconds.

"Do you want to go home?"

"I'm not sick. At least, not at the moment." She'd felt a couple of twinges earlier, but a pack of *água e sal* crackers had taken care of that.

"I don't mean to your apartment here at the hospital. I'm talking about Rio Grande do Sul."

A ripple of fear went through her, and she pressed her spine against the back of her chair. "Are you threatening to fire me?"

"What?" His eyes shut for a moment, fingers going to the bridge of his nose and pinching. When he looked up again, his gaze had softened. "Hell, no. I'm not threatening you, Sara. The hospital has been cutting costs for a while. That means no extraneous personnel."

"But the mobile clinic…" Was he saying they'd decided to do away with her job?

"Is an experiment. It's not guaranteed to continue. If there is the slightest glitch along the way, they could scrap the entire project."

A glitch. As in her pregnancy. Oh, Lord. She put herself in Sebastian's shoes for a second. A new nurse was hired to work with the illustrious Dr. Texeira and came up pregnant with his child soon afterwards. At the very least it would raise some eyebrows. Not many hospitals would tolerate questionable behavior on the part of its staff, especially if it affected its reputation. Even if the hospital wasn't affected, Sebastian could be. Especially if the news came out at just the wrong moment.

"I'm so sorry, Sebastian. I swear I didn't know about the pregnancy before I got here, or I never would have come."

"I believe you. The timing just—"

"Sucks."

One side of his mouth went up. "That's one way of putting it."

"I don't want them to squash the project." Which was a surprise, because a few days ago she had been wondering if she could even do this job. And then she'd seen what had happened with Talita Moises. Without the mobile clinic, she might never have sought treatment. And she probably would have died of an infection, somewhere down the road. Yet now she had a good chance of survival.

All because of the clinic.

"I don't either. But you're right. It's not worth risking your health or that of the baby." His fingers sought out the pencil again. "I'm sorry to say that Adam Cordeiro and Lucas, the doctor who runs the favela clinic, already know. It came out during a meeting. They won't say anything, but the wider the circle gets of those who know—and they will know—the harder it will be. Natália has to know at the very least. Any pharmacist who fills a prescription will know. Ultrasound technicians. The list goes on and on."

"I'll move to another hospital."

He shook his head. "As big as São Paulo is, most of the doctors know each other, and the pool of hospital administrators is even smaller."

"So what do you want me to do? Do you *want* me to go home?"

She couldn't believe she had even asked that question. It might be the easiest solution, but it wasn't what she wanted in her heart of hearts.

"Not unless that's what you want."

She leaned forward and put one of her hands on his desk. "I don't. I really think I could do some good here."

"I think you could too. I'm toying with an idea, but you probably aren't going to like it."

"I don't understand."

"I asked you if you expected a proposal when you first told me. A question to which I got a resounding no." He covered her hand with his own. "But think about it in the bright light of day, Sara. It's the perfect solution. There are several husband and wife teams that work at the hospital. If we did it quietly, and I told the hospital administrator that we had already been 'involved' before you came up here, no one would be the wiser. It would be the truth, to a certain extent."

She swallowed, finally understanding. "You want to get married. Why not just tell the administrator I'm pregnant? Surely this has happened before."

"Maybe. The administrator stressed that things needed

to stay professional between us. And since you're here doing a temporary *estágio*, it may be misconstrued as my taking advantage of my position."

"But you didn't. There has to be some way to explain all of this."

"If you can think of something, I'm all ears."

She racked her brain, but came up empty.

Sebastian squeezed her hand. "If you really want to stay here, I think it's what's best for the patients."

"So you'll make a noble sacrifice."

"No. I've never claimed to be noble." He blew out a breath. "I'm trying to help. To figure out a way that not only keeps the Mãos Abertos program up and running but also keeps you from losing your job."

"I'll go work at another hospital in the area."

"I already checked. The answers were all the same. No one is hiring. A lot of the health-care sector is operating in the red, and that situation doesn't look like it's going to improve anytime soon."

He'd already checked. Had already thought of sending her away to a different hospital to save his own ass?

No, he'd said it was to keep her from being sent home. She could only imagine what her dad would say. Actually, knowing her father, he'd probably travel up to São Paulo and give Sebastian a piece of his mind—if not worse. She'd been planning on keeping the baby a secret from him, at least for a while, so why was it any different that Sebastian wanted to keep the situation quiet?

It wasn't any different. It just hurt that he didn't trust her not to say anything. Realistically, though, if she stayed the whole six months, she was eventually going to show—and the secret would be out. And he was right about the list of people who would know once she started prenatal care.

But to get married because of it?

"I can't see myself marrying someone I don't love."

"And rightly so. I've seen where that can lead and it's not pretty. This would just be temporary. For maybe a year or two until well after the baby is born and your *estágio* is over. Then we get a quiet divorce. Just like lots of other couples."

Did he even hear himself? Her parents had been married for a long, long time, and they'd been happy. It was what she'd once hoped for herself. So to go through a sham of a marriage seemed disrespectful to her mom's memory somehow. And yet what else could she do? Abortion wasn't common in Brazil, but even if it was, she wouldn't choose that route. She wanted this baby.

There were several other married couples, he'd said—some of them probably had children—so they would just blend in with the crowd, was that it?

Maybe he was right.

He'd said it himself, this wouldn't be forever. And she certainly didn't have a boyfriend any more or even a distant prospect that could give her the cover story Sebastian wanted her to have.

"A year or two is kind of ambiguous. If I agree to this—and I haven't said I would—I would want to have a definite time frame so there are no misunderstandings on either side." Not that she expected Sebastian to fall head over heels for her and refuse to give her a divorce. No, it was more as a reminder to herself that he wasn't promising her roses and forever.

Sebastian's head cocked to the side. "How about we split the difference and say eighteen months, then? Can you stand to carry my name for that long?"

"Our situation wouldn't be any different than it is now,

would it? Just a fake marriage to keep our situation from ruining everything."

"The marriage would have to be legal, that's the only way any of this will work." He frowned. "And the situation wouldn't be any different, but your living arrangements would."

"I'm sorry?"

"Don't you think it would look kind of odd for a married couple to live in separate apartments?"

"I'm not sure… You want me to move in with you?" Surely that wasn't what he was saying.

"My apartment is big. You would practically have your own place with a few minor adjustments."

"How minor?" She was rapidly losing control of the situation. Was she actually thinking of going through with this? Of marrying a man who was practically a stranger?

Her mouth twisted. That certainly hadn't stopped her from sleeping with him. From carrying his child.

He'd said he wanted to be involved in the baby's life. What better way than to have said baby living under his roof for a few months after it was born? Except her *estágio* was only listed as being for six months. Was he inviting her to stay past that date? Maybe it was better not to ask.

"There are two bedrooms." He paused. "They share a bathroom, though. There's another one down the hall, but it's not a full bath. We'd have to work out a schedule for showering."

A shared bathroom. She could only imagine hearing the water running in there as he took his shower and picturing him naked. With water streaming down his…

She gulped. That was no minor adjustment. She would

have to invest in earplugs. Or something. "There are locks on the doors, right?"

Up went his brows. "Afraid I might try to sneak into your room while you're asleep?"

The thought of that made something in her tummy shift sideways. She covered it with a laugh.

"Of course not! I just don't want to walk in on you when you're in the bathroom."

"Yes, there are locks, Sara. Strong enough to keep out even the big bad wolf."

He might have meant it as a joke, but his words hit far too close to home for comfort. Because in that particular story the big bad wolf only wanted one thing. To devour Little Red Riding Hood. And he would do anything it took to get her.

Only Sebastian didn't want her. Not really. He just wanted to make sure his clinic stayed in business. And that she wasn't sent packing—although that was probably all part and parcel of making sure his pet project continued operating. Either way, she should be grateful. And she was. He was risking an awful lot for her. The least she could do was listen to his proposal and give him an honest answer.

"Tell me exactly how you expect all of this to work."

A week after making his crazy, impulsive suggestion, Sebastian found himself in a courthouse, reciting words that meant absolutely nothing to him. Worse, he was promising that he would keep to those words. Natália was there as a witness, although she had tried to talk him out of it several times. "This is too fast, Sebastian. It doesn't feel right."

It didn't feel right to him either. But once he'd decided, and Sara had agreed, there was nothing left but to go through with his scheme. As stupid as it now seemed.

Sara had asked that her father remain out of the loop. At least for a while. Once she got through her first trimester, when most miscarriages happened, she would tell him. As if getting married in secret would go over any better with him than it had with Natália.

This was seeming less and less like a good idea and more like a recipe for disaster.

Unless they could keep it together and do exactly what he'd said they would do: stay together until the baby was born and then for nine more months after that. When he broke it down like that, it didn't seem like such an eternity.

Who was he kidding? It already seemed like an eternity.

Wasn't it a small price to pay, though, to continue saving lives in the *favelas*?

Sara took the ring from his sister with a smile that wavered just slightly. That was okay, because everything inside him was wavering. And not just slightly, either.

Taking his hand in hers, she slid the thin band onto his ring finger. The ring he'd placed on hers moments earlier glittered an accusation at him. What would his child think of this once he or she was old enough to understand?

The same thing he'd thought when he'd found out the truth about his parents' marriage.

Hopefully he and Sara would exit this arrangement as friends, if nothing more. That was more than he could say for his mom and dad.

He glanced at Sara's face as she parroted the words the justice of the peace spoke. Her eyes were somber and unhappy.

Hell, he had practically forced her into doing this. He should have just asked her to go home. Oh, he'd blathered on about the project and it being canceled—and that was important. It was. But he'd also realized that if she left, he might never even see his child. There'd be no reason for her to seek him out. Especially if he'd sent her packing back to Rio Grande do Sul. And that killed him.

She took a breath, hesitating just a brief second longer than necessary. Sebastian gave her hand what he hoped was a reassuring squeeze, since he couldn't ask her if she was okay.

She did look at him then and returned the pressure.

A sense of relief went through him. He wasn't quite sure why—maybe he'd needed a little reassurance himself.

Then the stranger pronounced them husband and wife, inviting Sebastian to kiss his new bride. Natália glanced at him, brows raised in challenge. Fine. She thought it was too fast? That he was having second thoughts? He'd show both her and that smug official.

Cupping Sara's face in his hands and registering her slight gasp of shock as he did so, he lowered his head and planted his lips on hers. Only her mouth was a little sweeter than he remembered. A little more pliable. A lot more, in fact. If he hadn't known better, he might almost believe she was…

Returning his kiss.

He blinked, pulling back in an instant—somehow managing to fake a smile as he leaned down again and kissed the tip of her nose. There. Playful. That's how he would get through all of this. She was the mother of his child, but she was not his lover. He could treat her like a distant relative or a…

His glance went to Natália and a rock dropped to the

pit of his stomach. No, what he felt for Sara was nothing like the easy affection he held for his baby sister. It was more like the uneasy yearning that happened when he was around his mother and father. A wish for things to be different. Not good.

Natália came over and hugged his new wife, while sending him another silent glare over her shoulder. She mouthed, "This is wrong." Then she turned around and left the room. Well, there was nothing keeping her. She'd already signed the document that made all this legal.

But legal didn't necessarily make it right.

His plan was to talk to the hospital administrator as soon as they moved Sara into his house. He wasn't quite sure what his angle was going to be yet, because the man would undoubtedly ask if this was why he'd been so eager to start the project.

And then Sebastian would remind him that he'd been pushing for a mobile unit for the last two years. And it only made sense that he'd want to share something that was so important to him with those he loved.

Loved. That was a laugh.

The justice of the peace shifted, maybe sensing that the atmosphere in the room was darker than it should have been.

Sara saved him from trying to make small talk by glancing up at him. "You ready to head out?"

"Yes." He thanked the government official, and they walked out the door and into the blinding light of midday. He held a hand over his brow to shade his eyes, looking for his car. "That wasn't as bad as I thought it would be."

"Wasn't it?"

Sara's voice had a sad quality to it that he didn't like. Had he really done the right thing? Natália didn't think so.

"Hey." He took her hand and stopped her. "It's going to

be all right. Eighteen months will go by fast. And you'll have the baby to worry about soon enough."

"I know. It just seems dishonest somehow."

She and Natália were evidently reading from the same play book.

"Not dishonest. Just necessary."

The glare from the sun kept him from seeing her expression.

"Do you really think the administrator is going to buy our story?"

"He should, if we put on a united front. I'm pretty sure he's not going to fire one of the hospital's two oncological surgeons." He hesitated. "Would you be willing to roll part of your salary into mine? I can make up the difference. But if Paulo Celeste thinks he stands to gain something from the arrangement, he'll be much more likely to overlook any slivers of doubt. I'll talk to him."

She blinked. "Shouldn't that be 'we'?"

"I think it will be easier if I do it alone."

Pulling her hand away, she shook her head. "It's my life too. You talked about presenting a united front. How can we do that if I'm not even there?"

"He's been known to yell." Something that always made Sebastian distinctly uncomfortable, since his parents did that routinely.

"I'm a big girl. I think I can handle it."

She might be able to, but could he?

"If you're sure, I won't try to stop you."

He saw a flash of something that could have been teeth. "You can ask my father how easy it is to stop me once I have my mind set on something."

"That bad, huh?"

"The worst. He says I'm more stubborn than a steer during cutting and branding season."

"I have no idea what that even means."

She tilted her head and gave him a look. "No? Where I'm from, everyone knows what that means. I'm sure you city guys have a similar expression."

"Not really." Especially not since that sassy little look she'd just sent him had arrowed straight down to his groin. Probably remembering that kiss a few moments earlier.

"Sure you do. 'More stubborn than...'" She gave a little hand flourish that told him to fill in the blank.

Cornered, he forced his sluggish brain to think of something. Anything. "More stubborn than a V-fib that refuses to be converted."

"Okay, I'm not sure I like being compared to a deadly arrhythmia."

She was right. It was a stupid comparison. And a stupid game.

"Let's just go get your stuff and move it over to my apartment. And then tomorrow we'll tackle telling the hospital administrator."

"Are you sure you don't want to wait a few weeks? Until we see if the pregnancy is even viable?"

"Someone is bound to mention you moving out of the hospital apartments. And then it will be harder to explain away."

"I guess you're right. I just hate lying to people."

"Let's just concentrate on what's true, okay? It's true that we got married, is it not?" He turned and started walking back toward the car.

"Yes."

"It's true that you're moving into my place, right?"

"Um—yes." She caught up to him a few yards later. "But we don't love each other."

"When was the last time you asked a newly married couple if they loved each other?"

"Well…never."

He unlocked the passenger side door and waited until she climbed inside. "That's right, because you just assume they got married because they fell in love. The hospital administrator will assume the same thing. I doubt he'll even ask."

"I hope you're right."

"Don't worry. As soon as I mention combining incomes, the dollar signs in his eyes will block out any objections he may have. He might even be happy for us." Sebastian carefully omitted the fact that he planned on making up the difference in her salary and putting it aside in a special account. And if she was able to carry the pregnancy to term, he would sock money away into a college fund. That news could wait until they started their divorce proceedings, though.

"And if it doesn't?"

"Then we'd better have an alternate explanation ready."

All he had to do was think of one. Between now and tomorrow morning.

CHAPTER SIX

NOSSA! SARA COULD see why the condominium building was called the Vista do Vale, because the scenery from the twenty-fifth-floor balcony was spectacular. Sara had never been inside an apartment this luxurious. It certainly didn't feel like it was situated in a valley from where she was looking. After living her entire life in her parent's one-story house on the ranch, she felt kind of queasy about how high up they were. Or maybe that was her pregnancy. Honestly, it was probably a little bit of both.

"Where did you say the fire escape was?" She called back to where Sebastian was setting her two large suitcases on the polished marble floor of the foyer.

He came through the double sliding glass doors that opened to an outside living space. A space that was almost as big as her whole nurse's apartment at the hospital.

"I didn't, but see that platform hanging over there?"

"Where—? Oh, no!" She'd noticed the contraption hanging a few floors below them. Panic went through her system, the queasiness growing exponentially.

"Relax, Sara. I'm kidding. They're in the process of polishing and repairing the tile on this side of the building."

"In that?" No one in their right mind would stand on what appeared little more than a wooden platform with a thin line of metal railing encircling the outside. Even as she looked, it seemed to sway in the breeze. Her nausea spiked. There was no way she would go out in something like that.

She could tell the difference, though, in the cobalt tiles that had been polished and those that had collected years of dust and grime from the city below. Even the "before" view, though, oozed opulence and wealth.

"The company has many years of experience in this work. They know what they're doing."

She glanced down again, and then backed away, only to bump into Sebastian, whose arm went around her to brace her. The warmth of his touch soothed her rapidly fraying nerves. "Seriously, we could get out if there were a fire, right?"

"There are stairs, in case the elevator goes out."

"Have you ever had to use them?"

"I have. More than once."

"Deus do céu." She pressed both palms against her stomach. "Why?"

He turned her around to face him, hands still on her shoulders. "Hey, are you okay?"

"I think so. I just didn't think this would all be so…" She couldn't find the right word, so she settled for waving her hand to encompass the inside of his condominium. "How long have you lived here?"

"Not long. I moved here about a year ago."

"And you've already used the stairs more than once?"

His thumbs trailed over her collarbones as he peered into her face, as if seeing something that worried him. "I was kidding. I only went up and down them for exercise when I knew I wouldn't have time to go to the gym."

Her whole body sagged closer to him. "Well, you could have said that right away."

"I had no idea you were afraid of heights."

"I've never really had a chance to test out whether I was or wasn't. I think the tallest place I've ever been was the waterfall at Iguaçu."

"You really only notice the height out here. Inside, it just feels like a regular living space."

Regular living space? Was he kidding? There was nothing "regular" about his apartment. "I'll take your word for it." As much as she tried to keep her voice neutral, even she could hear the ironic overtones behind her comment. Besides, that continued brushing movement of his thumbs was beginning to warm her up in ways that worried her.

Maybe he read her thoughts, because he grinned and put his hand under her elbow. "Come on back inside, and I'll show you where you'll be staying. Since you're such a fan of heights, maybe I'll take you to the observation deck of the Banespa building. You can see a lot of the heart of the downtown area from there. You can even see this building from it."

Groaning, she let him lead her back inside. "Are there stairs there too?" She could see this being a common litany for her time in São Paulo.

"There are, but we'll want to take the elevator. Once we reach the thirty-third floor, we'll have to go up two flights of stairs to get to the deck."

Okay, so the fear was still there, but there was also a glimmer of excitement. Maybe it was from the gentle way he'd calmed her fears out on the veranda. Or because he wanted to take her to see parts of the city.

He's probably joking, Sara. You don't need to take any of this too seriously.

Because doing that could make for a whole lot of heartache. Especially since her wonky hormones were making her feel a little off—a touch lovey-dovey about everything—as it nurtured those maternal instincts. She had to remember that none of her emotions were trustworthy at the moment. And Sebastian would be horrified if he thought she was looking down the road and picturing them as an old married couple.

Not that she was. Even if the way he'd looked at her a few minutes ago had made her want things she couldn't have.

Good thing they had set up some ground rules.

"Well, we'll see. With the mobile clinic and your regular rounds at the hospital, you'll probably be too busy to do much of anything outside of work."

"We have to eat lunch or dinner sometime." He threw a glance over his shoulder as he headed toward the foyer.

"We?"

"We'll be working most of the same hours, and we're newlyweds, remember? It stands to reason that we would want to eat together from time to time. Like Adam and Natália do. Or the other married couples who work at the hospital."

"The two couples who were at your sister's wedding. They both work at the hospital as well?"

"Kind of. Marcos does, as you know. You'll be seeing a lot of him around the oncology department. And his wife, Maggie, works there as well. Lucas and Sophia do quite a bit of relief work in poorer parts of the country, and of course Lucas runs the clinic in the *favela* we were at the other day. But, yes, it seems that Santa Coração is a breeding ground for romance, my sister included."

Okay, so if he had caught the irony in her earlier words, she had definitely caught a hint of sardonic derision in his tone.

"You disagree with people falling in love?"

"I don't disagree with their decisions. I'm just saying that I tend to be a little more skeptical. I've witnessed some train-wreck marriages that never should have taken place."

Was he talking about theirs? This whole sham had been his idea, not hers. Maybe he was already regretting having suggested it. Or warning her not to get too attached. He needn't bother. Maybe she should try to reassure him on that point.

"Train wrecks have to be lifted off the tracks at some point. They're not permanent."

"Sometimes there are extenuating circumstances for them to linger." He reached down and picked up her luggage, no longer looking at her.

Oh, God. He *was* talking about them—about her pregnancy. Maybe she should have insisted on a prenup to make him feel better about everything. And here she was acting like a starstruck teenager about his apartment and the city in general. No wonder he was nervous.

"Hey." She caught at his arm, the biceps tightening beneath her touch. "Stop for just a minute, please."

Sebastian set her luggage down and turned to face her, his eyes a dark molten mass of—anger? "What is it?"

She took her hand off him in a hurry.

"If you're worried about me trying to extend our arrangement, don't. I'll sign a prenup or a contract, if you want. It's not too late for either."

"What are you talking about?"

She shrugged, needing to look away from those huge pupils. "I'm talking about this farce. I didn't want to do it in the first place, remember, and I only agreed in order to—"

"No. I'm sorry." His hands went to her shoulders once again, gaze softening. "I wasn't referring to you at all.

I know you didn't try to trap, coerce or whatever other words you think are rattling around in my head right now. I'm talking about my folks. They haven't been the greatest example of marital bliss. Natália and I both know they stayed together for our sake. And now they just—stay together, probably because they've been married for so long. But they're not happy. I don't remember them *ever* being happy."

"How awful." She tried to switch gears, but all she felt was a huge sense of relief, mixed with sadness. "Surely they must love each other. Some couples just show it differently." Her dad was a good example of that. He had always been a man of few words, but he had loved his wife deeply. So deeply she didn't know if he would ever marry again.

"I don't think the word 'divorce' is used as a weapon in most homes. I was surprised when Natália decided to get married at all. Especially as quick as it was."

"They seem very happy. At least from what little I've seen. Natália and I are friends. Surely she would have mentioned something if there was trouble in paradise."

"I'm sure they're fine. I just wonder how long it can— Forget it. I shouldn't have mentioned any of it."

She reached up and covered one of his hands with her own. "Yes, you should have. It helps me understand how hard this whole situation is for you. But we don't hate each other. At least, I don't hate you."

One side of his mouth went up and his fingers tightened their grip on her shoulders before he let go of one and caught her hand. "You probably should. I keep telling myself I should have checked those condoms when I put them on, but I wasn't quite myself that night."

"Neither of us were. Knowing about your parents helps

me understand. And I don't hate you. I hope we'll come out of this as friends."

"Hmm—friends." His smile slid just a bit higher. "That can be a loaded term. My sister and Adam started out as friends. Look what happened with them."

This time he was joking. She should be elated that they'd gotten everything out in the open, but there was this vague sense of loneliness rolling around inside her. "Not all friends become lovers."

His thumb stroked over the palm of her hand, sending a shiver through her.

Careful, Sara.

"No, they don't. But former lovers can become friends, don't you think? We just have to make sure we don't go on any more drinking binges."

They were in trouble, then, because the low thrum of his voice was as intoxicating as any liquor. And his thumb, still scrubbing across her palm in a soft back and forth motion, was making her nerve endings tingle in spots far removed from her hand. Was he doing that on purpose? If so, she should tell him to stop. Except it felt good. Intimate in a way that rough, grabbing hands could never be.

"Well, since I'm not allowed to drink until after the baby is born, there's nothing for either of us to worry about."

Right?

"Nothing at all." Sebastian's voice deepened, laced with a tension she hadn't heard since—

That night at the bar. Right before he'd swept her off to that motel.

Deus! It had to be her imagination. She was letting it run wild. If she just tugged her hand, he would release her and all would be right with the world.

But even though her brain tried to tell her arm to slide backward, it stayed right where it was.

Okay, Sara, try something else. Hurry!

Before she could, his mouth kicked up sideways in a half-smile that drove the wind from her lungs.

"Do you do that on purpose?" He let go of her hand, his index finger traveling up to her lower lip and making it wiggle slightly. The touch went through her like an electric shock. It took her a second to find enough words to answer.

"Do what?"

"Puff that out when you're nervous about something." He let his hand drop back to his side, although his gaze stayed put.

She sucked the errant lip back over her teeth before realizing how ridiculous that was. "No. At least I don't think I do."

"I noticed it for the first time at the wedding."

He had? Her insides quivered with heat. Was he doing *that* on purpose?

She tried to clear her throat, but it came out as a weak puff of air that sounded more like a sigh. Maybe because that's what it was. Time to change the subject. "You were going to show me the bedrooms?"

No, wait. That huskiness in her voice wasn't right. And that low pulsing in her belly—the one telling her to do strange things—had to belong to someone else.

"You lip is doing that thing again." He shifted closer. "And there is nothing I would like better than to show you the bedrooms. Except for maybe—this."

His head lowered until he was hovering just above her mouth. *"Posso?"*

Deus. Did he have to ask?

"Yes." She drew the word out, letting that *s* roll across

her tongue, everything inside her screaming for him to close the gap between them and kiss her.

Then he was right there, his hand moving to cup her chin. This was no tentative, questioning touch. It was mouth to mouth and beyond, a display that said this had been just as much on his mind as it had been on hers.

She opened to him, shuddering when his tongue slid easily inside, his exploration turning into long, lazy movements that left no doubt as to where his thoughts were. *Graças a Deus*, that was a relief, because hers were in exactly the same place.

His arm went around her waist, hauling her against him, widening his stance so she fit between his legs. And, yes, that hard ridge of flesh was right where she expected it to be: cradled in the soft flesh of her belly.

The bedrooms. His. Hers. She didn't care which, but she needed to be there. But to say anything, she would have to pull her mouth away from the sweet thrill of having him inside. And she wasn't willing to forgo that. Not yet. In fact, she closed her lips around him, relishing the groan that followed soon afterwards.

He wheeled back in a rush, separating himself so quickly that she just stood there dazed for a second.

What? No!

Just when she thought he had come to his senses, he reached down, his arm going behind her knees and scooping her feet out from under her. He gave her a little toss to settle her against his chest, leaving her to clutch at his shoulders. "Do you still want to see where I sleep?"

All she could do was give a single nod that had him striding down the hallway, past one closed door and stopping in front of another.

She licked her lips, his taste still as fresh as it had been seconds earlier. When he made no move to go inside, she asked, "Do you need me to get the door?"

"Mmm…" He leaned down and kissed her again. "No, just anticipating what's going to happen once it's open."

He wasn't the only one. But she was getting impatient, and a little afraid he might back out at the last second.

She unhooked one of her arms and reached toward the ornate silver lever, her fingers barely able to brush against it. Sebastian obliged by tipping her far enough so she could grab it. She pushed down, the latch releasing and allowing the door to swing in.

"Waiting is highly overrated."

He gave her a heated glance, chuckling. "Oh, but the pleasure is that much sharper when it finally arrives."

The words made her shiver. Did that mean he meant to draw this out?

He moved inside the room and set her on the edge of a huge bed, his presence preventing her from closing her legs. That was okay, because the way he was standing was pure invitation. All she had to do was…

She scooted closer, fingers sliding up his thighs only to have his hands grab both of hers.

"What are you doing, Sara?"

"Didn't they teach you anything in sex education class?" She gave him what she hoped was a sexy grin.

"Oh, I have plenty of education. Want to see?"

He spread her hands so they were wide apart and then bore her back onto the bed. His kiss was immediate. Almost aggressive. And her hips arched high, trying to find him.

He lifted his head to look at her. "Since you don't seem interested in slow and easy, let's go fast and hard, shall we?"

One leg spread hers even further, settling his length in the opening he'd created.

"Yes!" This time when her hips went up, they connected with him, a jolt of sensation careening through her. She repeated the movement, her pleasure centers engaging in an instant. Okay, this was good. A little too good. On her third foray around the sun she slid along him, eyes fluttering closed as she ventured closer to—

He edged away. "I changed my mind."

"What?" Her eyes snapped open.

Her reaction was met with a rough laugh. "Just kidding. Let me get my zipper down, okay?"

She sucked down a relieved breath. "No protection needed tonight."

"Oh, no? I think you might need a little."

She tried to figure out what he meant, but her brain was too clouded with wanting him. "A little what?"

"A little protection. From me."

Evidently he'd gotten his zipper down because his fingers were at the top of her waistband, undoing the button and sliding the fastener. But when he went to tug her pants down, he could only get them past her hips. Her spread legs prevented them from going any lower. "Won't. Work."

He leaned down and bit her neck. "Want to bet?"

"No. A bet isn't what I want right now."

"I think I know exactly what you want." He pushed her legs together and then hauled her pants and underwear off. Then he was back again.

Up went her hips, just like before, seeking him.

This time, he found her instead and plunged home in a rush that drove the breath from his lungs. Sweet, sweet heat gripped him, massaging the ache right out of his flesh and replacing it with a need to drive into her again and again.

Forcing himself to count to ten, he only made it to five before those sexy hips were at it once more, trying to locate the very relief he'd been hoping to delay.

Damn, he hadn't even gotten her shirt off. And maybe they wouldn't make it that far, because his muscles were starting to take on a life of their own, her movements coaxing an equal and opposite reaction from him.

Soon the pace quickened, the thrusts growing quicker, getting wilder. Her head tossed from side to side as he hovered over her, his elbows braced on either side of her arms. Then he dove deep. Stayed there.

Her grip on him tightened. Squeezed.

Deus do céu. He wasn't going to be able to hold on much longer.

Her hips suddenly bucked up and back, her hands going to his butt, nails digging in. The sharp pain sent him over the edge, but not before he felt that blessed series of spasms that signaled her orgasm. That was it, he was off like a shot, pumping like a wild beast, his body erupting right along with hers.

He kept that ecstasy going as long as he could, until gravity stuck suckered tentacles on his flesh and began to drag him back to earth. He tried to resist, because he knew as soon as he landed, his first thought was going to be—

He hit with a bump.

And there it was. That raging, damning thought that happened every time he was around her:

How in the hell could he have let that happen?

CHAPTER SEVEN

"YOU'RE MARRIED? CONGRATULATIONS." The hospital administrator barely looked up from his papers.

Okay, so this wasn't the reception he'd expected. No conflict of interest speeches or comments about there needing to be oversights.

Maybe finding out that Sara was pregnant wouldn't have been such a big deal either. Although the administrator had been known to come down on anyone who might give the gossip columns something to chew on. Some of their more conservative sponsors were pretty strict about the hospital's reputation. That included its staff.

Paulo was all about keeping things running as smoothly as possible and making sure the income and expenses were lined up in neat little rows. Sponsors and benefactors had to be kept happy.

"As of two days ago, yes." He didn't even want to think about what they'd done on their honeymoon night. In fact, that was why he was here alone, instead of presenting that united front they'd talked about. He hadn't been able to face her at the apartment. Not yet.

He'd been pretty careful to come home when Sara was already in bed and leave before she got up in the morning. That had meant taking naps in his office during the day, but it was the only way he could function.

"Good, good. Make sure the nurses' housing department knows that there's an empty apartment available. And make sure Human Resources knows about her name change for tax purposes."

Name change. He'd forgotten about that. Damn.

"Right, I will." The sooner he got out of this office the better. He was going to have to tell Sara that it went well, but maybe he wouldn't let on just how well it had gone. "Thank you."

The man waved him away, before looking up suddenly.

Sebastian tensed, waiting for the ax to finally fall.

"If you could write me up a statement on how things are going with the mobile clinic, I would like to use it for publicity. Maybe along with a congratulations announcement and a picture of the happy couple. We've had a couple of weddings over the last year or so. It might make for some good visibility for the hospital."

What the hell? Oh, Sara would just love that. And the man would probably get a big kick out of knowing they hadn't really spoken much over the last couple of days. Just some business stuff. But that would change tomorrow when they had to meet to do their rounds in the *favela*. There was no way to maintain silence when you were trapped together in a vehicle for an entire day.

"I'll check with her and see what she thinks."

The man's eyes narrowed slightly. "I would think that as a new hospital employee, she would be glad to help in any way she could."

A veiled threat? Not happening. And Sebastian wasn't about to let it slide by unnoticed.

"Would you care to rephrase that, sir?" The hospital might think it could do without Sara, but could it do without both of them? There were only a handful of on-cologists that could do what he did in the field of osteo-sarcoma.

"I stated that badly. You're right. Ask her if she would be willing to be photographed with you for hospital pub-licity. We're asking our other married couples to do the same for our Valentine's Day campaign. If she'd rather not, I won't push it."

"Thank you. I'll ask her and get back to you."

With that he headed out the door.

Only to barely miss crashing into Adam.

He matched his step to his friend's. "Did Paulo Celeste try to talk you and Nata into doing pictures for some kind of wedded bliss publicity stunt?"

"Yep, he's hoping to feature all the couples in the hospital for a Dia dos Namorados ad. Why? Did he say something to you about it?"

Okay, so Paulo had been telling the truth, it wasn't just him and Sara. He could understand that since Brazil's version of Valentine's Day would be here in a few months.

"Yes, he asked if Sara and I would pose next to the mobile clinic."

"Ironic, isn't it?" His friend shot him a glance.

"What do you mean?"

"Just that after all the objections you had about me and Nata, you end up married a month and a half later. Your sister has a few reservations about how it all went down."

He gave Adam a half-grin. "I would tell you to mind your own business, but since that seemed to be your line several months ago, I won't bother."

"Yeah, and somehow the request never made any dif-ference, no matter how nicely I asked."

He laughed. "Nicely? I remember some pretty heated moments there toward the end."

"And who started those moments?" Adam stopped at the bank of elevators and pushed a number into the console, waiting to see which elevator assignment came up on the screen.

"I'm not afraid to admit it." He slapped his friend on the back. "I'm also not afraid to admit when I was wrong about something. Natália seems happy. Really happy. I'm glad for both of you."

"Thanks. And you, Sebastian. Are you happy?" The letter E pinged on the screen. "Don't answer that. Just know that I want the same for you as what Nata and I have."

As his friend went over to Elevator E, Sebastian sighed. Some people didn't find happiness as easily as others. He'd already resigned himself to that fate. And since history seemed to like repeating itself, he knew better than to hope that it might get any better. His best bet was to hope it didn't get any worse.

It was worse. Sara barely said a word to him when she met him by the mobile clinic the next day. He couldn't blame her. He'd avoided her for the last three days. Mainly because he didn't have a clue what to say to make things better. He'd promised himself—and her—that it was a marriage on paper only. He'd even assured her there were locks on the doors, because she hadn't trusted him to keep his hands to himself. And rightly so. Less than an hour after they'd arrived in his home, he'd been all over her.

Was that what his father had been like as he'd had affair after affair—allowing his baser instincts to run the show? Wasn't that what had gotten Sebastian into this quandary in the first place?

Droga!

He paused before starting the vehicle, even though the heat was beginning to cause perspiration to bead on his forehead. "Sara?"

"Hmm?" She stared out the window as if something out there fascinated her. Since all that was there was a bunch of parked cars, he was pretty sure she was just avoiding interacting with him. He couldn't blame her.

"I think we need to at least try to get past this."

This time she did glance his way. But only for a second. "Past what?"

Was she kidding him? "What happened the other night."

"I'm already past it. Way past."

Great. He hadn't been able to work his way through things, and yet she acted like it hadn't meant any more than... Maybe she was too worried about something else. The baby?

"Are you feeling okay? Not sick?"

"Not today."

Okay, he was a first-class jerk. He'd been worried about his own comfort, while Sara was probably downing crackers by the dozen. "Morning sickness?"

"Not today."

"Well, then, when? Yesterday, dammit?" A flash of irritation went through him. He was just trying to help—to fix whatever was going wrong with their plan—and she was shooting him down as soon as he opened his mouth.

There was no way he could survive eighteen months of the silent treatment.

She swiveled in her seat and faced him. "Why does it matter? Did you ever talk to the hospital administrator?"

"Yes, as a matter of fact. He's thrilled for us."

She paled. "Are you serious?"

"I'm sorry. I don't know what is wrong with me."

He touched her arm. "And, yes, I'm serious. He wasn't upset. Just the opposite, actually. He'd like to feature us in some kind of promotion for Dia dos Namorados along with Adam and Natália, Marcos and Maggie, and some of the other married couples."

This time she laughed. Or it started out as a laugh, and swiftly changed to a weird keening sound that ended in a sniffle.

He put a finger under her chin, turning it toward him. "What's going on, Sara? Besides what happened the other night. Or is it because of that?"

"No, it's not about that at all. Well, it is, but not in the way you think."

"I have no idea what you're talking about."

"I'm talking about my dad."

His heart gave a painful thud. "Your dad? Is he okay?"

"He's fine. It's not his health I'm worried about." She closed her eyes for a moment. "He's coming to visit. Next Monday, in fact."

"What?" There was no way he could have imagined this happening. Or maybe he could have, if he hadn't been in such a damned hurry to screw up his life. And Sara's. No more drinking for him. Ever.

"Yes, and I haven't told him. About us. About the baby. I was going to wait until I was further along, but since I'm not in the nurses' dorm any more, he is certainly going to figure something out. Because I know good and well he's not going to expect me to be living under the same roof as you."

Her father probably wouldn't be thrilled that he'd taken his daughter to a motel right under his nose either.

"We'll figure something out." When he'd thought about things getting worse, never in a million years had he imagined them getting this much worse. Not only was

Antônio Moreira's daughter married, she'd married his oncologist, and she was now pregnant with that oncologist's baby. What a mess.

He started the truck, setting the air-conditioner to high as he tried to think through this thing logically. His lips twisted. An easy task, since everything about their marriage *reeked* of logic. He decided to be honest. "I'm coming up completely blank."

"I know. Me too. Barring asking you to move out of your own house, I have no idea how to fix this."

"Exactly how would me moving out solve anything?"

"I could say I was house sitting for a friend."

The muscles in his mouth jerked sideways in a smile. "Some friend, this friend."

"You know what I mean."

"And here I thought this was all about me."

Her head tilted. "What was?"

"I thought your irritation was because of what we did. Never mind. If you think my moving out temporarily will be the best solution, I'll do it."

"No. I was kidding." She smiled. "Okay, half kidding. But we were going to tell Daddy eventually. And someone at the hospital is bound to spill the beans. We'll just get it over with and do it when he gets here. We fell madly in love and decided to get married."

"In a matter of weeks. You think he's going to buy that?" Although maybe it was better to just throw it out there and see how he reacted.

"If I know my father, he'll probably be over the moon. That's part of why I didn't want to tell him right away. Well, making sure the pregnancy has time to take root was a big part of it, but I also don't want him to be hurt." She sighed. "He always wanted me to find the love of my life like he did. He's going to be so disappointed when he hears we're getting a divorce."

"He can't expect everyone to have the same kind of luck as he did." His parents certainly hadn't. And Sebastian didn't see himself having that kind of luck either. He already knew he didn't, if this was anything to go by. His parents had felt forced into marriage, kind of like he had. Only in trying to stick it out, they'd made themselves—and their children—pretty damned miserable. It looked like he really was a chip off the old block. His dad would be proud.

"I know. I just hate being the one to shatter his illusions. I've already disappointed him once, in that area."

He wasn't sure what she meant by that last sentence, and didn't feel like asking. "If what you said is true, he may be so happy to meet his grandchild that a lot of the extraneous stuff will fly out the window. Especially if we make sure that our split is as amicable as possible."

"I hope so." She took one of the pamphlets that advertised their clinic services and fanned herself with it. "Do you think we could start driving so that the airconditioner works better? I'm about to be steamed in my own skin."

"Of course. Sorry."

"Don't be sorry. It's just a relief to not have you flip out about this."

"Why would I flip out?"

"Um. Because not only did your one-night stand get pregnant. And not only did you marry her to save her job and your pet project, but now her dad is coming to visit and expects to see his little girl put on a happy face."

"You want us to put on a good show for him, is that it?"

"I can't ask you to do that."

He pulled out of the parking lot and onto the busy street. "Of course you can. It won't be that hard. We both have to work this week, so the only time he'll see us is when we're home." He flashed a look at her. "Damn. When we're home. He'll have to stay with us, or he's going to know something is off, which means…"

She nodded her head and glanced sideways at him. "We're going to have to share a bed again. Only this time it will be completely chaste."

He waggled his eyebrows at her. "Not necessarily. Especially since your lip is doing its cute little puffer fish imitation."

"Oh, no. That was your last hurrah, mister."

"My very last one? Forever?"

She laughed, although it came out sounding a little choked. "Hasn't it gotten us into enough trouble?"

"Yes. It has." He popped his shoulder joint to relieve the ache building in it. "But it was at least a little fun, wasn't it?"

"Maybe a little."

He had to content himself with that, because the tone of her voice gave her away. It hadn't been a "little" anything. And Sebastian, Sara, and her lower lip all knew it.

Talita Moises met them at the door. "You were right. About everything. I'm having surgery to try to scrape that silicone junk out. Or at least try to fix things as much as possible. At the very worst they'll have to remove both of them. I wasn't sure how I felt about that, but there are worse things."

She'd taken a one-hundred-and-eighty-degree turn from where she'd been last week, when she'd said she didn't want to lose her breasts.

It was kind of hard to say "Congratulations" to a

woman who might be facing a double mastectomy. "How do you feel about that?"

"I should be sad, but I'm not. I'm just relieved it's not cancer. The doctor said my diabetes might cause some problems in healing, but he's hopeful. I won't know ahead of time whether I'll come out of surgery with boobs or without. The doctor said there was really no way to tell until he gets in there and sees how much damage has been done. I'll just be so glad not to have to deal with this any more that I don't really care what he has to do."

It was kind of surreal, hearing the change in Ms. Moises' attitude toward a possible mastectomy. Of course, Sara had changed her mind as well, hadn't she—going from swearing Sebastian to secrecy about her pregnancy and their marriage to agreeing to sleep in the same bed as him the whole time her dad was here? But only as a way to pretend that they were a happily married couple.

Pretend, Sara. You need to remember that!

Sebastian glanced her way. "Have they set a date for surgery yet?"

"The doc is squeezing me into his schedule, so it will happen in two weeks."

Right after Sara's father left to go home.

The woman clasped her hands together, picking at a piece of chipped red polish on her thumbnail.

"What's wrong?" She'd seemed happy enough a minute or two ago.

"I'm worried about where my grandson will go if something happens to me."

Sara laid her hand on the woman's shoulder. "Like I told you last time, nothing is going to happen to you."

It was dumb to promise something like that, she knew it, but somehow the words just came out of her mouth.

"It might. I'm no fool. And I don't have any relatives left."

"None?" A flash of pain went through her heart. She couldn't imagine being totally alone in this world. Sara had her father. And friends back home. And she would soon have a child.

But not even Talita was totally alone. She had her grandson. "How old is he again?"

"Twelve. He'll be thirteen in two months."

"Hmm, let me see what I can do."

Sebastian sent her a warning look. He was right. But she'd already blurted it out. It wasn't like she'd promised to adopt the boy or anything. And a mastectomy wasn't brain surgery, where the outcome wasn't certain. Not that any surgery was certain. But surely it wouldn't hurt to give the woman one less thing to worry about. If worse came to worst, maybe they could house the boy while his grandmother was in the hospital.

Somehow she didn't think Sebastian would like that. And there might even be a hospital rule against it. She would have to check. But, in the meantime, she could ask around and see if anyone would be willing to look after him for a week or so.

"Would you do that for me?"

There was such hope in her eyes that Sara couldn't bring herself to say no, even though she never should have said yes in the first place.

"I will. I'll see if I can find someone, and I'll let you know."

Talita grabbed her hand in both of her own. Tears ran down her cheeks. "Bless you. And thank you. You can't know how grateful I am."

She could know. It was written all over the seventy-eight-year-old grandmother's sweet face. And she didn't care if Sebastian was glaring daggers at her. He could go stay at a hotel if he didn't like it.

Although it would be the second time in a day that she'd asked him to do just that. But there had to be some kind of compromise that would work for everyone. The last thing she wanted was for a government agency to step in and take a boy away from an obviously loving home.

She and Sebastian would be sleeping in the same bed next Monday when her father came to visit. Why not extend that a little bit, since their patient's surgery would be in two weeks, right about the time her dad went back home. It couldn't hurt to ask.

Right. She had a feeling it was going to hurt at least a little once she left this house.

If not physically then emotionally, because Sebastian was probably going to let her have it with both barrels.

But what else could she do? If the patient didn't get the surgery she needed, she might die of infection at some point. And if she didn't feel secure in thinking her grandson would be well taken care of, then she might refuse to go through with it. No, Sebastian was going to agree to this. The same way that she'd agreed to this cockamamie marriage. And if he didn't, then she was going to make sure the next two weeks were some of the most miserable of his life.

CHAPTER EIGHT

THEY'D NEEDED THE BREAK.

At least that's what Sebastian had told her. She had an idea this was more for his benefit than for hers. But it didn't matter. She was going to be traveling to the top of a really tall building. Again.

But at least there hadn't been one of those freaky window-washer contraptions strapped to the outside of the Edifício de Banespa.

Evidently people were only allowed five minutes at the lookout area and then had to leave. Even so, there was a line of people waiting to go up in the elevator. A lot of them were couples or lovers. In fact, everywhere she looked there were people linking arms or caught up in their own world. Not her and Sebastian. After the busy day spent in the *favela,* she had gone home, showered and gone to sleep almost immediately. They had the day off today, so he'd suggested they come here.

He probably just didn't want to be home alone with her. And that was a good idea. Less chance of things taking a wrong turn. Again.

"Ten people, please." The elevator doors had opened and the guard was ushering sightseers into the elevator. He counted down until he reached Sebastian. "Ten. You're the last one, sir."

"We're together. I'll wait."

And it was true. They were together, but not by choice.

Except it had been, or she wouldn't be standing in a line with this man and wearing a gold band on her finger. Her thumb went to the back of it, sliding back and forth over the smooth surface.

The guard found a single person to take the last spot. Suddenly she envied that young man. He could just go up there and not worry about a partner. Or whether he regretted taking the leap that she had. One that was changing a lot more than just her name.

Her father was coming in less than a week, and they had a photo shoot to get through before that. "It could be worse," she muttered.

Sebastian tilted his head. "What could be worse?"

"Just thinking about the timing of the photo shoot. It would be worse if my dad were here, because he'd want to see us do it."

His mouth ratcheted up. "I don't think that's a requirement for marriage any more."

"Oh!" Her face flamed with heat. "I didn't mean that."

"I know what you meant." He paused, his smile fading. "Have you thought about how you want to break the news to him?"

"No, but I guess we should sit down and make some kind of plan."

"You're going to wait until he arrives?"

"I hadn't really thought about it. Do you think I should tell him before he gets here?" How big a shock would it be to arrive and find them sleeping in the same room? Probably a pretty big one. "Are you going to tell your parents?"

His lips tightened. "No."

"Not at all?" Shock and—yes, she could admit it—a

tinge of hurt came over her at the cold way he'd said the word. He'd mentioned his parents didn't have a happy marriage. Was he afraid that they would be upset over his choice? Or did he just not care what they thought?

"Not at all. They won't ever visit, so there's no reason to."

"And what about their grandchild? Will you keep that from them too?"

Just then the elevator opened and people from another group exited. "The next ten, please."

Saved by the bell. Or the elevator. They all piled in, the fit a little tighter than she expected it to be. She tried to shift her bag in front of her and ended up elbowing the man beside her in the stomach. He gave a sharp *"Mmph"*.

"So sorry," she murmured.

The doors closed with an ominous whoosh, and people jostled each other, trying to find an extra inch or two of space. Sara, on the other hand, stood stock still, too afraid to move.

A sense of claustrophobia prickled along her spine, sending shards of discomfort spiraling into her brain. It sent a message back: escape!

Only there was nowhere to run. *Deus.* Her heart rate sped up. What had she been thinking, letting him talk her in to coming here? They weren't even at the top and she was already a bundle of nerves.

She twisted around, needing to reassure herself that he was there, as steady and calm as always. She couldn't remember seeing him frazzled. Ever. Even when she'd told him she was pregnant, he hadn't gone off at the deep end and flipped out like she would have expected him to do.

There he was. That rock-solid body and deep brown eyes.

When his glance met hers he frowned, his head tilting in question. She was being ridiculous. But when she turned back to face the ticking numbers, an arm snaked around her waist, drawing her into his narrow circle, back from the crush of people. And just like that her heart slowed its frantic pace and the buzzing in her skull turned into the lull of background noise. She leaned her head back against his chest in relief, allowing the warmth of his body to seep through her. His arm tightened further, and she slid her hands over it, afraid he might let go.

A minute later the doors opened and people spilled out onto the concrete surface of the viewing area, all of them anxious to see as much as possible in the five minutes they were allotted.

"Thank you," she said in a soft voice as she pulled out of his embrace. "It was a little close in there."

His hand slid down to grip hers. "I thought you were about to ask me to boost you up to the hatch in the ceiling."

"There was an escape hatch? Now you tell me." She grinned up at him, startled when something dark went through his eyes. His fingers released their hold.

"I always make sure there's a way out."

Was he talking about elevators? Or relationships?

Had her ex-boyfriend done that same thing? Had his escape been planned the whole time?

It was probably better not to think about that. What if Sebastian decided he wanted no part of fatherhood after the baby was born? Or when he or she was five years old? Ghosting her as easily as her ex had. After all, São Paulo and Rio Grande do Sul were several states apart. How long before the traveling back and forth to see his child became a chore, and the visits ground to a halt? Or if he chose to remarry and start another family with someone else?

The thought had her struggling to catch her breath.

Before she could walk away, though, he reached for her hand again and gripped it tight, holding her in place.

"What?"

"If you thought my apartment was high, this is even higher. How close do you want to get to the edge?"

Okay, she had remembered that, and yet she hadn't. Her body relaxed, thankful to have something else to fix her thoughts on. "How many flights of stairs are there?"

"More than you want to think about."

"Great." She took a deep breath. "Okay, how close do *you* want to go?" As long as he was holding her hand, she would be fine, right?

"I want to go all the way to the edge and back, but I'm willing to restrain myself if that's not what you want."

A shiver went over her. Why did she keep hearing double meanings behind everything? Maybe because the low thrum of his voice always gave her crazy ideas. Or maybe it was simply because she was at the top of a building, where the air was impossibly thin. Did she trust him? If he pulled her all the way to the guard rail, was she going to have a meltdown?

No. The way he'd held her in the elevator had made her feel safe. Protected. Just like the way he was holding her hand right now. Just like when he'd made love to her. "I don't want you to hold back. Let's go together."

He threaded his fingers through hers. "Okay. Together."

They walked over to the guard rail, and her free hand clenched around it.

"Still okay?"

She hadn't quite trusted herself to look yet. "I think so."

"Here." He moved around behind her and wrapped his

arms around her middle, just like he had on the ride up. Her unease disappeared almost immediately.

"I love it up here," he murmured, his chin coming to rest on the top of her head.

She allowed her eyes to focus and…

Oh, boy.

The view was horrifying and beautiful all at once. As far as the eye could see, there were buildings upon buildings upon buildings.

The ranching town where she came from had apartment complexes, but nothing like these. Nothing like this gorgeous *vista*. She didn't look down. Instead, she kept her gaze pointed toward the horizon. "You said we could see Vista do Vale from here."

"Yes, the condo is…" His voice paused for a second. "Just off to our right."

She turned slightly to the right, but everything was one jumble of shapes that seemed to go on forever. "I don't see it."

"Let me see if I can show you." He shifted until his cheek was pressed tight to hers. "It's the cobalt and white building about ten blocks out and at your one o'clock. It's one of the tallest in the group."

She looked a little bit closer, using his instructions to narrow her search, except all she could concentrate on right now was the feel of his skin against hers. She started chanting inside her head: *Cobalt and white. Cobalt and white. Cobalt and…*

There, she could see it! "It looks so small from here."

His cheek scraped across hers as he nodded, the rough edge of his whiskers awakening nerve endings she'd rather remained dormant.

"Don't forget it's located in a valley and it's some distance away. Perspective can get skewed."

Yes, it could, because with him so close that his body seemed to enfold hers, she realized it would be far too easy to get used to this. To go from thinking of their marriage as a necessary evil to something that was comfortable and…exciting.

She breathed in deeply, his scent mixing with that of the city. São Paulo seemed to have soaked into his very pores. He was as grounded here as she was in Rio Grande do Sul.

She'd do well to remember that. She'd always known her move here wasn't meant to last forever. It was to help her learn ways to help people like her father.

Neither of them said anything for a few seconds as they continued to look out over the downtown area. She did her best to enjoy these moments and not think about the future.

"How much time do you think we have left?"

If he had said seventeen months and twenty days she wouldn't have been surprised, but he didn't. "Only around two minutes."

"It's all going by so fast." A flash of sorrow hit her right between the eyes as she realized she meant that in more ways than one. "Right now I just want to stay here forever."

The warmth of his breath made wisps of her hair flutter. "Everything comes to an end. Or it should."

The cynicism behind those words made her ache inside. "Not everything. Not life. Love. The birth of children."

"Even those things don't last forever."

"The cycle does, though, don't you think?"

"Yes. Some of them. But they're usually the ones you don't want to continue."

A small commotion on the other side of the viewing

area caught her attention. A huddle of people suddenly broke apart and a young man, maybe in his thirties, staggered out of their midst. His eyes were wide and terrified, face red. He slumped to the ground almost immediately. Someone screamed, "Daddy! What's wrong?" The words were in English and a tiny girl leaned over his chest, patting his face with chubby little hands.

Without a word, Sebastian released her and jogged toward the group, leaving her to hurry after him. Even before he got there, he was taking charge of the situation. He switched to English. "I'm a doctor. What has happened?"

A woman knelt down beside the girl, trying to pull her back, but it only caused her to wrench against the restraining hands and cry even harder. "I don't know! He just suddenly grabbed his throat as if he was trying to cough." The sheer panic in her voice was unmistakable.

Sebastian leaned over the man, putting his head to his chest. "Was he eating something?"

"Just this." The woman handed him a package that said "Soja Torrada"...toasted soybeans.

"Does he have allergies?"

"No. Not that I know of." Tears started pouring down her cheeks. "Can you help him?"

In an instant, Sara was at the man's head. Every second was critical. The man's breath wheezed in partially and then went silent. He'd stopped breathing.

The woman fell to her knees beside them, clutching the child to her chest. "Oh, God, someone do something!"

"Sara, tip his head to the side. I'm going to try something."

She did as he asked, instinctively turning him to face away from the mother and daughter.

Sebastian put one hand over the other, placing the base

of his palms on the man's abdomen just under his chest. Already the victim's face was turning dark as his circulation pumped unoxygenated blood through his system.

Thrusting his joined hands sharply toward the man's diaphragm, while Sara made sure his mouth was open, the first attempt yielded nothing. By this time there was a crowd around them. Even the man from the elevator was there, no longer counting the minutes. He repeated the attempt, then a third time, his compression even harder. Something flew from the man's mouth and landed on the ground a few inches away. A nut.

Sebastian had been right.

Hoping the man would start breathing on his own, alarm swept through her system when he lay lifeless on the concrete. No rise or fall of his chest, no improvement in his color. It had been less than a minute since he'd collapsed.

Sebastian put his fingers against the man's neck. "I have a pulse, but it's weak."

Working as a team, they straightened his head, the oncologist beginning mouth to mouth while Sara counted the puffs of air as they went in. When they reached seven, Sebastian paused and listened. Still nothing.

"Do you want me to take over?"

"Just count." With that, he went back to breathing for the victim.

Come on. You can do it!

She wasn't sure if she was willing the words to Sebastian or to the man on the ground.

"Seven."

Pausing again, he lifted his head.

This time there was a weak gasp, and then another. Suddenly the man took a huge gulping breath. After the third one, his eyes fluttered, but they didn't open.

His wife—if the ring on her finger was any indication—grabbed his hand. "Max! Can you hear me?"

Still a little blue around the mouth, he barely nodded, then his eyes opened, seeking the woman and child immediately. One arm reached toward them.

Relieved murmurs went up all around them. One person clapped and several others joined in. It was a little too soon to assume everything was going to be all right, though.

The man's mouth opened, but Sebastian stopped him with a quick shake of his head.

"Don't try to talk." He glanced up at the elevator attendant, who was standing a few feet away. "We need to take him down with as few people as possible. Can you have an ambulance waiting for us?"

"Yes, of course." The man walked a few steps away, speaking into a cellphone.

Sebastian turned toward the woman. "His name is Max?" His English was fluent and easy, while Sara struggled to keep up with the strange words.

"Yes. We're here on holiday." She gripped her husband's hand. "Is he going to be all right?"

When the child whimpered again, Sebastian reached over and tugged a lock of her blonde hair, giving her a reassuring smile. "He should be just fine. Don't worry, okay?"

The gesture made Sara's chest ache. Would he one day comfort their child like this? His words from a few minutes earlier came back to her, making the ache grow. Or would he walk away from them, thinking this was one of those cycles that should end?

He glanced at her. "I want just the family and us on that elevator. The fewer people the better."

"I'm…okay." The croaked words came from the man on the ground.

"You need to go to a hospital and get checked out. We work at one not far from here." He paused as if trying to gather his thoughts. "It's for the best."

"Max, you need to go," his wife said. "Please."

He gave a short nod, not trying to say anything else.

Already he had pinkened somewhat, but Sebastian was right. They needed to make sure he hadn't aspirated anything else. Even a tiny piece of food trapped in a person's lungs could cause inflammation or, worse, aspiration pneumonia.

The girl scrambled out of her mom's grip and landed on Max's chest, her small arms going around his neck. "Daddy. I love you!"

He returned her hug, his arms snug around her back, even though it was obvious his strength hadn't completely returned.

"Let's get you out of here. Do you think you can get up, if we help?"

Max glanced up at them and gave another nod. "Think so."

With Sara on one side and Sebastian on the other, they levered him up and slowly walked to the elevator, the crowd parting around them with more clapping.

She could only imagine the fear of being in another country and going through a crisis like this. Actually, she could imagine at least a little bit. Her own crisis wasn't life or death, but she was away from the only home she'd ever known, thrust into a strange city, and then discovered she was pregnant.

And what had been the result of all of that? Sebastian had attempted a metaphorical Heimlich maneuver, hoping to avert disaster for the program. Only unlike in

Max's case, where the rescue attempt had worked, Sebastian might have unwittingly thrown them into a situation that was far worse. They would find out when her father came to visit. A tough old cowboy, he had an uncanny ability to see through people as easily as he could judge a steer. He'd warned her about her boyfriend, but she hadn't listened, too infatuated with the idea of love to pay attention to the warning signs. Until it had been too late.

Would her dad realize that this was just an act?

He would be devastated, if so.

They got onto the elevator, and although he tried to wave off their help, Sara kept her shoulder wedged under Max's arm. Sebastian did the same while his wife stood in front of him, still holding his daughter in one arm. She touched his face, murmuring to him in soft tones. He nodded yes or no to whatever she was saying.

Behind Max's back, Sebastian's hand touched Sara's elbow. She leaned her head back slightly to look over at him.

"Thank you," he mouthed.

There was something in his expression that made her stomach cramp. She sent him a nod and a slight smile.

When they arrived at the ground floor and the doors opened, there was indeed an ambulance waiting. The emergency crew came forward with a gurney, while Sebastian filled them in on what had happened and what he thought the prognosis was. There wasn't enough space for all of them to ride, and the trip through São Paulo wouldn't be a walk in the park anyway because of the huge amount of traffic. But this was no longer a life or death situation, so Sebastian didn't need to ride with them. He did give Max's wife his card, telling her to call him if they needed anything while they were at the hospital.

As they loaded her husband in through the doors, she used her free arm to hug the oncologist, whispering something into his ear.

When the EMTs helped her and her child into the back of the ambulance, Sara came up to stand beside him. "What did she say?"

His jaw was tight, and he appeared to be battling some kind of raw emotion. "She said, 'You just saved my whole world.'"

Pinpricks needled the backs of Sara's eyes. "She loves him very much."

"So it seems."

She nudged him with her shoulder. "Still think everything comes to an end?"

"I'll have to get back to you on that."

The ambulance pulled away from the building and forced its way into the snarls of traffic, siren wailing and horn giving off long blasts of sound. Then they were swallowed up by the never-ending sea of vehicles. "They should be okay."

"Glad we went up?"

"Oh, yes. And very glad you didn't boost me up to that escape hatch. We were right where we were supposed to be."

He turned and looked at her, his expression unreadable. Then he leaned down and kissed her cheek. "Yes. We were."

CHAPTER NINE

SEVEN COUPLES WERE lined up outside the hospital, each of them awaiting their turn with the photographer. And Sebastian felt like the biggest kind of fraud. Every single one of these people thought their unions would last forever, judging from the arms casually slung around waists and subtle touches. His marriage, on the other hand, had an expiration date built right into it. Eighteen months. No more. No less.

He never in his wildest dreams imagined he would marry for the sake of a child.

Unlike his mom and dad, though, he refused to linger in a marriage built on the wrong motives. He'd told Sara the truth when they were at the top of the Banespa building. Oh, in the aftermath of that choking crisis yesterday, when Max's wife had murmured those heartfelt words to him, his world view had quaked in its foundations a time or two. But the old cynicism had returned.

Ha! But that sure hadn't stopped him from coming to this photo shoot and pretending to "love the one he was with". And Sara didn't look any happier about the arrangement. She was standing with her eyes focused on the ground, not even looking at the poses the first couple was given.

He couldn't blame her. There was mushiness right and left, along with a lot of gazing into each other's eyes.

What the hell had he been thinking, agreeing to any of this? He was not cut out to smile and pretend. He was... stoic. That was how he saw himself. None of the histrionics that had gone on in his childhood home. In fact, the quieter and more invisible he became, the better it was for everyone. Especially his sister, who had been fragile for most of her teenage years because of the cancer. He'd protected her from a lot of the drama. At least, he hoped he had.

Maybe that's why he'd been so quick to jump in and offer marriage to Sara. That protective instinct had never been totally snuffed out.

In fact, it was kicking in right now like it had yesterday, when they'd talked about escape hatches and when he'd held her out on that balcony. Pressed his cheek against hers.

It had all felt too good. Too real.

But it wasn't real. He needed to remember that.

He leaned down and whispered, "We can just leave, if you want." To hell with what the hospital administrator wanted. There could just be one less picture in their precious promotional article.

"It's already too late."

At least, that's what he thought she'd said. The words had been so soft, he couldn't be completely sure.

Too late for what?

"Are you feeling okay?"

She motioned him over to the side. "Remember when you asked me about my dad? And you asked if I was going to tell him before he got here? Well, I decided to go ahead. So I told him. About the baby. About us."

Okay, he wasn't sure what that meant. She'd told him the truth? Or she'd given him their cover story?

"He knows what, exactly?"

"Well, it would be kind of awkward for him to get here and say, 'Oh, by the way, I'm sharing a bed with the man who was your doctor.'"

Ah, okay, so that answered that. She'd told him that they were married.

"What was his reaction?"

Her head cocked to the side. "He was happy. Horribly, terribly happy."

The words "horribly" and "terribly" fit the situation. But to put them together with "happy"? That just seemed like an oxymoron. "In other words, he bought the story."

"That's what I just said."

Another couple was called to the forefront. Sebastian had no idea where they were in the queue.

"So that's a good thing, then. It should make his visit a piece of cake."

"No." She looked at him like he'd lost his marbles. "He is going to expect me to be like him and Mom. And—and—" Moisture rimmed her eyes, just like it had yesterday. Only this was for completely different reasons. And he'd caused it. All of it.

Damn! In trying to help her, he had made things infinitely worse. Which was why she'd said it was too late. It was done. And they were stuck.

Except that in eighteen months she was going to have to go through the explanations all over again. And he doubted her father would be quite as happy.

Unless they chose to stay married.

Um, no. Then he *would* be following in a set of footsteps that he despised.

"It'll be okay, Sara. We'll figure this out." He put his arm around her shoulders.

"Sebastian and Sara Texeira?" The call cut through the air like a knife and every head turned in their direction.

Hell, could this day get any worse?

He unhooked his arm from around her and linked their hands—to keep up the pretense. "Let's get this over with," he muttered, trying his best to plaster a pleasant expression on his face. It wasn't easy when every muscle in it felt stiff and frozen.

A second later, Sebastian was seated on a little stool with Sara standing behind him, her fingers curled like claws into his shoulders.

"Can I get a smile from the bride?" The photographer's mop of black hair flopped to the side as he peered out from behind his camera.

A few seconds later, a titter of nervous laughter came from those still in the area. Sebastian glanced up and over his shoulder to see what Sara was doing. Oh, Lord. Her lips were cranked skyward in the most unnatural expression he had ever seen. And that sexy bottom lip was nowhere to be seen.

The photographer got up and made his way toward them. "Okay, it's normal to be nervous. Maybe we'll try something without a smile."

"I'm sorry…" Sara started, only to have the man give her a wide grin that was much more spontaneous. A little too spontaneous, if you asked Sebastian.

Sebastian's frown grew when the photographer came up beside her, using cupped palms to tilt her head downward and to the right. "We'll just have you look at each other, how's that?" His hands kept fiddling with her pose, touching her arm here. Her waist there.

When he leaned a little too close, steam gathered in Sebastian's head.

Camera boy was beginning to really get under his skin. Did he know she was pregnant? Was he even an adult? He looked like a gangly kid from where he was sitting.

"Dr. Texeira, can you kind of peer over your shoulder at your wife?"

He did as he was asked, seeing the nerves still alive in Sara's face. He reached up and laid his hand over one of hers to reassure her.

"Yes, that's it. Hold it just like that."

Sebastian nodded at her and tightened his grip just a touch, feeling her relax, a lock of hair falling over her shoulder. With the sun behind her, she looked soft and radiant and—beautiful.

And there was that lip. Puckered just right.

At that second, he heard the tell-tale click of the camera. It went again and again, as they stared at each other.

Her eyes. Her upturned nose.

That sexy mouth.

"Okay." The sharp clap of the man's hands broke through whatever had been holding him in place, and he blinked.

Swallowed.

Sara took her hands off his shoulders and shoved the errant lock back over her shoulder.

"Let's try something a little different."

Sebastian frowned. "You mean we're not done?"

"I want just a couple more shots, and then I'll let you pick one to take home with you." He studied them for a second or two. "Why don't we have—Sara, wasn't it?"

When she nodded, he continued, "Sara, why don't you come and sit on your husband's lap."

"Excuse me?"

"Here." When the man acted like he was going to reach for her hips, Sebastian pre-empted him by gripping them and tugging sharply. She tumbled onto his lap, her arms going around his neck to keep from careening onto the ground.

Their cheeky photographer just laughed. "That's it. Just like that. Hold it."

Sebastian's right arm anchored her in place, while the man studied them from a couple of different angles. When she whispered, "I'm going to kill you," he just smiled.

"Better that than me killing that damned photographer." He kept his voice low enough so that only she heard him.

As if on cue, the guy was back, standing directly behind Sara, tilting her head back and resting it against his abdomen for a second. The muscles in Sebastian's neck went stiff with rage. This was no longer cheeky. It was unprofessional and inappropriate. When his gaze clashed with the photographer's the man's eyes widened slightly, and he took a step back. "That should do."

He took three more pictures, and Sebastian had to give it to the man. Inappropriate or not, he knew exactly how to play up Sara's features. With her head tilted back, the long line of her neck was on display. Her hair fell in a curtain that went past his hip, almost touching the ground. Her eyes were closed, probably from embarrassment, but to a casual observer it probably looked like she was waiting for his lips to slide over her throat. And if they had been alone, he would have been tempted to do just that. He would have bent over her and used his mouth to—

"Okay, that's it. Thank you."

Sebastian almost groaned aloud. Parts of him had

woken up unexpectedly, putting him in an awkward position. Sara's back came up as she straightened and her hip pressed hard against him. Air hissed through her lips, and she jerked around to stare at him. She'd felt his reaction.

Lord, how could she *not* feel it?

Her brown eyes crinkled at the edges.

"Can you get up?" Her voice shook slightly as if holding back laughter. Oh, she thought this was funny, did she?

"What do you think?"

"I think you already are." She popped off his lap, leaving him to somehow uncurl his body in a way that didn't reveal exactly what this little photo shoot had cost him. To his surprise, Sara stood in front of him, giving him a chance to collect his senses and put his life—or rather his body—back into some semblance of order.

"If you'll go over to the computer and take a look at the shots, while I get the next couple set up, that would be *bacana*. They're right on the monitor in the order they were taken. Just select the number beside the image you like best and write it on the card with your name."

They actually had to look at the photos? Great. But at least it gave him a chance to send blood flowing back into his head, rather than pooling in his groin.

They moved over to where the camera was set up. The shots were there, just like the man had said.

"Do you have a preference?"

When he glanced over, Sara was staring out at the landscape.

He chuckled. "You might actually have to look at the screen in order to choose."

"Ugh, I can't."

So he did it for her, and what he saw took his breath away. That stilted grin picture was there, but as soon as his eyes tracked to the first posed shot, he knew the photographer had done his job a little too well. The ones of her behind him showed a loving couple gazing deeply into each other's eyes. One right after the other, the angle of the camera lens changing just slightly between those three shots. When he came to the images of her on his lap, his throat tightened.

He'd thought she was beautiful when she was standing up? These pictures were magazine-worthy. Sebastian was staring down at her, his lips curved just slightly. And she looked totally lost in the moment, carefree and happy, one of her legs lifted off the ground to help her keep her balance. He remembered those long slender calves wrapped around his waist less than a week ago.

Damn. He wanted it. Wanted her. All over again.

"This one." He tapped the monitor.

As if fighting an inner battle, her eyes swung toward the screen. Her hand went to her throat. *"Misericórdia."*

Have mercy? It should have been him asking for mercy.

"Do you think your dad will believe it now?"

"*I* almost believe it." As if realizing what she'd said, she glanced quickly at him. "You're a very good actor."

He hadn't been acting. And in the shot he'd chosen—the very first of the lap pictures—he could still see a trace of the anger in his face over the photographer's hands being on her. He was almost in a swooping position, ready to protect what was his.

Only she wasn't.

And he'd better not start wishing she was, because he was the last person she needed. She deserved someone who actually believed in love and fairy tales. Who wasn't afraid to show emotions like anger and frustration. Who wouldn't always wonder if he'd married her for herself—

or because of what he'd done to her. Didn't they used to call that "doing the honorable thing"?

There was no honor in marrying for that reason.

Irritated at himself for even letting his thoughts wander in that direction, he scribbled the number down on the card. "I think we're both pretty good actors when we want to be. One more task to cross off the list."

He stood up, his body once more firmly under control, and he flipped the card onto the small stack of cards of the couples who were already finished with their photo shoot.

Well, so was he. He was finished. And *pelo amor de Deus*, he'd better damn well remember that.

They weren't the only ones who'd chosen that picture. The day her dad was to arrive, a huge publicity poster appeared in the entryway of the hospital. Perched on an easel, it proclaimed:

> *Hospital Santa Coração:*
> *A place where hearts are healed—*
> *and love is found.*

And the image at the very center of the poster was their lap dance.

Heavens, had Sebastian seen this yet? She hoped not, although how could he have missed it, as he'd been called in early to treat a patient? Maybe they'd just put the poster up.

The pictures of the other smiling couples surrounded them, but it seemed the photographer had put them all in much more conventional poses, reserving the most embarrassing one for her and Sebastian. The guy had made her feel a little uncomfortable, but even worse was Sebastian's reaction to it. For a brief second, she'd wondered if he was jealous. And then there was his...*reaction.* A very physical kind of reaction. It had nudged her as she'd moved to get up, shocking her. She'd had her eyes firmly closed to block out the experience, because she'd felt a familiar tingling awareness when she'd stood behind him and he'd looked up at her with those sexy hooded eyes she loved so much.

Loved?

No, not loved. She was only thinking that because of that huge, glaring word on the poster. It was sending a subliminal message, burrowing into her brain like a screwworm.

No matter. In the three hours since Sebastian had left the apartment, she'd gotten her things and moved them into his bedroom. Thank God his bed was huge—larger than any bed she had ever seen before. She could just put a stack of pillows between them and it would be as if they each had their own island to sleep on. She would simply get dressed in the bathroom in the very unsexy garb she had purchased for just this occasion. Not that they would be tempted to do anything with her dad practically sleeping in the next room. She was being ridiculous.

Shaking herself back to awareness, she wandered over to the elevators, trying to keep her head down and hoping no one recognized her as she headed to her appointment. Although she looked totally different in that picture than she did in real life. At least she hoped she didn't carry around that besotted expression everywhere she went.

They were supposed to pick her dad up at the airport at five this afternoon. Sara had tried to convince Sebastian to just let her go on her own, but he'd insisted, saying her father would think it was strange if she arrived by herself.

"He'll just think you're working."

His brows had edged up. "But I'm not."

"But you could be."

They'd gone back and forth a few more times before she'd slumped into a chair in the living room. They'd finally compromised. He could go with her to pick up her father, but he wasn't allowed to go to the prenatal exam he'd talked her into.

She took a deep breath. It was going to be okay. Her dad was only going to be here for a week. Sebastian wanted to do a little blood work on him and check his cancer markers. He didn't expect there to be any changes, but it didn't hurt to do a quick check. "Thank you. I owe you."

He'd given her a strange frown she still didn't understand. It was almost as if she'd said the wrong thing. But that didn't make any sense. It was a figment of her imagination. Much like their marriage.

Within seconds the elevators shuttled her to the correct floor, where Natália stood waiting for her. She swooped in for a quick hug.

"Hey, *moça linda*, how's married life treating you?"

God, she felt like such a liar. This was Sebastian's sister and one of her closest friends. "Oh, you know. We're still trying to figure things out, just like any other married couple."

"Okay, then," was all she said. Natália didn't believe her—and who could blame her? As someone who was also recently married she probably saw right through the sham. Or had Sebastian already told her it was all a farce?

"Are you sure it's not too soon to do this?"

"Nope. If you're eight weeks, we should be able to see something. Maybe even the heartbeat, if we're really lucky."

She nodded, following her down the hallway, doing

some quick calculations in her head. She'd been in São Paulo for... "Maybe a couple of days over eight weeks."

"I thought so. That was right about the time of my and Adam's wedding. I had no idea you and Sebastian even knew each other that well."

Squirming inside, all she could do was nod again. "We went out to get a few drinks after the wedding and things just...happened." No need to mention the reasons behind it.

"I know how it is. I have to admit I feel a little bit responsible. Sebastian wasn't himself once he found out about me and Adam. He was still acting out of sorts and moody at the wedding."

What was she trying to say? "We're both adults. He didn't take advantage of me, if that's what you're implying."

"Oh, God, no. Sebastian could be raging drunk and he would never lose control of himself."

That was funny, because Sara remembered them both being kind of out of control. Although Natália was right. She couldn't really recall many times when he'd totally lost it. Hmm. The night they'd had sex in his bedroom *could* be considered one of those times. And then when the pictures were being taken. And— It didn't matter. It was what it was. There was no wishing that things were different. They weren't and they never would be. He'd made that perfectly clear.

And Sara was fine with that. She had to be.

She decided to change the subject. "Can you do the ultrasound yourself?"

"I can. It might be better if you and an OBGYN do it, but I should be able to find something. We'll take a traditional pregnancy test as a back-up, just in case."

Ten minutes after Sara had peed into a cup, she found

herself lying on a table, ultrasound wand gliding across her belly. "Let's just see if we can find little Billy."

Sara rolled her eyes, trying to act nonchalant about the whole thing. "How do you know it's not a girl?"

"I don't. Billy can be a girl or a boy's name." The wand hit a ticklish spot, making her squirm. It then went back over the same spot.

"Are you doing that on purpose?" She choked out a laugh. "Let's change places and see how well you like it."

The second the words were out of her mouth, her laughter died a hard death. "I'm sorry. I didn't mean that."

There was silence for a couple of beats, then her friend smiled. "It's okay. I came to terms with the fact that I can't have children a long time ago. Actually, we're thinking of adopting at some point."

"That's wonderful." She shifted on the table.

"Let's try the left side." When Natália changed her location, she went "Bingo" within seconds. "There, do you see?"

Her friend pointed at a small blob on the screen, then fiddled with something, moving the transponder again. "Oh, Sara, look."

"Is something wrong?" Had she found some kind of horrible deformity?

"Nothing is wrong. Your baby's heart is beating."

She stared at the monitor, straining to find what the neonatologist was talking about. Then she saw it. A tiny quick movement. Rhythmic. Continuous.

A heart.

Her own swelled, and she was afraid to look away for fear that little flutter on the screen would suddenly stop. "Is it okay?" she whispered.

"As far as I can tell, everything is perfect. You need to have a real examination, though."

"I will." She swallowed, suddenly overwhelmed. "Okay, I've seen enough. Thank you."

Natália switched the machine off and the screen went dark. She had to bite her lips not to ask her to find the baby again. It was okay.

There really was a baby in there.

Her friend wiped the gel off her abdomen and pulled the gown back down.

"Thank you." She hesitated. "Could you come up here, please, if you're all done?"

"Sure thing." She moved to stand by her shoulder. "Do you feel better now?"

"Yes, a little. Can I sit up?" When Natália nodded, Sara jammed herself upright. "I can't believe I'm really pregnant."

"You really are, according to your body. But, then, you already knew that, didn't you? It's why you got married."

She put her legs over the side of the exam table, her hands clasped in her lap. "He told you."

Rather than continuing to stand, Natália hopped on the table beside her. "He didn't have much of a choice. I was all over him about marrying so quickly."

"He was trying to protect his project, and actually protect me too. He thought maybe they would remove me from the team if they thought there was any kind of impropriety."

"Instead you ended up getting roped into the Dia dos Namorados campaign."

She examined her toenail polish to keep from having to look directly at her friend. "That was a hoot, let me tell you."

"I bet. I saw the poster downstairs. If I didn't know better, I would think you two were in love."

"The photographer somehow pulled stuff out of his hat that wasn't there. Some kind of airbrushing trick."

"With your skin, I would be very surprised if he had to do anything."

A scoffing sound came up from her depths. "I barely even know him, Natália."

"You're carrying his child."

"Last time I heard, you didn't have to know anyone at all to carry a child. There are lots of ways to get pregnant."

"Yes, there are. And yet you looked pretty darned happy to see that baby's heart beating."

"I was. I'm not sure why. I should be frantic. Or horrified." And yet she was none of those things. She hadn't had time to sit and think about it. Until right now when she'd seen living proof that a baby was growing inside her.

The only thing that horrified her was the thought of her dad figuring out that her marriage wasn't built on love but on convenience and self-interest. They'd taken the picture from the campaign and had it framed, putting it on the mantel like they'd talked about. Just something to reassure her dad that she was okay. That she *would* be okay.

And she would be, no matter what happened between her and Sebastian.

"I think my brother is a lucky man."

Shock rippled across her nerve endings. "We're not going to stay together, Natália."

"You don't know that for sure." Her friend gave her hand a squeeze.

"I do know. We set a date to divorce after the baby is born."

"Well, that's interesting." If Natália was surprised,

she didn't let on. She just hopped off the table with an enigmatic smile. "Just remember. Plans change. So do people, if you give them some time."

Sara sighed and then got dressed before following the neonatologist to the door. Once there, she stopped for just a second or two and then gave a sad shrug. "Not these plans, Nata. And not these people."

CHAPTER TEN

SHE'D PUT A bunch of damned pillows down the center of the bed. Under the covers so they formed some kind of blockade.

Against what? Him?

Did she really think he couldn't just roll right over them and land on her side?

"This is more than ridiculous. You know that, right?"

Her muffled voice came from the far side of the mattress where she lay teetering on the edge. "I just didn't want to accidentally move to your side and crowd you."

"Crowd me. On a king-sized bed." Even he could hear the irony dripping from his voice. He was lying just on the other side of the barrier, but even if he stretched his arm as far as it could go, he wouldn't be able to reach her. And that was probably the point. But she couldn't stay there all night. In those long flannel pajamas in the dead of summer.

Her father's flight had been delayed twice before finally landing at almost midnight. They hadn't had much time to talk. Used to rising at the crack of dawn, the older man had dozed most of the car ride back to the condo. Once there, he was tired enough that he'd kissed his daughter and shaken Sebastian's hand with muttered congratulations.

The man hadn't asked a single question. About any of it. But he had no doubt that those would come tomorrow. Especially since they were scheduled to do blood work and a quick health check. And then he and Sara were supposed to head over to Tres Corações to meet with Talita, whose surgery had been moved up by a week. Natália and Adam had agreed to take care of Jorge until his grandmother got out of the hospital. Thank God, because he didn't think he would be able to survive having Jorge and Sara's dad here at the same time.

"I move around a lot in my sleep."

Yes, he knew she did. He'd slept with her before.

And yet as much as he was ridiculing her, he had to admit she was all kinds of adorable with her dark hair flowing across the white of his sheets. He laid an arm across the mountain of pillows. Nope, couldn't reach her. But he could tease her. At least a little.

"I had to turn the air-conditioner way up. I don't normally wear this many clothes to bed." Actually, he didn't normally wear any. The pajama bottoms were for her benefit. He didn't think she would appreciate him coming to bed naked, even if she had seen him that way before.

She gave a weird cough. "It is kind of warm tonight, although Daddy thought it was chilly in the apartment. He doesn't use anything but fans at home. It's taken a little getting used to for me as well. The hospital I worked at before I came here had air-conditioning, but it was broken most of the time."

He propped his hands behind his head. "It sounds like you loved your life there."

"I did." She rolled over to look at him. "I always loved watching my dad rope steers. He always seemed so— strong, you know?"

He really didn't, since his dad had never been someone he'd looked up to. "He's still a strong man."

"It scared me, seeing where he was a year ago when
the cancer caused him to break his leg. I thought he was
ready to give up."

"But he didn't."

"Thanks to you and Natália." She scooted closer to
the barricade and leaned up on her elbow, her long hair
just touching the mattress. Now he could reach her, if he
wanted to. He forced himself to stay where he was, content to hear the sound of her voice.

It was almost—normal. Was this what some couples
did every night?

"It was all Natália. She was the miracle worker in this
case. Her surgery was similar enough that it made your
dad think he might have a good outcome as well."

"And he did."

"Yes, he did."

She fiddled with the fabric on one of the center pillows. "I appreciate everything you've done for us. His
surgery. My position here at the hospital."

He didn't like where this conversation was headed.
The last thing he wanted from her was her gratitude. It
made him wonder things like whether she'd slept with
him the night of the wedding because she'd been trying
to pay a debt.

No, she wasn't like that. And since she was a nurse,
it was unlikely that she'd been indulging in a little bit of
hero-worship. He'd never encouraged that with patients,
and he knew the boundaries that needed to be set and
kept. So what had happened with Sara?

He'd gotten good and drunk. And she'd been so beautiful, carrying an air of vulnerability that he hadn't understood. Still didn't, in all honesty. But beneath all of that

lay a heat and fire he hadn't expected. It had consumed him that night. Burnt him alive.

The ashes were still glowing, waiting for the slightest breeze to tease them back to life. Even those silly chaste pajamas couldn't extinguish it. Or her attempt at a pillow levy bank.

Right on cue, something in his body stirred.

He moved, so that only the bridge of pillows was between them. "The program needed you. I needed you."

It was true. In more ways than one.

"And I needed it." She gave a heavy sigh, plumping the pillow beneath her hands. "The opportunity came at just the perfect time."

He could barely see her over that damned mountain she'd created.

"Don't you think this is idiotic? We're expecting a child together."

"It just seems kind of funny with my dad in the same house." She lifted her head a little higher to peer over the pillows at him.

"He's not right next door. And the rooms in this place are pretty damned soundproof. He couldn't hear you if you screamed the place down."

She blinked at him. "Why would I do that?"

"Guess." Parts of him lifted higher than ever. "I know exactly what you sound like."

"Sebastian!" Her voice was a shocked whisper.

"He can't hear you. But if you prefer to play it safe..."

All of a sudden he didn't want safe. He wanted dangerous. And forbidden. And the woman lying less than a foot away was even more beautiful than when he'd first laid eyes on her.

"Play it safe?"

Did he hear a glimmer of disappointment? All he

knew was that he wanted to go down this road just a little further. Tease her just a little bit more.

He reached under the covers and plucked one of the pillows, sending it sailing over the side of the bed. The first brick in her flimsy little fortress—gone. "Safe—as in if we're very, very quiet, your dad won't hear us at all."

She squeezed the pillow she held tighter. "I don't remember either of us being all that quiet."

Parts of him were now pulsing, demanding he listen. "I'm always up for a challenge." He reached over and took the pillow from her and tossed it behind him, putting them face to face. "How quiet can you be? I bet I can come without making a single sound."

Her loud gasp made him chuckle. "Oh, not good. You're already failing the first part of the experiment."

Reaching out, his fingers encircled her wrist and tugged her onto the pillows, flipping her on her back. "But I can think of a very, very good use for these. And it has nothing to do with keeping us apart and everything to do with bringing us together."

With that his head came down, and he found her mouth, taking it in a kiss that seared his own senses, even as she squirmed to get closer.

He wanted her. Father or no father. The fact that she was carrying his child made it even sweeter.

Fingers swiftly parted the buttons on her pajama top and his lips moved to the first of the pink nipples he'd uncovered. Sucking it hard, he relished the way her back arched as she pushed toward him. The tiny moan she gave turned him to molten lava, making him release his hold to look down at her. "Shh. I need this. And I think you do too."

Straddling her hips, he gathered her wrists in one hand and carried them over her head. "You do, don't you?"

He whispered the words against her lips. "Need this as much as I do?"

She gave a single nod. "But please be quiet."

"I will." He stretched out on top of her and parted her legs, pressing himself hard against the heart of her, "I guarantee it. But I can gag you, if you're worried about yourself."

Sara bit her lip when he ground against her again. Then she leaned up and kissed the side of his mouth. "I won't be the one making any sounds."

"It's too late. You already did."

The back and forth whispering was intimate. Sexy. And his body was aching for her. Mouth against her ear, he slid slightly to the side, leaving just enough room for one hand to skate down her still-flat tummy and edge beneath the elastic of her bottoms. He went past her panties, and curved around until he was just where he wanted. She was hot. Wet. And he'd done almost nothing except talk.

Well, he was all done talking. Sitting up, he stripped her of her bottoms, laying her bare to his gaze.

Deus! He didn't ever remember being this hot for a woman.

His fingers moved up to her face, then captured a strand of her hair. He drew the blunt end down her nose and across her lips, which parted. His erection twitched and strained.

"Time to make good use of these pillows." He stacked them three high, while she watched. "Now. Come here, Sara."

As soon as she got on her knees, he took her pajama top and slid it down her arms before moving behind her. His fingers trailed down her spine, curving up under arms and cupping her breasts. "So perfect." He squeezed the nipples, leaning down to bite the side of her neck.

She gave a tiny whimper, not much louder than their whispered talk had been. But it was enough to tell him it was time.

"Lie over the pillows, baby." He put a hand between her shoulder blades and applied slight pressure. She obliged, her body aligning perfectly so that her hips were elevated, while her torso lay flat on the mattress. His hands squeezed those perfect ass cheeks, before moving up to grip her hips, one hand going down to release himself.

Taking a second to position himself, he found that moist heat he'd discovered earlier.

Bracing himself, he thrust home, burying himself inside her silky flesh.

That tiny whimper came again. He leaned over, pressing his front to her back and scooting his hands underneath her. One at that tight puckered nipple and the other at the nub of flesh at the V of her legs. He flicked both, pulling his hips back and then plunging forward once again. Her breath rasped in and out as he repeated the act. He couldn't hold it together much longer. Not any longer, in fact.

Changing tack, he gripped her nipple between his thumb and forefinger and began a rhythmic squeeze that matched his thrusts. He buried his lips in the hair at her nape as her whimpers grew more frantic. "I love the way you squeeze me. Like this." He tightened his fingers around her in both places, still pumping hard and fast. And just like that she fell apart around him, her body convulsing as she buried her face in the mattress and made all kinds of sexy muffled sounds. Unable to stop himself, he plunged deep and let the ecstasy take hold, pouring everything he had into her, teeth gripping the soft skin of her neck.

He was done. Completely done.

Satiated, he lay there and took stock of the situation. He heard no movement from any part of the apartment. No sense that they'd been discovered. Sara's back was soft and supple, her muscles completely relaxed.

Maybe he wasn't so done after all.

They could have fun with this. A whole lot of fun.

He pulled out, smiling as she gave a breathed protest. He licked the spot on her neck that he'd just bitten. "Don't worry. We're not finished." With that, he flipped her onto her back, hips still elevated by the pillows. "But let's try it this way this time."

With that, he lifted her to his mouth and watched as he got ready to ravish her all over again.

She loved him.

Sitting across from him at the breakfast table, she felt the same trill of fear she'd felt last night as she'd listened to him sleep. Those deep easy breaths that had spelled total contentment. How was she going to give him up in eighteen months?

Maybe she didn't have to. He couldn't have made love like that without feeling something for her, right?

"Do you want some eggs, Daddy?" She held a plate out toward her father.

Sebastian had seemed distracted this morning. Oh, he talked easily enough with her dad, but it was almost clinical. He asked questions about his health as if he were any other patient.

And she'd caught her father glancing between her and Sebastian with open speculation in his eyes.

Surely he couldn't have guessed.

"Everything looks great, honey." He took the bowl and served himself a healthy portion. It made her smile.

Breakfast had always been important in their house. Her dad worked long hours and claimed he needed food and plenty of it to sustain him throughout the day. In reality, Sara thought he did it because it made her mom so happy to cook for him.

A pang went through her heart. What would her mom think of her daughter's deceit?

She would be so disappointed. She was a firm believer in telling the truth whenever possible. Everything about Sebastian and her relationship had been built on a lie. From that time in the motel, when they'd both had too much to drink and she'd been looking for a way to ease her heartache, to their marriage, to those pictures and beyond.

Only what she'd felt for that lost boyfriend paled in comparison to how Sebastian made her feel.

Unbidden her eyes went to the mantel where that photo was on display. A sense of nausea slid up from nowhere, gripping her stomach and squeezing tight. She took a bite of toast.

"Everything okay, sweetheart?" Sebastian's voice carried a question. Only it too was a lie. Sweetheart? She wasn't his sweetheart. Maybe she would never be.

She forced a smile. "Fine." She took another tiny bite, hoping the dryness of the bread would soak up whatever pool of acid was forming in her belly. She swallowed. Then gulped again when it did nothing but add to her troubles.

"I'll tell you the truth. I was mighty surprised to hear that you two had gotten married. Especially since Sara's last boyfriend was a big city man as well. Although I think that one knows better than to ever show his face at the ranch again."

"Dad!" She was horrified that he was even talking about this right now.

"What? I'm just glad to see that there are still some good men out there. And I'm sure you got married for the right reasons."

Her eyes shot to Sebastian's, who laid down his fork a little too carefully. "I think it was."

She almost snorted. Of course he thought it was. He'd been saving his project.

"Love shows up when you least expect it, though, isn't that right?" her dad went on.

This time Sebastian didn't even attempt to answer. Didn't attempt to even pretend that their marriage was based on that particular emotion. Her heart squeezed so tight she could barely breathe.

She needed to stop this. Now.

"Daddy, I think you're embarrassing him."

Her husband's eyes met hers. Cool and indifferent. As if last night had never happened. "Not at all."

"Sorry if I'm speaking too plainly. She's my only child. I want to make sure she's happy."

Happy. Now, there was a fickle word. And what a difference twelve hours could make.

"I understand."

"Adding a baby so soon will add some stress, but I know you two can work through it." Her dad smiled at her. "Your mom wanted more children, but you were it for us."

Why was he saying this? Her hand went to her belly in a protective gesture.

Sebastian saw it, his gaze hardening slightly. "Lots of people only have one child."

"Yes, they do. But it was the one thing that Dalia wanted that I couldn't give her. Even after thirty years of marriage, it was still hard for her to accept. I would have sold my soul to give it to her."

"Oh, Daddy, she loved you for you."

"I wasn't perfect. I think sometimes she just stayed with me because of you."

An odd sound came from the other side of the table. She glanced over to see that Sebastian's jaw was rigid, white lines forming on either side of his mouth.

"That's not true." She said it in a rush, trying to circumvent a disaster in the making. She remembered Sebastian talking about his parents and how they had stayed married for the sake of the children. "You two loved each other very much."

"Yes, you're right, of course." He forked up a bite of eggs and chewed for a minute or two, looking at her with a frown. "I'm sorry, this has nothing to do with your relationship. I know you'll have a long, happy marriage just like your mom and I did."

Her husband picked up his fork again and stabbed at a piece of ham on his plate. He said nothing. Didn't try to reassure her father, didn't try to reassure her. Because there was nothing he could say without tossing one more lie onto an already stinking pile.

If anything, he seemed to be studiously trying to avoid looking at either of them.

In that moment, Sara realized it was hopeless. They were not going to have a long, happy marriage. Because he didn't love her. It was never going to happen. She was pretty sure her dad might even realize that. He'd hurled those barbs like little jokes, but they'd caught at Sebastian's throat and given him a bad case of laryngitis. Maybe it was better that he didn't try to defend his actions.

Her nausea increased fourfold and her gaze returned

to that picture. How carefree she'd looked in it with her head thrown back and her husband smiling down at her as if he—as if he loved her.

Only he didn't. He'd as much as admitted it.

Her eyes pricked with tears. She'd been living in a fantasy world. Oh, not at first. She'd sworn she could handle this fake marriage and all it entailed. Sebastian had sure been able to.

Her dad had it all wrong. They'd married for the worst of reasons. It hadn't even been about the baby. It had been trying to save both of their asses from the possible consequences of their actions. Consequences that might not have even come to pass. They should have just confessed and let the chips fall where they may.

And now she'd committed the ultimate sin. She'd fallen in love with the man.

And in seventeen months—if they even made it that long—he would walk away from her without a second glance. Just like her ex had.

"Hey, you two." Her dad was looking from her to Sebastian. "Did I commit some kind of faux pas? I'm not really acquainted with the rules in the big city."

Sebastian laid his fork down once again. "Of course you didn't. I just have a big case I'm working on that has taken all my energy. In fact, if you'll excuse me, I need to get to the hospital."

"Of course." Her dad stood to his feet. "I think Sara was going to take me to see some tall building that she says will give me a great view of the city."

"The Edifício do Banespa." Her husband's glance landed on her, before skipping away. "Yes, it has a great view."

A great view. He could have been talking about any normal building. There was no mention of how he'd held her tight against him during that long elevator ride. Or how he'd pressed his face close to hers as they'd looked for this very building.

Who was she kidding? He *was* talking about just another building. Because that was all it was to him.

She had to close her eyes for a moment to fight to keep the contents of her stomach inside her. Seventeen months?

There was no way. She wouldn't last that long.

Sebastian would guess the truth long before then. Hadn't he realized how scared she'd been on that trip to the top? He would realize she loved him in a month, if not sooner.

And it would drive him away long before she was ready.

What choice did she have?

She could leave.

She could wait a week or so after her father left and then she would follow him—tell him that she realized she really had married Sebastian for the wrong reasons. He would be devastated, but he would get over it. Just like she would.

She followed them to the door, plastering a fake smile on her face that resembled the macabre grin she'd had in the first picture of the photo shoot. But nothing she tried made it look any more natural.

Because nothing about this situation was natural.

Sebastian would make a great father, and there was no way she would keep him from his child, despite her words in his office all those weeks ago.

Wow, had it only been weeks?

At the entrance, Sebastian leaned over and kissed her on the cheek, but the light touch seared like the branding iron her dad used on his steers, and she jerked away from it.

"See you when I get home," he said.

"Sounds good. Drive safely." The words had a sour taste as they came out of her mouth.

Oh, God, how was she going to sleep in that bed again after all they'd done in it?

She didn't know, but she'd better figure it out. Or else she needed to confess the truth to her dad and get out long before then.

Maybe even before Sebastian came home from work.

He closed the door behind him without a backward glance.

Yes. She and her father could just leave. Go to the Banespa building. Look at the city, and then over lunch she'd lay it all out.

She could raise a child alone. People did it all the time. And she was positive there were plenty of people who loved someone who didn't love them back. This was her second time around that particular block.

Knowing it didn't make it any easier, though.

Her dad glanced over, his smile fading in a hurry. He wrapped his arm around her waist. "Sara, what is it?"

"Oh, Daddy…" Turning, she buried her face in his familiar shoulder and burst into tears. Between sobs, she said, "I've made the biggest mistake of my life. I got pregnant. And he doesn't love me. He never has, and we just did this to save my job and his project, and it was never supposed to be real, but now it is. And I don't know what to do."

He didn't try to put a stop to the incoherent babbling or tell her to back up and start again. He just held her as she poured her heart out to him in a long stream-of-consciousness torrent. When she finally wound down, he took hold of her shoulders and held her away from him, studying her face.

"You love him."

"Yes, but didn't you hear me? He doesn't love me back. And he won't stay with me once this marriage runs its course." She didn't go into Sebastian's parents or how he hated that they'd stayed together in a loveless, bitter union. And that's what their marriage would turn into as well: a dry empty husk. Oh, the sex might keep him coming back for a little while, but it wasn't enough to build a real relationship.

And did she really want a man to stay with her just for the pleasure he found in her body? Bile washed up her throat all over again.

No, that was not what she wanted. And that was not what she would settle for.

So, is this the end?

Yes, it was. And she'd better get used to it, because like Sebastian had said up at the top of the Banespa building.

Everything eventually came to an end.

Even their marriage.

CHAPTER ELEVEN

"ARE YOU SURE this place is safe?"

Sebastian had a new nurse.

And no wife.

"We'll be fine. The people we're treating aren't hit men." Irritation bubbled up in his throat, most of it directed at himself.

A month after coming home to an empty house, he still couldn't believe Sara had just walked away without saying a word. And when he'd tried to call her, Antônio had answered and bluntly told him not to call back until he figured it out.

Figured what out? He had no idea what the hell he'd even done wrong.

Really?

His behavior at the breakfast table had been atrocious, but he hadn't been able to stand listening to Mr. Moreira talk about how wonderful his marriage was and watch Sara sink further and further into herself. It was all Sebastian's fault. He'd practically shoved this marriage idea down her throat and forced her to go along with it. Had basically threatened her with losing her job if she didn't.

What kind of person did that?

His father, that's who. A man who lied and cheated

and went to motels to have cheap sex with women he didn't love.

Sebastian had done exactly the same thing. And he'd compounded it by lying and cheating to get what he wanted: the Mãos Abertas project.

He'd gotten it. And lost his self-respect in the process. And a friend.

A friend?

Hell, he had no idea what Sara was to him.

It didn't matter in the end, because she was gone. He'd simply told Paulo Celeste that she'd gone home to help her father for a while. He hadn't elaborated any further than that. And surprisingly the man hadn't asked questions, he'd simply assigned him another nurse. Another punch to the gut. He could have avoided all of this.

And his baby?

That was still a huge unknown. Sara had told him he could be a part of the baby's life as long as he was sure he could be there for the long haul. Well, she must have changed her mind about that. There'd been no word on how either of them were doing.

Don't call back until you figure it out.

"What's the woman's name again?"

"It's right there in the chart." He fired the words at her and immediately regretted his attitude. It wasn't her fault he'd screwed up his life. He took one breath. Then another. "Sorry. Her name is Talita, and her grandson's name is Jorge."

He turned down the narrow street that led to her house, finding the crude board fence with ease. Maybe he needed to do something about that. Surely he could spend a few hours fixing up some things around her house. And it would give him something to think about besides his sorry state.

"Someone actually lives here?"

Something about the nurse's words made his hackles rise all over again. It wasn't all her fault. Santa Coração dealt with wealthy patients for the most part. This was a foreign world to many of them—to most of the staff as well. Besides Marcos and Lucas, there weren't many people who had actually spent a large amount of time in a *favela*.

Well, if she wanted to work with him, she'd better get used to it and fast. "Yes, someone does. Do you have a problem with that?"

His grouchy attitude was back with a vengeance.

"No. Of course not."

Well, at least he'd knocked a bit of the haughtiness from her voice.

He turned off the truck and got out. This was more of a courtesy call than anything. Talita had had a double mastectomy three weeks ago. She'd healed well, and the doctors told her she shouldn't have any more episodes of lipogranuloma.

She was still working on her blood sugar, which was why they were here.

At least, that's what Sebastian told himself.

"Do you want me to bring her chart?"

"Sure. Why not."

Veronica Cantor's mouth thinned, but she didn't say anything else as they arrived at the entrance and Sebastian clapped three times.

Within seconds, the door was thrown open by Jorge, who held his fist out for a teenage version of a handshake. Sebastian bumped his own against it with a smile. "How have you been?"

Jorge looked past him at the Mãos Abertas truck, probably looking for Sara. He hadn't said anything to Talita about the break-up, and he was swiftly realizing that coming here might not have been the best idea.

"Who is it?" The grandmother's voice came from inside the house.

"It's Dr. Sebastian and some…" Jorge looked the nurse up and down and Sebastian got ready to give him hell if he said what he thought the kid was thinking of saying. But to his credit, the boy filled in the blank with the word "lady".

"Well, don't just keep them standing outside in the heat."

Jorge ushered them in, not that it was much cooler in the house. But a fan in the living room at least moved the air around enough to take his mind off the oppressive humidity.

Talita, seated on her customary floral chair, glanced at Veronica and then at him. "Where's Sara?"

"She went home." Those simple words came out of his mouth before he could catch them.

He wasn't here to check up on her. He was here to— He had no idea.

Don't call back until you figure it out.

Talita motioned her grandson over. "Why don't you take Nurse…?" She sent Sebastian a glance.

"Her name is Veronica Cantor."

The older woman nodded. "Take Ms. Cantor to see the game system Sara sent for your birthday."

Sara had sent him something? Hell, Sebastian hadn't even known it was the kid's birthday.

How did she do that? Make everyone feel special?

Until they were no longer on her radar.

Veronica shot him a glance, and he nodded at her. Talita was either going to lecture him or console him.

He didn't need to be consoled.

He just wanted to be left alone.

Ha! Wasn't that what Sara had done? Left him alone?

Dammit, maybe he shouldn't have come here after all.

As soon as Veronica and Jorge had left the room, Talita waved a hand at the ragged faux leather sofa next to her chair. Suppressing a roll of his eyes, he lowered himself onto it, but decided to go on the offensive. "How are you feeling?"

"I'm fine. How are *you* feeling?"

She'd turned it around on him, the emphasis on the penultimate word making Sebastian laugh. "Are we really going to do this?"

"Do what?" The older lady batted her sparse lashes at him.

"What do you want me to say? Sara decided she wanted to go home. So she went."

She and her father had slipped out before he'd even gotten home from work. The day after they'd made love.

Don't call until you figure it out.

That phrase had been knocking around in his head ever since that phone call.

"Why did she decide to leave?"

"I don't know."

Talita stared at him long enough to make him wince, her lips twisted in thought. "I wondered why the postmark on Jorge's present said Rio Grande do Sul. Is that where she's from?"

He nodded, not sure where she was going with this. "Her dad is a *gaúcho*."

"When is she coming back?"

This was one question he knew the answer to. "She's not."

Antônio hadn't said it when he'd called, but the intimation was plain enough.

"I'm sorry."

"Me too." It was true. He was damned sorry. And he had no idea why. It should make his life a whole lot easier.

Maybe he didn't want easier.

She was gone, so it didn't really matter what he wanted.

"Did you tell her you love her?"

"No, of course not, I—" Too late he remembered Talita didn't know the real reason he'd married Sara: so that people like Talita could get the surgery they needed.

Only the project hadn't been sunk the moment she'd left. It may not have been sunk even without marriage. Although it still could have caught up with him.

Could have?

It had. Sara had left.

He kept coming back to that. Why did it matter that she was gone?

Talita gave him a sharp look. "You didn't think you loved her, did you?"

He shook his head, not even bothering to answer.

"But you do."

His brain caught on the words. No, he didn't. He couldn't.

It was impossible, because...

There was a gaping hole where that missing word should be.

A thunderbolt struck him in the chest.

He did. He loved her.

Which was why he couldn't seem to get past the fact that she'd left him high and dry.

Don't call until you figure it out.

Was this what he was supposed to figure out? That he loved her?

"Yes. I do." He shrugged. "But I guess she didn't feel the same way."

"She married you, didn't she?"

"Yes, but only because she felt she had to."

Which was the very reason he'd been so hung up over this whole thing. Why he'd set an end date. Because he hadn't believed that a marriage built on that premise—on a pregnancy—could last.

He still wasn't sure it could. His parents' marriage had, if you could call that miserable existence something that "lasted".

Talita leaned over and looked him in the eye. "Are you that blind? The last time I saw you two, it was written all over her face. The way that girl looked at you said it all."

He frowned. "The way she what?"

"She looked at you the way my Henri used to look at me."

"How did he look at you?"

A dreamy look passed across her face. "As if I was his whole world."

His throat clogged. Wasn't that what the woman at the top of the Banespa building had said?

You just saved my whole world.

He fought for something to say that wouldn't sound cheesy or patronizing. Or hopeless. He settled for simple. "How long were you married?"

"Twenty-five years. One child. And one grandchild."

Five years less than Antônio Moreira had been married.

Had Talita really read something in Sara's expression that had led her to believe she loved him?

And if she did?

Could he actually be happy with someone—with her—for thirty, forty or however many years they lived?

Yes. He thought he could.

He and Sara were not like his parents. He couldn't remember even one serious argument—oh, there'd been little ones, but not about things that mattered. They'd laughed together, worked together—made love together.

Veronica poked her head around the corner. "Can I come out yet?"

"No!" Talita and Sebastian both said the word at the same time. The older woman giggled like a girl when the nurse retreated back into the bedroom.

"So what are you going to do?" she asked.

"Her father told me not to bother calling until I figured something out."

She leaned closer. "I think you just did."

"I think you're right."

"He's probably wondering what took you so long." She crossed the stub of her left leg over her right. "So I'm going to ask again. What are you going to do?"

"I'm going to go down there?" Why he made a question out of it, he had no idea.

"You're damn right you are. And don't come back until she believes you, you hear? No matter how many times you have to say it."

He leaned over and kissed her cheek. "I hear you, Talita. Loud and clear."

Sara slid her hands into matching oven mitts and opened the door to the stove. The casserole inside sizzled. *Escondidinho*—one of her favorite dishes. It should be making her mouth water, and although the meat pie topped with puréed manioc smelled delicious, all she felt was a rock where her stomach should be.

It had been that way ever since she'd come home. Because she'd run away from a difficult situation without saying a word to anyone. How was that any different from what her ex had done to her? It wasn't. But it was too late to go back and fix it.

Her father had been supportive and wonderful about everything, but over the past month she'd caught him staring out the window. When she asked him what he was doing, he said, "Nothing. Just thinking."

Probably wondering how he was going to survive toddlerhood all over again.

No, her dad said he was looking forward to having little feet running all over the place, and she believed him.

Clap! Clap! Clap!

Ugh! Not again! It seemed every time she turned around, one of her father's employees came over from the bunkhouse to ask some question or other.

It wasn't like her dad not to be out working the ranch. He still had to be careful with his leg, but two weeks ago he'd gotten a tentative okay to start riding a horse. At a walk. But he'd seemed more interested in that stupid window.

Was he worried that the cancer had come back? They hadn't had the chance to do the blood work Sebastian wanted.

She took off the oven mitts to answer the door, but her father beat her to it. Good, whoever it was could get the answer right from the source. She turned around to finish her lunch preparations, even though her stomach was still doing somersaults inside her. Just another month until her morning sickness should be over.

If that was even what this was.

The door clicked open.

"What in the hell took you so long?"

Sara's brows shot up as she took another step toward

the kitchen. She'd never heard her dad greet anyone that way before.

"It took me a while to figure it out."

She stopped dead in her tracks.

Deus. She was having some kind of stress flashback. That voice wasn't real. It couldn't be. Her guilt was making her hear things.

"And have you?"

Okay, that was her father's voice. It was okay. Just her imagination. She started to walk again.

"Yes. I have."

No. It wasn't her mind playing tricks. She swung around toward the door, but her father was blocking the view.

"Daddy?" she called out.

He glanced back and smiled. "There's someone here who wants to talk to you."

Her hand went to her throat. "Is—? Is it—?"

A man stepped around her father's form. "I hope it's *my* name you're searching for."

Sebastian. It was really him.

"What are you—? Why are you here?"

Her dad gave her a strange knowing smile. "Is that any way to talk to your husband? I think you should at least invite him in for lunch."

Lunch? *Lunch?*

She was having some kind of breakdown, and he was worried about missing a meal? He was acting like he'd been expecting Sebastian for ages.

The image of him looking out the window day after day came to her. Was this why? He'd expected Sebastian to appear?

Her dad swept past her, giving her arm a quick squeeze.

"Hear him out, okay? He's traveled a long way to see you. And to say it."

To say what? That he wanted a divorce?

Deus, that's what it was. He figured if she was no longer working at the hospital, there was no reason to keep up the pretense. She should have expected this.

What she hadn't expected was for him to come in person. He could have simply sent the paperwork by certified mail or something.

Once her dad was gone—listening from the kitchen, no doubt—Sebastian closed the door then slowly made his way over to her as if—as if he wasn't sure.

This Sebastian was different from the one who knew what he wanted and went after it. Or maybe she was still trapped in that hazy dream state from when she'd heard his voice at the door.

But he was here. This was a flesh and blood man. Her dad had seen him, had spoken with him, so he was real.

She lifted her chin. Okay, then. It was time to face him and get this over with. "Did you bring the papers?"

He nodded.

Her mouth popped open to help her force air into her suddenly aching lungs. "If you have a pen, I'll sign them and you can be on your way."

He rolled his shoulder in a way that made it pop. Her eyes burned. It had been forever since she'd heard that sound—since she'd heard his voice.

"Maybe we're talking about two different sets of papers." He pulled a sheaf of documents from a long white envelope, then his eyes came up and met hers. "I want to get married. Again. In a church."

Pain ripped through her chest. So soon?

"To who?"

One side of his mouth tilted up. "Do you have to ask?"

She guessed she did, or she wouldn't have voiced the question. But he was smiling. That sexy heart-stopping twist of lips that made her insides go all gooey.

It hit her. There was only one person he would be saying that about. She hoped.

She took her index finger and curved her hand around until it pointed back at herself, her eyebrows raised to make it a question.

"Yes, Sara. You."

"You want to marry me? Why? I thought you were coming to ask for a divorce."

"I don't want a divorce."

"You don't. Is it because of Mãos Abertas?"

He set the papers down on a nearby table. "It has nothing to do with the project. It has everything to do with you."

"The pregnancy, is that it?"

Why did she keep firing questions back at him as if unable to believe his request could be related to something besides all the obvious choices? Because the only other option was…

Surely not.

"This isn't about the baby. Or the project. Not this time. This is about you. And me. I want you to come home."

Home. As if that was where she belonged.

He reached for her hands. "I love you."

"No, you don't."

His head tilted. "I think I would know."

She tried to tug free, only to have his grip on her tighten.

"Please, stop. I already told you I wouldn't keep the baby from you."

"I love you. I'm going to keep on saying it until it sinks into that pretty head of yours."

"Did my dad put you up to this?"

"No, but when I tried to call you the day after you left, he told me not to call again until I figured it out." He lifted one of her hands to his lips and kissed it. "So I didn't call. I came instead. I love you."

Maybe he was really going to keep saying it.

"Are you sure?"

"I wouldn't be here if I wasn't." He nodded at the side table. "I brought proof. Unless you don't feel the same way about me."

"I did." She blinked a time or two to clear her vision. "I mean, I do, but are you sure you really want this?"

"I'm more sure of this than I've ever been of anything." He reeled her in until she was flush against him. "Marry me."

"But what about not being able to see a relationship lasting for decades?"

"I'm out to prove myself wrong. And you're going to help me do it." His fingers sifted through the hair at her nape. "Because I already know the outcome. We're going to last for the duration."

Muscles in her body that had been tensed relaxed against him. "That could be a very long time."

"I'm counting on it." He smiled. "And on having a few more babies along the way."

"More babies?"

"Does that scare you?"

"No. It makes me happy." She believed him. Her arms went around his neck and she raised her face for his kiss.

It was the same sweet fire she remembered, and it injected warmth to her very core.

"I want a real wedding. To make a real commitment.

Not because of any baby or babies, but because I want you to be my wife. My forever wife." He took her hand where her wedding ring was and slid it off her finger. At her shocked gasp he hushed her with a kiss. "Don't worry, I'll put it back on. At a ceremony, which will happen here at the ranch, because this is where it all started."

Their mouths met again. Clung. The promise of a lifetime full of love and happiness shimmered around them.

He pulled back, his lips still touching hers. "Do you think your dad would be shocked if we shared your bedroom tonight?"

"I doubt it, but that's not what I want."

When he made to take a step back she did what he had done earlier and tightened her grip. "I have something very different in mind."

"You do?"

"Mmm." She stood on tiptoe, rubbing her cheek across his. "Yes, because you said it all started here at the ranch. Well, that's where you're wrong."

"I don't understand."

"Think about it, Sebastian. Our relationship did not start here. And I want to spend the night in the place where it all began."

He stood there for a second and then his brows slowly went up.

"I see you're beginning to get the picture," she said.

"You want to spend the night at the—"

"Shh. We have to be very, very quiet." She knew he would get the reference to their shared night.

He lowered his voice to a whisper. "You want to start this new phase of our relationship in a sleazy motel? Remember, we now have a baby in tow."

"And I think our baby would say, 'Thank you very

much,' don't you? Since that's where he or she got their start."

He chuckled, biting her lower lip and sending a sharp pang of need through her belly that spiraled lower and lower.

"Do I think so? Oh, I do, Sara. I do indeed."

EPILOGUE

BABY SILAS TEXEIRA came on a stormy day.

But the one thing that wasn't stormy was Sebastian's heart. As the sound of thunder rumbled just outside the hospital, he leaned his head against his wife's, relishing her tired sigh as she whispered, "Love you."

"I love you." He kissed her cheek, his hand going to their baby's tiny back. "And I love our life."

He did. His heart gave a couple of hard beats. He'd worried so much about his motivation for staying that he'd realized he'd lost his way for a little while, almost never getting the opportunity to feel the joy that came with discovering a person in tiny bites. Those moments in time that were meant to be savored and enjoyed.

Yes, he'd jumped into marriage for the wrong reasons. But he was staying for all the right ones.

"Can I call them in?"

"Yes. Please do." She tried to drag her hands through her hair, but he stopped her.

"You look beautiful."

"No, I don't. But no one will be looking at me, anyway." She laid her hand on top of his. "He's amazing, isn't he? This little creature came from both of us."

He grinned. "Maybe we'll leave out some of the details of how he came to be, though."

"I want to go back to that motel every anniversary."

"Sorry?"

"We belong together. I want it branded on our souls, etched in our minds. The motel will just make the process fun."

"Little pitchers." He pretended to cover Silas's ears. "And I don't think it's appropriate to try to seduce me in front of a newborn."

She smiled back at him. "*Try* to seduce you?"

"Okay, so that's pretty much a done deal." He wanted her. All the time. Not because of the sex, although that had been pretty damned amazing. But because of Sara herself. She touched a part of him that no one had ever reached. And he couldn't get enough of her. Her ex-boyfriend had done Sebastian a huge favor in leaving, although if the man ever came back, he was probably going to meet the wrong end of Antônio Moreira's branding iron.

He kissed that cute lower lip. "I think we'd better let some people in here before the room starts to steam up."

She nodded, sighing as she gazed down at their child. "I guess we can share him."

"We might be facing a mob scene if we don't." He moved his lips to her cheek before forcing himself to stand up. "I'll go get them."

He ducked into the hall, and fifteen heads turned toward him in bright expectation. Marcos and Maggie, Lucas and Sophia, Sara's dad, of course. His sister and Adam.

Then his chest tightened. Because a little off to the side was Talita Moises in her wheelchair. Jorge stood directly behind her.

Talita, who had read Sebastian the Riot Act and brought him to his senses. Her blood sugar was finally under control once again. It looked like she would be there for the rest of Jorge's childhood and into his adult years as well.

He was just getting ready to ask everyone to follow him when one of the nurses from the front desk came barreling toward them. "You are not going to take all of these people in there at once, are you, Dr. Texeira."

Funny how that hadn't been a question but a statement. This particular nurse was known to be ruthlessly protective when it came to her patients. He could understand that. He was pretty protective of Sara as well. But this would be good for her.

He wasn't above a little bargaining to get his way. Unlike his dad, though, this was for a good cause. "How about if I take them all in, but we stay half the amount of time. They'll be in and out." He did a quick head count. "I think since most of us work at this hospital, we know how important it is for patients to get their rest. And since I'm her *husband*…"

For a second, he thought she might veto even that bargaining chip, but although her lips tightened, she gave a brusque nod and glanced at her watch. "Half the time would put you at five minutes."

"Five minutes sounds perfect." He led them down the hall and opened the door. While the rest of the group went in, he waited until Talita and her grandson wheeled up next to him. Laying his hand on her arm, he lowered his voice. "Thank you. For everything."

"I could say the same for you. If it wasn't for Mãos Abertas, I might not be here. How can I ever repay you?"

"You already did. Just by doing us the honor of being here."

"That girl is your whole world, isn't she?"

"Yes, Talita, she is."

"I knew it." She leaned up and pressed her lips to his cheek. "Don't be a stranger, okay?"

"Never."

Then she and Jorge went in to join the rest of the people who were busy oohing and ahhing over the baby and Sara.

As he stared at the gathering, a burst of gratitude sizzled inside him. He was a lucky, lucky man.

He went to the head of the bed and draped his arm on the pillow above Sara's head, watching as she laughed at something Natália had said. He was rich beyond his wildest dreams and it had nothing to do with money.

"Two minutes," he said, feeling a little like the elevator man at the Banespa building.

The nurse was right, though. Sara might look perfectly content, but she was exhausted from giving birth.

Besides, he wasn't quite as willing to share her and Silas as he'd thought. These moments were precious. Irreplaceable.

"Sebastian." His wife's voice carried a chiding tone he knew all too well.

"Nurse's orders."

Natália stepped forward and kissed Sara's forehead. "He's right. We shouldn't tire you out." She gave a pseudo-whisper. "We'll come back when your bodyguard is at work."

"I work here." Sebastian's dry response wasn't lost on anyone. They laughed, but all followed his sister's lead and congratulated them and filed out one by one. Talita and Jorge lingered a moment longer.

"You have a beautiful baby there, honey."

"Thank you." Sara squeezed the older lady's hand. "I hear you're the reason I still have a husband."

"Oh, he would have realized he was being a fool eventually. He just needed a big kick in the behind to understand it sooner rather than later."

"Can I call you whenever he needs another kick?"

"No need," said Sebastian. "I have learned my lesson."

Talita smiled and put her arm around her grandson's waist. "You have to come and eat at our house, once you're out of the hospital."

"Nothing would make us happier, right, Sebastian?"

"Absolutely."

Jorge smiled. Always quiet, he nodded toward the baby. "I could show him how to do things someday. Like maybe ride a bike."

Sebastian had probably heard Jorge say maybe ten words the whole time he'd known him. And the thought of this shy, retiring boy being willing to come out of his shell in order to help Silas made something in his throat grab. He coughed, trying to rid himself of the sensation. Then he put a hand on the boy's shoulder. "Silas would be very fortunate to have a mentor like you."

"Like a real mentor?" The boy stood straighter.

"Yes. Like a real mentor. He'll need one. So you'll have to set a good example."

Talita reached up to ruffle the teen's hair. "Oh, he will. And now we'd better be on our way." With a last flurry of hugs, Jorge wheeled his grandmother from the room, leaving Sebastian and Sara alone with their baby.

He kicked off his shoes and then settled into a nearby chair, propping his feet on the bed.

"You've been awake as long as I have. You need to go home and get some rest."

He reached for her free hand and gripped it tight. "I don't need to go anywhere, *querida*. If you're here and the baby is here, this is my home."

* * * * *

LET'S TALK
Romance

For exclusive extracts, competitions
and special offers, find us online:

 facebook.com/millsandboon

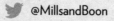 @MillsandBoon

@MillsandBoonUK

Get in touch on 01413 063232

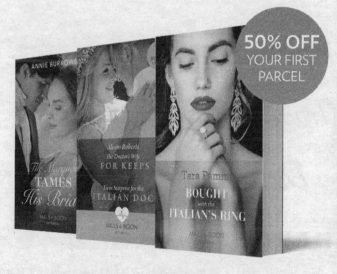

JOIN US ON SOCIAL MEDIA!

Stay up to date with our latest releases, author news and gossip, special offers and discounts, and all the behind-the-scenes action from Mills & Boon...

 millsandboon

 millsandboonuk

 millsandboon

t might just be true love...

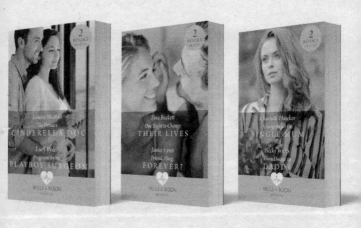